Praise

"A beautifully written epic nov
acters and haunting scenes."

—John Rechy, author of *City of Night*

"Sexier than a stable of *Playboy* bunnies, more adventuresome than a Greek romance, able to confound expectations on every single page, Dora Levy Mossanen's first novel, *Harem,* is truly astonishing."

—Robert Hellenga, author of
The Sixteen Pleasures and *Blues Lessons*

"Compulsive reading right from the start. Gorgeous imagery and outrageous characters whose stories grab you and hold you enthralled till you've turned the final page."

—Robin Maxwell, author of
The Secret Diary of Anne Boleyn and *Virgin*

"*Harem* transports the reader to another time and place. As I turned the pages—I was not aware of it—it seemed as if I was on a journey that I did not want to end. Not only are Mossanen's characters magical story tellers, but this debut shows she is one herself."

—M. J. Rose, author of
Lip Service, In Fidelity, and *Flesh Tones*

"An important contribution to the growing canon of women's mythology in contemporary literature. From the first sentence I was as captivated as I used to be as a child when my mother read me fairy tales from around the world. The quality of myth that the author achieves is stunning."

—Christin Lore Weber, author of *Altar Music*

"Dora Levy Mossanen's *Harem* lures us into a language as opulent as its world, filled with solitudes and lush tapestries of human frailty, love, and ambition."

—James Ragan, poet and author of *Lusions*

"A rare and beautiful novel."

—Maureen Connell, author of *Mary Lacey*

"*Harem* is a succulent feast with a rich cast of characters."

—Ann Rowe Seaman, author of *Swaggart*

Harem

a novel

DORA LEVY MOSSANEN

SCRIBNER PAPERBACK FICTION
Published by Simon & Schuster
New York   London   Toronto   Sydney   Singapore

SCRIBNER PAPERBACK FICTION
Simon & Schuster, Inc.
Rockefeller Center
1230 Avenue of the Americas
New York, NY 10020

SCRIBNER PAPERBACK FICTION and design are trademarks of Macmillan Library Reference USA, Inc., used under license by Simon & Schuster, the publisher of this work.
For information regarding special discounts for bulk purchases, please contact Simon & Schuster Special Sales at 1-800-456-6798 or *business@simonandschuster.com*

Designed by Kyoko Watanabe

Manufactured in the United States of America

1 3 5 7 9 10 8 6 4 2

Library of Congress Cataloging-in-Publication Data is available.

ISBN 0-7432-3021-3

For Nader
and for
Carolyn and Negin
My Partners on this Magical Journey

Acknowledgments

This magical journey would not have been possible without the faith, encouragement, and wisdom of many.

I am indebted to John Rechy, brilliant author, mentor, teacher, and friend, whose invaluable insight and guidance were indispensable to *Harem*.

Alev Lytle Croutier's beautiful book, *Harem: The World Behind the Veil*, supplied important historical facts that stirred me to write about the fascinating world of harems.

I owe much more than thanks to my writer angels, Paula Schtrum, Joan Goldsmith, Alex Kivowitz, and Maureen Connel, whose comments while reading and rereading *Harem* were critical, and Ann Rowe Seaman, whose perceptive observations and belief in Rebekah and the rest of the cast kept my spirits and my pen flying.

My gratitude to Dr. James Ragan, head of the Master of Professional Writing Program at the University of Southern California, for his endless encouragement and wise guidance.

A million thanks to Mark Gompertz, Trish Todd, Chris Lloreda, and Marcia Burch, for their enthusiastic support and outstanding expertise. I am infinitely grateful to my remarkable publishing team: Debbie Model, Laurie Cotuamaccio, Brad

Foltz, Francine Kass, Kim Palladino, and Erin Saunders for their invaluable contributions.

I am grateful to my parents, Sion and Parvin Levy, and to my sisters and brothers, who were always there even when I could not be.

Leila Michaela—my blessing—arrived when I needed her most. Thank you.

I have been inspired by the protective spirits of my grand-parents, Doctor Habib Levy, who left me with a wealth of stories and wrote many more of his own, Zoleika Levy, who provided voice to my most beloved characters, and by Heshmat and Abraham Shenassa's benevolent shadows.

Words cannot describe my gratitude for the unconditional support and encouragement of my husband and daughters. Thank you, Nader, Carolyn, and Negin.

I owe special appreciation to my agent, Loretta Barrett, and to my editor extraordinaire, Marcela Landres, whose courage, enthusiastic guidance, and astute remarks were essential.

Harem

1

*R*ebekah of the violet eyes heard a voice that would haunt her the rest of her life.

"I know she's only ten. I'll be patient."

She hugged her doll and tossed on her pallet. The heat, the flies, and the soothing words of the strange man in the next room interrupted her sleep. Visitors were rare in her home. Her widowed mother left at dawn to wash other people's laundry. In the evenings, Rebekah learned from her mother to bake pistachio cookies and crispy rice, to differentiate between aromatic herbs, and to flatter the man who would one day take care of her.

Rebekah pressed her ear to the makeshift wall.

Her mother's cough shattered the silence.

As if the cough had originated from her own lungs, Rebekah clutched her chest.

"She's the prettiest girl in Persia. I'm saving her for a rich husband."

Suspended between wakefulness and sleep, Rebekah heard the man's melodious persistence, promises of china dolls and lace skirts, chickpea candies and saffron halva, fantasies peculiar to her dreams.

ço

Soon after, Rebekah and her mother went to the house of
bougainvillea to visit the Ancient Zoroastrian, a clairvoyant
who had witnessed the rise and fall of dynasties. She was the
only person alive who had seen a time before evil was introduced into the world, a time when the great prophet Ahura
Mazda of goodness ruled.

At the end of the alley of pomegranate trees, Rebekah and
her mother approached the single room buried under lavish
flowers. They parted the branches, searching for the low
entrance, and nudged open the door that was never locked.
Lingering at the threshold, they waited to be acknowledged.

The old woman sat cross-legged next to a brazier heaped
with blazing coals on which seeds of rue crackled and smoked,
permeating the air with anticipation. The Zoroastrian's ash-
colored skin stretched taut over fragile bones. She had lost all
her hair to the ravages of time. Her purple eyelids concealed
inquisitive eyes.

Rebekah's mother averted her gaze from the turquoise
amulets that hung around the woman's neck, and the red
chicken eyes that were set in gold and glared at her from the
Zoroastrian's pierced earlobes. "Holy One, I've promised
Rebekah's hand in marriage. She's here to ask for your blessing."

The Zoroastrian did not lift her head, open her eyes, or ask
any question. She had gazed into her fire and had seen Rebekah
and her mother approach. The old one had clutched her bony
knees and had chuckled out in glee. She had shifted closer to
the flames to better inhale the scent of pearls, silk, rapture, and
bliss. Neither the mother nor the child was aware that marvelous miracles were about to occur in Rebekah's life.

"Rebekah's fate is sealed," the Ancient Zoroastrian murmured in a voice that had retained the vigor of youth. "Her

future is embellished with crowns and jewels. A life of lust and passion, conspiracy and love. At times, it will be difficult, but never, ever hopeless."

The Ancient Zoroastrian set her veined hand on Rebekah's head. "May Ahura Mazda bless you and may he grant me more years on this earth to revel in the impending miracles."

⋘

In the synagogue of the One-Eyed Rabbi, Rebekah's mother folded a parchment and handed it to Rebekah. "This is signed proof you're a married woman." She pressed her lips to her daughter's golden curls. "Your husband is rich. You'll live in comfort."

Glancing at the parchment that dangled from her fingers, Rebekah knew she had to accept her fate. She was sad but not scared. Promises of toys and veils and sweets, of kindness and patience and love reverberated in her head. Her mother had married her to the stranger with the sweet voice.

"Your husband will not join you in bed before your first menstrual period," her mother whispered, tears in her voice. "Since I won't be here for long, you must demand that he keep his word."

For the first time Rebekah understood the gravity of her mother's endless coughing and the terrible wheezing in her chest, and why she had found it necessary to discuss the importance of a wife's responsibilities.

Rebekah held her mother's hand as she led her past the stalls in the bazaar toward her husband's house. The ground was thick with chicken feathers, horse manure, and decayed melon rinds. The cries of the vendors of ice water, hookah pipes, and hot tea filled the air. Lopsided poles held white canvases that sheltered vendors from the fierce sunshine. Goods were exhibited at the entrances—strings of figs suspended overhead, roasted nuts and dried beans overflowing canvas sacks, cones of sugar perched on sloping counters. The green-grocer in his skirted robe, belted at the waist with a multicolored shawl, lifted his cone-shaped hat and scratched his shaved head. He wet his henna-tinged forefinger in his mouth, then smeared his saliva on Rebekah's cheeks to scare away the evil eye. From an assortment of persimmons, pomegranates, and yellow melons open to the flies and street dust, he chose a pomegranate, quartered it, and offered her a slice. "For the violet-eyed beauty."

She bit into the bloody fruit, sucked on the seeds, and tasted the familiar tang of powdered nutmeg and ice flowers. She dropped the rest in her pocket to save for her husband.

They reached the end of the Alley of Ezekiel the Cobbler. "This is your home," her mother whispered. "Your husband is thirty-four years old. He'll take care of you."

Her home was the color of mud. From behind an iron fence that protected the house, she saw jasmine bushes, a walnut tree, and a patch of arid land.

"Rebekah," her mother said. "Look! Enough space for you to plant geranium and flowering almond and myrtle like your garden back home."

"Water our garden, Madar. Don't let it dry like this."

At her mother's touch, the gate groaned open. Rebekah stepped into the smell of hot coals. She pressed her nose to her mother's chador to inhale her scent of caramelized sugar and licorice.

Her mother squeezed her to her breasts. "You'll never be alone. I'll always be looking over you," she said, releasing her and walking out the door.

Rebekah ran to the window and peered out through the curtains, past the rusting iron gate. Clutching her doll in one

hand and the parchment in another, she watched her
mother's wide hips disappear around the turn of the alley. A
bird fluttered against the window. The breeze ruffled the
leaves of the ancient walnut tree. She turned around to look
for the stranger, her husband with the lullaby voice of a storyteller.

Heavy, gold-colored drapes darkened the room. Silver
masks, features frozen in laughter, stared down at her from a
mantelpiece above a massive kiln in the center. Her stomach
churned at the glitter. She averted her gaze from the flames in
the hearth, from the poker; mesh glove and thongs suspended
from hooks hammered into the cracks in the baked mud walls
around the furnace.

"I am Jacob the Fatherless." A fat man with crossed eyes
that quivered under heavy brows faced her.

His grating voice shattered her dreams. This was not the
man with a voice like music.

His hand that smelled of burning metal grabbed her doll
and sent it flying toward the kiln. She rushed to catch the doll.
Flames licked the cotton face and devoured the wool dress.
Rebekah leaned over the ledge that faced the kiln and thrust
her hand into the fire. Jumping back, she stuffed her fingers
into her mouth to soothe the burnt flesh. Her doll sizzled into
black smoke, gray ash, nothing.

Jacob the Fatherless bowed in mock courtesy and straightened, lifting his stomach with a groan. Spidery legs sprouted
from his swollen body, and dark, knotted curls framed his
bloated cheeks. "I am a blacksmith—a creator," he said, his
crossed eyes struggling for balance. "I melt iron into any shape
and alloy I want. All my life I've worked toward a day when
everything I melt will turn into gold."

Her mind reeled, trying to contain the scream that choked
her. Why had her mother abandoned her to this man?

He spat into the fire, tilted his head, and paused to relish the sizzle. "Your mother negotiated a bargain. She married you to Jacob the Fatherless. A man born without a father."

Her mother's lessons came to her rescue, and she gazed at Jacob with wet, violet eyes, blew on her hand, and fluttered her lashes, pretending fascination.

"Soon I'll become the richest man in the Jewish Quarter. Do you know why? I'm one of the few who endures this fire. The heat has ignited a permanent furnace in my heart. Even in my sleep, flames lash behind my lids." He shot another stream of spittle into the flames, then stared back at her. "I know a secret that will make me eternal like gold—remain forever in one form or another, liquid or solid. Then, like God, I'll never die. Do you understand, Rebekah?"

Rebekah did not.

But that evening when she watched him melt objects in the man-sized furnace in the bedroom, she understood fear. Fear of the kiln, the fire, the madness in his eyes, the heat that turned into beads of sweat on his face while he molded metals into knives, cauldrons, and pots. In the kitchen, he nailed metal sheets on the counter and the wall behind the wood burner, in the dining room over the table and stools, in their bedroom on top of the baked-mud floors.

Past midnight, his eyes raked the house for scraps to feed his voracious flames. He formed ornamental trinkets from the remnants of metal and locked them in a box. He dangled the key in front of her face.

"Who are the trinkets for?" she asked, curiosity overcoming her fear.

He unbuttoned his coat and dropped the key in the secret pocket of his vest, stroking the place where it was buried. "One day you'll know."

When dawn glanced through the window, he nodded

toward one of the pallets that flanked the kiln in the bedroom. "You may retire now."

He occupied the other pallet. He tossed about, grumbling for hours, then raised himself and approached her. He lingered overhead, tapped his small, feminine feet against her pallet. Lifted the blanket and stared down at her. She squeezed her eyes shut and pretended to be asleep. Pressing his thumb on the artery at the side of her neck, he counted the pulse of her fear. The acrid odor of liquid iron flowed from his hands and stung her nostrils.

"Open your legs!" he ordered.

"You promised!" she cried, her eyes springing open, her hands struggling to escape.

"No one," he growled, "extracts promises from Jacob the Fatherless."

"You gave your word of honor!"

"Honor! What honor?"

She fought to keep her thighs locked. "Madar!" She screamed, certain the urgency of her pain would summon her mother.

He thrust her thighs open and mounted her.

His howls sounded like a wolf's, and his moans like those of wounded animals. Or were those her cries, her pain, her loss? Where was the man who had asked for her hand, who had promised to be patient?

Blood burned her thighs.

"Never, ever grow," he panted, emptying himself.

♊

By twelve, Rebekah's violet eyes had acquired a defiant spark, her curls the sheen of gold, and her lips the blush of wine. The burned skin on her fingers had the pallor and snug fit of an old glove that had, at last, conformed to her hand, and like her, had learned to cope with and survive the world of Jacob.

Her veiled gaze followed him as he shuffled around their home. Even in his absence, she didn't dare search the house for the gold bullion he amassed with the money he earned melting iron. Every evening he sent her into the garden before he made sure nothing was missing, then he changed the hiding places of his wealth. He sat down to dinner, calling her back.

Tonight he fished a large bone from a bowl of hot stew. The heat did not penetrate the thick skin of his fingers. He slammed the bone on a metal plate to empty the marrow, soaked bread and mint in it, and devoured the concoction. He stroked his bloated stomach, stuffed a skewer of ground kebab with mint leaves into his mouth, and belched. A smile of contentment hovered on his face. He complimented her on the freshness of the mint she picked daily, reminding her that without his money that bounty would not have been possible.

She looked forward to the hours she spent cultivating her herbs, not only because her patch of land evoked the home she longed for, but also because from behind the railings she could observe the dancing Gypsies. Rebekah fed the earth with left-over stew and chickpea paste and sprayed the leaves with a mixture of honey and wine to attract the praying mantis. On Fridays, when the first chorus of cymbals, tambourines, and shakers rang about the neighborhood, she walked to the fence, expecting the Gypsies. Colorful, flowing skirts and sleeve ruffles came into view first around the bend of the alley, then plump, feminine figures twirled and spun and swayed in dances Rebekah captured again in her dreams. The vegetation in her garden doubled in size and turned a deep, glossy green, and the dances in her dreams developed and matured in ways she did not understand. What she found out was that something as innocent as a bunch of herbs concealed a secret that helped her subdue Jacob. The taste, the scent, the sizzle of burning mint must summon his lust for gold and pacify him. If he did not chew or smell mint, he seemed to appease himself with her body.

Selecting a sprig, she inhaled the tangy-sweet fragrance. Was it addictive? She touched a leaf to her tongue, tore and chewed on it, tasting its bitter tartness. Why did he prefer it toasted? She held the leaves over the embers on her stove. In her mouth, it was like fire, the acrid taste of her burned fingers. If only she could muster the courage to ask the wandering Gypsies if mint regulated some part of the body. Added to a man's sense of virility? Dampened his cruelty? Made a tight-fisted man sometimes generous?

Even Jacob, at times, strove to be generous. One warm Saturday evening, when nightingales and the scent of jasmine lured Rebekah to her herb garden, Jacob arrived with a rolled parchment.

"The plan for our new house. I'll build it even farther from the garbage pit."

Rebekah realized the importance of owning a home far from the pit, a mound of garbage in the center of the Jewish Quarter around which makeshift stalls displayed fruits, nuts, and spices. She missed the inviting scents and friendly voices; the comforting closeness of people, her mother's avid bargaining as she selected provisions. Didn't her mother know she was not allowed out of the house alone? Why didn't she visit? Did Jacob forbid it?

"Come inside, Rebekah," he called out. "Sit on my lap, while I explain. I'll build our house at the end of the Alley of Lanterns, where a plot of land is so expensive, your little mind won't grasp its value."

"Can I choose the furniture?"

"No," he replied.

"The fabrics for the curtains?"

"What do you know about fabrics?"

"My mother says I've a talent for colors."

"You have none."

"Yes, I do."

His fleshy hands slid under her hips, raised her high in the air, and dropped her to the floor.

"Madar!" Her breath twisted in her lungs.

"She can't hear you," he barked.

Lying flat on her back, his shadow a dark blanket between her and the light of the oil burner, she swore that one day she would destroy Jacob the Fatherless.

ൟ

Dawn after dawn, she splashed cool water on her face, tossed a chador over her head, and walked with Jacob to the Alley of Lanterns to watch him build their house with his own hands. He dug her an *estakhr* behind the house, paving it with turquoise tiles and filling it with fresh water from a well he had dug.

"Your private *estakhr!*" he announced, pausing for her appreciation.

Rebekah watched the sun dance on the golden waters and her heart beat with anticipation. Could the Ancient Zoroastrian's prophecy of jewels and love and happiness come true in this house?

Jacob lifted a finger. "You must always swim fully dressed, or I'll flog you to death. Even the stars of heaven must not set eyes on a single toenail of yours. Be chaste and virginal at all times, except in my bed, when you'll transform yourself into a whore. And I'll reward you by treating you like a queen."

The next evening, Jacob arrived home carrying a dress of crushed velvet, a pair of kid boots, and a chador of China silk.

He flung them at Rebekah's feet, stepped back, and slapped his thighs with gleeful pride.

Rewarded for the evenings she had surrendered her body to him!

She slipped back into the kitchen to serve his dinner: shank, bone marrow, and mint. Tonight, as every other night, she hid a portion of the meal. Her loneliness was easier to bear if she imagined a time when the stranger with the sweet voice would knock on her door and ask her to collect provisions for the road because they were, at last, leaving for a safer place.

"Where's the mint?" Jacob demanded when Rebekah returned with the steaming stew.

She hurried back to the kitchen. Delicate leaves, slender sprigs, lush bunches of mint had become her friends. Most of his waking hours, while he labored over the kiln, he chewed or smelled mint she picked from her garden. It seemed she had trained him, like a dog, to associate the taste and smell of mint with that of liquid gold. Now the scent of mint made him feel as omnipotent as when he melted gold, so that he didn't seem to have to copulate with her as often to validate himself.

She heard his approaching steps, heard him linger at the door, enter the kitchen. She did not move. There was nowhere to flee. He was behind her, his stomach flattening her against the wood burner, his breath on her neck, his voice calling her a whore-wife, his hands tearing her vest, groping her buttocks, dragging her back into the room, pushing her down on the pile of garments he had purchased.

Not only had he thrust early womanhood upon her, but he felt he had made up for it with a heap of expensive fabrics and sheer veils she despised.

Her gaze roamed the ceiling, forming shadows of fantastical animals and birds and plants, a world where the pain of Jacob's body on top of her and the bitterness of his broken promise to her mother did not matter. A place where the Ancient Zoroastrian's miracles would come true, where she would whirl around as free as the dancing Gypsies.

"Say you're my whore-wife!" Jacob's voice came from afar.

"Never."

"One day you will," he moaned, crushing her into velvet and silk.

Soon, she thought, he will rise and go about his work. For a few hours, she would be left alone in the refuge of her imagination. She tugged the chador of China silk from under her head and studied its shades of orange, red, and yellow. The colors of fire. She threw the veil over her face to inhale the smell of silk and dye and shame.

Jacob's breathing settled. He lifted himself and tossed a coat over his naked body. "Wait right here. I've a surprise for you."

Her palm sliding over her body, Rebekah watched her husband leave. Her hips were slightly fuller, her breasts beginning to ripen, and so was her shame.

"Come out," she heard Jacob calling from the garden.

She buried her face in the rustle of silk. She would not go out. She did not need any more garments or jewelry or perfumes that reeked of disgrace, favors that fed her grief.

Through the silk and velvet that covered her ears, she heard him summon her with the tone reserved for times he believed he was indulging her. Had he mistaken the humiliation on her face for gratitude? When his voice curdled with irritation, she lifted herself.

She leaned naked against the doorway. The breeze carried a biting coolness, and the moon sailed in a cloudless sky. A raucous noise came from behind the house. The stamping of hooves?

Jacob emerged into the garden, pulling a donkey by a rope tied around its neck and muzzle. Her breath caught at the most beautiful sight she had ever seen. The animal's pelt was the color of onyx, with a goose-white band that stretched from its muzzle all the way down to its lush and restless tail. With every jerk of the rope, the donkey turned its neck, thrust its red tongue out, and spat at Jacob. The animal's hard kick sent Jacob flying to the ground. Rebekah pursed her lips to stifle her laughter. She felt an immediate affinity with the stubborn donkey.

Jacob ran after the donkey, pulling the animal around to face her. "This is the only male who may glance at a single strand of your hair."

Rebekah was ecstatic. She had found another who would spit at Jacob. She saw that the animal's penis dangled almost to the ground. To spite all signs of masculinity, she named him Venus.

2

*R*ebekah watched her husband's silhouette disappear into the steel-gray fog as he embarked on his morning visit to the house that had become an obsession; back to creating a gaudy monstrosity he had decided to sell in order to buy more gold bullion to feed his kiln.

She wore her extravagant attire and ran to the stable. She scrubbed Venus, rubbed his pelt with animal fat, braided his tail, and laced donkey-beads around his hind legs. From his neck, she suspended an amulet of turquoise and a satchel of gum arabic to ward off the evil eye. This would be her secret daily ritual. She would never alter the ceremony until Jacob's gifts—skirts and dresses and veils—were stained with Venus's spittle and inherited the odor of manure.

Tears swam in the animal's eyes. Were they for her? She touched her lips to the donkey's, brushed her cheeks against his neck, and swept her scarred fingers over his tongue. "You're my only friend," she whispered.

Venus nuzzled his ear against her shoulder. His sweeping tongue was a cool balm. The thumping of his heart gave her courage. She pressed her nose against his hide to stop the stink of iron she carried with her. The comforting smell of domestic animals emanated from him. "Would you still love me if I became a wife-whore?"

The donkey's flank shook against her cheek. His ears pointed up. The odors of rain and hay and sweat assailed her. Lightning drenched the stable with violent shades of purple. Heavy boots crushed the hay behind her. She pressed her eyes shut and held the reins tight.

Jacob the Fatherless approached. He stared at her flushed face; at the stained silk and velvet clothing he had bought her. She prayed he would curse her, because his silence carried more poison than his words. He jumped back to escape the kick Venus aimed at him.

His voice was steady: "Don't move until I return."

Venus knelt and rested his head at her feet.

She heard Jacob descend into the cellar under the stable and then climb back up the steps. The crackling of hay and the tinkle of metal preceded him.

The iron box that held the metal trinkets he had fashioned in their first days together lay cradled in his arms.

He dragged her out of the stable and into the house, strode to the hearth, and tossed a bunch of mint into the fire. His nostrils flared. He touched himself between the legs where he was growing hard. Opening his vest, he removed the key from its secret pocket. The key scraped in the lock. He pushed the box into her arms.

"Put these on!"

Bafflement and dread paralyzed her.

"Raise the lid."

She did not budge.

He snapped the lid open and lifted the ornaments one by one. "The tools of a whore!" he proclaimed. "Deck yourself befitting the harlot you are."

"I'd rather die."

"Say your last prayers then," he hissed, his hands circling her neck.

"No one listens to my prayers."

His fingers squeezed harder.

"I can't breathe." She gasped, her lungs about to burst. "I'm dying."

He released her.

Her eyes sprang open. An expression, a certain slyness she did not comprehend but feared more than the hardness, altered his face as he gazed at her for a long time.

"Do you want to leave?" he asked.

She hesitated, suspicious, then asked, "This house? Forever?"

"Yes. You may go, on three conditions. You'll leave right now. You'll take nothing. And the donkey remains behind."

She flew to the door and flung it open, refusing to throw a second glance at what she was abandoning. She ran straight to the stable to say her farewells to Venus. She grazed her cheek against the animal, looked into his eyes, pressed her mouth to his ear. "Please, please, don't be angry. I'm leaving, but can't take you."

His eyes mournful, the donkey turned his neck and spat at the entrance to the stable.

Bewildered, Rebekah spun around, certain Jacob had followed her. An accusing emptiness confronted her. Venus emitted a long, grievous bray. She held the bridle and pressed her face to the donkey. Jacob would kill Venus if she left. Rebekah slumped on the hay. She had no alternative; if she stayed he would kill them both. She had to return home to her mother and demand to meet the man who had left behind a voice that would not die. She stood up, wiped her tears, and brushed the hay off her skirt. "Forgive me, Venus. Good-bye."

She hurried back to the house to pick up her chador. She

pushed the door that had been left open, and entered. Jacob
had not budged from the center of the room. He stood with the
box cradled in his arms, a triumphant smirk on his face.

Did he think she would not leave without Venus? She ran
to the bedroom, snatched her veil, tossed it over her head, and
rushed past Jacob toward the door.

"I forgot to tell you," he called behind her. "Your mother
died last Sabbath."

She whirled around to scrutinize her husband's expression,
and she realized he was telling the truth. Now she understood
why her mother had not come to visit.

He thrust the coffer, tools of a wife-whore, back at her.
"You've nowhere to go. I'm your only hope."

She shuffled into her bedchamber, dropping her clothing in
a trail behind her, certain the Ancient Zoroastrian's holy fires
foretold nothing but lies, certain she would never again laugh.

Rubbing musk on her upper lip to overpower the smell of her
loss, she drew out the tin ornaments and studied them to discover which part of her body they were intended for. Rows of tin
bangles on both wrists and ankles; metal bells on chains around
her neck; brass bullion hanging from her earlobes; silvery ropes
girthing her waist. She stared at a pair of dangling copper rosettes
with streamers. What was she supposed to do with these? The
rosettes did not have snaps for her ears, or pins for her hair, or
clasps to hang on some part of her body. They were two identical
vessels. She pressed them to her nipples. They fit. Each trinket
planted a fresh kernel of shame. She was no longer a daughter, a
wife, but had been transformed into Jacob's concubine, a vessel
to receive his waste. Avoiding the mirror, she painted her lips
scarlet, lined her eyes with charcoal, and doused herself with a
perfume of spices Jacob had bought her. The odor offended her
even more than the cold jingle of metal against her flesh.

She entered the room and approached Jacob.

"Arouse me!"

She balanced herself on her toes, lifted her arms overhead, twirled her hands, and tossed her curls back, imitating the dancing Gypsies.

He clapped his hands in glee. "Faster! Faster!"

She spun beneath the oil lamp. The metal floor under her tapping feet sounded like drums. Every swing, every sway, and every ripple exaggerated the reflection of light on her ornaments and bounced off his hungry eyes. She was a silvery doll; the pliant curve of her buttocks carved against her veil. The flash of defiance in her eyes stoked his passion.

She averted her gaze from the deranged masks on the mantelpiece. The tips of her fingers traced her rosette-clad nipples as she lowered herself onto her knees, swaying backward, her long hair brushing the floor.

A roar originated from his chest. He clutched his swollen penis. "Open your legs."

She braced herself against the enormity of his weight.

With every spurt of his lust, he threatened to bar her from heaven if she did not cherish his seed. "You'll give me sons. Your only salvation from the fires of hell!"

The kiln shot sparks against the soot-blackened walls. Did the fires of hell have voices like the ones in the hearth that roared at her with silent mouths: *You are a weakling, afraid of freedom, Rebekah?*

Smoke and tears burned her eyes.

The raging monsters melted onto the iron at the bottom of the hearth only to flare up again with threatening echoes: *God gave you the choice. You refused. You have lost Him.*

"No!" she cried, startling Jacob out of his rhythmic frenzy.

"Say, 'I'm your whore,'" he gasped. "Louder. Louder."

She turned her face from him and, for the first time in their married life, touched him of her own volition to silence him.

"I'm your whore," she whispered. Her shame ripened into guilt.

॰॰

At fourteen, the seed of Jacob the Fatherless stirred in her.

Jacob held a glass of clear liquid in one hand, and in another he clutched a small bundle he unwrapped to expose a mound of flesh she could not identify.

She bent closer. Was this another gift? She sprang back at the offensive odor of stale blood.

"Foreskins!" He chuckled.

A surge of bile stung her throat. She clamped her palm to her mouth, afraid to vomit on the treasure her husband so proudly offered. What was she to do with foreskins?

"Is your stomach empty?"

"Yes," she murmured.

He held up the glass. "Warm castor oil!" He thrust a foreskin deep into her mouth. "Wash it down with oil and don't you dare vomit."

Rebekah's translucent skin turned crimson, and her eyes a deep purple as she fought the bitterness that poisoned her while the foreskins of other women's sons made their way into her entrails.

"Now my beautiful wife will give birth to a virile boy," he announced, sustaining the kiln with scraps of metal. "My son will be born into a world of gold."

Rebekah begged God to come to her rescue. She had cursed, pleaded, threatened, and surrendered to no avail. Maybe if she became more pious He would listen. Although she had never before thought of lighting the Sabbath candles, now she transformed every sundown into her own private Sabbath. If her mother's God granted wishes on the holy day, she would will every evening into one. Facing the candles, a veil thrown over her curls, she prayed for a boy, so that Jacob would have pity on her and not dispatch her to hell.

ॐ

Rebekah went into labor at noon. Her husband was out melting iron.

The midwife, who visited at dawn, noon, and dusk, murmured incantations under her breath, boiled a pot of water, cut strips of calico, and examined Rebekah. "Child, if you don't stop trembling, your baby will be afraid to enter the world. What are you scared of?"

She was terrified of her prayers coming true, of giving birth to a boy, of dying, of being thrust into the unknown. She should not have pleaded for a son, a boy would be nothing but an extension of Jacob the Fatherless, following in his steps, melting, burning, and destroying everything in his path. In her dreams, she had given birth with ease to a girl, but the pain of delivering a boy had split her in half. Rebekah shut her eyes to blot out Jacob's demons.

The midwife rested her hand on Rebekah's forehead. "It won't take long. The mouth of your cervix is as open as the face of a large coin. Now take a deep breath and push hard."

Calling upon Abraham, Isaac, and Jacob, the midwife thrust her hand into Rebekah to turn the baby around and facilitate its delivery. Rebekah bore down hard, feeling herself widen, a pain far worse than the one she had experienced in her dreams. She was giving birth to a boy.

The child was born silent.

Rebekah's eyes sprang open. Had Jacob's cruelty killed the fetus? "Is it a boy?"

"A girl, my child."

"Why isn't she crying?" Rebekah asked.

"She is smiling."

The midwife set the infant on Rebekah's stomach. God was merciful; He had not forsaken her. He had forgiven her nights with Jacob, pardoned her transformation into a whore. He had given her a girl. A daughter. An ally, a friend. She, in return, would prove she had garnered courage from His generosity and would raise her daughter to become a devout Jew. She would watch her day and night until they planned their escape. She must start searching the house for Jacob's wealth, the gold bullion and coins. She would need money to travel with her daughter to a faraway place, to a world with no evil, no iron, no fire, no boundaries.

She smoothed her daughter's cheek, touched her lips, inhaled her innocence. A sweet faintness enveloped her, a haze, a welcome exhaustion. This was worth the humiliation of choking on bloody foreskins, worth all the nights she had danced for Jacob, contaminated herself with his odious perfume, and suffocated under his body.

Her daughter would be educated—above all the girls of the Jewish Quarter. She would learn to express her feelings. She would read her the *Rubáiyát* of Omar Khayyám and teach her to recite poetry. She would allow her to choose her own man. A man who would smell good to her. On her wedding night, dignitaries and important people of the neighborhood would file past, offering their congratulations and gifts of lacquered rosewood and filigreed jewelry. Her daughter would move into a rust-brick house like the one at the end of an alley, away from the garbage pit, in the most affluent part of the Quarter. She would have her own private bedchamber and a maid to wash the laundry in the *joubs*.

The echo of Jacob's steps came from afar.

Rebekah's dreams vanished.

She had given birth to a daughter, only to thrust her into the evil world of Jacob the Fatherless. Into the horrors she herself could not escape.

Jacob banged on the locked door with his metal-soled boots. He demanded to see his heir. A hard kick sent the latch flying from its hinges.

On twig-like legs that had grown strong from carrying his bulky body, he strode to Rebekah's pallet. She lay in sheets soaked with sweat and blood, the infant pressed against her bosom.

The room submerged under a cloud of fear, the smell of blood, birth, and iron. Jacob the Fatherless loomed in the center.

He snatched the child and raised her overhead. His crossed eyes quivered as he stared up. "Lord!" he cried to the heavens. "How dare you act against my will!?"

The midwife grabbed the child from him and ran out.

Jacob's ashen face turned to the kiln. He pulled on the metal mesh glove. He lifted the poker from its hook and jabbed it into the hearth, goading the flames.

Rebekah watched the tip of the poker blaze. An ember began to blossom. It was beautiful, like rosebuds about to bloom. She'd adorn her daughter's hair with roses, scatter petals in her cradle, on the pool, on Venus's saddle, and fill up bowls she'd set around the house.

Jacob the Fatherless stabbed the poker into the fire, retrieved and examined it, returned it into the hearth. He raised the poker. Spat on the tip. Held it to his ear. Relished the sizzle of dying spittle.

Rebekah pressed her palm to her heart. What was he trying to do now? He must not spoil this hour given to her. She promised God to repay His kindness by continuing to light the Sabbath candles, and to attend services in the synagogue of the

One-Eyed Rabbi. After services, she would allow herself some
vanity and flaunt her daughter's beauty. They would ride Venus
through the bazaar for the people to see that her daughter had
ivory skin and full lips like her mother and that she was not
cross-eyed and sour like her father.

Jacob approached the bed.

As if she were watching a fantastical dream, Rebekah connected the image of this menacing stranger to Ahriman, the
devil who resided in the Ancient Zoroastrian's dry, musky
scrolls. But this devil did not have bat wings or horns. He had
small, feminine feet buried in large boots, which he now
planted beside her mattress. He towered over her. His stare
pierced through her naked body.

He held the poker above her. The heat felt unbearable.

"Please," she pleaded, "leave me alone."

Jacob the Fatherless drove the tip of the poker between her
breasts.

᳇

Lifted on the wings of a breeze, she soared away. The skies
became lucid. Crystalline objects, china dolls, emerald car-
riages, and porcelain animals floated in weightless sweeps. On
the luminous horizon, veiled spirits pointed out an arbor of jasmine crowned with candle flames. A company of messengers
awaited her at the foot of the arbor and lured her forward.
Faster, they whispered, in voices that reverberated in her chest,
there is little time till dawn, when we must fall silent to hear
the prayers and praises of the living.

Rebekah sighed, contented. She would forgive her mother,
forgive her husband, make this place, where fires did not rage,
her home.

The echo of her daughter's name came from remote places.

She had not named her daughter.

Who had? She listened.

Gold Dust!

Jacob the Fatherless called her baby Gold Dust. Why? What did that name imply to him? Was he identifying her with gold so as to tolerate her presence? If she stayed here Jacob would convert her daughter into a motherless whore.

Rebekah plummeted into the acrid stench of burning flesh in her bedroom. Jacob was gone. The hearth was cold. The poker swayed on its peg.

"Our holy mothers are merciful, *Khanom!*" the midwife cried. "Your heart had stopped. We thought you were dead." She laid the baby on Rebekah's bosom.

Gold Dust's hungry mouth searched for Rebekah's nipple, intensifying the pain. Rebekah did not cry. She had passed through heaven and hell and had returned to save her daughter. She could not allow herself the comfort of tears.

Later she would think that because she did not scream out the pain, the poker had scorched her permanently, leaving a brand that turned hot or cold with her feelings, a padlock that imprisoned the ache in her chest, destroyed her faith, but in return supplied her with the spirit to fight.

 *3*

*J*acob the Fatherless gazed at his three-year-old daughter, searching for a resemblance to convince him she was the true offshoot of his blood.

For the last three years, he blamed Gold Dust for his inability to face the incriminating eye between Rebekah's breasts, the curse that prevented him from touching her. The damning stare was so terrifying that after Gold Dust's birth, the only way his passion stirred was through Rebekah's dancing.

Rebekah fluttered around him, pretending to dust the furniture.

"This creature is not my daughter! Whose fair complexion did she inherit?"

Rebekah set a plate of mint on the table and wondered what his distorted mind was concluding now. It pleased her to watch him struggle with his tormented self, to survey his increasing obsession with gold and mint, to observe him recoiling from the crimson blush of the brand he bequeathed her that had triumphed in its own subtle ways. His fears and delusions were intensifying, stripping him of his last vestiges of power.

"Whom did you fornicate with?" he demanded.

"I hardly leave the house."

"Whores find ways," he replied, unable to look into the bottomless indifference in her eyes. "I'm tired of raising a bastard. One day I'll pour liquid iron down her throat."

Rebekah lifted Gold Dust from his lap and walked out of the room. Was Jacob capable of such atrocity? Would he kill his own daughter?

Rebekah went to seek the help of the Ancient Zoroastrian.

"Ancient One," Rebekah said, hardly able to bear the heat between her breasts. "Could you devise a mixture to protect Gold Dust, if she were to consume liquid iron?"

The Zoroastrian did not lift her head, open her eyes, or ask questions. She had gazed into her fire and had seen Rebekah approach on her donkey. The old one had chuckled and had rubbed her palms in anticipation. She remembered a time when she had predicted amazing marvels in Rebekah's life. Seven years had passed. Rebekah was seventeen now. Although she had lost her faith in the holy fire, she had not lost hope, and that fountain would give birth to many more miracles.

The syrup was brewing in a treated cow udder. The liquid, thick and milky, consisted of the outer layer of pearls and seashells crushed and soaked in the roots of cypress, myrrh, and agaric, which bonded the ingredients and made them indigestible. The Zoroastrian handed the udder to Rebekah. "This liquid does not mix well with alloys. For thirty days, feed it to your daughter through the teat, only one drop, then increase the amount to a palmful for another twenty-one days. It will coat her digestive tract, so that even liquid iron will not burn her."

Rebekah examined the pregnant udder. The teat felt warm.

"No more than a palmful," the ancient one sighed. "Be cautious. More will seep into her blood and poison her."

Rebekah cupped the treasure in her hands.

"Go!" The ancient one whispered, "The hand of Ahura Mazda aid you and remember that after pain there is always laughter."

Every evening, before she put Gold Dust to bed, Rebekah squeezed a drop from the teat into her mouth. She watched her daughter drink hot goat milk, the steam rising from her throat, with no sign of pain on her face. She saw that she swallowed from Jacob's soup without wincing. She marveled at her increased resistance to hot liquids and hoped the elixir had created a protective shield inside her daughter.

ৡৢ

Rebekah's panic-stricken voice echoed around the house. "Gold Dust!" Her bed was empty. Where had Jacob taken her? To force liquid iron down her throat? "Gold Dust!"

Jacob sat by the kiln, Gold Dust on his lap. He thrust her into Rebekah's arms.

"What did you do to her?"

"The devil afflicted your daughter with a curse," he shouted, running out of the house.

Rebekah pressed her ear against her daughter's heart. Her bones were singing. They had turned into flutes. Melodious vibrations filled her marrow. Sad notes drifted out of every pore.

Had the music scared Jacob from acting upon his threat, or had the Zoroastrian's elixir saved Gold Dust from the liquid iron Jacob had forced down her throat?

"Gold Dust," Rebekah whispered. "Did you drink something very hot?"

Gold Dust stared at the door, then touched her throat.

"Jacob's gone. Don't be afraid. Do you hurt here?"

Gold Dust opened her mouth. A viscous residue mottled her tongue and throat. Rebekah rubbed Gold Dust's tongue with her finger and put it in her own mouth. Was this the caustic taste of iron, or the taste of her own fear?

"Help me, Gold. Was it hot?"

"No," Gold Dust replied. "It was bitter."

Rebekah cuddled her daughter on her lap and tried to decipher the melodies of her bones.

When Gold Dust was sad or in pain, her music resembled the melancholy notes of a sitar; when confused, the jarring beat of tambourines; and when happy, the playful chime of bells. In the ensuing months, Rebekah realized that her daughter's music was the manifestation of her emotions.

Her feelings had been transferred into her marrow to be protected by her bones.

Rebekah set out to teach Gold Dust to restrain her music. "Imagine going through life with your bones singing in the presence of friend and foe. Learn to hold back your music like you do your tears and laughter."

Her honey-colored eyes wide with wonder, Gold Dust listened.

"A woman must recognize her weaknesses and strengths," Rebekah continued. "Yours reside in your bones. That's why they ache when you're sad and sing when you're happy. Manipulate your music to your advantage."

Gold Dust was an astute student. She learned to plug her bones in the presence of strangers and compose happy tunes when her mother needed cheering.

Ultimately, the joyous or melancholy notes of her bones replaced her tears.

❧

Rebekah went to the local well to cleanse herself of her monthly blood.

She wailed out to the treetops, to the squawking crows, to the gurgling streams. The Ancient Zoroastrian had promised to linger as close as a prayer to Gold Dust. But she had broken her promise. Gold Dust could not cry. How could she bear this life without the comfort of tears?

The water in the well grumbled. Crows fell silent. Rebekah placed a plug of wool soaked in the juice of weeping willows inside her. One day, her brand might lose its intense pulsing and the ability to intimidate Jacob. He would copulate with her again. But she would never again give birth to his offshoot, sons or daughters who forget to cry.

She returned from the well. Jacob recoiled from the violet ice in her eyes. He went to his kiln and spent hours making love to iron, molding metals, smelting copper mixed with tin to create bronze implements. He tossed them all into the fire.

"I want gold with no trace of the base alloys," he thundered, as if his voice would force God into compliance.

Rebekah served his dinner of stew gorged with the bones of beef. He sat at the table and banged the bones on a metal plate, soaked *sangak* bread in the marrow, and stuffed his mouth. "Soon I'll become immortal like gold," he barked, sucking his teeth in search of mint leftovers. "Do you understand, woman?"

"No," Rebekah replied, "but I've faith in you. I'm certain you know a secret I don't." Has anyone lived forever? she wondered, her brand sizzling. It was hard enough to protect herself from him; it was becoming impossible to shelter Gold Dust.

"If you had any brain in your thick skull," Jacob said, "you'd understand the concept of immortality. When gold melts it's altered into liquid, when it cools off it becomes solid again. In both states it remains tangible and never vanishes into nothingness like humans do in death."

Rebekah felt the room turn cool. A breeze fluttered through her hair. Jacob's lips moved, but she could not hear him. She was riveted by an idea revealed to her. Why had she not thought of this before? The weakness of men lies in what they cherish most. She tossed a bunch of mint into the flames. The room turned warm again. She wiped her forehead.

Jacob banged on the tabletop with a butcher's knife. "Where are you, woman? Did you hear me?"

Rebekah soaked more mint in the bone marrow he devoured and tossed a plateful of herbs into the furnace. "I understand now. Gold survives even in fire that's known to destroy everything. But how can *you* become gold?"

Jacob rubbed his bulging organ. "Whine like your beloved Venus, and I'll tell you."

Let him flog her. Kill her. She was ready to die. But she would not whine like a donkey.

"Deck yourself with my jewels first."

Her chilling gaze was aimed at him like a curse.

"Go! Or I'll drown Gold Dust in the well."

Rebekah ran to retrieve her coffer of trinkets. She would protect her daughter even if she had to whine, even if it would take her hours to rouse Jacob to such ecstasy that he would exhaust himself without touching her.

She emerged unafraid of Jacob but surprised by the hardness that filled her. Had she lost all feeling? The metal ornaments Jacob had designed covered most of her naked body, dangling from her ears, neck, waist, and ankles. His latest gifts, bronze toe rings, hurt her feet. From a rope around her neck hung a copper medal fashioned to the size and circumference of her brand to conceal it from Jacob.

"Open your legs!" he cried.

Rebekah stretched out on the carpet and spread her thighs.

"Wide! Don't you have hands?"

Her fingers revealed the dark blush. His stare stabbed like daggers.

"Moan!"

She arched her back, raised her mound, sighs rising from her throat.

"Louder!"

Animal sounds sprang from the pit of her stomach; dew glistened on her body. Her buttocks trembled with the tension of holding herself exposed to him.

"Now get up and dance for me!"

Underneath the oil burner, Rebekah spun on her toes, curls flying, breasts swaying. With a flurry of ringing metals, she whirled from one corner to another, gathering fistfuls of mint from bowls around the room and tossing them into the flames. The smell of cremated mint permeated the air.

She dangled her breasts in front of his eyes, swung her rosette-clad nipples over his knees, teased him with one, then the other, her body pliant from years of dancing. He twisted in his chair. Sweat beaded his nose. His eyeballs rolled up, leaving two white crescents behind. She clutched him. His moans intensified. A single squeeze sent him into painful convulsions.

You son of a burned dog, empty yourself clean because this will be your last release.

"Don't you dare grow old on me," he panted.

"I won't," she replied, her voice sweet and sticky. "If you teach me how to become immortal."

꩜

Jacob stood in front of the kiln, his back to Rebekah. She held on to the door frame, one palm resting against her heart. Tonight you'll turn into gold. Have courage. Be a man. Defeat the fire, she begged silently. If she could only toss more mint into the flames, erase the last traces of doubt; remind him of his virility, his power to triumph.

She had to muster courage, brace and ready herself for the unknown, guide this night into the one she had been awaiting.

Jacob the Fatherless removed his boots, stepped out of his calico pants, and tossed off his shirt. He dropped his vest on the metal floor; the key tinkled in the pocket. The light shone through his naked body. Rebekah's heart gave a joyous leap. She had learned the workings of his mind. He would face fire like a warrior, with nothing between him and the flames. He shifted. Hesitated. Did he sense her presence? She stood motionless. Silent.

He whirled around. Met her gaze. The fire galvanized his stare. Two opaque marbles locked with her eyes. His tiny pupils were dark pinheads.

"Don't become immortal. Please. Don't leave us. We need you." Approaching the bowl of mint, she unbuttoned her blouse. She flung the herbs into the flames. "Think of us, your children."

His nostrils flared and the lines on his face hardened with his resolution to oppose her.

She advanced, her breasts almost brushing against his chest. The odor of mint saturated the room. He was virile, invincible. Would he garner the courage to forever preserve this moment?

She tossed off her blouse. Her nipples stood erect.

He started back, alarmed at the glow between her breasts, the outer ring pulsating. He pressed his palms to his eyes.

Jacob the Fatherless raised one foot, then the other, and climbed over the ledge that separated the kiln from the room.

He stepped into the flames.

His back caught fire. The hiss of searing hair, skin, and flesh filled the room. In a slow-moving nightmare, the flames enveloped him. He turned around to confront her. Behind the blazing screen, his mouth opened into a smile, then melted into a grimace. The fire smothered his scream. His distorted face began to dissolve.

"You were not gold after all," Rebekah murmured to the heap of fat at the bottom of the kiln.

She picked a sprig of mint and stuck it behind her ear to stave off the stink of the Devil.

4

The next day was hot. Even the sun could not find refuge behind the sweltering clouds. Rebekah ran out into the alleys. Clutching her daughter's hand and tearing strands of her own hair from their roots, she wailed that the black plague had consumed her husband. He had shivered and sweated and vomited until his feet had turned blue. He couldn't control his bowels; his skull had shrunk; his eyes wouldn't shut. He couldn't even drink a drop of water, she screamed. What an agonizing death! She addressed the populace as if her words were meant as a benediction. "May this never happen to you."

Mothers snatched their children into the safety of their arms; men sneaked away, women slipped behind tree trunks.

"Jacob wanted to be buried in the privacy of his backyard," Rebekah sobbed. "I need strong hands to wash the corpse and dig a grave."

The crowd of many able, healthy men, and young women, who could help with the cleansing and burial ritual, averted their eyes. In fear of contracting the plague, no one came to Rebekah's aid. Some sneaked away, others fidgeted with the tassels of their religious shawls. A few counted their prayer beads, their eyes raised to heaven in search of a savior. Some, like Heshmat the Matchmaker, who had found new cud to chew on, whispered that since Rebekah never had a happy marriage, the great show of distress she displayed was no doubt to hide some secret shame that time would reveal.

∾

Eighteen-year-old Rebekah locked herself in her house, a seeming recluse from a pitiless world. She would dodge the curious questions of neighbors: How did the plague consume Jacob the Fatherless? Why didn't his wife and daughter contract the pestilence? How did she manage to bury that heavy body? Time would cloud their memories. They would forget. When Gold Dust reached the marrying age, Rebekah would emerge into the bazaar, reappear with such splendor the community would have no choice but to acknowledge them. She'd flaunt her daughter's beauty and find her a young man who had been taught to respect women.

Rebekah set to work searching the house for her late husband's fortune. She tore the casings off the mattresses and pillows and emptied them of feathers. She pried loose the bricks from around the kiln in her bedroom and dug under the metal floors of her kitchen. She went to the stable and burrowed under the straw and mud. She descended to the basement and rummaged among the tools and molds her husband had used to fashion her jewelry.

He had left behind nothing but the stench of the burning kiln, the stink of his rancor, and the shame of poverty.

Overnight, Rebekah became a poor woman.

Soon nothing was left of the donkey but skin and bone.

Rebekah sold her jewelry, fancy clothing, and the box of trinkets: tools of a whore. When she had nothing more to barter, Gold Dust began to suffer from malnutrition. Her stomach swelled like the belly of their earthenware jar, her tongue became lined with cracks, her hair fell out in fistfuls, and she moaned endlessly.

When weak cries of hunger replaced Gold Dust's sweeping laughter, Rebekah's heart broke. She had endured her brand with patient dignity. She had crawled on all fours and whined like a donkey to protect her daughter. She would not allow her to die from hunger.

The night of Noi, the darkest and longest night of the year, when the owls never blink for fear of missing Beelzebub's pranks, Rebekah folded a sack under her arm and went out to the garbage pit. The sky was an expanse of black velvet with no moon to soften the sadness. The air was stagnant. No breeze to transport the aroma of flowers or the stench of the pit. Not even the drone of crickets disturbed the silence, or fireflies lightened the impenetrable gloom. She raked through the garbage from where the filth and poisonous fumes brought contagious diseases and white worms that caused a bloody affliction of the intestines. The feel of her fingers and a keen vision—cultivated by having watched Jacob work—told her what to choose. She left with a sackful of tins and metal scraps to melt in the blacksmith's kiln that operated in the center of the bazaar. She swore never to light the fire in her bedroom.

She first fired the medal her husband had fashioned to conceal her brand from him, then, imitating him, she melted metals and poured them into molds. She fashioned kitchen utensils, decorative pins for women, and cheap ornaments for little girls. She would continue this until she saved enough money to buy fabrics and become a bundle woman.

A phantom under the tent of night, a sack swaying over one shoulder, she visited houses at the fringe of the Jewish Quarter.

She spread her objects on the ground, sold six spoons to one family, a set of forks to another, a bracelet to a pregnant woman who had peeked into her belly in her dreams and seen a daughter there. Rebekah sealed her lips shut and opened her palm, accepting any amount offered her. Sometimes she was robbed; at other times a charitable person would offer more than the worth of her merchandise.

She came to be known as the metal-woman who bartered in the dark. Those who lived at the outskirts of the Jewish Quarter saw the glint of one eye peering through the fold of her veil, and even they would not recognize her if they saw her in daylight.

By the time the sheen of Gold Dust's coffee-colored hair had returned, and her eyes had acquired the sparkle of health, Rebekah had accumulated enough money to buy fabrics. She let it be known she would pay well for superior materials embroidered with costly threads. Women rushed to the bazaars and spent their life savings on wires of silver and threads of silk soaked in liquid metals to weave fabrics with exceptional luster. Rebekah had an excellent eye for acquiring materials that women had to have. The name Rebekah the Bundle Woman found its way out of the Jewish Quarter and reached the ears of affluent Muslims who were not afraid to spend money on their vanity.

But the echo of Jacob's voice refused to abandon Rebekah. Not even the stars of the sky should set eyes on a single toenail of yours. Venus is the only other male who will glance at a single strand of your hair! She went from door to door, the burning between her breasts and the need for revenge eternal.

One night, a male client, in exchange for spending an hour with her, offered her more than enough to frame the tapestry of her lofty dreams. Rebekah dumped her sack of metals into the garbage pit. A whore's disgrace was already stamped on her.

Why not profit from the shame and amass a respectable dowry for Gold Dust?

Rebekah had a cobbler stitch her sandals with soles that imprinted FOLLOW ME on the dirt road. Then she made it known to her male clients she would readily entertain them if they promised to fade from her life without leaving behind so much as a whiff of their intimate scent.

༄

Around the baths and in the back stalls of the bazaar, tales about a mark between Rebekah's breasts circulated among her men. They swore that the mark changed shape with her emotions, glowed when she made love, and burned to the touch when she was angry. The exact shape remained a mystery to all save Rebekah and her men, who whispered they were certain "the thing" was a supernatural phenomenon. Rebekah's evenings grew busier as curious men—single, married, fathers, and grandfathers, Jews, Christians, and Muslims—rushed to visit this marvelous gift of God: a violet-eyed beauty who wore nothing but a mark between her breasts and a sprig of mint behind her ear.

Common men came in search of an hour of excitement; scholars came who wished for nothing but a space to rest their weary minds, and an occasional warrior came who felt a need to boast of his triumphs. Rebekah learned of the peculiarities of men, what transformed an ordinary man into an exceptional soldier and what caused the fall of great kings.

Rebekah was selective, receiving mostly wealthy men. Occasionally, if a poor soul came knocking on her door, she would oblige for less than her usual price if he had a pleasing voice. She was still young and full of hope and believed she would one day unravel the mystery of the voice that continued to haunt her.

5

*T*he lucky patterns in the slush at the bottom of the coffee cup, the feminine curve of Gold Dust's hips, the inviting sway of her walk, her expansive laughter and inquisitive questioning told Rebekah her daughter was ready to be presented to the world.

Rebekah set out to search for the most educated bachelor in the Jewish Quarter. Wisdom, she had decided, granted a man confidence and ease in his relationship with women. Illiterate men like Jacob made up for their ignorance by stifling a woman's soul. Rebekah's search was brief. Not many families in the Quarter were well off and had an educated son the right age for Gold Dust. Rebekah learned that a merchant, Rouh'Allah the Spirit of God, and his son, Ebrahim, lived in a residence of real fired brick, an extravagance where baked mud and straw were common.

She went to inspect the merchant's grounds. The house was built at the end of an alley and below street level, with steps leading down to the entrance, so the Jew beaters, who periodically invaded the Quarter to harass and rob Jews, would not bother with the maze of dark alleys and steep stairs that protected the merchant's residence.

Keeping herself out of the range of light that spilled out, Rebekah peered in through the lace-covered windows. From her vantage, she half saw the main hall. An oil burner, with brass arms holding flaming cups, hung from the center of the ceiling. Every room connected to a round hall by a passageway she detected when doors were opened momentarily.

She acquired the habit of prowling around the residence. Ebrahim, the merchant's son, was a handsome youth with green eyes, black curly hair, and skin the color of raw almonds. He wore eggshell pants, opal capes, and dove-gray shirts. He liked his sweets with a pinch of saffron, obvious from the yellow tinge of the rice cakes and chickpea candies. He made a face at the brown, hard-boiled eggs and fried eggplant served on Sabbath. He never touched the Friday *gondy* of meat and chickpeas, but enjoyed rice *polo* with diced carrots and red beans with a touch of turmeric.

He was a voracious reader, not only of poetry he recited from leather-bound books; he also studied the lives of renowned warriors, and listened to music from foreign lands that was too sophisticated for Rebekah to understand.

Gold Dust would spend the rest of her life in this house. She was young and pliable and would easily learn the ways of the rich.

Rebekah taught her daughter to bake rice bread and chickpea candies with saffron and discouraged her from boiling Sabbath eggs. She bought her numerous books of poetry and volumes of history that talked of the lives and habits of men such as Aristotle, Cyrus and Darius the Great, and Tamerlane, the Mongol. She taught her to read. Salvaging strips of white and cream-colored cloth from the materials she sold, Rebekah made Gold Dust flowing skirts and clinging blouses.

Rebekah returned to the merchant's house to make sure his son still lived there and had not been married off. She hid behind the window and watched Ebrahim. His books were heavier. He had grown into a scholar. Often, she heard the murmur of discourse between him and his father, who occupied a seat in a corner of the room, far from her vantage. She took pains to conceal herself. The merchant might think she had come to invite him to her bed to make a few *dinars*. Even a whore could feel shame.

Yes. She could be humiliated despite having convinced herself that her body was only a means of supporting her daughter, despite her refusal to allow guilt to choke her life, and despite the stamp of her FOLLOW ME sandals, which to the world was a whore's invitation, but to her, a grand ruse to discover the man who would redeem in her heart the fall of all men.

That man knocked on her door at dawn when the gray skies still hovered overhead. He stood clutching a coin. A stunning youth with platinum hair humid from the sweat of excitement, and green, scintillating eyes wide with fear of his first encounter with a woman. He held his trembling palm out to assure her he would pay. His beauty sent Rebekah's heart into a flutter.

He was no older than thirteen.

She led him into the warmth of candles and incense and slipped off his loose robe, the vest under it, the prayer shawl from around his waist, all the time careful to keep her hands off his bared skin. She would prolong his excitement—her own too—enjoy this boy, so different from Jacob the Fatherless, who had robbed her of her innocence. This princely boy would be resilient to her touch, ready to be advised, grateful for the guidance of a woman of twenty-five.

She stepped back, her gaze caressing his elegant features, his every trembling muscle, his beardless face, the innocent outline of his lips. When, at last, she stepped close, his skin, even under the tips of her numb fingers, felt vibrant with anticipation. She kissed his emerald eyes shut to allow him respite from the heat between her breasts that his stare could not turn away from.

His voice shook. "Let me see your mark."

She whispered, "It's a wedding brand. Don't gaze at it too long, it will burn your eyes."

Her tongue slid over his body, feeling the hardness between his thighs, the beat of the arteries behind his knees. The moisture on him, the wetness in his mouth tasted sweet. She rose on her toes and hid his face between her breasts.

Imitating her, his tongue drew circles on her chest, her swollen nipples, around the brand that burned with desire.

She grabbed a shock of his silver curls and forced his head back, locking her eyes with his. "Part your lips," she whispered, taking his luscious mouth in hers. Her hands cupped his buttocks, embracing him, crushing him against her, her tongue probing his mouth.

A spurt of semen wet her belly.

He sprang back full of apologies.

She smeared his seed on her brand. "Your first lesson is never to apologize for spilling yourself."

She allowed him time to rest, fanning the flies away while he fell into a deep sleep. Then she lay down next to the cold hearth where the metal floor was warm from their bodies and offered herself to him, hoping to regain her dignity.

She opened herself to him with such innocent surrender the boy experienced a courage he did not know he had, and, as if he were an experienced man, thrust his hardness at her while she moaned with pain as if it were her first time.

Before he left, she knew he was no longer a green boy, nor she a spurned woman.

At the door, he whispered, "I've worshiped your wedding brand all night. It hasn't burned my eyes."

"It won't, if you care."

Every Sabbath eve, Moses, the boy, returned. When he did not have money, he brought a branch of jasmine he had picked from the neighbor's garden, a slice of rice bread he had stolen from the kitchen, a strand of fake pearls his mother had left unattended. Rebekah welcomed him. Surrendered to him. Gave him refuge between her ample thighs.

He, in return, taught her to inhale and taste the many scents that inhabit the world, to give them the proper name and color, and to learn to smell the body and soul with all of their sweet and stinking hues.

"I miss your brand when I'm away," Moses complained.

She licked his eyelids shut. "It brings bad luck."

"You're wrong," he said. "It makes you different, loving and courageous."

"Then let me give you one." She went to her coffer and came back with her sewing box and the container that held her ointments and dyes. "Don't look," she whispered, holding a needle in the candle flame to decontaminate it. She sat him on the mattress and pressed her ear to his chest, listening to the beat of his heart.

Her needle traced a design above his left nipple, pricked the border of the figure and the insides, drawing blood. He sat motionless as she retrieved a satchel of henna from her box and smeared it on the pattern, mixing it with his blood.

She raised a mirror and displayed his tattoo. "There!" she said, blowing on his chest. "My gift to you. A permanent love brand to remember me by. Now you have two hearts to love with."

"But hearts are not this color."

"It's the color of overexposed blood—like mine."

One Sabbath eve, like every other, anticipating Moses, she locked her door, refusing all visitors. Late into the night, before she retired, she unlocked the door, certain he would come. He was one of eleven brothers. He helped support his family. He might have had to work late.

Moses never came.

Her body ached for his grateful gaze, kind hands, and bloody love tattoo, but she was not sad. He had transformed her into a different woman, a tutor of love, a benevolent matriarch to a large contingent of adolescent boys who would happily steal to pay her for secrets that would convert them into seasoned men.

"If the fire didn't destroy your soul, Jacob," she repeated every time she parted her thighs, "this will." And the words turned into a tenacity that goaded her life.

6

*R*ebekah the Bundle Woman appeared in the Jewish Quarter with a sprig of mint stuck behind her ear to stave off the stink of the Devil. Her silver chador shimmering in the sunlight, her golden hair flying out of the fringes of her veil, she blew passionate kisses to those she liked and batted her eyelashes flirtatiously at those she did not. Clad in layers of lace, and emerging for the first time in daylight, Gold Dust perched on the saddle behind her.

Women secured their chadors over bitter mouths, yanked their children away, and fled the scene of shameless beauty, blinding glitter, and brazen gestures. They questioned the morality of a world where a whore dared not only bare her face, but also stir envy in chaste wives.

Men crowded around Rebekah to stare at her violet eyes, the shade of dusks, full, sensuous lips, and hair the color of daffodils.

"Today," Rebekah sang out to the wild jingle of her multi-bangled wrists, "I shall reveal a secret I've guarded for years." Then, to their amazement, she cupped her mouth with her hands, as if to keep her words from the ears of the Almighty. "Eleven years ago, I returned from death because I couldn't bear the grief of deserting my daughter. What a boring way to depart, sweetloves. Next time, *I* will decide when to die, and it will not be at the hand of the Devil."

"Tell them the story," Gold Dust whispered, tossing back her almond-brown hair, which swayed against her cheeks, and raising amber eyes that had a slight twist. She, too, wanted to learn the story of the Devil. In the privacy of her home, she no longer dared ask the question she had been grappling with all of her young life.

Rebekah stroked the donkey's neck. "Patience, child. Mysteries have a revealing season of their own. I'll say more when you are older."

Then, with an elaborate flourish of her arm, she announced, "I shall go down in history as the first woman who dared defeat the Devil."

Her words sent another shock through the crowd of men who had lingered behind. Their stares followed her as she steered Venus toward the labyrinth of alleys that led to the house of the wealthy merchant.

With their layers of lace, glittering veils, and glass-studded skirts, their legs flanking the donkey, the woman and child had a liveliness about them that mocked the somber alleys and the sadness in Rebekah's heart.

Mosquitoes buzzed around, and winged cockroaches were crushed under the donkey's hooves. Beggars followed Venus. Afflicted with *kachali,* the boys had lost their hair, and their bare skulls festered with a crust of dried blood and pus. Those who had a few lice-infested strands left scratched their heads as they implored alms. This was not the inviting bazaar Rebekah remembered when she had visited with her mother. Today the call of the vendors sounded sad, the smells carried the odor of decay. Rebekah tossed out two silver coins and swore to do all in her power to save Gold Dust from a future where human sweat and the hacking coughs of consumption were the only tools to arouse pity so as to gain a few dinars to support a large family.

Thankful for this mission that distanced her temporarily from her home, a gravesite of memories, Rebekah chanted to her daughter, "I'll teach you how to become a woman and how to elaborate on your music when a man is present, so you'll charm him forever."

Gold Dust reached out slender arms and hugged her mother's waist. A melody suffused with sadness, like silk moths floating in the air, rose from her bones.

The feel of her daughter's embrace added to Rebekah's resolve. The important journey she had ahead of her sharpened her senses.

"Madar," Gold Dust asked, unable to contain her curiosity. "Where are we going?"

How could she explain that although Gold Dust was the daughter of the infamous Jacob the Fatherless, and the offshoot of a whore, she was certain her daughter's redeeming qualities would render her ambitious journey a success.

"Imagine," Rebekah replied, "you're traveling to unknown destinations where you're promised extravagant treasures—but only if you keep your bones calm until we arrive, a wise and necessary practice throughout your life."

A sigh of resignation filled Gold Dust's marrow. Once her mother began to speak in riddles, Gold Dust knew she had lost her to a secret scheme.

The music of lute and tambourine came from afar. The acrobats! Gold Dust had heard them before, but was never allowed to go out and watch the acrobats. Her mother had recounted tales of a father and son who swallowed air, and spit fire, draped poisonous snakes around their necks, and thrust their heads into the mouths of bears.

"Can we visit the acrobats?" Gold Dust now asked.

"We don't have time," Rebekah murmured, engrossed in her plan. Her nipples rose with anticipation. She hooked the reins around her wrists and rubbed her palms to warm them up and cup them over her breasts. She buttoned her vest. It would not do to visit the merchant with stirred nipples and the moist aroma of a just-awakened woman wafting off her.

Venus started into a trot. At the opposite end of the alley, two men gazed at the approaching donkey. One bent and reached for an object on the dirt road.

"Madar," Gold Dust called. "Look out!"

Rebekah covered her face with the chador, but was unable to dodge the horse manure that smashed against her veil.

"Whore! You defile our innocent boys. How dare you show your face in daylight!"

Gold Dust jumped off the saddle, gathered pebbles, and ran toward the men. Rocks flew. Yells pounded in her ears. "Bastards! Sons of whores!" Then, even in her anger, she fell silent, ashamed she had uttered the word she had promised herself never to voice in her mother's presence.

Rebekah's heels goaded Venus forward. She leaned over and helped Gold Dust vault the donkey. "My brave one, control your temper. Remember to be a lady."

"Whore!" The narrow alley swallowed the word, spitting it back at mother and daughter.

Rebekah bent from the waist and blew playful kisses at the men. "I'm an honorable whore in need of dishonorable pimps. Would you oblige, gentlemen?"

Venus maintained a steady pace. Brushing past the men, the donkey turned its neck and aimed a sticky wad of spittle at them. The veil spattered with manure fluttered in the air and landed at their feet.

Rebekah's laughter lingered in the mist as Venus disappeared around the corner.

She checked herself, sniffed between her breasts, under her arms. The chador had saved her attire.

"What is a whore?" Gold Dust asked, resting her cheek against her mother's back. Of course she knew. But even at her young age, she had learned to plead ignorance and save her mother embarrassment.

"A whore is a woman who has the honor to sacrifice her body and soul for the comfort of her child," Rebekah replied, kicking the animal into a canter.

At the end of the narrow alley, they faced steps, flanked by pots of jasmine, that led down to the merchant's residence.

To Gold Dust, the rust-colored house seemed plucked out of her mother's many tales—a spacious castle, with lace-draped windows, behind which hid a mysterious world she could not even begin to fathom.

Rebekah counted six cherry trees away from the merchant's house and tied Venus to the trunk of the seventh. She hoped the animal was far enough not to offend the elegant landscape. She untied her bundle and removed a simple black chador she had borrowed for the occasion. She spread the veil over her head and her glittering clothes. In the alabaster of her face, her eyes were scintillating worry-jewels. She had come to offer her daughter to the altar of men, to power and wealth, to one of the few who had raised a scholar in this bleak place. She had come to offer her daughter to the only boy who deserved her. Would he, one day, redeem in her eyes this monstrous alliance referred to as marriage?

Gold Dust frowned, exaggerating the dimple in her chin. "When you have that look, something goes wrong. I'm coming with you."

"Have I taught you nothing?" Rebekah said. "Behave like a lady of substance. You'll enter with appropriate pomp and elegance after you've been invited." She whirled around and started down the path, certain she had made the right choice in bringing her daughter along. If all went well, she wanted her nearby.

Gold Dust's gaze followed her mother's retreating back. She slumped under a cherry tree. The ground was dotted with the plump fruit. Gathering a handful, she tied the stems to weave an anklet. The music of the acrobats was nearing. She could walk to the end of the alley and return before her mother missed her. Gold Dust laced the cherries around her ankle, lifted herself, and dusted her skirt. She followed the music, counting the trees, so she could find her way back.

Not far from the main street, the acrobats skipped around; the son, perched on his father's shoulders, played the tambourine.

Gold Dust raised her gaze to him and her child-heart exploded in her chest. His complexion was so fair and his eyes so blue, she mistook him for one of the angels in her mother's tales. His copper-colored curls and dazzling smile and the music at the tip of his fingers shattered her heart further.

He vaulted into the air, somersaulted once, twice, and settled at her feet like a cat. His hands skipped on his tambourine and his toes on the ground as he danced in circles around her. She saw the tambourine flip high into the air, spin and twirl, then swoop down and encircle her like a musical embrace. Kneeling, he drew a sword, tied with a golden rope around his waist, and with the tip severed her cherry anklet and dropped it into his pocket.

He frolicked around a cherry tree, cut off a branch, genuflected, and held it up to her. "Your eternal servant, Soleiman the Agile."

"Gold Dust," she whispered.

"A beautiful and becoming name, my lady. I shall remember Gold Dust as long as I live."

"Someday I'll marry you!" she blurted out, hugging his gift and running away, stunned at her audacity and at the ridiculous words that had tumbled out of her mouth.

༄

Rebekah tucked her stray hair inside her chador and wished she had a mirror to check herself. Maybe this was not the right time to visit the merchant. What if he personally came to the door? She might lose her bearing if she came face-to-face with the grand man without the proper introduction from a servant.

She held her veil tightly under her chin and started down the sand-covered steps. Horrified, she stared at the imprint of FOLLOW ME the soles of her sandals had embossed on the sand. She removed the sandals and concealed them under one of the jasmine pots. She fought the urge to turn back, forget her absurd plan, her bare feet, her daughter.

Her daughter!

Racing up and down the stairs, she wiped the imprints off with her feet.

At the door, she raised her knuckles. Stealing her hand away, she pressed her palm to the brand between her breasts. In an ancient act of prayer she had thought forgotten, she brought her hand up to her face, creating a dome with her five fingers. She only knew how to pray to herself.

Her knuckles drummed too hard on the oak-wood door. Before she had composed herself, the door opened. She came face-to-face with a servant, shaven head reflecting the sunlight, arms folded against his chest. A look she knew too well darkened his eyes.

She locked her fingers and struggled to control the habitual cooing that threatened to creep into her tone. "Honorable *Agha,* may I talk to the master of the house?"

"His Honor is not available." The servant stepped back, indicating he expected her to remove herself from the threshold.

From her vantage, the hall behind the servant seemed endless. Costly Kashan rugs and columns of alabaster flanked the doors at both sides of the corridor. "Your Honor!" she shouted at the top of her lungs. "I am Rebekah, the wife of the late Jacob the Blacksmith. I am here to see you!"

The servant pushed her from the entrance and tried to shut the door. If only she had saved a handful of manure to smear on his indignant face, she thought, her bare foot preventing the door from closing. Only the deep flush of her cheeks betrayed the pain in her toes.

She cupped her mouth with her hands and turned toward the neighborhood. She would lure every wealthy man out of his sanctuary, every pampered woman from her lofty throne, force them to acknowledge parts of the Quarter they preferred to ignore, acknowledge Rebekah the Whore at the merchant's doorstep. "Your Honor, I'll not leave until—"

The merchant appeared at the end of the hall. He stood tall, chestnut hair brushed behind his ears. A cape of camel's wool with ruby trim draped his shoulders. A chain of onyx worry beads wrapped twice around his right wrist. He clapped his hands, the sound hardly audible. The servant hurried toward him.

The murmur of the merchant's order and the servant's protests reached Rebekah; she pressed the back of her hand to her lips to blot off cherry unguent. With a fingertip, she rubbed off excess kohl from the rims of her lashes. She checked to make sure her vest was fully buttoned.

The servant bowed her in, leading her into the formal area. She lowered herself onto a divan pointed out to her and adjusted her veil to cover the curls she was in the habit of

flaunting. She congratulated herself. It had not been that difficult after all. None other than the master himself had received
her with respect. But why? Why had he allowed her into his
home without the slightest questioning? At the thought that
he might have invited her out of charity, the translucent skin
of her right fingers shrank. The merchant reached for her hand.

Moisture fused her palm to his.

His gray eyes lingered on her lips, bosom, bare toes. His gaze
swept the length of her body. "I am Rouh'Allah the Spirit of
God."

His voice overwhelmed and unraveled her, caused her
immense hopelessness. An honest and candid tone. Intimate.
Even considerate. A deep respect evident, despite her occupa-
tion. The ring echoed in her ears in the ensuing quiet.

She formed words with her lips, but her voice lost its way
in her throat. She hurried to her feet. "So kind of you, Your
Honor . . ."

"Dear lady." He held her disfigured hand. "Please don't
stand on ceremony with me. I know you well."

She had a strange premonition that if she opened her
mouth she would blurt: I am Rebekah, Your Honor, Rebekah
the Whore. No. She might softly whisper: I am Rebekah, Your
Honor, an honorable whore. Would this voice that made her
shiver and want to spill out the secrets of her life whisper back:
An honorable woman, my dear, in fact a desirable woman?

Rebekah blushed. Her fingers were on fire. She had to
absolve herself, disclose why she had chosen her profession,
why she considered herself more respectable than many wives
who were forced into submission. But beyond all, she longed to
hold on to his voice, which inflamed her brand and rattled her.
In the shadow of the curtains his face was only a silhouette.

She slipped her hand out of his and stuffed it in her pocket.
How should she handle this novel sensation, the touch of this

man? Most of her life she had been slapped. Bruised. For his tenderness she had no name. Rouh'Allah's words drifted to her:

"I've grown closer to you as I watched you, late at night, behind these windows. I would leave the curtains open for you. Please! Don't distress yourself on this account. No harm done, none at all." Night after night, he had seen her peek through the window. He had at first believed she would eventually trample upon her pride and knock on his door to take a closer look and maybe even inspect intimately the wealth she could never attain. But when time passed and she had not tired of her secret visits, he had concluded that some tender emotions stirred her and that she came to observe him. He positioned himself on the divan in a safe corner from where he could better watch. The thought of calling on her had occurred to him. He had brushed it off. One visit would ruin his reputation and consequently his son's, who was of marrying age. But the heaviness he felt in his heart when she skipped her visits gave rise to deceiving solutions: he would invite her in and spend a few hours of harmless exchange; he would only share a meal with her; he would discuss the trading of materials and give her advice . . . he would . . . he would . . . When the struggle rendered him sleepless, he dispatched his servant to Rebekah to buy a piece of fabric he did not need. When he discovered she was well and healthy, his disappointment at her absence was endless. Now she had come. The passion in her voluptuous body, violet eyes, and red toenails blurred the stern prohibitions of his society. "I was hoping you would gather the courage to knock on my door."

Rebekah pressed her palm on her brand. What source did he expect her to muster courage from? She was a coward who had lost her ability to see and hear.

Rouh'Allah clapped his hands, allowing Rebekah time to recover and arrange the chador around her. Delighting in her flaming cheeks, which transformed her into a vulnerable girl, he controlled the urge to cup her face in his palms. A desire he had thought lost in his many years of solitude welled up in him.

The servant entered with a tray of peeled fruits, warm sweetmeats, and roasted pistachios.

Rouh'Allah set the plates at Rebekah's feet. She inhaled his scent as the borders of his cape brushed against her. Without having to touch her nose to his skin, she knew he smelled right. She picked a handful of pistachios and began shelling them in quick succession as if the crackling would erase the merchant's tone, which had thrust her into a flurry of clashing emotions.

Rouh'Allah tore his stare from her bare toes and took in her henna-tinted fingertips, the vein that throbbed at the curve of her neck, beneath the glass-bead necklace that sparkled like her eyes, the mint leaves that peeked from behind her ear. His gaze stopped on her plump breasts, embraced the rise and fall of her bosom. Were the tales about the mark in the center of her breasts true? If only he could touch his lips to her bosom, caress her wounded fingers, smooth her glass-studded skirt over her thighs, brush her toes against his mouth.

Rebekah's fingers fluttered over the buttons of her vest. Her nipples shriveled with humiliation. She raised her eyes and was surprised to meet the uncertain gaze of a man who might desire a virtuous woman. Later she would tell herself that if she had not been drowning in the highs and lows of his voice, she would have noticed the defiance of a man who had at last come to terms with a dilemma he had been struggling with for some time.

He smiled. Opened his mouth to say something. Brushed invisible particles from his robe. Could this grand man be nervous in her presence?

"Years ago," he said at last, "I had asked for the hand of the prettiest girl in the Jewish Quarter, a girl with violet eyes and golden curls. But, alas, your mother chose a man much wealthier than I for you. My loss."

﹏

The last decayed threads that linked her past to the present snapped. Long ago, she had lost faith in God. Today she lost faith in her mother, who had married her to Jacob the Father-less, who had branded her and dispatched her to hell.

Now, after years, the padlock of her heart had gathered rust, become hard and impossible to unlock. The grief inside her chest persisted, as fresh as at the moment of Gold Dust's birth. With the pain had come rewards. Gold Dust. Eternal youth. The ability to sniff the Devil from many *farsangs* away. The capacity to cherish the scent of forests and ancient cypress that drifted from the merchant's cloak with every flutter of his arm as he moved closer to her. But she had not learned to recognize love.

"Fate has its own logic," Rouh'Allah murmured.

Rebekah swallowed her tears. She set the pistachio shells on the corner of a plate and noticed the gold-trimmed edge. That extra bit of opulence depleted her last vestige of courage. Why did he have to evoke the past? She was sad. She was angry. If she did not start talking, she would rush out and never look back. "Your Honor," she blurted, "I came here for a reason from which I believe both of us would benefit."

At once, the merchant returned to a relaxed posture and threw one leg over the other. "I promise to do whatever is in my power to facilitate your wishes."

"I've come to ask for the hand of your son, Ebrahim, for my daughter, Gold Dust."

Rouh'Allah sat motionless. Blood drained from his face. He counted every onyx prayer bead as it slid down the thread, gathered in his palm, and coiled like a snake. He rose to his feet, patted the hair at his temples, struggled to comprehend.

"*Agha*, allow me an explanation. After months of thought,

I've realized that Ebrahim and Gold Dust are meant for each other."

He looked down at Rebekah; his eyes turned dark, grappling with the shock of having to shift his emotions, of having to unravel the anger that took him by surprise. He had high hopes for his son. He had chosen his bride, the daughter of the only judge of the Jewish Quarter who argued legal matter in the royal court, and who had the power to facilitate Ebrahim's entrance to the single reputable university in Persia. Suddenly, he was irritated by this woman, who, even now, her lashes shadowing her flushed cheeks, mesmerized him.

Rebekah raised her head slightly toward the man. He was pale. "I know all about your son," she whispered above the lump in her throat. "He is young, educated, handsome. But you've never heard of my daughter's merits. Although, to my great chagrin, I'm sure you've heard about me."

He waved his hand as if the subject was inconsequential. The glass clink of his beads continued. A pool of black tears piled in his palm.

Rebekah stole her gaze from his furious fingers. "I've been tossed into this profession because of a past molded for me by my mother and husband when I was a child. When I opened my eyes, it was too late. Ill reputation sprouts like weeds but is hard to discard. So I took charge of my life and saved for a respectable dowry for Gold Dust. But I'm not here to talk about money. I've come to tell you of my daughter's merits, which few girls have. She is beautiful, intelligent, artistic. At the age of eleven, she cooks, sews, keeps a house. She's the only literate girl in the Quarter. She recites poetry. She studies the lives of warriors and knows the ways of men." Rebekah stopped to give importance to her next announcement:

"And her bones create heavenly melodies."

Her gaze was unwavering. Her hands no longer shook. Her

voice was strong. "Her husband won't need to guess her moods. The music of her marrow will reveal her innermost feelings."

The merchant let out his breath. Despair replaced his anger. He murmured as if to himself, "How fascinating, how utterly celestial. What a lucky man her husband will be. To unravel the feelings of a woman."

His smoky eyes filled with pain for a mother who had to bear the shame of doing what no other had and to personally solicit a husband for her daughter. His heart filled with bitterness against himself. If he had had the courage of this woman, he would have approached her long ago, given her shelter, embraced her daughter, and spared them both this agony.

Rebekah shifted under his closeness. "Your Honor, I assure you Gold Dust is very different from me . . . you understand? I swear, she'll never . . ." A hush fell over the hall. She was pleading. She had never done this before, and she would never again.

Rouh'Allah turned from her; his cloak agitated the air. He could not bear to watch this proud woman humble herself. He went to the window, glanced out, bent closer as if he had discovered someone there. Drawing the curtains, he paced back and forth, rubbed his hands, raising the screech of his worry beads.

Rebekah's eyes followed him as though his every step were connected to iron chains that pulled at her heart. She took in the hardening of his jaw, the fast throb of his left temple.

"My dear lady, wait right here," he said, and with long strides left the hall.

She should not have come. Now she had lost the man whose voice had embellished her life with hope. She did not know whether to mourn a loss or rejoice at a triumph. The merchant must have left to invite Gold Dust into the house. Yes. He had seen her behind the window. He would return, leading her by the hand, assuring her he would be the kindest father-in-law. Rebekah hugged her knees to her chest, counted the peeled fruit, the roasted pistachios, the warm sweetmeats on every plate. She picked imaginary threads from the folds of her skirt and wove a wedding veil for her daughter. She searched the colors on the Kashan carpet and identified each with the feelings they symbolized to her.

She lowered her knees as Rouh'Allah's determined footsteps approached. There was such ease in his stride and understanding in his eyes that the knots in her insides loosened. He would invite her daughter after he had discussed the matter with Rebekah. She prayed her nipples would not respond haughtily to that instant of relief.

He dropped a pouch in her lap. The jingle of coins broke her. The flash of yellow blinded her.

"Add this to your daughter's dowry. Ebrahim is seventeen. He'll soon leave for faraway countries to complete his education. By the time he returns, your lovely daughter will be happily married and raising children." He buried her hands in his. "We are all victims of our rigid beliefs." He bowed from the waist, offering his arm and thinking of his own hypocrisy. If she ever changed her mind and wanted him, for her, he would break his strongest convictions.

Rebekah accepted the arm presented to her as he led her through the corridor, now as dark as her heart. Years ago, her mother had chosen the Devil over Rouh'Allah the Spirit of God. Today, for her daughter's sake, she had aspired to select Ebrahim over devils that populated the world. They had both lost.

At the door, she thrust the pouch at the merchant. "Thank you, sweetlove, I don't accept charity."

7

When Heshmat the Matchmaker sent word to Rebekah that she had received her message and that she had an appropriate suitor for Gold Dust, Rebekah removed the sprig of mint from behind her ear and sniffed. Once again, she felt a pang of guilt for her profession, which would always scare young men like Ebrahim away from her daughter. Nevertheless, word from Heshmat was welcome. She dealt with affluent and respected members of the Jewish Quarter. For the last few years, on every occasion, Rebekah had gifted Heshmat a stretch of silk, muslin, or lace, hoping to secure a grand match for her daughter.

Rebekah aired the mattresses and cushions, unplugged the hole at the bottom of the small *estakhr* in her backyard, scrubbed out the slosh, and filled the pool with fresh water. She searched her bundle and chose colorful fabrics to decorate the corners of the cushions that leaned against the walls. The matchmaker would want to see if Gold Dust was versed in domestic chores, among the most important the trimming of herbs, radishes, and spring onions. Rebekah taught Gold Dust to identify and wash cilantro, coriander, and mint. Rebekah poured tea in narrow-waisted glasses and set them on a tray for

Gold Dust to practice carrying back and forth without spilling a drop.

Gold Dust watched her mother's swinging walk, improved her own by flipping her hair back seductively, then announced, "I don't need a matchmaker. I'll marry Soleiman!"

Rebekah snatched the tray from her. "What in the Devil's name are you babbling? Did you leave home without my permission? Soleiman is an illiterate acrobat with no future but skipping around like a clown and begging for pennies."

"He's better than the men who visit you," Gold Dust replied, stroking her breasts like Rebekah, and wondering why her mother had started slapping the cushions.

"Take your hands off yourself," Rebekah ordered, "and forget the dark creatures who come to me. These brutes lack insight into their feelings. They pay for love, hoping to purge their infirmities with sex." Her cheeks flaming, she spat at the door from where her clients came and went, the same men from whom she learned to fight, surrender, and survive. She was becoming a warrior of life.

Melancholy notes rose from Gold Dust's bones.

"Can't you see these men's dark skins?" her mother cried out. "Their hair is tar-black. Their eyes opaque. The evil in their heart taints their whole being. Keep away from them. I accept their money to save you from a life like mine. Now dress up and don't enter the room unless I call you to serve tea. The matchmaker will be here soon." Rebekah felt helpless in the face of her own child. Helpless in her endless effort to house prostitution and integrity under one roof. Helpless against the discrepancy of her own beliefs. She did not have faith in marriage, yet struggled to marry her daughter off. Was a barren spinster's life preferable to a wife's?

Gold Dust's bones lost their harmony. Confusion replaced sadness. Why was her mother angry when all she, Gold Dust,

desired was Soleiman, who was different from the men her
mother despised? In the only other room that was not locked in
the house, Gold Dust lifted a piece of shabby cloth nailed from
the ceiling to divide the place. Although her mother forbade
her to enter this area, too, she often sneaked in because she was
fascinated by her mother's pallet. An incense burner on a stool
smoked idly. Colorful jars and vials caught moth-filled rays
that, through a hole in the ceiling, poured in sunlight, flies,
mosquitoes, and rain. She inhaled the oil scents of almond,
coconut, and sesame—perfumes of rosewater, attar of jasmine,
and essence of ice flowers. Ice flowers with golden, waxy petals
that clung to sturdy leafless stems. Memories surfaced. Her
insides surged.

Mysterious shadows wrestled and grappled, became one,
then tore apart when she peered from behind the partitions into
this dim cubicle. Awake a good part of the night, she tried to
block her ears against the sad moans, groans, angry cries,
screeching snores. And, at times, her mother's curses. Did they
hurt her? Alarmed, she had once lifted the divider. Red as a
pomegranate, her mother had sprung up, her hair flying, a
specter cowering behind her. She had slapped Gold Dust in the
face.

The rest of the night, Gold Dust grappled with her bones,
struggling to suffocate her music, to plug the sad notes by shut-
ting her eyes and imagining cotton replacing her marrow, the
echo audible only to her. She would lie awake, images populat-
ing the screen of her mind. Her mother would come to her
once the last man left. She would cuddle her in her secure
warmth and render life to stories with extravagant gestures.
She would recount the attributes of warriors who triumphed in
wars because they had gained knowledge of the mysteries of
life. She had favorites, such as David, a poor shepherd who
hurled stones from a sling with such force and accuracy that he

felled the giant Goliath and himself became king. Gold Dust thought that one day Soleiman would become king, too.

Rebekah repeated the triumphs of Teymour the Lame, a Mongol leader who, despite his handicap, rose to become the fiercest conqueror in history, and she sang the praises of Rostam, a legendary Persian warrior. She reminded her daughter that life was like war and soldiers could teach her more than anyone else.

The noises of the night momentarily forgotten, Gold Dust hugged her mother and dozed off to her soft murmur:

"One day, you'll meet an honest man who'll come to you in the light of day. He'll be fair and kind and sensitive. Not dark-colored like men who buy love in hiding. That day, you'll know true love. Don't ask me what it is. I don't know. . . ."

But Gold Dust knew. She had found love in the fair-skinned acrobat who had eyes the color of cloudless skies.

Waist-belted to a wheelbarrow that carried his massive wife, the matchmaker's husband, like some kind of ass, galloped into Rebekah's house. Unfastening the leather straps from around his waist, he drew labored breaths as if he were suffering from the last stages of consumption. Slumping on a cushion, he cursed his never-ending job. When he did not haul his wife from one house to another, he shoved a pot under her when the need arose, or stuck a pillow behind her back when she fell asleep in the wooden wheelbarrow he had built after she had come down with a mysterious illness that had caused her hair to rot and had loosened her teeth.

The matchmaker tossed her veil off, raised the hem of her skirt, and wiped off drops of sweat from her face. The small house suffocated under the acidic smell of her armpits. Her voice rattled through layers of phlegm. "Where is Gold Dust? I don't have time."

Rebekah curled her lower lip and winked at the husband. "First your proposal, sweetlove. Tell me about this man. Is he educated?"

Heshmat the Matchmaker huffed, trying to find a comfortable position for her crossed legs. "I hate small formalities! And please don't 'sweetlove' me. Your daughter needs a husband. I have one. What else is there to say?"

"Well," Rebekah sighed. "Is he educated? Is he rich? Is he young? Handsome? Versed in love?"

"Put a pillow behind my back," Heshmat ordered her husband. She lifted one giant breast, removed a handkerchief concealed there, and blew her nose with great force. "My dear, your daughter is not exactly the Queen of Sheba. Can't you see her eyes? One faces east, the other west. And don't forget, she's already a year or two above the marrying age."

Rebekah sailed into the kitchen and came back with sherbets perfumed with the attar of roses. She offered a glass to the husband, then bent close to Heshmat's ear. "Let me worry about my daughter's age . . . and if you were a man, you'd appreciate the sensual twist of her eyes. Now, the information, sweetlove."

Heshmat withdrew from Rebekah's searing breath. "He's handsome, yes, take my word. Good-looking, with silver at the temples, most distinguished." She aimed a meaningful look at Rebekah. "And he has a respectable profession, which is more than I can say for some of us."

Rebekah touched the glow between her breasts. "How old is he?"

"Oh, come, come, why does that matter? Don't tell me you really believe she's some kind of gold dust?" Heshmat hiccupped broken cackles. "Anyway, he's a butcher, he'll bring home not only bread, but choice meat, lamb hooves, sweet-breads. . . ."

"How old is he, sweetlove?" Rebekah inched her way to the corner of the room. "I've a feeling he'll need to consume lots of sweetbread to stiffen his own limp meat." She rested her hands on her hips, pleased at the matchmaker's livid cheeks.

Heshmat raised the flab of her stomach to let air circulate under the folds. "With a mother like you, what kind of a hus-band do you expect for your daughter?"

Behind her back, Rebekah clutched a pillow. "His age?" she demanded, all music abandoning her voice.

"He is only sixty-five," Heshmat croaked, her eyes round-ing. "If your daughter is woman enough, she'll easily produce sons."

The pillow came down on Heshmat's head, sending dust around her startled face and filling the room with the smell of her armpits. She raised her hands to ward off the second, the third, the fourth blow.

Rebekah turned to the matchmaker's husband. "Please remove this woman from my home!"

8

Heshmat the Matchmaker's rumors spread in every corner of the mud houses, the fly-infested bazaar, and the humid baths: "Rebekah killed her husband with the same iron-stuffed pillow she hit me with. The blows reduced his brain to pulp. She buried his body in the stable where she houses her spitting buffoon-ass, who consumes wine instead of water."

Calling upon others to condemn Rebekah, Heshmat went from house to house and hissed, "What do you expect of a woman who defeated the Devil and wears sprigs of mint to endure the stink of her shame?"

Old memories emerged from the labyrinths of the past, and the inhabitants of the Jewish Quarter relived the incident of Jacob's death, which at the time, in fear of contracting the plague, they had conveniently ignored and eventually filed away.

Now, years later, in hope of absolution, and with the aid of the matchmaker, they seized the chance to prove that the true sinner was Rebekah. Heshmat had unearthed Rebekah's secret, at last. Why would any man in his right mind wish to be buried in his own backyard? A whore who experienced no guilt and defiled young boys was certainly capable of murder.

The merchants approached Rebekah only to ask for the price she would pay for their fabrics. Her Jewish customers sneaked in through the back. To spite them, Muslims made a point of entering from the front door. Young boys came to her disguised as girls.

Cruelty and indifference did not shock Rebekah. She did not call upon Abraham, Isaac, and Jacob, the fathers she had never known. She was the only one she could rely on, and she had her own plan.

On the first day of the week, at the noon hour when the streets were crowded, Rebekah and Gold Dust vaulted Venus, decked in his most colorful saddle and crown of ostrich plumes.

"Hold your head high, Gold," Rebekah sang defiantly, soliciting the attention of every pedestrian. "The world is your dais and you are the main performer." She yanked on the reins and vaulted off the saddle. "Learn the delicate art of walking and the feminine rounding of your shoulders. Your eyes should harbor secret dreams, and your tongue murmur passionate words. Now breathe as if you are in pain."

Perched on Venus, Gold Dust shut her amber eyes and with her tongue moistened lips that were full, but not as full as her mother's. She glanced expectantly around the alley, praying her blue-eyed acrobat would appear with the music of his tambourine and his pliant body twisting and bending in unbelievable configurations.

"Exhale softly, very softly," Rebekah encouraged, "like the footfalls of kittens. And flutter your lashes like the wings of nightingales."

Gold Dust licked her thumb and forefinger and wet her lashes, fluttering them. Her palm glided up her knee and rested on her thigh. Not even her mother was aware that Gold Dust performed for an invisible fan.

Wide-eyed, the populace watched a girl of eleven not only

imitate her mother's ripe sensuality but embellish it with a slight parting of her lips, a delicate arching of one brow, and a mysterious lighting of her eyes.

As if she had just ended an exhausting show and had to refresh herself, Rebekah removed the sprig of mint from behind her ear, waved it about, and brought it to her nose. Then, with a great sway of her breasts, she bowed to the crowd, whose anger blazed at the gall of this child and woman's provocative show.

Pleased with her student's progress, Rebekah dug her sandals into the donkey and steered him toward the Ancient Zoroastrian's home. "Gold, ask the old woman about good and evil and secret of the *Gathas,* the seventeen hymns of Zoroaster. She loves to teach. It's an implicit requirement in return for her help."

A visit to the Ancient Zoroastrian was a significant event. For her mother to solicit aid, no doubt, a monumental phenomenon was about to transpire. "You never need anyone's help," Gold Dust said.

"You're a woman now," Rebekah murmured. "Advice from a clairvoyant won't hurt."

They entered the house of bougainvilleas. The Ancient Zoroastrian sat huddled next to a brazier. Her round, opal eyes quivered as if disconnected from their sockets and rested with no sign of surprise on the two. "I was expecting you, Tinkling Child!"

Rebekah stuffed Gold Dust's hand into the Ancient Zoroastrian's lined palm. "Holy One, she just had her first menstrual period."

Gold Dust recoiled from the loose folds that hung from the woman's arms and resembled gray dough. She was amazed the old one didn't cover herself like other women. She feared her hands would, of their own accord, spring out of the woman's and snatch a piece of her flesh to mold it into a less offensive shape.

Rebekah elbowed Gold Dust, motioning for her to start.

Gold Dust had learned her lesson well. "Ancient One, how did evil first come to our world?"

By some miracle, mossy decades suddenly dropped from the old woman and in a strong voice she cried, "That was a terrible time when demons burst upon the world. Zahak, the demon of Deceit, his body brimming with lizards and scorpions and other vile creatures, had the audacity to offer sacrifices to heaven to allow him to depopulate our earth." She struggled to regain her breath. Staring at Gold Dust, she searched for the virtue of inquisitiveness, a trait she cherished above all else.

Wonder replaced the tremble in Gold Dust's voice. "Holy One, where is Zahak now?"

The Ancient Zoroastrian stretched her lips in a dry smile. "Don't ever lose your curiosity, Tinkling Child." She was fond of this girl, who at a young age had cultivated the art of questioning. "Zahak is on Mount Damavand, where the hero Thraetaona imprisoned him. He will remain there until the end of history. Then he will attack again, devour creatures, and smite fire until the resurrected Keresaspa will eliminate him. Then good will overcome evil, poverty will not be a shame, and women will find love in noble hearts, not in power and overflowing pockets. . . ."

Rebekah's disapproving touch weighted the woman's shoulder down. She was not here with her daughter to hear lessons in ethics and imaginary worlds of moral hearts where power and wealth were scorned.

The old woman felt the pressure of Rebekah's hand. Her gnarled finger traced the outline of Gold Dust's waist, her young hips and slim thighs. "You are maturing, child. Would you like to know what Ahura Mazda has inscribed for you?"

"I would be honored," Gold Dust replied.

The Ancient Zoroastrian's gaze probed the fire, her tongue wriggling in and out of her toothless mouth as if it were a fish tossed ashore. "Holy flames and beneficent light, which banishes the darkness of your adversary Ahriman, show me the truth. High heavens, deep oceans, and mighty mountains, reveal Mazda's sacred flames."

Rebekah stared into the fire. "I see them. I see wisdom, power, wealth . . . and much more. . . . What is this I see?"

Tall men with flowing capes and fancy aigrettes surfaced, then melted back into the fire. Naked men with hard bodies and kind eyes quivered into being, carved their shapes into the flames, then faded.

"I see a tightrope walker with hair of fire," the old woman murmured.

Gold Dust jumped up to inspect the images for herself. Rebekah's grip held her back.

Rebekah's eyes hurt. Mud shanties quivered next to mansions, muddy streams next to flowing rivers, the pit next to a hill of precious stones. Ululating women whirled around, their faces hidden behind costly veils, their bodies decorated with silver and gold. Was this the king's harem, where sultanas covered their faces in the presence of alien men? The harem!

Why had she not considered the safe haven of the harem? A future beyond the Jewish Quarter, the pit, and the house of a whore. The palace jealously guarded its secrets, but the few facts Rebekah knew were encouraging. The harem housed at least three hundred concubines with their attendants, tutors, readers of poems, keepers of the jewels, the baths, and the schools where women were placed under supervision to go through apprenticeships and master a variety of skills. That sanctuary could offer her daughter liberties marriage could not.

The company of women without the limiting yoke of one man. The security of a roof and financial assurance without the insulting debts and obligations of a demanding husband.

From her pocket Rebekah clutched a fistful of seeds of wild rue and flung them into the flames. She summoned the strength to influence fate. The seeds popped, raising a cloud of smoke. Clawing at her bosom, she cried out, "I see a commanding presence clad in a splendid cape!"

A flush of anger stabbed at Gold Dust. Her mother had grabbed her life and was molding it without considering her, Gold Dust's, personal wishes. Sitting there helpless, as if she had no hand in her own future, she longed to douse the flames with water and laugh when the man with the splendid robes drowned. She rose and stared into the fire. "I don't see anything!"

Rebekah turned a purple storm on her daughter. "That's because you're too young. Go beyond the illusion of your five senses; call upon your sixth, seventh, eighth. You can't see the sun on a cloudy day. That doesn't mean the sun isn't shining. You'd swear the sun rises at dawn and sets at dusk. An illusion. The sun never sets. Is the world flat? Is the sky blue? Do you think the creatures that share my bed are men?"

Gold Dust sank back onto the carpet.

Invisible forces overwhelmed the Ancient Zoroastrian. The other woman's will had clouded her ability to prophecy. The flames licked the thatch roof without burning it. Was this an indication from Ahura Mazda? The old woman's voice regained confidence. "NOW! The time has come. She must find her mate!"

"Yes," Gold Dust agreed. "I'll find my own mate, and I don't care for power and money."

Rebekah lifted her arms. "May the ears of the Devil go deaf, and the eyes of the ignorant be illuminated." She raised her face toward an unknown force and with authority declared: "My daughter will lounge on jewel-studded divans."

Gold Dust shuddered. Her mother had ascended into another realm. She seemed to levitate. The veins at her temples throbbed. Her arms spread out like bat wings and the mark between her trembling breasts glowed. Gold Dust had the urge to kneel and kiss her mother's toes as if she were a divine being.

ꙅ

Rebekah's footsteps bounced on the dirt roads. Gold Dust had fallen into the ceremonious gait she acquired when she was angry. Even now, away from the Ancient Zoroastrian, her mother seemed oblivious to her and stepped to the rhythm of her own schemes.

Rebekah raised Gold Dust's chin. "Do you know what day it is?"

Gold Dust glanced at her mother. "A day like every other."

"No. Today the black eunuch visits the Jewish Quarter!"

On the fourth day of every month, Narcissus the Great Black Eunuch came to call on Sharaby the Wine Maker. Rebekah was aware of the importance of the chief eunuch. He was the only man who could approach the Shah at any time. He was the private messenger of the Shah and the Court Minister and had free access to the Bibi Sultana, the Shah's mother. Above all, the eunuch screened and selected girls for the harem.

Since the consumption of alcohol was forbidden in Islam and no Muslim was allowed to sell spirits, Narcissus purchased his alcohol from Sharaby the Wine Maker. The aroma and taste of Sharaby's wine, which fermented in large clay pots in his basement, was known throughout the country. Narcissus preferred to visit the wine maker in daylight, when the spirits of the night shut their ears and eyes to the happenings of the mortal world. Narcissus did not fear the Jews. They would not dare disclose his visits to the outside world or care to meddle in his private affairs, and most welcomed an extra coin added to their resources.

Rebekah did not care about the chief eunuch's secret or his coins. At the moment, she needed her daughter's cooperation. "We have a surprise for him," she said.

With her rising anger, the twist in Gold Dust's eyes grew more pronounced. She thrust her head back, sending her hair flying in defiance. "If it has to do with my future, go and surprise him on your own."

"I shall do no such thing," Rebekah declared, overwhelmed by doubt. Had she weighed the repercussions of letting her daughter go? Being left alone with her memories and the kiln of ashes in her bedroom? Was she sending Gold Dust into a world of danger and intrigue? Into a golden cage? Was the sheltered harem preferable to a miserable alliance? Yes. Her daughter had no chance in a community where a respectable name was essential to secure her future. First Jacob, then Rebekah herself, and eventually Heshmat the Matchmaker had robbed Gold Dust of the possibility of a decent life among the Jews.

"You'll join the harem," Rebekah announced.

Gold Dust's mouth went dry. She fell on the dirt road, folded her arms over her chest, and pretended she was dead.

Squatting next to her, Rebekah begged, as if trying to convince herself. "It's every girl's wish. You'll be showered with gifts, have beautiful dresses and jewelry, the most delicious food. You'll learn to dance and play instruments. You'll have company your own age, you'll never be alone."

Gold Dust half opened her eyes. "I've heard the Shah poisons women who don't give him sons. He has so many wives, he locks them up in a cage and forgets to visit them."

Rebekah tucked Gold Dust's hair behind her ears. "What

ridiculous lies. The Shah is too busy to meddle with his sultanas. Now get up. We must hurry to greet the great eunuch."

Gold Dust refused to budge.

"You'll have servants. You'll sleep at night without being bothered by men. You'll be respected."

Gold Dust pressed her eyes shut and turned her back to her mother.

"For my sake," Rebekah pleaded. "If you become a powerful sultana, you'll save me from this life."

"How?"

"Money, my child, is the solution to everything. You'll buy me a house in the center of the city. I won't need to work. I'll be respected . . . no more horse manure."

Gold Dust heard her mother's pain. She evoked her nights, the curses rising from the darkness, the whore-cry of the alleys. She sprang up and dusted herself off.

They entered the bazaar, and Rebekah checked the area, choosing the entrance to the Street of Lanterns as the best spot to wait. Although the hub of the Jewish Quarter had five alleys branching out from it, the Street of Lanterns, the first to be installed with oil lamps, was the only route wide enough for horses to pass through.

Young and old craned their necks, jostling each other to catch the first glimpse of Narcissus the Great Black Eunuch.

The voice of the palace crier came from afar. "Go blind! Go deaf! Here comes the chief eunuch of His Holiness the Shah."

The populace pressed their palms to their ears so they would not hear words that might transform into slander and averted their gaze so no commoner would set eyes on His Eminency.

A distant clatter of hooves silenced the idle chatter.

The high soprano of the eunuch came from afar and floated in waves of ancient poetry.

The populace eased their palms from their ears to better

hear the sweet music that spoke of balmy nights and dew-filled dawns and of love and nightingales and the scent of jasmine.

The Great Black Eunuch, on a massive white stallion, galloped through the entrance of the alley. The mount's haunches scraped chunks of baked mud from the walls. Its luxuriant white tail swished flies away.

With lowered lids, Rebekah watched the eunuch approach. He was clad in a magnificence she could not even conceive in her dreams. The splendidly pompous scene splashed color on the tapestry of her life, promising possibilities beyond the gates of the Jewish Quarter. She clutched her bundle of fabrics, her fingers itching to test the silk of the eunuch's red turban, pinned with a cluster of blue sapphires, and the lavish satin paisley of his pants. At every opportunity the eunuch heralded his arrival with the singing voice he was proud of. But she had heard that when he spoke his tone was squeaky, high-pitched like a woman's, a constant embarrassment.

Gold Dust first stole a glimpse, then stared at the eunuch in surprised disappointment. He was ugly. The bright colors of his attire, under which his flabby stomach jiggled, transformed him into a clown. His face was puffy. He had short legs, and his teeth were yellow.

The eunuch dug into his pockets and tossed coins into the air. Silver flipped up, then fell down at the feet of hungry-eyed men, women, and children. Some scrambled to grab the coins. Others clung to the shreds of their dignity.

Rebekah rushed in front of the horse.

The eunuch yanked at the reins. The neighing animal rose into a regal dance.

An awesome silence fell over the dusty air.

Rebekah knelt and unfastened the knots of her bundle. Her veil slipped off her hair. The flaps of her vest fell open against her lace-clad breasts. With a flourish of her multibangled wrists, she spread out her fabrics, ribbons, and trims. She focused her gaze on the eunuch and cupped her palm over her bosom. "Pardon my impudence, Your Honor. I've merchandise fit for the harem—silk, satin, and cotton muslin, embroidered with wires of gold and silver. I've sheer fabrics, transparent and light, woven with threads that shine in the night."

The eunuch stared into her violet eyes and felt a stab in his groin, a sensation he had almost forgotten. He felt a stirring in his heart, which he had thought lost forever when he was gelded like a calf and robbed of his manhood. Not even later, when he had fled a world of rape and slavery and had entered the harem of the Shah, a forbidden world where true men were not allowed, for fear of setting eyes on the Shah's sultanas, had he experienced such potent yearning.

It seemed another lifetime when that ruthless *hakim* had rested a hand on his shoulder and had snickered, "You will lose your manhood but not the desire for a woman."

In his quest for fulfillment, Narcissus had inserted ravenous gerbils in his anus, drunk potent aphrodisiacs laced with saffron, walked around with ivory marbles attached to his crotch, and smeared his groin with sea horse ointment and deer antler extract. But he was as far from consummation as the first day he was cut. And his constant longing was eternally fanned in the harem, the world of women in which he resided. Now this bundle woman stirred welcome desires in his veins, and filled him with hope of a universe resonating with possibilities.

"Whore!" A single cry shattered the silence.

"Whore!" "Whore!" "Whore!" A chorus of voices joined the first.

The palace crier burst out into his proclamation: "Go mute! Go dumb!"

Rebekah grabbed the horse's bridle, lowered the animal's head, and kissed its eye. Her hair uncovered, she winked at the eunuch. Kneeling, she gathered her fabrics and folded them on the scarf she used as her bundle. As hard as she had convinced herself that she had grown a thick shell through which embarrassment did not penetrate, now cold sweat beaded her forehead and she had to brace herself to confront the populace, the eunuch, and especially her daughter.

An alien object on the dirt road attracted her attention. A piece of pale alabaster. Had the hooves broken a piece off the foundation of a house? Strange. Houses were not made of stone around the Jewish Quarter. There were no stone pavements. Maybe in another place, the alabaster had lodged in the horseshoe and had been carried here. She picked up the stone, surprised at its shine and smoothness. A symbol of better worlds. She threw it on her fabrics and tied her bundle.

She rested a hand high up on the eunuch's thigh. "Remember me, sweetlove. I'll come knocking on your door."

"Away, woman," he squeaked, struggling to harness his tone, and wishing he could sing to her instead of order her off. Rearranging the arrogant sneer on his face, he kneed the horse in circles around her.

Gold Dust struggled to keep her eyes level and her head high. She jabbed at a man whose guffaws hurt her ears. She was about to rush to Rebekah's rescue when she flung her veil off her shoulders, plunged her fingers into her curls, arched her hands overhead, and thrust her breasts forward. And to the jangle of her bracelets, she burst into a sensuous dance, her sandals imprinting FOLLOW ME on the dirt road. Gold Dust retreated.

The eunuch closed in on the full-hipped woman whose every swing sent a delicious stab between his thighs. He reined the mount alongside her, bent down, and cried, "Away, brazen woman!" Then he burst into a song, sending the horse into a canter.

Rebekah's hands dropped to her sides. She took a few steps

to follow the flying horse, to ask for a token to authorize her entrance into the palace. He was gone. Nothing left but loud insults and the ring of the last words he had whispered in his flight: "Will you fulfill the promise in your eyes . . ."

The misery, anger, and pain Rebekah had learned to conceal in her soul were now reflected on her daughter's face as she forced the words above the grievance of her bones. "Madar, I don't want to go to the harem."

Rebekah wrapped her arm around Gold Dust and steered her away from the crowd. They all fought against her. Her daughter, the Jews, the demons in her own head. They would not allow her even her dreams. Was it not enough that she was torn between holding on to Gold Dust and letting her go?

The echo of hooves died behind them. "Gold," Rebekah said, "I want you to believe in fate, but also remember that it needs a helping hand. That's all I did today."

 *9*

*R*ebekah dug out a clay pot hidden under a bed of straw in the stable. She emptied four coins onto her palm—testimony to years of dinar-pinching to save a dowry for her daughter. Gold Dust would no longer need a dowry. Once Rebekah found a way to penetrate the palace and befriend the eunuch, he would invite Gold Dust into the harem.

The chief eunuch searched for and selected suitable virgins from among whom the Shah chose a few to share his bed. The sultanas lived a comfortable life. A few managed to climb the hierarchy within the harem and amass a fortune by trading opiates and calming herbs with the outside. Could a girl from the Jewish Quarter, the daughter of a whore, become a woman of high rank, like Nakhshe-Del, who, for many years, had ruled the Turkish Empire? What about a girl whose bones played music? There might come a day when she, Rebekah, would knock on the merchant's door, his servant bowing her in with great respect. She would focus on Rouh'Allah the Spirit of God's smoky eyes and say, "Remember Gold Dust? She's a well-known sultana in the Shah's harem." Rebekah smiled sadly at yet another fantasy. Nothing in her life had turned out the way she had imagined. Only one thing was certain. No one could hinder a woman who had taken destiny into her hands.

She knelt to tie her bundle before venturing into the city. Feeling a hard object under the fabrics, she sprang back, never knowing what dangerous tricks would be played on her. She picked up the fabrics and gave each a hard shake. The piece of alabaster she had found next to the eunuch's horse tumbled out. Intricate inscriptions were etched into the stone in a foreign language. Did the rock belong to a building of prayer? Did it have value? She would show it off to her men. She dropped it with the coins into her pocket and mounted Venus.

Rebekah entered the bazaar and called on every stall. In back of their shops, salesmen handed her the fabrics their wives had embroidered in their spare time. She examined the merchandise as she slapped off shameless fingers that crawled up her skirt. Then she vaulted Venus and entered the residential areas, knocking on the door of spinsters and widows, and whispering, "It's the bundle woman." She inspected vibrant fabrics, offered from behind half-open doors as if, by hiding their faces, the women would protect their chastity. Rebekah, however, had memorized every telling line on the palms, every brown spot on the hands, every ugly mole on the fingers. When she walked the streets, she was in the habit of first checking people's hands, and in time she had learned to couple them with their owners.

Silky-soft fingers reached out from behind a curtained window. Rebekah examined a piece of square cloth embroidered with wires soaked in saffron-water to create a rare vermilion color. A hunting scene with the Shah's likeness adorned by fantastical plants was stitched with such detail it resembled a framed painting. Rebekah recognized a rare work of art. "Name your price," she whispered.

"It's priceless. I've dyed the threads with my blood and glued them with my tears."

Rebekah was familiar with that desperate tone. It seemed to rise from her own heart. She dug into her pocket and retrieved one of the gold coins, planting it into the open palm, then closed her own hand over the clenched fist. "My friend, thank whoever you believe in and include my daughter in your prayers."

༉

At dawn, Rebekah embarked on the ride toward the palace. The journey was short, but full of hazards. Any woman daring the open road to the king's residence would have had to disguise herself as a man. A Jewish woman, especially one as notorious as Rebekah, would not have chosen that path, even while escorted. But Rebekah was safer than most men. The supernatural aura that encircled the mark between her breasts had transformed her into a mystic curiosity her enemies preferred to avoid. Still, she was well prepared. The whip she held in her right hand lashed out to frighten the hungry dogs that barked at Venus's heels. Her eyes did not blink for fear of missing the slightest movement from behind trees and ruins and in doorways.

A clatter of hooves startled her. She untied a slingshot from around her wrist and out of her pocket retrieved a fistful of cork pebbles. With a hard kick and a yank at the reins, she sent Venus into a trot and directly into the heart of a group of men clad in black. She recognized Jew beaters who roamed around, searching for Jews who had the audacity to brave the alleys at dawn. She aimed acid-soaked pebbles at their faces.

Their retreating howls of pain filled the gray. "The evil sorceress!"

"The Jewish whore." Rebekah's teasing laughter rang out, provoking, impressing, and adding another tale of triumph to the many she recounted, with great embellishment, to her men.

She tied Venus to a tree, shouldered her bundle, and walked toward the palace grounds. She stood back to catch her breath. A shimmering mirage of turquoise, the reflection of the palace quivered on the surface of the River of Dreams that enclosed the foot of the hill and the back of the palace. Isolated logs drifted on the water. To innocent observers, this was a deceiving facade. But Rebekah was aware that beneath the calm surface of the river lurked riverain sharks, the most ferocious of their kind, and one of the few species that resided in fresh waters. This part of the king's domain, guarded by the sharks, was impenetrable.

Rebekah started uphill. From a base of alabaster, the edifice rose to greet her—walls and portals of glazed blue and green tiles with cut-glass inlays reflected multifaceted lights, a grand world poised on a vast hill.

Numerous blazing domes of gold and silver crowned the various quarters and houses of the palace. Endless steeples, towers, minarets, and gates marked courtyards, political halls, and entrances to the chambers. Elaborately tiled arches decorated the upper levels. Two towers flanked the grounds. On the right stood the mud-brick Pigeon Tower. Hundreds of pigeons flew in and out of the intricate honeycomb brickwork on its roof. The birds deposited loads of dung, which fed melon fields around the royal hills. On the left rose a massive domed structure, shaded by a high wall—the Ice House. On the coldest nights of winter, streams were diverted from the surrounding mountains into ditches that coursed into pools under the rammed-earth and mud-brick cistern. Throughout the summer, layers of ice were skimmed off the surfaces of the ponds for use in the palace.

Above the palace facade, carved in stone, loomed a bas-relief portrayal of the Shah astride a bull, holding the animal's horns victoriously. There was a regal quality to his stance, his

powerful legs hugging the bull; his muscular arms stretched
rigidly, the stone fingers clutching the horns. Was this his true
likeness? She waved her hands in front of her eyes, pressed
them shut. For an instant she saw Gold Dust riding the bull,
her flying hair etched into the stone, her triumphant smile
carved above the portals.

Rebekah looked around. The Gates of Bliss were etched in
gold on a marble arch. This must be the entrance that connected the harem to the outside world. She pinched her cheeks
to give them a flushed tinge and coughed to irritate her throat.
Her pace slowed, her back slumped, and her breath came out in
gasps. She limped toward the guards who flanked the gates like
two colossal statues carved out of coal. She crumpled at the feet
of one man, her arms curling around his ankles. Her chador
spread out like a peacock tail about her generous hips. Startled,
the guard knelt, trying to free himself from her grip.

"Honorable *Agha*, I've not eaten for many suns." She circled her arms around the guard's neck and raised one knee to
his crotch. Her lips nipped the wiry hair on his chest. "I'm so
hungry, I could eat you."

"I'll get you food," the guard offered, embarrassed at the stirring in his groin.

"An honest woman needs a source of income, not a single
meal. I sell fabrics. Honorable *Agha*, allow me into the palace."
She untied her bundle and spooled out a silk scarf, draping it
around the guard's neck.

"On your way, woman!" the man roared, grabbing Rebekah
around the waist and planting her on her feet. "No one is
allowed into the palace, except by invitation."

"I've been invited, sweetlove. The Great Black Eunuch
himself invited me."

At once, the men came to attention. "You have evidence?"

She fumbled in her pockets, her mind racing. Important

members of the palace had an emblem, coin, or token they gave to a guest to present at the gates. Not even peddlers were allowed in without the permission of the chief eunuch. The sovereigns from Gold Dust's dowry jingled in her pocket. She pressed a coin into the palm of each man. "Call the eunuch, sweetloves. Leave the rest to me."

One of the guards started toward the palace. The other dropped the coin in his pocket and held his partner back. "The eunuch won't like this."

Rebekah bolted past, through the Gates of Bliss, and into a courtyard bordered by tall cypresses. She searched for the private entrance to the harem: on her left, a long road forked into dark corridors; on her right, a silk tunnel stretched from an entry toward a pair of heavy portals. That must be the route the sultanas took, so they could come and go without being seen from the outside. She ran toward the silk underpass.

"Cover up! A stranger is infesting the harem," the guards called out as they tried to catch up with her.

Past vestibules carpeted with Esfahan and down shadowy halls lighted by reflections of alabaster walls, Rebekah hurried. She must be advancing into the belly of the palace, into the innermost heart where vestibules grew longer, dimmer—chambers opened into others, and partitions whispered, swinging shut behind her. The harem must be at the end of these twisting labyrinths, far and safe from the outside. The echo of "Cover up!" trailed her.

Out of the shadows, mute as phantoms, two giants startled her. She struggled to bat her lashes, pout her lips. Fear paralyzed her. The ominous eyes hollow as empty wells, and the blank expression on the eunuchs' faces, were proof her seductive skills would fail. She winced at the pain of her arms being twisted behind her back, the anger of being searched by ruthless hands crawling up her thighs, between her legs, tearing her

pants, moving up her breasts, lifting each, an instant of surprise at her nipples erect with indignation, up her armpits, into
her hair, and back down, patting her buttocks, plunging into
her pockets.

The eunuch guard stroked the alabaster, fished out the
stone, raised it close to his eyes. Displayed it to the other man.
They started back. Freed her arms. She had no notion what had
occurred, why they stared at the stone, why they had lost their
composure, barked accusations at each other.

Their voices shook. "Many, many pardons, *Khanom*. Why
didn't you show us the great eunuch's stamp? Where are you
going, *Khanom*? Shall we guide you?"

From Pearl Hall, the central chamber of the harem, Narcissus the Great Black Eunuch heard commotion. He moved
through the vestibule as fast as his opium-ravaged bones
allowed. He came face-to-face with Rebekah. He glared at the
guards, gazed at Rebekah, tried to decipher the cause of the
tension. He controlled the urge to strike the men out of his way
and send them directly to the penitentiary. "The bundle
woman," he screeched, as though for the last few weeks he had
not been courting her in his every dream.

Since the day Rebekah had rested her hand on his thigh
and aimed her luscious eyes at his crotch, he had sunk into her
net, and had begun to encourage the impossible fantasy that
she might one day bring back the feelings he had once had as a
young boy. Now, as her veil slipped off her head and her glistening lips parted, he felt such vigor he itched to touch himself
to ascertain that his organ had not grown back. He dismissed
the guards with a wave of his hand and led Rebekah through a
vestibule of glazed-tile walls painted with images of soldiers
with childlike faces. They moved toward the inner quarters and
the remotest part of the palace. He stepped aside to let her
enter Pearl Hall.

Brushing against him, she lingered on the threshold. "If you press your ear to my chest, you'll hear the gratitude in my heart."

"Go in!" he ordered. "Before I change my mind. And don't forget you're the first Jewish bundle woman to pass through these doors."

The partitions opened into a world of bright colors, snatches of sun-starved flesh, and husky whispers of lounging sultanas. The bodies seemed entangled into a blend of brocade and satin and pale skin glancing through lace. Rebekah tried to separate the whole into comprehensible parts.

Of the three hundred and sixty-five sultanas who resided in the harem, many were present in Pearl Hall. Women napped in each other's arms; some shared a single hookah pipe held between the plump thighs of a sultana who sat cross-legged in the center; some checked their complexions for blemishes; others laid their heads in generous laps to be caressed, and their hair braided.

Numerous small girls, dressed as women, scurried around.

No boys roamed the hall. Why? It was customary for boys to remain with their mothers until they started their tutoring.

Was it possible that with all the sultanas available to him, the Shah had not fathered a single son?

Rebekah's gaze settled on two women. One sat on a dais in the center and above the rest, her body spread out in lazy folds. Her thick brows, drawn from one temple to another, were raised like the wings of a lark. A dark mustache adorned her upper lip. The Bibi Sultana, Rebekah thought, the Shah's mother. The other woman, tall and lanky, with a face as round and as pale as a moon, knelt in front of the Bibi Sultana, offering the older woman sherbet, arranging her full skirts, and fanning her with peacock plumes. Was this the Bibi's favorite, or the present favorite of the Shah? Rebekah reminded herself to watch out for these women.

Rebekah spread her fabrics on the Esfahan carpet and began chanting their merits.

Pearl Hall came alive. Women swarmed around Rebekah. The hours when peddlers visited the harem were the highlight of the week. Taken by the vibrant colors of the threads, the sultanas fought for the best pieces, snatching them from each other, and hiding them in the pockets of their swelling pants. After the initial haggling, the purchase of fabrics, and the absorption of gossip from the peddlers, the sultanas would spend many more hours with their dressmakers, designing cloaks for the evenings of storytelling, for the afternoons of napping, and for the few mornings they strolled the gardens. Their most magnificent attire lay folded in chests, awaiting the Shah's invitation. Three hundred and sixty-five sultanas prayed for his summons; most never received it.

Ecstatic at the reception she received, and aware of the hawkish eyes of the Bibi Sultana, Rebekah went from one woman to another, draping a shoulder with velvet, a waist with satin, and a neck with lace. She measured the fabrics by holding one end to her nose and the other in her outstretched hand, then cut the edge of the fabric with her teeth and ripped it in a straight line. She stepped over lounging bodies, too deep in opium dreams to care for worldly goods, around plump girls playing with porcelain dolls, and found her way to the center of the room and to the Bibi Sultana. She prostrated herself and kissed the edge of the dais at the sultana's feet. "My *Khanom*, has none of my merchandise pleased your sacred being?" She dug into her bundle and fished out her masterpiece.

The black eyes of the Bibi Sultana narrowed. She wiped sweat off the dark mustache she treasured because of the masculine air it gave her. Reaching out a bare, lumpy arm, she snatched the material. In her forty long years in the palace as the most important woman and with access to the best available goods, she had not encountered such fine work. The vermilion-colored embroidery depicted a hunt. The Shah in full battle regalia and with a haughty expression speared a dragon. Fantastic plants with curled arms and tangled roots adorned the edges.

She folded the piece, turned to the tall, lanky sultana, and with a gravelly voice coughed, "Moon Face, pay this woman."

Moon Face's knees and shoulders jutted out through the sheer fabric of her floor-length veil, giving her the air of an awkward animal with no command over its extremities. Rebekah placed her palm on her bony chest to hold her back. "My *Khanom*, accept this as my modest gift."

Moon Face's blood-red lips trembled as she pried open a satin pouch. Who was this woman who had caught the Bibi's interest? She exchanged glances with Gulf Lily, her private eunuch. With his giant bulk, the light from the lanterns reflecting on his shaven ebony head, he resembled an ageless statue. He was dumb but not deaf. Years ago, he was castrated so he could attend upon the women of the harem while they bathed. His tongue had been cut off, so he would not recount their secrets, but he made up for that loss by the elegant language of his eyes and hands, which now danced in reply to Moon Face's concern.

"Bring more of this kind!" the Bibi declared.

Rebekah raised her fingers to her eyes in a gesture that assured the sultana she would obey as if it were a command from her cherished eyes.

The Bibi flung the chador away from her massive body and raised her short skirts above her pants. "Am I too thin for these fabrics? Should I gain more weight?"

"You are ample and voluptuous," Rebekah assured. "Like a ripe melon."

The Bibi displayed two rows of gold teeth. She chose a rice cake from a plate, bit half off, and offered the remainder to

Rebekah. The bundle woman hurried to accept this token of friendship. A rumble of anger bubbled in Moon Face's throat.

Narcissus entered the hall and with a repetitive wave of his head indicated that Rebekah's time was up. She thanked the ladies and followed him to the exit. Under an oak archway, inlaid with tortoiseshell, and before Narcissus had time to collect himself, Rebekah unpinned the diamond cluster on his turban and untied meters of fabric the color of amber. She lured out a stretch of yellow satin from her bundle and coiled it around his head and pinned the brooch back at an angle. She bent and kissed his forehead.

His plump arms hugged her waist. His head rested on her bosom, listening to the laughter in her chest. He gave her another stamp with his image engraved on it. "You are now the official bundle woman of the harem."

Careful to conceal her brand from him, Rebekah unbuttoned her blouse and lodged the alabaster cube deep between her breasts.

He shuddered at the ivory flesh bared to him, the crescent of one nipple exposed. "If I were a man, I would have invited you to my quarters."

"You are more than a man," she sang. "Don't let anyone tell you otherwise. Now I've got to hurry to my daughter. She's in her budding years. I shouldn't leave her alone. She's warm-blooded like me." She lifted the eunuch's hand and with the tip of her tongue licked tiny circles on his palm. She turned to leave, took a few steps toward the exit, then glanced back. "Narcissus, will you consider my daughter for the harem?"

He struggled to unruffle himself, stop the tingling in his palm, the quiver of his body. "No! No! There's no place for another sultana in the harem."

"What a shame, sweetlove. I would have loved to prove your manhood."

10

On the fourteenth dawn of the month, when the copper boilers of the *hammams* were hot and ready, the trumpet bearers of the baths sounded their horns. Out of mud shacks, depressed hovels, flimsy huts and shanties, Jews emerged carrying bundles slung over their shoulders, perched on their heads, or trailing the ground behind them. They filled the dirt roads, obscure figures slipping past the garbage pit and the closed stalls of food and spices, past beggars who started their day by delousing their children, and headed toward the two baths circled by lopsided mud walls above which vapors grayed the dawn.

Mounted on Venus, Rebekah and her daughter took the narrow alley out of the Jewish Quarter, away from the stink of the garbage and from Heshmat the Matchmaker's slander. To Gold Dust's sleepy questions, her brooding mother replied that they were on their way to a place of plenty, a place of dreams.

Suddenly, Gold Dust was wide awake. After their encounter with the eunuch, her mother had never stopped discussing the harem. They were going to the palace! "Madar, are we staying there?"

Rebekah tossed dry bread to a pack of hungry dogs yelping at their feet. "Only you, Gold."

Gold Dust fought to harness the tumult of her bones. "I don't want to stay without you."

"May the Devil go deaf. Don't let him hear you, Gold. You don't have many choices."

Gold Dust had always seen her mother in control, an impenetrable mask on her face. Now her hands trembled, her posture was rigid, and the glass studs on her skirt reflected a melancholy tinge on her face. Gold Dust concentrated on counting the anemic oil burners outside the Quarter. She slapped mosquitoes against her face and wondered if they were the kind that caused the shaking plague. Listening to the rhythm of her mother's breathing, she tried to focus on the present—her mother would take care of the future. She rested her cheek against Rebekah's back.

"Keep your head up," Rebekah ordered. "If you ever have a choice between people hating or pitying you, always choose hate—always."

Gold Dust raised her head and held her shoulders as high as her mother's.

Beginning to feel the heat of the past, Rebekah mumbled under her breath. She yanked on Venus's reins and stopped under a dust-shrouded plane tree. She faced her daughter. "One other warning, Gold. Remember that marriage is an alliance to enslave and shame women."

"Madar, have you seen the acrobats?"

"Yes. Why?"

"Soleiman the Agile has a fair complexion and blue eyes. He'll never shame me."

"I didn't raise you to hand you over to a bare-assed acrobat, Gold. Not all fair blue-eyed men are kind. Men are fickle; they come and go. You and only you must remain the ruler of your heart; that's the secret to survival."

Gold Dust did not need to be reminded. Early in her life, she had learned that men left behind dim memories that did not fade with time—her mother's men did, the man with the smell of iron did. But he had left behind more than faint memories. He had left behind a kiln her mother refused to ignite and a male donkey she had named Venus. "To spite Jacob!" she had replied one of the few times she was inclined to answer. "To prove that even his donkey has no balls."

"Who was he?" Gold Dust had asked.

Her mother evaded the question as if the words were vapors that, if left unattended, would evaporate.

Rebekah twirled a strand of her daughter's hair around her finger. "Gold, fall in love with yourself. Demand the world as your right. Take advantage of your singing body. And don't give yourself easily, or you'll lose respect."

Gold Dust felt pride. Her mother was initiating her into womanhood. Imitating Rebekah, she stroked her breasts, flicked her hair back, and slid her tongue over her lips. "Madar," she whispered, "if it'll make you happy, even if he's a dark man and locks his women in a cage, for you, I'll marry the Shah."

The Shah?! Gold Dust had uttered the name as if she would settle for no less. The Shah! Not even in Rebekah's loftiest dreams had she considered the king himself for her daughter. Rebekah tried to chase the thought away. It was madness enough to wish her Jewish daughter to join the harem. Grand ambitions, Rebekah knew, would only reduce her to a bitter woman. She repeated the Shah's name as she stared at her daughter.

Gold Dust was not beautiful in the conventional way. Her features were not perfect. But the whole worked so well one rarely noticed her wandering left eye or the slight flare of one nostril. Her coffee-colored hair framed high cheekbones and flattered her amber eyes. She had pale skin and angry cheeks that flamed with her emotions. Her wandering eye added mystery to the ripe look she had mastered. She had the allure and expansive laughter of a woman and the innocence and questioning glance of a child. Her words concealed the doubts of a child, but the language of her body, the slight tremble of her buttocks, the thrust of her budding breasts, and her dancing gait were those of a woman.

She would be irresistible to a man who had perfection flung at his feet.

The Shah?

The name roamed the labyrinths of Rebekah's mind and settled in her heart.

Why not?

Why not break the confining walls of convention her ancestors had raised around her? Why not let her ambitions soar?

She dried her eyes. A hardness framed her profile.

"Rebekah's daughter will become queen!"

ⵣⵙ

They reached the palace gates. The sky was the shade of persimmons. They sat on the ground, waiting—Rebekah concealed in a shimmering veil of sequins and rhinestones, Gold Dust in layers of dove-colored chiffon. Rebekah had saved strips of material, remnants from the rolls she had sold, and had stitched them into a multilayered skirt with a clinging top that traced Gold Dust's young body. A cascade of ivory lace fell over her hair and face.

With the first cry of roosters, Rebekah cupped Gold Dust's shoulders in her hands and drew her close. Rebekah was rendered speechless by the enormity of her decision, Gold Dust by the fear she might never see her mother again—was she allowed to visit? Rebekah smoothed her daughter's hair, adjusted her blouse. Gold Dust grabbed her mother's hands, but the words she had readied stuck in her throat.

Rebekah stepped back and with the scrutinizing stare of an experienced woman checked her daughter's simple but snug dress, the rounded shoulders slightly exposed, the eyes sparkling through the lace tumbling over her face.

She came forward and unveiled her daughter.

"You will be the first woman to enter the harem with uncovered face."

A breeze brushed against Gold Dust's naked cheeks. She raised her hands to the sky. She liked this freedom. Her gaze swept over the River of Dreams, where the colliding logs now sounded cheerful.

The palace guards opened the gates, honoring the eunuch's stamp and the familiar figure who visited the harem on the first day of every month.

"Who is this girl?" one of the guards asked.

"My apprentice," Rebekah sang.

Silence shrouded the palace. They were ushered through an overwhelming opulence. Alabaster columns supported mirrored ceilings, and chandeliers threw rainbow colors on bas-reliefs that depicted battles, love scenes, and mythological beings from Ferdowsi's *Epic of Kings*. Esfahan, Tabriz, and Kashan carpets sprawled on marble floors.

"The Great Black Eunuch is in the servants' quarters," the guide said.

"Lead us there," Rebekah replied, hoping to catch the eunuch in his chambers, where the intimate and more humble surroundings would be more conducive to her request.

Past intricate webbing of halls and vestibules, a door

opened into a corridor of soot-covered walls. The odor of stale oil and mildew invaded them.

The Great Black Eunuch, his face puffy from the prior night's opium suppository and from his constant consumption of raw sugar, filed past young apprentices, awaiting their morning inspection. The eunuch stared at a boy no older than twelve. Dark, curly hair framed his brown, bony face.

Narcissus turned to his assistant. "Prepare for the bastinadoes."

With a display of exaggerated pomp, the eunuch's assistant pulled the boy out of line, stretched him on a wooden frame, and bound his hands and feet.

One. Two. Three. Narcissus flogged the soles of the servant. The shrieks sounded inhuman. One. Two. Three. The boy's body jerked with every lash.

Gold Dust plunged into a nightmare. She controlled the urge to seek her mother's hand. She saw the boy's extremities stretch to the limit, his body vibrating like a bowstring. The soles of her feet burned. Each blow seemed to vibrate in her marrow. She was not sure whether the whimper she heard originated from her or from the boy.

The assistant repeated in a monotonous voice, "All ye boys observe and learn! All ye boys observe and learn!"

Rebekah nudged the guide. "Sweetlove, what did the poor soul do?"

"Newcomers are subjected to the bastinado as a way of discipline and for others to watch and learn."

When the boy's shrieks turned into sobs, Narcissus ordered him taken away.

A group of eunuchs, their torsos naked, awaited their turn for inspection. Narcissus checked the crotch of each eunuch. When he reached the last one in line, Narcissus stopped. His hand slipped back and forth between the eunuch's legs. A finger traced a slight bulge there. His hand plunged inside the alarmed man's waistband and into his pants.

Narcissus turned to his assistant: "He has become a man again! Recastrate him."

Gold Dust made up her mind. She would not stay in this strange place. She rose on her toes and whispered, "I'm leaving."

Rebekah's arm circled her daughter's waist. "This is the dark side of the palace. You'll never see it again. Wait until we get to the harem. You won't believe the beauty."

Gold Dust didn't care for the beauty, the Shah, and the fat, beardless man who flogged boys. The injustice of her mother forcing her into this world. She asked, "Do you love me?"

Startled, Rebekah stole her gaze away from her daughter. What was she supposed to answer to this simple question? That her love was so great it had been transformed into a madness that fueled her life, that her love had churned into a rage that was the source of her vigor, a love so immense she would suffer the pain of separation? "Hush, child!" she whispered as Narcissus shuffled toward them. "Bad things happen even in heaven."

Gold Dust pursed her lips. Another time, she would repeat her question and demand a satisfying answer.

The eunuch surveyed Rebekah's full-figured allure, then gazed suspiciously at Gold Dust's bare face. "Why are you here so early?"

Rebekah brushed her veil off her head, but kept the gauze that draped her lower face. "With your permission, I brought my daughter, Gold Dust, for your inspection."

"What permission!" he croaked, stamping his legs in anger. "I never gave any."

Good. Gold Dust inhaled deeply. Did he think she was dying to enter this prison? She had to escape before he tied her

up and flogged her, before her mother left her, before the drumming of her heart punctured her ears. She searched for an exit.
"Madar, I'm going."

"My apologies," Rebekah cooed, grabbing the back of Gold
Dust's skirt and stopping her in her place. "I took the liberty on
my own. Would you please me by considering her as part of the
harem?"

Gold Dust's body jerked toward her mother. Lines had
etched themselves around her mouth. Gold Dust was familiar
with that unwavering look. Now even fate could not deter her.

Rebekah refused to be intimidated by the eunuch's huffing
and puffing and petulant waving, which sent his stomach into
a quiver. Although aware of his tremendous power, she was also
aware of the terrible sexual cravings he struggled with. "I'll offer
all of myself at your feet, Narcissus," she whispered.

He examined Gold Dust. Her complexion was too rosy and
her hair cut too short. Her left nostril flared more than the
right, giving her an arrogance reserved for dignified spiritualists
like himself. Reluctantly, he confessed to himself that he liked
her amber eyes but not the twist in her left one, which made
him think she stared at a distance beyond his reach. The dimple in her chin was quite charming and so was her seductive
stubbornness. But what fascinated him most about this girl was
the mysterious, sporadic hum of disapproval that seemed to
emanate from the vicinity of her body.

He gazed at her uncovered face. Which group of sultanas
would she fit into? The harem was suffocating with women of
all sizes and temperaments. But as hard as he tried, this girl
defied categorization. Might that not save him from his
predicament?

For some time now, sameness, a horrid flatness, had crept
into the Shah's life. He had been noticing the Shah's glazed
stares, the many nights he passed alone, and the absence of gifts

he used to send as a token of gratitude for the girls he, Narcissus, chose. The Shah was ready for a change.

"She is not beautiful," Narcissus muttered, "and she has not inherited your voluptuous hips."

No, Rebekah thought, and she might never learn to stir to life the dead emotions of a eunuch. "Stay here, Gold," she ordered, the glare in her eyes stopping her daughter. "I'll be back." Then she lifted the fine gauze from her face and asked Narcissus if he would show her his private quarters. Her arm hugged the eunuch's soft shoulders. "Narcissus, please call for someone to watch over Gold Dust until we return."

Narcissus felt Rebekah's hand melt into his flesh, her breath warm his lungs. Her smell tasted of honey and molasses. He clapped his hands.

A girl of eighteen appeared and stood with bowed head, her long lashes brushing anemic cheeks. Gold Dust pinched her nostrils shut. The palace exuded the musky odor of mold and age. The Shah was everywhere, baked into glazed tiles, engraved on porphyry and malachite columns, in combat with man and beast, wielding the spear, bashing a head, or hoisting a scimitar. His face was brutal and distorted. His stone eyes followed her. She glanced at the girl's colorless complexion, her eyes the shade of water, her lips drained of blood.

"Is this the true likeness of the Shah?" Gold Dust asked.

"His Holiness appears before his subjects at a distance. No one has depicted him truthfully."

Gold Dust dashed out of one of the many branching corridors.

෴

Rebekah and the Great Black Eunuch passed the inner court and the kitchens and entered the lodging of the eunuchs. He unlocked a door framed with elaborate carvings of wooden animals with bulging eyes of ruby.

She brushed past him like a breeze, feeling a hard object against his side. She raised an eyebrow. "What's this?"

He mumbled unintelligible words. His cheeks trembled. He turned his eyes from her scrutinizing stare.

Her fingers traced the plush velvet of his cape, the satin lining, the ermine trimming, the slippery silk of his billowing pants, and rested on his waist. She grabbed the solid object.

He slapped her hand away, but like leeches her fingers stuck. "Can you keep my secret?"

She fluttered her lashes and slid her tongue over red lips. Yes! She would treasure his secret, tuck it away in her heart, and produce it at the right time.

"Promise," he begged, imploring clemency from the spirits of the dead.

She touched her bosom. The shape of her mark began to change. "I swear by all my ancestors."

He reached under his sash and the elastic of his waistband and retrieved a small jar full of brine.

Rebekah shut her eyes; her fingers sprang to her mouth; the mark between her breasts throbbed.

He held up the glass container, checking its contents, then turned it in circles in front of her face.

She opened her eyes again, her breath labored, sweat trickling down her cleavage.

He displayed the glass on the palm of his hand. "Our Muslim tradition demands we bury the whole body to attain heaven."

"Poor, poor Narcissus. Your manhood is pickled in a jar!" She touched him between his legs. "I'll show you there's more here than what's preserved in brine."

"It's useless. I'm not a man."

"I shall prove otherwise."

"What arrogance makes you think you'll succeed where others failed?"

She pressed the discolored skin of her palm on his mouth. "The arrogance comes from this burned hand you've been staring at." She uncoiled his turban and the sash around his waist, removed his dagger and cape, vest and pants, then led him to the floor-bed at the corner of the carpeted room.

"What caused this burn?"

"Don't ask questions. In return, I'll raise your passion to such heights you won't want to return."

He snickered. "I don't want arousal. I've enough of that. Passion without release is like enduring castration over and over again."

"Will you tell me about it, Narcissus? Do you want to?" She knew he would. She recognized his need to communicate his pain. She herself, in her capacity as a healer, had learned to listen and to hoard secrets and to use them to her advantage. "Talk to me, Narcissus."

"It happened in the desert, the operating hall of slave traders. Can you believe they said a prayer over me when they saw the bush of mature hair?"

They shaved him, then tattooed a red narcissus on his pubis, a decorative substitute for what he was about to lose. White ribbons were bound around his stomach and upper thighs to prevent excessive bleeding. They bathed his genitals in hot pepper-water.

"I thought I'd burst into flames. But worse was still to come."

"Poor, poor Narcissus," Rebekah cooed. "Pox on their house! How could they do this to you?"

They wound another stretch of cloth tightly about him, starting at the tip of the penis and going inward to the roots.

With a quick flash of a razor, they severed his penis and testicles.

His screams erupted to the seventh heaven.

The wound was cauterized with hot oil left on a single burner all night. They inserted a pewter needle into the opening of the root of his penis and applied puffball fungus and alum, then shrouded the wound with calico saturated in water and secured with strips of a fabric known for its blotting quality.

Narcissus wiped his forehead dry and stared at the shuddering Rebekah, expecting her to flee like the others before her. She steadied herself, aimed her distressed stare at him, and whispered, "Go on, Narcissus, my heart is breaking for you."

"They held me from the armpits and walked me around the desert until I was about to dry up and crumble."

Then they buried him up to the neck under the hot desert sand, the most effective balm in the world. They did not give him water. If his passages swelled up, he would not be able to urinate and would be doomed to an agonizing death.

For four suns and four nights he hallucinated, the desert sand and hungry-eyed slave traders chasing him. Mirages of gelded calves loomed, disintegrated into the haze, and reappeared to haunt him with endless bleating. The pain, thirst, and the impossibility of relieving himself were unbearable. After the fourth sun had set, they unwrapped the strips of cloth and pulled out the needle. A spurt of bloody urine flowed. They raised their heads in a prayer of thanks.

"And as a priceless gift, they handed me this crystal jar. See the relief cut around the edges? I'm luckier than other eunuchs. With a lucrative trade of organs, only honest slave dealers give the owner back his parts."

Narcissus hugged the jar that housed his manhood, his only hope of redemption preserved in brine.

"Narcissus," Rebekah said gently. "I promise you release

today. But on the condition you admit Gold Dust to the harem. If you don't keep your promise, I swear on everything you believe in that this will be your last."

She lowered herself next to him, forcing him down, pressing her palm to his mouth to stop his feeble protests. Kneading his hairless thighs, she felt his flesh respond as if it were warm dough in her hands. His body, liquid and buttery, devoid of muscles, gave way to her touch; a pale film of moisture covered him. She parted his thighs. He was bare between his legs, a bloody narcissus tattooed on his pubis. She controlled the urge to vomit. The opening of his urethra gaped at her. Nothing there. No penis. Clean-cut.

Rebekah squeezed a pillow against the eunuch's mouth to stifle his howls. She uncapped the tumbler of coconut oil she carried in her pocket and lubricated her fingertips, rubbing his neck and shoulders, softening the knots, her touch soothing, never rushed. His lids were growing heavy, his eyes drunk. Her fingers circled his temples; the slightest pressure kept him alert. She needed his concentration.

Her breath was warm. "You are a man; feel yourself hard inside a woman. She wants you, is tightening around you, cries with pleasure. . . ."

Animal moans sprang out of his mouth. His fingers searched between his legs to grab the absent penis Rebekah had rendered life to. She prevented the shattering of his fantasies by holding his hands back, licking his fingertips, burying them between her breasts. "Feel the contractions; she can't restrain herself. . . ."

Saliva dripped from the corner of his mouth as he bit on his tongue, sucked on his lips. Rebekah understood the vacuum there. She must fill it up or he would tear his lips and return to the harem bleeding. She guided her nipple into his mouth.

Her touch slipped down his stomach, circling his navel, into his hairless pubis, around the urethra, testing, appraising. His writhing and moaning led her to his sensitive points. She searched for the anal cavity, his muffled groans rising, her touch caressing, probing, pressing, advancing deep where the eunuch himself had never dared. He bit on her nipple, puncturing the skin. Her fingers played faster, a pitiless, fiery, sacrificial dance hatched by the enormity of her pain and her desire to triumph.

His moans turned to wails as he pleaded for a relief that seemed remote. Rebekah wavered. Her life and that of her daughter depended on this instant.

She unlocked his teeth from her nipple, turned him around, and came down on her knees, spreading his mounds. A shudder ran up his spine. The thrust of her tongue let loose the raging fire he had repressed all of his adult life.

He stiffened, let go of the pillow, sighed, went limp. She wrapped him in the covers. He would need hours to recover from the deep orgasm she had induced from his lust gland. She straightened up, her veil draping her shoulders, her face damp, her mark flushed.

"You are mine, Narcissus," she whispered. "You are all mine!"

11

*T*he shriek of peacocks came from the gardens and echoed off the walls, as Gold Dust rushed through a set of swinging partitions and found herself in Pearl Hall. The bright array of colors and the glitter of precious stones mesmerized her. Everything seemed suspended in time, every motion lethargic, every word a mystery. Was this the harem? Engulfed in a cloud of opium. Overwhelming in its strangeness. Calming in its sluggishness.

A sultana pointed at her. Heads turned. Whispers developed into murmurs. Little girls, dressed like adults, abandoned their mothers' laps. The spell broke. Gold Dust whirled around to escape. A eunuch appeared behind her to guard the swinging doors.

Honey was the first to notice Gold Dust lost by the back entrance. Honey's ink-black hair and slanted eyes sparkled. An ebony teardrop, tattooed at the corner of her left eye, gave her a melancholy air. Sultanas who preferred their own kind were fascinated by Honey's fleshy mouth, which curled and twisted and sucked on her own tongue as if in search of nectar.

Honey stared at Gold Dust, a vision in white, her face

naked, her bold hair short, her skin as lucid as seashells. Despite the presence of the Bibi Sultana and forgetting all precautions, Honey tiptoed toward the stranger. She thrust her fingers through Gold Dust's hair; one forefinger slid over her lips and lingered on the dimple in her chin. The blushing cheeks of this stranger told her she was a virgin. Honey decided to become her mentor, to have her before the other sultanas befriended her.

Gold Dust slapped Honey's hand away, puzzled at her dancing lips, the curious, probing fingers, the blue-black tear that smiled or cried at the corner of her eye.

"Soon the Bibi will scream," Honey whispered. "Don't be afraid."

The sultana's touch both invaded and calmed Gold Dust. She wanted to accept her admiration, yet escape her brashness. She looked around to find her way out beyond the smoke of opium. It was too late. Pearl Hall had awakened. She was trapped.

The Bibi Sultana narrowed her hawkish eyes and demanded to know who had intruded upon the harem. Moon Face hurried to unravel the mystery. Honey circled an arm around Gold Dust, hanging on to the delicious moments of secrecy. The sultanas, smelling intrigue, shook their boredom off and chewed on sugar cubes to revive themselves.

The Bibi Sultana's voice rumbled, "Who is this girl? Where is Narcissus?"

Behind a tall sultana, whose pale complexion loomed above the others, Gold Dust saw her mother appear.

Rebekah forced a path through the sultanas. For months, the eunuch had directed her into Pearl Hall through the main entrance, and she had never noticed the back doors where Gold Dust now stood bewildered. The tension in the air, the echo of the Bibi's voice, the menacing storm in Moon Face's eyes, and the audacity of Honey's fingers alarmed Rebekah. She hoped it would not take the eunuch long to wake from his orgasmic stupor and come to her aid.

Rebekah opened her arms to her daughter. As if it were the most natural thing to say, she announced, "You have found a new home, Gold."

The relief Gold Dust had felt at her mother's appearance vanished.

Rebekah saw in her daughter's eyes a glint, an icy stare, she believed had been buried with Jacob the Fatherless. She stepped back as if she had been struck.

The Bibi Sultana shifted on her dais, motioning Moon Face to stop fanning her. Nothing must distract her from the dramatic confrontation about to unravel.

Pearl Hall held its breath.

"Madar, I'll stay." Gold Dust's words broke the expectant silence. "I'll stay to punish you. So you won't impose your desires on me again."

Rebekah waved a bangled wrist, a futile attempt to arrest her freshly emerging qualms. "Gold, it's *our* desire, not mine. . . ."

"No, Madar." Gold Dust's stare was unwavering. "Yours. I have other desires."

Narcissus entered with a rhythmic gait. The flush on his black complexion alerted the women that a monumental event had transpired in his life.

He gauged the gathering in the room, the ominous silence. Even the little princesses had stopped playing and hugging their dolls to their chest, and now lingered around the hall. He went to the Bibi Sultana and kissed her hand. "My apologies. I wanted to surprise you with my latest trophy. But apparently she found her way before I could make an appropriate introduction."

The Bibi glared at the eunuch. "You have a way of spoiling delightful moments."

Rebekah went to the Bibi Sultana and prostrated herself, murmuring her apologies for disrupting the calm of the inner quarters. "I shall leave immediately, my lady."

"Take your time to wish your daughter farewell," the Bibi said. "She's an ignorant creature, but once I'm done with her, she'll be a different woman."

The brand between Rebekah's breasts turned into ice. She had not fully considered the dangers of the seraglio. Now it was too late. Once the Bibi Sultana wished a girl to join the harem, no force could change that.

"Gold," Rebekah whispered, "listen well, even if it's the only advice you'll ever follow. Never submit to the pitiless clutches of the brown addiction. Never become part of the opium-filled hours here."

The Bibi's final decree had stripped Gold Dust of her last trace of anger. Her bones shuddered at the fear thrust her way. "Please, don't forget me here."

"You are the air I breathe, Gold. How could I forget you?" Rebekah glanced at her right hand, the skin translucent as onion peel. She felt the heat between her breasts as intensely as the moment she was branded. She touched her thigh, where she still carried the heaviness of the gold pouch Rouh'Allah of the melodious voice had once dropped in her lap. Would this decision become another load she would lug the rest of her days?

"Madar, are you allowed to visit?"

"Listen to me, Gold," Rebekah whispered. "Relatives are not, but I'm now the official bundle woman of the palace, so I can visit you. Don't be afraid. I won't abandon you."

The eunuch decided to expedite matters before the Bibi Sultana lashed out at the two women who whispered in her presence. "I shall now," he announced, "withdraw with the girl to communicate with the spirits. I'll return with the decision of the higher powers."

The Bibi Sultana curled a finger and motioned the eunuch to her side. "This one better find favor in my son's eyes . . . or else one of these nights your head will roll in the Courtyard of Horses."

Narcissus, too, heard the stirring of three hundred sixty-five dissatisfied women. He, too, sniffed the bitterness of an unused harem, the putrefying of fertile organs left to nothing but frustration. He, too, foresaw the biggest threat of all: the danger of the Shah's slipping back into his old ways, finding his pleasure in the arms of the beautiful half-man whom the Bibi Sultana despised. Rebekah had appeared just in time. She had introduced fresh blood into the harem.

12

*T*he Great Black Eunuch locked himself in his room. Drowned in a hypnotic trance, he rocked in front of an incense brazier, inhaled herbal fumes, and consulted with the spirits. When he left the room, his breath exhaled the morbid odor of a creature that had been fasting for many days, but the determined line of his jaw spoke of a man whose mind was set.

He presented Gold Dust to the Bibi Sultana as she sat spread out cross-legged on the dais and suffered the eunuch to go through the proper introduction. He spoke of Gold Dust's unusual beauty, her charming qualities, and above all assured the Bibi that he had examined Gold Dust and found her a virgin.

With watery gray eyes that had retained the keen vision of a preying hawk, the Bibi gazed at Gold Dust. She thrust a tattooed fingertip at the girl's cheeks, stomach, and buttocks to test their firmness. She slapped her twice. Gold Dust held her head high. Tears flashed in her defiant eyes. The Bibi Sultana raised her hand. Gold Dust did not blink. She seized the hand in midair. Narcissus shuddered. The sultanas gasped. The princesses giggled. Honey sighed at such boldness. Moon Face snickered behind her palm.

"You may join the harem," the Bibi croaked, her mustache trembling. "I'll personally rub your arrogant snout in dust."

Her anger snuffed out by the hate on the Bibi's face, Gold Dust prostrated herself. "I'll forever be your servant."

"Never forget that you are just that."

Narcissus was relieved. The Bibi had accepted Gold Dust, welcoming the challenge of crushing another young girl. Now he would not need to reveal the marvel of sitars humming in Gold Dust's throat. He would disclose that secret to the Shah with preparation, great pomp, and a begging palm.

ℭℴ

Gold Dust began rigorous training in palace etiquette, dance, poetry, music, and the Islamic culture. With every lesson she learned, Gold Dust shed a tear for the home she missed, and another out of fear she decided to keep from her mother: the tales of twenty-five women, the castoffs of the Shah.

Every sundown, after the sultanas put their daughters to bed, Pearl Hall swelled with lethargy induced by opium pills. They called it *keyf*, the ultimate fulfillment. The sultanas floated in opium rituals, puffing on the gurgling hookahs, sinking into smoky fantasies, caressing each other, and telling legends of lands beyond the latticed windows.

Gold Dust, alert and conscious, fought to harness the sighs that threatened to rise from her disjointed bones. Her mother had warned her against submitting to the merciless brown addiction. But, hearing the sultanas' stories, she wished she could lose herself in their opium dreams that made them forget their distant homes.

ℭℴ

Gold Dust followed the rough voice of Moon Face, the sooth-ing murmurs of Honey. The reason for the Shah's wavering moods, and his periodical need for solitude, the two women agreed, was the years, not long ago, he had spent in the Cage, a tower close to the palace, but off-limits to everyone, save cer-tain eunuchs and a handful of deaf-mute guards, whose eardrums had been punctured and tongues severed.

The Shah was too sensitive for a prince, his father, the late shah, had decided. His firstborn son was unworthy of wearing the crown. The late shah had locked the kind-hearted heir in the Cage with thirty other princes, his younger sons, whom he feared might rebel and claim the throne. And from then on, if a sultana became heavy with child, he had her tied up in a sack and hurled into the river. The late shah suffered from madness that had afflicted Persian kings because of their constant fear of invasion. Once Persian culture flourished and harmony pre-vailed, an attack from remote countries was imminent. The resources of Persia—carpets, iron, and copper—were a con-stant temptation to other countries, especially to an empire on another continent that harbored pale, blue-eyed scoundrels, and a gray, gloomy climate.

While the late shah had wandered the halls of the palace, struggling with the rapid process of aging and rambling about better days, his son, in the Cage, lacked for nothing but free-dom. He had women who had been stripped of their childbear-ing organs; he had baths that were kept warm throughout all hours; he had musicians and clowns who performed at the snap of his fingers; he had a young, fair-complexioned, exquisite boy called Hazel-Boy, who took care of his personal needs.

Wide-eyed, Gold Dust asked, "What needs?"

Honey pressed her palm to Gold Dust's mouth. "My sweet, don't ask dangerous questions." She slipped her fingers between Gold Dust's legs.

Gold Dust struggled to comprehend a world where no secrets were honored, no privacy allowed. Narcissus had warned her that if any man or woman touched her she would be spoiled for the Shah. She brushed aside Honey's hand.

Moon Face wiggled her finger into Gold Dust's waistband, snapping the elastic. "Be kind to yourself. No one will reward you for abstinence."

The Shah will, Gold Dust thought, shifting away from the women.

"The Shah learned the art of falconry and the cultivating of roses."

He rode up to the chain of the Alborz Mountains to practice falconry and seized two peregrine falcons and one gyrfalcon from their nests, on the summit of the Damavand volcano. He tamed them, placing hoods over their heads and slipping brails around their wings to prevent them from fluttering. On their legs he attached jesses with bells. In a dark room, he puffed on a hookah pipe to calm the birds and remind them of his presence. After four sunrises, he lit a candle. The gradual illumination helped the falcons adjust to their surroundings. When they lost their fear and picked food from his palm, he perched them on his shoulders and on his heavily gloved forearm. They were trained to listen to the beat of his heart, to remain calm when he was, and to flutter wildly when he was angry or afraid.

His newfound serenity was shattered the day the Great Black Eunuch and his private army entered the Cage. All the princes but the young Shah crouched behind their divans, certain that the executioner had at last come.

"You are now the ruler of Persia," the Great Eunuch announced, prostrating himself and kissing the Shah's slipper. The eunuch held up a vial of earth. "Allah bless your father's soul. The curse of madness consumed him."

Following the eunuch to the Hall of Ceremonies to pay one

last homage to the body, the prince was told his late father had, after hearing the rumor of another invasion, for a week ingested only myrrh and balsam to ensure the preservation of his body, then had drunk a vessel of bull's blood, which coagulated in his throat and choked him. His body was covered with camphor and wrapped in a sevenfold winding sheet, the face included, as prescribed in Islam.

At the gravesite, the Shah threw earth from his father's grave onto his own head, as was customary for sons to do.

The sultanas sighed behind the screen of opium.

Honey stroked Gold Dust's hair. "The few who were intimate with the Shah believe he still craves the lazy days of his youth when threat of invasion did not penetrate the Cage."

He managed to overcome his lethargy and rule the empire with rare compassion. But when the moods overwhelmed him, he withdrew, tending to his roses and coming back to the palace saturated with the smell of earth and roses.

Then he fell in love with Pari, a dainty dark-haired sultana. He built her a private quarter with a garden he personally tended to. His love for her manifested itself in the roses he bred, Persian ebony-tipped ones and others from distant continents. He produced a hybrid he named Pari. Its fame traveled the world. Gardeners from near and far came to Persia to learn the secret of a black rose with ruffled, onyx-colored petals, and purple capillaries, the fragrance of which was mute at dawn and shrieked at sunset. The Shah refused to share the mystery of Pari's rose. Even the royal gardeners were not aware of the origin of the seeds that were delivered in secrecy every No-Ruz, the first day of spring.

Then Pari died.

Gold Dust leaned closer to Honey and asked, "How?"

Moon Face, paler than usual, directed a stormy stare at Gold Dust. "Someone pushed her off a cliff into the River of

Dreams." Rage distorted her face as she pointed a finger at Gold Dust. "She should not have occupied another sultana's place."

Gold Dust recognized Pari's murderer.

Surely the whole harem knew. Why else was Moon Face so obvious in her unspoken demonstrations? Gold Dust realized she, too, must seal the secret in her heart to protect herself from Moon Face.

"Is Pari's death," Gold Dust asked, "the cause of the Shah's moods?"

"From that day on, they grew darker," Moon Face murmured, her breath bitter with opium and hate. "They come and go with no predictability. It might be lost love, the fear of another invasion, or the curse of madness that manifests itself in mistrust of others and ends in death."

Honey directed a warning glance at Gold Dust. "Moon Face forgot the real reason for the Shah's moods." Her hand slipped between Gold Dust's breasts. "Would you like to know?"

"Yes." Let Honey fondle her, Gold Dust thought, a bait in exchange for precious information: the king's strengths, weaknesses, needs, likes and dislikes. Even faults, to reduce him to the rank of ordinary men. Then she would understand him better.

"Listen well!" Honey's breath was on Gold Dust's neck, a murmur in her ear: "It's the shame of his failure to produce boys."

Trying to plug the joy in her bones, Gold Dust stifled her excitement. At last she had located the Shah's flaw. He had no sons! That's why boys were absent from the seraglio.

She pulled a mask of innocence over her features. "Why is it shameful not to have sons?"

Moon Face snickered. "With no heirs, the lineage will die with the Shah. A tragedy. A great shame."

Both women, for different reasons, tried to scare her away from the Shah. But they had added mystery and fascination to the image Gold Dust had created of him.

No sultana had produced an heir to the throne! If the Shah chose her as a favorite, under the custody of the Mistress of the House, she would be bathed, endowed with private quarters, a barge, a carriage, and slaves.

She would bear the king's first son. She would rise above the other concubines to become his wife. The queen of Persia.

"Snuff out that light in your eyes," Moon Face barked. "Experienced women could not bear him sons."

Gold Dust cast her eyes down. Let Moon Face think what she may. Although most sultanas were more skilled than she, none had a mother like Rebekah. Surely, among her mother's many magical mysteries and potions, one would help her produce an heir.

Moon Face reached out bony fingers for the bowl of rock sugar. "Honey is your salvation. Enjoy her before you shrivel like the rest of us." She set her head on Gulf Lily's lap.

The eunuch's glance swept the length of her body, her lean thighs, sinewy arms, boyish breasts. The enormity of his love could, at will, summon the many tastes of his beloved, even the flavor of aged wine he imagined pumped in her veins. To endure the memories that remained as painful as on the first day, his fingers played a silent lullaby in Moon Face's hair. He knew his mistress well, the fury in her eyes, the twitch at the corner of her mouth. The past was seared into her heart. She conjured bygone incidents at will—especially her days with the Shah.

๑๛

He had sent one hundred and two silk dresses to the harem. Narcissus had marched around and had called out the names of a handful of sultanas, handing each a robe. "The Shah will spend the noon hour with you."

Like bees in search of nectar, the women buzzed around the

halls, swarmed into the baths, and peeped through the latticed windows to accustom their eyes to the light. When the muezzin called the faithful to prayer, the sultanas followed the eunuch past the Hall of Felicity and the Hall of Entertainment, and entered the vast Pool Room. They were disappointed. They had anticipated a day of outing, a warming of their blood, a thawing of their desires. But the Shah had preferred the indoors. They dipped their toes in the water and glanced at the latticed screens from behind which the Shah was in the habit of spying on them.

Eunuchs handed them glass balls that distorted their images, pearl chains that shimmered, and quicksilver orbs with mirrored triangles. The sultanas dove into the water fully dressed. They held the strings of pearl between their lips, passing them from mouth to mouth, sheathing their teeth in fear of breaking the strings. They gazed at their distorted reflections on the glass balls and tossed them from hand to hand.

A hush fell over the hall. The women stared at each other. Their silk garments floated about them, their breasts exposed above the surface. The water had unglued the seams. They stifled giggles, thrust their breasts forward, arched their backs, and began dancing. A show for the king.

Moon Face balanced herself on her toes, exposing the triangle of her pubis to the invisible Shah. Her face swayed above the stem of her long neck. She bit on a string of pearls; iridescent dots punctured the water. Chasing the pearls, she caught them between her lips and concealed them in her mouth. Among a family of pearls, one matured in a poisonous oyster. Neither the color nor the size differed from other pearls, but if ingested, it instantly killed.

The Shah would see her swallow the pearls. Gamble with her life for him.

He invited her to his quarters.

In the privacy of her room, she mixed rosewater, almond paste, and rice flour for extra whiteness. The Shah liked pale women. She fumigated her room with sandalwood until her pores emitted the scent of dry tree barks. Not smiling for fear of cracking the hardened mask on her blank face, she appeared at the threshold of his chambers. A satin pouch draped down her arm. The Shah had had women with manly breasts, with child-like hips, with fleshy buttocks, with skins the color of coffee or ivory. With her unresponsive face, shaved eyebrows, bloody lips, and long-legged body, she was unlike the others.

She pried the neck of the pouch open and removed a stick of incense and lit it with the flame of a candle. The aroma of musk and sandalwood permeated the room. Her soulless eyes never leaving the Shah's, she lubricated her toes with almond oil, her fingers crawling between the shallow valleys, lingering, sliding back and forth, and drawing tiny circles as if to dislodge a dark secret. She had come informed about his petty inclinations—even his obsession with feminine toes. When he raised an eyebrow, she knew her animated toes fascinated him. She searched her pouch. A flesh-colored object, molded from wax to the shape and measure of the Shah's organ, lay in her palm. Would it please him that she had exaggerated the size of his sex?

She transformed herself into a wild animal, sucked, licked, then forced the organ into herself, sighing, trembling, and twisting. He embraced himself, his hand sliding up and down his shaft.

She had performed for him in the evenings and sometimes at dawn. One night she had pressed her mouth to his. Was it the taste of cherry unguent? The icy feel of her flesh? Or the disillusionment of consummation?

He had banished her from his bed.

13

Gold Dust followed the eunuch to the Receiving Hall, a long, rectangular room with heavy velvet drapes gathered with twisted ropes. The raised platform that held the Shah's unoccupied throne faced a balcony where female musicians performed in the evenings. Arches carved into the walls by master architects created echoes that produced the effect of a grand assembly of instruments when music played.

The eunuch checked Gold Dust one last time. She wore the ivory dress she had on when she first entered the harem. The toile outlined her breasts and tumbled down in ruffles. She had refused to cover her face and she wore no makeup. He recognized that as an added bait. Her hair, parted in the middle, framed arrogant cheeks. Two pearl drops swayed from her earlobes. The Shah would appreciate the simplicity, the unassuming sensuality. The eunuch left her standing in the center of the hall.

Gold Dust's startled eyes searched the hall for partitions, lattices, or peepholes from behind which the Shah screened his women. The fragrance of black roses betrayed his presence.

When time stood still and she thought she would never be rescued from the awkward waiting, a feeling of nakedness overwhelmed her. She resented being on display like a slave whose teeth were being counted in a bazaar. She wrapped her arms around her chest and came down on the carpet, hugging her knees. She would rather seem arrogant than be transformed into a helpless girl stripped naked by invisible eyes.

"Stand up and turn."

His voice was like thunder. She rose and spun on her toes. She twirled until the walls, drapes, and his throne rotated around her. When would he ask her to stop? She felt dizzy, was about to fall. She slowed down. Stood still in the center of the hall and tried to keep her balance. She settled back on the carpet and folded into herself.

"Impudent!" The word bounced off every corner.

She sprang to her feet and whirled around, searching for the origin of his voice. His laughter pounced at her from the many archways, magnifying her humiliation. Controlling the urge to press her palms to her ears, she gazed straight ahead as her mother had taught her. And without waiting to be dismissed, she walked toward the door.

"To learn obedience!" The Shah's voice reverberated. "You will serve us."

༄

Every dawn, Gold Dust examined the absent Shah's schedule, set the appropriate attire on the dressing stand, fanned the coals in the brazier, and brewed tea and rosewater for his mid-morning libation. The rest of the day she spent with the Mistress of Dancing.

She watched the mistress conquer the hall with painstaking accuracy, every motion calculated. Gold Dust set out to create her own version, more fluid, uninhibited, even reckless. She demonstrated what she had mastered.

The mistress stepped back in amazement. "Where did you learn to dance like this?"

"From you, my lady," Gold Dust replied.

The mistress was at a loss. The girl's style had not been taught in books, nor observed in the past. Oblivious to the world, she abandoned herself to her passions, flying around the hall like an untamed dervish, her hair wild, her toes hardly touching the carpet.

"Gold Dust," the Mistress of Dancing announced, "you're a born dancer. I'll never forgive myself if I restrain your natural freedom."

At sundown the Shah invited Gold Dust.

She wore a skirt of lavender damask, brocaded with silver flowers; a wide-sleeved smock hugged her bosom and closed at the neck with a clasp of rubies. She entered the hall with a breeze of perfumes and the exhilaration of being invited back. The hall was heavy with the king's scent.

She glided close to the walls, stroking with dancing fingers, performing for the king, but secretly searching for a crack, a door, a partition from where he might be watching. Her heart raced at the possibility of his emergence.

The spell of her dancing—the roll of her hips, the sweep of gossamer around her body—lingered in the atmosphere and roused a more potent scent. She listened to the silence. Had her dancing captivated him? Was this the stillness of respect, reverence, maybe even awe?

She evoked an image to suit his voice and his silences. The screens and stone carvings painted a monstrous portrait, but in his love for roses, for Pari, and in his attentive quiet, she found a man who would care.

The eunuch came to lead her back to the harem. She

snatched her arm away and planted herself in the center of the hall. "My shah! Allow me the honor of beholding your face!"

The once cherished silence left a mocking ring in her bones. Had he been absent while she poured her heart out? No, he was here. His scent had intensified with her performance and had produced a mild state of drunkenness in her. She launched into a fiery performance. She would force him to acknowledge her. The degrading shadows were unbearable. She had had enough of her mother's phantom-men.

He would hear her bones.

Yes, it was time.

She would release her soul into that room, lure the king out of hiding, and see for herself that he was pale-skinned and blue-eyed.

She fought to calm herself and evoke happy memories: her mother shimmered in her glass-studded chador, on the Purim holiday of masques, riding Venus, decked with the crown of scarlet feathers. And Soleiman, her copper-haired acrobat, offered her cherry blossoms.

A tinkling sensation spread through her body. Warmth permeated her marrow.

She drew a deep breath and let out her emotions.

A dissonant chorus burst from her. A world of warring notes collided, jarred her ears, hurt her heart. Her bones had shamed her. She bowed a hasty farewell and turned toward the exit, struggling to slow her steps, hold on to her dignity.

A moan came from behind a screen. A sigh. She hesitated, stopped, but did not turn around. She heard his breathing. The beat of his heart. And then she heard his voice:

"It was lovely."

Late that evening, when the pungent vapor of opium hung over Pearl Hall and the slaves nudged the sultanas out of their dreams, Gold Dust asked, "Why does the Shah hide behind partitions?"

Shifting away from the ever-present shadow of Gulf Lily, Moon Face raised eyelids afflicted with lethargy. "Because of some curious disease of the spirit, he concocts childish games to raise himself beyond the habitual languor of the Cage. It's his private titillation. As if he collects, one by one, the notes for some complicated music he'll play when he's ready. And even then, he'll play it only once. No one knows who the next victim is."

Gold Dust shuddered. "Why do you call yourselves victims? Why do you leave him with the taste of honey that turns to ash?"

"Because once the Shah has a woman and captures her with his intoxicating scent, resentment replaces his initial excitement. He resents relinquishing part of his manhood by wasting his seed in our womb. The moment a sultana is confident of his love and acquires a voice of her own, he punishes her with indifference until nothing is left but the aftertaste of his scent."

Gulf Lily brushed Moon Face's hair, cupped her chin, and raised her face as if it were an exotic flower. His eyes softened with unspoken words.

"Above all," Moon Face continued, "he loathes the fact that his women can't produce an heir."

"Does he blame the sultanas?"

"To blame himself is a threat to his manhood."

Gold Dust moved closer to Moon Face. "So why are the sultanas eager for his invitation?"

"That you'll not understand until you experience his touch and his addictive smell. It's what every woman prays for . . .

until she enters his lair." A spark of lunacy darkened her eyes.

A melody suffused with fear and sadness surrounded Gold Dust. Confusion brought tears to her bones. She didn't know whether to flee or wear her most inviting attire and roam the labyrinths of the palace in search of the Shah.

14

$\mathcal{G}$old Dust followed Narcissus into a secluded building behind the royal courts. They entered a bedchamber littered with costly tea sets, decanters, and perfume sprinklers. Beyond the latticed doors, drab with caked dirt, she saw a neglected yard. An exquisite bath of inlaid turquoise lay in a patch of over-grown weeds. There was such an air of negligence that suddenly Gold Dust felt lonelier than she had since joining the harem.

Narcissus set a bowl of yogurt and a slice of wheat bread sprinkled with sesame seeds on a dust-covered stool.

Gold Dust stared at her meager meal. "Narcissus, why am I here?"

"You'll find out soon. In the meantime, keep your stomach as empty as possible."

Seeing the puzzled look on her face, he burst out into a snicker that sounded like the cracking of ice. "A full stomach will make you sluggish. You won't be able to copulate in a sprightly manner."

After months of waiting, the time had come for her to meet the Shah. Was this a temporary station from which she would be called to him? Cautious hope filled her. Perhaps she had not

heard about this ritual because it was reserved for those wh
the king favored.

If only she knew what to expect in the person of the Shah,
she would not mind waiting. But jealous sultanas, the bas-
reliefs on the wall, and his silences and few words created the
image she had of him. Was he ugly? Cruel? Old? She didn't
even know his exact age.

She aired the sheets, set the filigreed tea sets in order, and
washed away the stale smell of spices and mold that clung to a
pile of Arabian towels. She welcomed the sweat that cooled
her frenzied thoughts.

She went out to the garden and pulled out the weeds that
populated what she thought had once been a rose garden. Was
this Pari's garden? Plucking a rose, she sniffed the dried bud that
had survived the elements. Ice flowers. Time had extracted
the natural scent of the rose and had left an essence that
smelled of ice flowers. Her stomach revolted at the recollection
of the perfume her mother kept at her bedside, at the memory,
now altered by time, of the men falling on top of her mother,
crushing her with their weight.

She shut her eyes and imagined the Shah appearing, roaring
with anger, the men fleeing. The king reached out to the girl
hiding behind a flap of cloth and led her out of the Jewish
Quarter, away from the dark-faced men.

Gold Dust lay out on the verandah, baring her breasts to the
sun. She envisioned the man who had loved Pari, who had
bathed her in a jewel-studded tub, and who had fled to his falcons to share the grief of her loss.

A shadow fell over her. She started up. Grabbing her veil,
she prostrated herself, kissing the floor in front of the man who
observed her with interest.

"You need not do this," he said, raising her gently from the
shoulders. His fragile features were sculpted to perfection. Sil-

he borders of his cone-shaped hat. He had a
and green eyes. A miniature silver bottle
around his neck. He lifted her chador and
her breasts. "For once," he said, "they were
..... You are stunning."

Why hadn't any of the sultanas ever disclosed how beautiful
the Shah was, that the color of his skin was lighter than ivory,
and his eyes deeper than emerald? Their jealousy was beyond
comprehension. Her anticipating heart fluttered. This man was
not weary of life. He had the curious eyes of children and the
considerate tone of men who care.

But he was so young. She began to calculate in her mind the
years since the Shah had been locked in the Cage. He must be
past thirty. The man in front of her was not much older than
herself. She stared at his hairless face with no shadow of
a beard. A face as smooth as a eunuch's. But he was too slim to
be one of the sexless who directed their bitterness into eating,
and he was too refined in his manners and attire.

He raised her chin with two tapered fingers. "Your restless
eyes tell me you'll be an astute student."

"I've been trained in palace etiquette."

"But not in the erotic arts," he replied, brushing a palm
against her cheek. "Nor in the art of the intimate chambers."

"Who are you?" she whispered, as if in the presence of a
deity.

"I'm Hazel-Boy, the man in the stories you heard. I spent my
youth in the Cage with the Shah, and I continue to serve him."
He toyed with the silver bottle.

Her eyes clung to his every move; she longed to touch his
face, experience for herself if it was as soft as she imagined. She
wanted to ask what was in the silver bottle.

"Cast your eyes down," he said. "And never smile too
broadly, lest it be taken for brashness."

She averted her eyes from his intimate gaze. Did he k. her from another time?

He cupped her elbow and led her inside. He nodded approvingly. "You have put the chamber in order. This place has not been used for years. Good. The decanter is on the right side of the tray; the cup handles face whomever you'll serve. Now bring the stool closer, uncork the decanter, and serve the wine without a single drop staining anything." He ran his fingers through her hair. "Don't look surprised. Many of us drink behind closed doors. After all, what is love without wine?"

His touch sent unfamiliar warmth through her bones. She kept still, as if a single word would be sacrilege to his caress.

His fingers paused in her hair, felt her shudder. "Listen to me, little one. It's important you understand what I have to say."

She would listen; she would understand; she would do anything. If only he would not leave her alone in this place with someone else's memories—costly objects that smelled of mildew and dead bushes that reminded her of ice flowers.

"We will spend five nights and five suns together. I'll tutor you in the ways of love, teach you to be a woman and respond to a man. But you must not fall in love with me. And you must remain a virgin."

She did not know whether to grieve or take offense. Did he assume she did not value her virginity? That she was desperate? They had just met. He was a common tutor, she a sultana with high hopes. No. She would not fall in love. She was destined for the king, who was taken even by the jarring music of her bones. "It was lovely!" he had assured from his hiding place. Then why had this last announcement from Hazel-Boy forced her to tear herself from him as if she had been captivated for ages? Realizing she stood there with the decanter in her hand, she began going through the motions of pouring wine.

"You must promise one other thing. Don't
 ̣ay have to show restraint. To you it might

 ̣ divan and removed his hat. Platinum-
 ̣ ̣ ̣ ̣ ̣ ̣ to his shoulders. The faint scent of roses
sweetened the air. "Now come closer. Unwrap my sash—without my turning around. Slip your arms around my waist and
fold the fabric."

Her breasts brushed against his chest as she circled her arms
about him.

"Your body may not come in contact with mine." He looked
down at her upturned face. "Lower your eyes. A lady never
stares. Now arrange the pleats, and never leave a pile of clothing around. It's in bad taste. Unbutton my coat from the top
and go down on your knees. Gracefully. First on one, then the
other knee." He lowered himself on the edge of the divan. "Sit
on the carpet and hug my slippers in your lap before you
remove the right one first. Do your job efficiently, in the least
time possible, but without seeming rushed."

Gold Dust lowered her eyes, aware that he was in the
process of removing his attire. Would the rest of him be as
smooth as his face? Would he have hair on his chest? Was he a
eunuch? Did she want to know? She raised her eyes. A silk wrap
was tied loosely around his waist. Snow-white down gleamed
on his chest. A henna-colored heart was tattooed above his left
nipple. She lowered her gaze to his legs—solid muscles of a
man. She rose against her will, or she would have crushed her
pride, pressed her face to his thighs, and said, "Tell me about
your tattoo. Have we met before? Have you been following me
around?"

He rested his hand on her shoulder. "You may not get up
until he permits."

She lifted her face and asked, "Who?"

Harem

"The Shah, of course. A wave of his hand will indicate ι you remain behind after eunuchs, servants, and other sultana. retire. Then you'll undress."

She watched him transform in front of her; his hair swinging, eyes scintillating, he spun on his toes, seeming slimmer, gliding about, his molded buttocks exposed through a slit in the loincloth. His palms stroked his own body, lingering on his chest—tattoo—and under the loincloth. He did not resemble a man as he floated toward her, closer, his breath warm on her forehead, lips, chin; closer, tantalizing, never touching, his hands tracing her aura, cupping the imaginary wreath on her head, the silhouette of her breasts, sliding a finger between her lips, eyes embracing, his mouth parting to accept hers. He stepped back. He was a man again. They had not kissed.

"Now undress as if you are in the process of a delicate dance."

With the pulse of his words, she undid her chador and it settled around her feet. Like rosebuds, her nipples hardened against the chill of the unknown.

His tone was a balm. "I'm pleased with your grace. Even more control in your movements. Smoothly, Gold Dust. Now remove your skirts. Good. Don't wriggle, glide harmoniously."

She stood naked in front of him. Her impulses were to turn around and flee, or rush to him and ask: Are you a man, a woman, or a eunuch? But she restrained herself, stepped out of the skirts and veil that circled her ankles, folded them, and placed them on the clothes stool. If only he would wrap his arms around her, talk to her and unravel her clash of emotions. It didn't matter who he was. What mattered was that he was different from the men she had gazed at through torn partitions.

"Have we met before?" she whispered.

"Why?"

)ice, and you stare as if you know me."

u since that morning your mother first

palace to introduce you to Narcissus. I've

ss in the harem."

. . ."

"I've been singing to you in your dreams." He went to the divan and lounged in full view of her, then drew her to him.

In the golden light that flowed through the windows, her fingers trembled as he pressed them to his lips, up his neck, and into his curls. The hair on his chest was like swan feathers, his tattooed heart warm. She pressed to taste his mouth.

"Not yet," he whispered. "Refined lovers don't rush."

She had passed many evenings of storytelling with the castoffs of the Shah and had heard only of a moody man who was anything but refined. "Is the Shah a tender man?"

"Men of rank have many facets. Only women who dare explore them will secure love."

"Tell me about his scent of black roses that causes drunkenness."

Hazel-Boy gazed at her with newfound admiration. She had, in a short period of time, discovered more about the king than many sultanas who spent years in the harem. He decided to share with Rebekah's daughter the king's most important secret.

"The king's fragrance of black roses is a blessing and a curse. At the initial stages of arousal, it causes a pleasant, heady drunkenness, but the more aroused he gets, the more potent his smell becomes, thrusting his partner into an inexplicable delirium of addictive lust impossible to withdraw from."

Gold Dust clung to Hazel-Boy. "Teach me to protect myself."

"You can't decrease its potency but can lessen its effect. When with him, don't breathe through the nose. Smell is an aphrodisiac. It causes us to fall deeply in love, sometimes deeper than is wise. He will caress you around the face because

the scent is strongest on his hands; try to avoid having ₒ
too close to your face. And remember the smell influences p.
marily the emotions. Treasure your sound mind, and it will
guard your heart."

"Have you protected your heart?" she asked, stroking his
tattoo.

"It's my love secret," he sighed, passing his tongue along the
shafts of her fingers. "Now moisten your fingertips in your
mouth and glide them over my body and familiarize yourself
with the sensitive nerves. Remember to breathe through the
mouth."

She felt Hazel-Boy's hard muscles, smooth chest, and the
beat of his hearts. A sigh, a moan, a whisper, a restraining
touch told her to linger or to advance. Her hand slid below his
waist and down his stomach. She sprang back.

His soothing kisses nibbled every part of her body, until she
calmed. Then he held her hand and guided it between his legs.

She felt hard scars under his stirred organ.

"Don't feel sad. They cut enough to keep me beardless,
embellish my feminine qualities, and soften my voice. But I've
been treated like a precious sculpture, handled gently in fear of
being marred. And I can satisfy a woman, which few of us can.
But, alas, I've taken an oath to never again become one with a
woman. I must show restraint."

His touch searched every nook of her body, uncovering
nerves she did not know existed—the throb behind her ears,
the pulse in the folds of her thighs, the plump curve of her buttocks. The bedchamber turned aglow. The past and the future
fused into a present she prayed would never end. She wrapped
her arms about his waist and melded her body to his, the silver
chain digging into her breasts. "What's in the bottle?"

"Close your eyes, little one, and rest," he murmured.
"You've learned enough for one day."

o recover from the effort not to divulge his
ɔr. How could he tell her that he, too, was
Quarter? That he, too, had known her

....s to a poor peddler of pomegranate juice
and a mother who struggled to raise eleven sons. His beauty did
not prove a blessing, but caused his greatest misfortune. On one
of his visits to the Jewish Quarter, the Great Black Eunuch,
captivated by Moses, offered his parents a fortune that could
change their lives. A fortune that could save Moses's siblings,
and promise him an opulent life in the Shah's palace.

So they gelded him like a calf.

"We lose one in five," he had heard the royal hakim, before
he had taken the knife to him. "Such a pity to lose this exquisite youth."

"There have been consultations with the magi," Narcissus
had assured. "He'll live."

As the mist around him had deepened, he had pleaded with
God to spare his life. He had been too young to comprehend
what the cutting would do to him.

He was luckier than most eunuchs. Before they had castrated him and locked him in the Cage with the Shah, he had
had the fortune to experience his first sexual encounter with an
exceptional woman. He was thirteen when he had heard of
Rebekah the Bundle Woman, a benevolent whore with a
resplendent brand between her breasts. He had stolen a coin
from his father and gone to Rebekah. The passionate evenings
he had loved her were forever treasured in the tattoo above his
heart. A spare heart to love with.

Now Rebekah's daughter lay next to him. He longed to love
her as her mother had once loved him, but he had strict orders
from a jealous Shah.

Gold Dust felt Hazel-Boy's warm breath, his lips too close.

She had remained in the harem first to punish her moth͜
then to avoid her fate. But since the beginning of this a͜
which now felt like an eternity, the rage to please a eunuch had
taken precedence over all else. She stared at the silver bottle he
did not separate from, and at the henna heart that seemed a
part of him. Maybe by the end of the week he would disclose
their secret.

She turned around and slipped closer to him, her back
molding into his body. His legs circled her thighs; his hands
cupped her breasts. Now she would never fall asleep.

A stream of light woke her, and the image of Hazel-Boy
came to her like a dream. She had fallen asleep after all. Reluctant
to break the spell, she half opened her eyes.

Naked, he lounged next to her, his head propped on one
hand, his gaze on her. He had awakened earlier and painted his
lips red and rimmed his eyes with kohl. A gossamer gauze fell
over his hair. "Today," he said, "I shall recount a love story."

His voice sounded fragile, feminine. He was a storyteller.
She would learn to be one.

"The Shah ordered a costly bath set between his rosebushes
where in the evenings he bathed Pari. The sultanas, hearing of
such an act of servility from a man known for his impatience
with women, could not contain their jealousy. On one of the
harem outings, Pari sat on a cliff, watching the River of
Dreams. It was a calm Persian day; all the elements were in harmony;
even the river was serene, the logs floating aimlessly
with no trace of sharks.

"Pari tumbled down the cliff and disappeared in the
river."

Gold Dust caught her breath. The river again. Its name was
misleading; so was its glassy veneer, which reflected a world of
green and blue, and the many logs that drifted on its tranquil
surface.

l," Hazel-Boy continued, "that one of the
1 pushed the favorite to her death. From
an was allowed inside these quarters."

re. She had replaced Pari in the Shah's
know that Moon Face had pushed Pari off
the cliff? "Hazel-Boy, why are you telling me Pari's story?"

"Because, little one, you must remember that those whom
the Shah favors must see with many eyes and hear with many
ears to survive."

"You'll protect me, won't you?"

He enveloped her in his warmth. "When this week ends, it's
best we go our own ways." He uncorked the silver bottle and
took a swallow from its contents.

"May I have some?" she asked.

"Stay away from the nectar of poppy seeds and other narcotics. For me it's a habit to pacify painful memories."

She rested her head on his chest and fell asleep.

She woke to a rare contentment. Since Hazel-Boy's arrival,
the bedchamber and yard had been transformed into her private sanctuary. She had grown into an adult in his company—
talking, eating, caressing, craving. Every night, the hunger
drove her insane as she fell asleep from sheer exhaustion, her
desire persisting in her dreams.

Today she had stepped beyond the threshold of girlhood.
She slipped out of the silk he had insisted she sleep in to feel
the stimulating effect of different fabrics and went to him,
kneeling down at his feet. Her tongue traced the path of his
veins, every muscle, every crevice. He shuddered and wavered
under her palate. Moisture glistened on him. His organ
responded. She held him in her mouth, savoring his pulse. His
fingers cupped the back of her neck, lingering, pushing himself
deeper inside her mouth.

He grabbed her hair and yanked her head back.

He tied his loincloth around his waist. "Don't force u break my oath."

He soaked a towel in warm olive oil and pressed it to her stomach to relieve her cramps. "One day you'll have a real man."

On their last morning, she woke to find his side of the divan empty. She threw the sheet around herself and ran outside. Her eyes shut against a stab of sunlight; she raised the cover to tent her head. When the fiery specks subsided behind her lids, she saw Hazel-Boy lounging in the bath. Like liquid gold, water fell from his fingers. Through the steam of sun-warmed water, his gaze swept over her. She would not think of farewells. She flung the sheet away and rushed to him, ignoring the sting of thorns on her bare feet.

"Don't race to open your legs like the Whore of Babylon," he commanded. "Control your steps, square your shoulders; don't lap like a lovesick dog."

She raised the sheet from the thorns and covered herself, blinking back tears of anger and frustration. It had been a dream, after all. He was like all other men. Kindness and devotion lived in her mother's tales, not in her home in the Jewish Quarter or here in the palace. She turned around to return to the bedchamber.

"Come here!" he ordered. "Take small, feminine steps."

Aware of every footfall, she went to him with stinging feet.

He reached out a box and snapped the lid open. "Rub my back with this."

Gathering a handful of ground pumice, she directed her anger into a vigorous rub. The roughness felt good under her palm. He did not move until his skin flamed red, and she thought it would bleed. Then he stood and cupped her face between his palms. He took her mouth in his. The force of his teeth left two scarlet dots on her lower lip.

blood and salt on her tongue and with all
 and disappointment, she slapped him on

nds and whispered, "Water is healing.

he helped her into the bath. The morning sun had warmed
the enamel and it felt pleasant against her body, which had
ached with desire a short while ago, but was now sore with
anger.

"We will resist each other until we can't bear it any longer."

In the wild splashing of water and against hard enamel, they
wrestled savagely in what was more like war than love. Limbs
and arms flailed, locked, and freed to resist again. She fought
with all the might of her shaken pride.

"Sometimes he'll make love to you," Hazel-Boy said. "And
sometimes he'll prefer to wrestle with you before he enters
you."

"Have you experienced the Shah's touch?" she whispered,
coloring with shame. "Did it bring the taste of ash into your
mouth?"

"Don't ask dangerous questions," he groaned, slipping his
fingers around her sex.

The forbidden honed their passion. All faded but the desire
to please. By some magical harmony, they experienced release
at the same time. He had broken his oath and he did not mind.
His secret would be safe with a daughter who had inherited her
mother's convictions. They lay back exhausted. Pinpoints of
light burst on the ripples around them. Their breathing
calmed. The water settled.

"You are strong and graceful and proud," he murmured.
"The king will love you."

The scent of spring in the air, slaves filled the baths with water, rubbed and kneaded the sultanas' bodies with warm oil and sprinkled their garments with jasmine and orange blossoms. The women left their quarters earlier than usual. It was the first day of spring, the New Year, and they were about to partake in an ancient drinking ritual. Colorful sherbets of fruit, essence of gardenia, or chamomile, perfumed with musk, ambergris, or aloes, shimmered in glasses with filigreed casings. Wrapped in flannel and carried on seventy mules, the sacred snow in the sherbets came from the great ice pits of Mount Damavand and had traveled for two months and six days to reach the harem. Since taste was first transmitted through the fingertips, all sultanas were trained to perform this ritual with grace and delicacy, using three fingers and hardly getting them soiled. Dipping separately each fingertip in the sherbets of eternal youth, they sucked on them, every move a skillful dance of precision. The right hand was used for food, the left for impure tasks. Later slaves delivered pitchers and basins for ablution.

This was Gold Dust's favorite ritual, reminding her of the days she had stolen into her mother's side of the room and inhaled her perfumes, the days before the scent of ice flowers brought bile to her mouth.

Now she felt proud; not only had Hazel-Boy tutored her, but she had gone through today's ceremony without a single discordant move.

The partitions were flung open. In a pompous procession, the Bibi strode in, accompanied by Narcissus and the Mistress of the House.

The hall submerged under an expectant cloud.

"Gold Dust has been chosen," the Bibi announced. "She was trained in Pari's quarters."

The Bibi's spies hid in closets, behind screens and drapes. It

m long to find out what had transpired
and Hazel-Boy.

glaring eyes, and bared fangs surrounded
torted their faces. Moon Face's lips were a
cy powder she used to lighten her cheeks.

had let the seemingly innocent Gold Dust into her confidence, only to be betrayed. No other sultana had been allowed
inside Pari's quarters. For that privilege, Gold Dust would pay
dearly.

"My son has honored you," the Bibi Sultana continued.
"The old Gold Dust is dead! Prepare the new sultana for the
Shah."

The black slaves lifted Gold Dust in their arms and carried
her into the baths, into a dense sulfurous vapor laden with gossip, into the murmur, laughter, chatter—the rare freedom of
hundreds of sultanas. The splash of water, running from brass
faucets into marble sinks, echoed against walls inlaid with
faience tiles. Slave women hastened to disrobe her so jealous
jinns and evil *ifrits* that hid in the clammy recesses of the baths
would not enter her pants and spoil her virginity. Rolling their
eyes, the slaves murmured incantations to ward off the jinns.
The sultanas click-clicked on stilt-like clogs, high wooden sandals that raised them from the wet floor where wicked spirits
lived. A circle of naked women caged Gold Dust. Such hatred
in their faces. Such darkness in their eyes. Where was her
mother now? Seek power but don't let it cloud your humanity.
Empty advice. Words from a woman who had never seen these
stone eyes and tight-pursed lips. How could she fight her enemies without becoming one of them?

They stretched her out on one of the platforms. Checking
her for the slightest sign of body hair, they smeared *vajebi*, a
depilatory mush of burning minerals, arsenic, and lime, on her
legs, arms, pubis, and underarms. Before the paste corroded her

flesh, they scraped off the hair with the sharp edges of mussel shells and washed off the residue with hot water from china bowls. They rubbed her with ginger and cloves to increase her powers of seduction and burned yellow Aleppo stone to perfume her skin.

The sultanas raised eyebrows lengthened with India ink and fluttered eyelids shaded with kohl and announced that she was ready for the Bibi.

Slaves mixed a sack of the finest henna, a preventative against perspiration, with ten egg yolks and half a cup of Turkish coffee. They handed the Bibi two brushes, one slim and the other wide with soft bristles. She slid her palm over Gold Dust's flat stomach, firm breasts, and slender neck. A pudgy finger found the wild throbbing of her artery. "Don't worry," she said. "My son is a matchless lover."

Gold Dust succumbed to the Shah's mother. Let the Bibi deck her as if she were a roasted lamb in need of garnish. When the time came, she would seduce the king with her own music.

The Bibi dipped the larger brush into the henna mixture and first dyed Gold Dust's pubis and four fingers' length above it, then the armpits. With the smaller brush, she painted her toes and fingernails, a jasmine above her navel, three even rings around her nipples, a beauty mark at the upper corner of her lips. The Bibi stepped back and eyed her creation. For the next forty days not even the strongest soap could wash off her work of art. She clicked her tongue, snapped her fingers, and smeared the residue of the henna on her own pubis.

Slaves balanced embroidered napkins and fresh towels on their heads and led Gold Dust past a vestibule and a series of warm rooms into the resting chamber. Curious women smoked water pipes, sipped gardenia sherbet, and nibbled slices of melon.

Gold Dust, her hair piled on top of her head to dislodge the last drops of water, lounged on cushions. She settled into muslin fragrant with essence of jasmine, gazed at wooden sandals that sank into Persian rugs, at gilded hangings encrusted with pearls, and dreamed of the sanctuary with a stable in the back housing a donkey that spat at anyone who dared stare at his mistress.

Moon Face sat cross-legged at the head of the chamber, stared at Gold Dust, and yanked at her own tresses.

15

*R*ebekah the Bundle Woman came to visit. The palace gates creaked. Halls were solemn. Specters lingered in the shadows. Narcissus averted his eyes. She planted her hands at her waist and cocked her head. "Not even a welcome peck on the cheek, sweetlove?"

He flung the inner doors open.

Under the domed arch, she held him back and gazed at his plump cheeks and raisin eyes. "What? Not a kind word?"

"Gold Dust turned all the sultanas against her," he said, stifling in his throat a cackle of joy.

Rebekah's heart died. Not her Gold. She had taught her to spread her net, to gather it with silver rings and hold on to her prey, to use sweet words to conceal her anger, and to master the music of her bones. Rebekah clutched the eunuch's sleeves. "You promised to take care of her."

"You're too good a tutor," he murmured, a tinge of resentment in his voice. "You don't need my help."

Rebekah glared at him. "If anything happens to my daughter, I'll pull out your guts and feed them to the vultures . . . your lust gland will go first."

♀

Gold Dust sat cross-legged on her pallet, a history book spread open on her lap. She stroked a melancholy-eyed gazelle, the animal's rough tongue grazing her cheek. The Shah's gifts didn't give her joy. She felt helpless against the animosity in Pearl Hall. Stares stabbed like daggers. Words poisoned like hemlock. She frequented the royal library in hope of gaining insight into the intricacies of Persian dynasties, the strengths and weaknesses of kings and the women who manipulated them. Her only friends were Honey, Hazel-Boy, and, to her surprise, the Bibi Sultana, who had come to prefer Gold Dust to Hazel-Boy.

The Shah had heard of her recurring nightmares of bowstrings slicing her throat. He ordered tasters to sample her food for poison, and cooks to serve her meals in Chinese green porcelain, which changed color with the smallest trace of poison. His most trusted eunuchs stood watch outside her quarters.

Early morning, and with no warning, the Shah had entered the harem and planted himself in the center of Pearl Hall. His hands clasped behind his back, he warned, "If the favorite is touched by anyone, we shall ban opium, sugar, calming herbs, and hookah pipes. Not even the Bibi Sultana will be exempt!"

It was unheard of in history for a king to penalize his mother for the mere reason his favorite was in danger.

Right there and then, the Bibi plucked her mustache, swearing to no longer sport the symbol that raised her to the level of men.

Moon Face donned sackcloth and locked herself in the House of Tears with mourning widows and barren women. She plunged into the act of sewing her own shroud.

The door opened, and Rebekah appeared, jolting Gold Dust out of her thoughts.

"What's the eunuch so upset about?"

Suddenly Gold Dust longed for the security of her mother's closeness, to be the child of sixteen that she was.

Rebekah stepped back to survey the bedecked sultana she hardly recognized. Surely the Shah had invited Gold Dust to his divan. Her eyes sparkled with grace and assurance. A chain of pearls circled her slender waist. She used more kohl on her left eye, so the twist seemed less pronounced, and had shaded one of her nostrils to even it out. A gold coin dangled from the tip of each of her braided tresses.

Rebekah sighed. "You'll become queen and won't need me anymore."

"I'll need you more than ever." Gold Dust glanced at her mother; the skin on her face was still firm. Not even a shadow had settled under her chin. Her eyes had retained their violet fire, and the mark between her breasts had not lost its luster. Was it true that those who returned from the dead never aged? To stop herself from probing into the past, she asked, "Teach me more about men."

Rebekah slammed shut the book that lay idle on her daughter's lap. "You won't find these intimate details in books. I'll disclose secrets men murmur in my bed, between my thighs, to my cleavage-eye—secrets that will help you confront life like a well-armed soldier."

Rebekah spoke of the hidden weaknesses of kings, of muscular bodies that became slaves to the female touch, of cutting words that concealed sweet invitations, of manly roars that were nothing but boyish whimpers, and of the power of the heart over the body. "And don't fail to listen to your bones. In the end, life is judged by highlights, not by days." She looked at her daughter and saw a woman. "Have you been chosen?"

"Yes," Gold Dust replied.

"Gold, I didn't prepare you for the evils in people's hearts because I was foolishly hoping you'd not need it so early in life. But the palace is a different world . . . things happen fast here . . . there's a force here I can't control the way I can at home."

Gold Dust did not reveal her fears. How she had caught Gulf Lily prowling around her quarters at dawn. How she had heard Moon Face order a delivery of iron of calabar, a deadly poison from Niger. How one of the tasters had drunk Gold Dust's tea laced with belladonna and had suffocated.

Rebekah heard the echo of solemn bells in her daughter's bones. "What could be so important?"

"I've not been called to the Shah yet."

"You will be, Gold, I have no doubt. Allow time to sharpen the edges of his passion, then he'll savor you as you deserve to be."

"Madar, tell me how to conceive sons."

Rebekah recalled the past. Jacob the Fatherless forced her to consume foreskins so she would give birth to sons. For the same purpose, Heshmat the Matchmaker sold a concoction from the dried gills of a rare fish mixed with ground pearls and alligator semen. Many of her visitors assumed a drink of dates aged in red wine and saffron added to their virility and the flow of semen that ensured sons.

Rebekah knew better. "Gold, sons are the fruit of passionate love between a couple. A man who desires a woman will not leave their love bed until he satisfies her, and she, in return, will surrender her intimate juice. It's essential for a woman to experience deep orgasm before her man ejaculates. The moist environment of her womb is conducive to the survival of the male seed."

16

*N*arcissus carried a velvet vest with gold trimmings, a flowing skirt of Arabian silk studded with crystal tears, and satin slippers with bows of colored gems.

Gold Dust stepped out of the tub of donkey milk and rubbed cucumber unguent on her armpits.

He draped a veil over her head.

"The Shah has summoned you!"

Gold Dust lifted the lace and handed it back to him.

"Since he'll claim your virginity, he must be the first to unveil you."

"I'm not ashamed of my face! I've already uncovered it myself."

"It's an essential formality," the eunuch croaked. He snapped open a box. A set of emerald necklace and earrings sparkled on a bed of velvet. "Do as I say, or you can't have this."

"I won't hide my face."

The eunuch slammed the lid shut. This girl's impudence was beginning to boil his blood over. Now that she was chosen as the favorite, he, the chief eunuch, had the duties of her personal eunuch imposed upon him. He would have to teach her a lesson or two before she dared raise her head too high, before she forgot who the true master was.

Gold Dust stared him in the eye. "You and I can become powerful allies, Narcissus. You through your connections in the palace, I through the Shah's heart."

"You've a long way before you conquer his heart," Narcissus barked.

She unlocked the box, gathered the earrings, and planted them in his palm. "From now on you protect me against Moon Face and I'll share my gifts."

The secure heaviness of emeralds felt good around her neck. She followed Narcissus past a courtyard strewn with straw meant to frighten away approaching evil spirits by the noise of crackling steps. Her heart brimming with joy-tinged fear, she entered the Secret Passage, a labyrinth of dark corridors and steep stone stairs that echoed the unspoken words of sultanas who had visited the Shah before her. She had never seen these tunnels that twisted under the palace. Did the underpasses lead to the outside or only to the king's private quarters? Had any sultana ever tried to flee from here? Could she escape their murderous jealousies? They climbed circular steps toward light and away from the smell of mildew. To her right, round windows, sealed shut by iron frames, lined the stone wall. The threatening pulse of the river could be heard through the heavy walls. What lay behind this fortress? She rose on her toes and peeked through the windows. Below, a ribbon of water embraced the back of the palace. The shark-infested river was the sole guardian of this side of the palace.

Was this the place from which the late shah, in fear of an heir claiming the throne, had thrown his pregnant sultanas into the river?

Breathless, his feeble body threatening to buckle under the strain of the long walk, the eunuch urged her on. He recalled every other trip he had made, each with a different sultana on his arm. Was he growing old, or had the sugar and opium made his bones brittle? No, it was the consequences of losing his manhood that had caught up with him, he reminded himself bitterly. Rebekah had succeeded in giving him back only a portion of his manhood. He visited her once a week, when the sun was high and daylight stripped him of any mystery that might condemn him in the eyes of spirits and mortal men alike. He galloped into the Jewish Quarter, on his tallest horse and wearing his costliest attire. He offered Rebekah gifts in exchange for the feats she performed on his lust gland, which for a few exhilarating moments made him feel whole again.

Despite his need for her mother, the inquisitiveness of Gold Dust irritated him. She asked too many questions, heard too much, saw with many eyes. "Stop staring at the river. These waters are dangerous," he said. "No human has survived them."

"Then why is it called the River of Dreams?"

"Don't let the name deceive you. These are dreams of death."

Death, she imagined, must be a form of escape like the river that snaked away into a world of no boundaries over which kings held no power.

They entered the private way to the Shah's bedchamber. At the threshold, she clung to the eunuch's sleeve. What if the Shah was as ugly and as cruel as Div, the white giant in her mother's tales? Act as a woman of substance does, her mother reminded. Gold Dust loosened her grip and raised herself to her full height. She fought to calm the child in her, evoke the woman.

The eunuch stepped back into the halls.

Gold Dust stroked the partitions that would unfold into the king's quarters. The mother-of-pearl and cabochon emeralds inlaid in silver filigree felt smooth to her touch, the netting of silver irregular. Like her feelings. Radiant in her delight to appear, at last, at the Shah's threshold, uncertain and scared of the outcome. Her fingers traced the silver latch, lifted it from the cradle, and held on to it.

She released the panels.

The chamber was draped with velvet curtains, their vermilion hue casting an illusion of blazing dusks. Carved furniture of oak and banyan were immersed in the same ruby shade. Black rose petals overflowed bowls of jade and agate. Fans of silver lacework agitated the petals. Three mahogany trapezes swung next to a divan. A brazier smoked idly. The Shah was absent. She was thankful for the chance to quiet her bones.

A potent and exhilarating aroma of black roses wafted toward her. A stirring came from a beaded lattice.

The Shah emerged from behind the curtain of beads.

He stood on the central arabesque of the Esfahan carpet, looming over her. Two hooded peregrine falcons perched on his shoulders, a gyrfalcon on his gloved arm. The sable trimming of his cape fluttered under the fans. A cluster of pearl-shaped diamonds flashed from the center of the snowy aigrette on his turban.

She harnessed the clamor in her disjointed bones. Yes. He was tall. She would have identified him the very first time she set eyes on him—even among a throng of men as massive and as olive-colored as he. His shaven brows, drawn with coffee sticks into perfect arcs, framed restless eyes. These were the eyes she had imagined of the man in the Cage, the man Moon Face would kill for, the man who sighed behind partitions.

He extended ringed fingers, the index crowned with a sharp cap of silver.

Her eyes acquired a will of their own, staring at his arrogant cheeks, fleshy mouth, large teeth that had inherited the flaxen tinge of his diversions: tea, coffee, and opium.

The falcons lowered their hooded heads to their master's chest. Their feathers stood up in anticipation. They had been trained to translate his heartbeat as a cue to pounce on a quarry. Were they responding to the tumult in her bones or to his pulse?

The Shah followed the trail of Gold Dust's gaze toward the finger dagger. He placed it on a stool, settled on his divan, and patted a space next to him. She approached with a seductive swing, her gaze brimming with secrets and as if drunk with wine. She was a rarity among sultanas who communicated with him through eunuchs. He had learned of her fear of the evil eye and that she believed it afflicted fortunate women; he had smiled at her fashion of arousal with herbs and oils in preparation for the day he would invite her; he discovered even the most intimate detail of her nights when, despite the temptation to stroke herself, she displayed restraint so as to save herself for him.

Yes. Tonight he would have her.

He had been assured by his spiritualists that a woman of small stature with tiger eyes and the boldness of a she-lion would bear him sons. This woman would end his shame. Years ago his father had predicted that he, the Shah, would cause the demise of the Persian dynasty. That curse had come true. He had tried and tried and had failed to sire heirs. Before long, he could not tolerate his own company, or that of the fruitless sultanas Narcissus selected for him.

In a silence saturated with the scent of black roses, he unwrapped his turban. Blade-straight hair the color of onyx fell to his shoulders. He had the olive complexion of men of the mountains; his muscles seemed carved from bronze. His chest expanded with desire, the breath of leather and tobacco on him. He buried her fingers in his massive palm.

His fierce grip startled her. She lowered herself onto the divan and set her head in his lap. She raised his hands and helped him uncoil her braids, feeling his effort to imitate her gentleness. His fingers were not used to delicate tasks.

Hazel-Boy had warned that the king would sometimes make love and sometimes wrestle with her. What would he do now? He seemed in one of his cloudy moods. She would await his next move. Then she would know how to react. His desire for her, and the smile on his lips, gave her confidence. His harsh hands and wild falcons frightened her. Where was the man who cultivated roses?

At his touch, she shuddered, and her temples drummed with the effort to contain the raucous symphony her bones were about to embark on. She would present him with a world different from the boredom of his palace, but she must proceed with care. He would invite her back, again and again. Until she mastered the deep orgasm her mother had promised would assure her of sons.

He saw her body shake and assumed she strove to generate music. "Sing for us!"

When the silence lingered, he roared, "Were the notes we heard a product of our imagination?" Was it the sign of the changing times that he began to doubt miracles? Why did he question her music when his body craved and ached for the melody that had soared from her the day he had heard her from behind partitions? A music that had lured him out of his weariness and allowed him a glance into an enigmatic world he longed to unravel?

"Be patient," she whispered. "Once my bones choose to sing, you'll forget the loneliness that haunts you since your days in the Cage."

Joy filled him at the discovery that she was familiar with his past. She could not have understood his isolation unless she had experienced one herself. He strove to control the habitual bluntness of his touch as he unraveled her last braid. Might this woman be the one to raise him beyond his lethargy, help him rediscover his true self and abandon the one he was reared to believe was his? Her intense hair tumbled on his lap. Her curls had grown since he had first seen her.

"Tonight," he said, "we are all yours."

She rose and gathered her hair at the nape of her neck, adjusted her skirt, and checked her face in the mirror where she saw the Shah's startled eyes. She whirled to confront him. "My love for you is different from what you are used to. It will not flame, then die away in one night."

He felt an inexplicable need to weep for a woman who had the conviction to vocalize thoughts that could send her to the House of Tears. Crushing her in his arms, he thrust his hands in her hair and released the coil. "Little one, man needs the company of more than one woman."

"And a woman?" she asked.

"If a woman has more than one man," he growled, "she is a whore."

"Why, my lord, is it man's nature and not a woman's?"

He banged his fist onto his palm. "If Allah desired the same freedom for a woman, He would not have afflicted her with a hymen, a sure guardian of her virginity."

"The concept of virginity is created by men to control, spoil, and violate women." She reiterated her mother's belief.

Despite his longing for this woman, her indiscretion was beginning to annoy him. "We shall be yours for longer than one night. But on one condition."

"You need only order, my lord."

He rose to his full height, flapping his cape like a whip and towering over her like an enormous god. A scornful smile skipped around his mouth.

"You must promise that the fulfillment of our desire need not be the death of it as it has been with others."

A shudder rattled her spine. Could she ever tame the king? Peel off layers of scab and touch the man? Her mother had taught her to tantalize, tempt, hold back until he was ready to promise his heart. Would he? Not only for one night, but until she was pregnant with his son?

She reached out and felt the Shah between the legs, taken by surprise at what she had imagined as smaller. Her laughter sprayed through the room like a shower of emerald beads.

He began to remove his cape. He must have her even if he lost his desire for her.

Surrounded by the flicker of long-stemmed candles, she tossed the cape back over his shoulders. "You, my shah, will remain fully dressed. Tonight I'll introduce myself to you. You'll know me intimately before you have me."

The promise in her voice made him retreat.

Petals of lace slipped down to unfurl about her ankles. Her alabaster skin gleamed in the candle flames. Her fingertips traced the oval of her face, the almond-shaped sockets of her eyes, her earlobes soft as peach fuzz, the wetness in her mouth, down to her fragile neck and firm breasts, sketching the curves. She knelt on the carpet, her hands acquiring a life of their own, sliding over her buttocks, up to embrace her breasts, crushing them together. Responding to tiny pinches, her nipples hardened. Her torso swayed, her shoulders grazed the carpet, her hair cascading about, her thighs unfolding to reveal her hairless mound. Her fingers parted the lips, exposing the pink of her sex that glistened as if brushed with nectar.

Fighting the urge to taste her, he watched her unveil, a woman bent on exploring her own senses. A virginal girl with bold hands, who did not exhibit the shame that came from ancient religions, outdated rituals, or the constraints of her home. He had had girls of ten. He had had mature women. None were so intimate with their bodies.

Gold Dust heard the heaving of his chest, felt the sweep of his eyes. She sailed to the brazier. Lifting a pipe, she stuck a piece of opium to the edge.

"Not now." He would remain alert. Understand this woman better.

"Draw deeply," she insisted, parting his lips and fixing the stem of the pipe there. "Tomorrow will be yours."

He dragged at the pipe, reclined and forced her down, searching her tiger eyes. The yellow of her irises reflected the temperament of a woman who would give him sons. "We are becoming impatient," he said.

"My shah, I don't want to follow the other sultanas."

His breathing became shallow. His chest settled into a soft rhythm. His hair, shiny as the mane of a purebred horse, cascaded over his profile. His penciled brows, wiped off, left dark shadows, beneath which his restless eyes quivered under closed lids, grappling with the demons of his dreams. His shaved brows exaggerated the sharp outline of his features, the high forehead, the straight-arched nose, the full lips distinctly contoured as if with a painting brush.

Was this the man she would one day love?

She pulled at the cord next to the divan. Narcissus entered, his eyes taking the room in. The Shah was asleep. The sultana was under the covers, a blush on her cheeks, her tangled curls piled high. He did not dare open his mouth lest he wake the king.

Gold Dust whispered, "Bring Honey to me before the cry of roosters."

Never! Narcissus shook his head. Never! Women who preferred their own kind had small penises between their female organs. The Shah would be furious. Narcissus opened his mouth. Gold Dust pressed a finger to her lips.

The eunuch drew his scabbard and made a motion as if to

slit his own throat, a silent demonstration of the danger they would face.

Gold Dust pressed two fingers to her eyes as a promise to protect him, and she rubbed her thumb and forefinger to assure him a reward.

Before the sun was up, Honey entered the royal quarters. Her eyes strained to adjust to the darkness.

"Come down on your hands and knees," Gold Dust whispered from the shadows.

Honey advanced, the carpet scraping her knees. The black tear at the corner of her eye crinkled with fear and anticipation. She would do anything for Gold Dust. Even spread her legs to a man if it would please her. Still, the outline of the Shah, lying dressed on the divan, alarmed her, and his biting smell of black roses nauseated her.

Gold Dust ran her hand through the king's hair. His eyes opened, gazing at the two women, one with a masculine body, small breasts, and fleshy nipples, the other voluptuous with rounded thighs, haughty breasts, and quince eyes.

Gold Dust rubbed almond oil on Honey's body and stroked unguent between her breasts. Honey's lips bloomed inside Gold Dust's mouth.

The Shah lifted himself from the divan and began to undress. How dare they!? He would force himself upon them. Break them apart.

Gold Dust lowered herself on her knees, slid her tongue up his thighs, around the edge of his coarse hair, and enveloped his penis in her mouth. Her tongue slapped in teasing motions until she felt the spasms coming. She drew back, staring him down with her unyielding gaze. "My shah, master your passion."

And the king held back. He was savoring the unfolding scene, delicious pain tugging at his nerves. He watched Honey shudder, her lust spent. He saw Gold Dust retreat in time to thwart her own climax. He marveled at his erection and was pleased he was able to arrest his own release. He was no longer the feeble prince of the Cage.

∽

The time had come. Longing and curiosity had replaced Gold Dust's initial desire to flee. She would join the king's solitude and the bitterness that fed it. She would be remembered as the sultana who saved the Persian dynasty.

Her marrow exhaled a lament, a burst of lustful notes that fluttered the candle flames and turned the room aflame.

The Shah awoke to the melody of her bones.

She slipped in and out of the netting of amber candle blush reflected on the walls; she skipped playfully, somersaulted, stretched her body into exquisite shapes, swayed her arms like willow branches, languid, curvy twists that transformed her into a houri-angel. She brushed her nipples with hashish. Careful not to harm her maidenhood, her fingers slid between her legs to stroke the velvet slit. Her complexion turned amber, her body moist with perspiration.

She unleashed her emotions and transferred them to the king's skin, where they sank through every pore and into his core. With a moan of resignation and with great strength, he came down on his knees, lifted her in his arms, and laid her on the divan. He prostrated himself at her feet.

Now she realized why the taste of honey turned into ash in the mouth of the discarded sultanas. Nothing was more addictive than the king bowing down in supplication, not even his perfume of black roses.

She coaxed him onto the divan and stretched herself out on him. The bittersweet aroma of tobacco and wine lingered on his tongue. To assure her orgasm before his, and before she became drunk with his scent, she glided to the top of the divan, raised herself on her knees, her thighs flanking his face, her own far from his hands.

His gaze prodded her darkness. His mouth embraced her, freed her, then suckled her again and again, his tongue lapping at her escalating passion, his nostrils devouring her salty aroma. He held her waist to anchor her shuddering body, and he drank and drank.

Lifting her in his arms, he set her on the divan.

She parted her thighs for him. He must come into her juices, which would assure a favorable environment for the survival of his male seeds.

He wet his penis in her mouth, then guided it into her firm grip, struggling to contain himself until he seized her virginity. His fluids mingled with her blood, her passion, his seeds, their impending tomorrow.

"Promise, you are only mine," she whispered.

"Only yours."

17

They surrounded Gold Dust in the baths, examined her abdomen, pinched her buttocks, and squeezed her waist. Her walk, her pointed stomach, and her luminescent eyes were ample proof she carried the Shah's son. The fruit of such intense passion could only be male. Since Pari, Gold Dust was the only sultana who had sustained the king's passion even after she had given herself to him and even as she grew with child. The women suffered a fresh threat. If Gold Dust gave birth to a son, the Shah would take her as his legal wife and pronounce her queen. When the heir to the throne reached the age of puberty, Gold Dust would weed the harem of sultanas who became pregnant, or powerful. She would choose her own entourage to replace the discarded sultanas who would rot in the House of Tears.

The Bibi Sultana's eunuch requested an urgent meeting in the privacy of the gardens. "We'll crush the bark of the tali tree in the favorite's food."

The Bibi held on to the branch of a weeping willow, took a deep breath, and slapped him with all the force of her plump hand. "I'll stuff the bark down your own throat." Not that she liked that arrogant Jewish pauper. But the girl had succeeded to mesmerize her son so completely he seemed to have abandoned Hazel-Boy, at last. Enough reason to support her until she, the Bibi, came up with a discreet plan to eliminate Hazel-Boy. Did her son think he would produce heirs with that half-man?

When word got around that Honey and Hazel-Boy roamed about with sharpened eyes and ears and threatened to go to the Shah, the sultanas moved their conspiracy to the gardens, under the cloak of darkness, bushes, and maple trees, behind fountains that smothered sounds. The harem lost its tongue but not its rage.

While Gold Dust passed her days and nights under the influence of calming herbs, Moon Face summoned Gulf Lily to the House of Tears to discuss ways to terminate Gold Dust's pregnancy.

"Ground glass in coffee," Moon Face whispered. "She'll bleed internally. There's no antidote for it."

Gulf Lily rushed to peek behind the partitions. He pressed a warning forefinger on his lips. My lady, it's a lengthy, agonizing death. The Shah will find out. He rested his palm on his heart. I worry for you.

Honey tiptoed around, spying on urgent whispering and bickering behind veils. She pressed her ear to the door of a sultana who had once been chosen by luck, circumstance, and cunning to adorn the Shah's bed. "Henbane or nightshade." She heard the lethal words.

Honey burst into the room and grabbed the sultana by the hair. "Over my lifeless corpse," she cried, about to uproot the woman's braids. "No poison in Gold Dust's food, or I'm going to the Shah."

"Who mentioned Gold Dust?" the sultana screeched. "How in heaven did you come to this ludicrous conclusion?"

Honey, her purple lips and black tear trembling with indignation, let go of the woman's hair.

Despite the threat of Honey, Hazel-Boy, and the Bibi hovering overhead, Gulf Lily and two other eunuchs convened at midnight in the Courtyard of Horses.

The eunuch with skin the color of turmeric offered: "Let's poison her with white arsenic."

"No," the other eunuch, whose bluish lids fluttered nervously, replied, "it leaves a telltale odor on the body."

"She could trip over the stairs of the Secret Passage."

"She rarely goes there alone."

"We could tie her up and yank the fetus out."

"How do you propose we do that without its seeming a blatant conspiracy?"

"Stop your idle schemes," the eunuch cried. "If the favorite dies, we'll all lose our heads."

Gulf Lily rose to his full height. The two eunuchs raised their eyes to the specter who towered over them like a massive tree. His hands skipped in silent discourse. Our safest choice is to afflict the fetus with a lethal curse before it sees the light of day. A curse so potent even if the child lives, its parents would wish it dead.

The eunuchs put their thoughts together and came up with a collective plot.

It was well known in all schools of sorcery that to annihilate the enemy one must first destroy the powers of her allies. Gold Dust had a formidable supporter. Rebekah the Bundle Woman. Narcissus was intimate with her. He would find a way to weaken the protective shield the woman had erected around her daughter.

The sultanas and their eunuchs went to Narcissus. "You can't ignore Gold Dust's growing power. Rebekah comes and goes without your permission. The king visits the favorite as if he were a commoner and without considering harem decorum."

They did not have to try hard. For some time now, Narcissus had been striving to remember when Gold Dust had first replaced him as the confidant of the Shah. Before Gold Dust, he had been so busy with the task of replenishing the harem with women, he had had no time to scratch his head. The Shah had rewarded him with costly gifts. Then Gold Dust had appeared and spun her web around the Shah. At first, Narcissus was showered with gold and gems. The Shah wanted to know Gold Dust's preference in clothing, ornamentation, and men. Now the Shah went directly to Gold Dust with his questions, as if a sultana who was incarcerated in a world of women could have her own opinion.

And unaware, Rebekah had fanned a rage in the eunuch's groin. The discovery of his lust gland made him ache for the feats his testicles could have performed. The constant preoccupation with his lost manhood consumed him more than ever. As long as he held a certain power, his loss was bearable. But now the other eunuchs and sultanas confirmed his fears. He was losing his grip on the harem. Rebekah and her daughter were stealing his sole weapon of survival.

It was time to beseech the spirits of darkness.

∞

Narcissus entered the Shah's quarters. He shuffled from one foot to another, wondering why he had been summoned. The Shah's dark brow and the intensity with which the falcons listened to his heartbeat petrified Narcissus. He cleared his throat. "The holy book I advised for the purpose of predicting the child's gender revealed that the favorite is bearing a son! The pages fell open to a section where the prophet drew his sword against the enemy and slew them with one blow. The lifted sword leaves no doubt as to the gender of the child."

The Shah's tone did not betray his joy. "The Bibi came to us with disturbing news."

Narcissus felt his heart turn into a block of ice.

"We hear there is a threat to the favorite's life."

Narcissus clutched the scimitar at his side. His determined look, the click of his heels, and his clenched jaw assured the Shah of his continued loyalty.

"You will follow the favorite like a shadow. At night you will guard her door as if it were your own life. If the slightest harm befalls her, we shall behead you with our own hands!"

The eunuch released the hilt of his scimitar. The Shah had facilitated his task. He would watch Gold Dust's quarters. He would guard her life as if it were his own. And he would let the eunuchs in at night. Their collective curse would produce such negative force that once liberated into her bedchamber, it would steal the fetus's spiritual force, causing illness, deformity, producing a weakling with no soul.

But the favorite would not be harmed.

She would remain healthy to enjoy the rest of her barren days.

The eunuch's eyes filled with consideration. "It may be wise, my Shah, to allow her to rest these last few months. She is deeply taken by you. It's not prudent to raise her heartbeat and warm her blood with your presence. And God willing, the Empire will at last have an heir. If your honor desires, I shall choose for your amusement other sultanas."

The Shah slapped the falcons from his shoulders, dispatching them to their perches. "For now, we shall do without women."

Narcissus went straight to the kitchens and ordered the cook to add hashish and the nectar of poppy flowers to Gold Dust's food.

18

A eunuch sat cross-legged next to Gold Dust's mattress and faced the Bowl of Forty Keys—a bronze vessel with forty incantations carved around the rim, each one appropriate for a distinct predicament. His yellow-tinged fingers traced the etching on the bowl. May this child be devoid of faculties. May this child have no soul. . . .

Gold Dust, under the effect of hashish and poppy seeds, dreamed of orchards where boys swam on foamy waves under a silver moon. Their laughter rang against a star-stricken sky ruled by an aging Shah, who concealed a vast emptiness beyond the surface of his rage.

She tossed in her bed.

The eunuch pulled his black robe over his head, throwing himself on the bronze bowl to cover the reflection of the moonlight.

Half awake, Gold Dust remembered her mother's warning to first sit, then turn in bed, so the umbilical cord would not wrap around her son's neck and choke him. She raised herself into a sitting position. She felt dizzy. Beyond the window the moon was the color of sin. Her eyelids were heavy. She must stop drinking those chamomile brews.

The eunuch heard the sultana's tossing. He counted the beat of her breathing. She had gone back to sleep. He stole out.

The night after, Gulf Lily entered Gold Dust's quarters. His eyes rolling in a hate-induced trance, he ordered Allah to end the life of the creature inside its mother's womb. He vowed to stack Allah's altar with sacrificial sheep and aromatic spices—but only, he begged, only if you keep Moon Face's eyes blind to my true emotions. Although I can't bear to see her in the arms of another, I could never look her straight in the eye if she found out the nature of my love.

Gold Dust grew round and chubby, craving sherbets with rosewater and ices with ambergris, enjoying long naps in the daytime and sleeping deeply at night. The Shah came to visit. He did not dare call her to his chambers.

The hakim had warned, "The favorite must bear this fruit to a ripe term or she might bear a mangled child unworthy of the throne."

Gold Dust listened to the hakim, to the Shah, to her mother, but primarily to her child. She would protect her son with whom she had formed a bond. She, too, knew it was a boy. In her dreams, she had seen the prince grow to become as handsome as his father, with dark hair and olive eyes. But her son would inherit her own fire. He would not need to hide behind mocking laughter and arrogant words. Her son would be brave and kind. His strength would lie in his sound judgment and the realization that the power he possessed was rightfully his and could not be snatched away. She would make sure of that.

Days dissolved into months and eunuchs kept their night-time vigil, dark figures blending with the shadows, almost invisible next to the velvet drapes, always muttering lethal words, sometimes rocking on their flabby bottoms, often motionless onyx statues.

Then came Narcissus's turn. The seraglio caught its breath.

On the first day of the month of Mordad, when the skies suffocated under the lingering heat, Narcissus slapped his book of magic shut, raised the lid of his opium box, and prepared to pass the night in the favorite's chambers. He broke a piece of opium from the chocolaty tube, rolled it between his thumb and forefinger, and dipped it in melted butter. He inserted it into his rectum. Despising the taste and pungent smoke of opium, he had discovered a way of enjoying an extended euphoria without experiencing the bitter tang. By the time he had passed the Courtyard of Horses and entered the harem, the delirious effect had seeped into his head. His eyes seemed loose in their sockets. His lust gland throbbed.

He exchanged places with the eunuch guard, tarried next to the door to collect his opium-tainted fantasies, unlocked the door, and approached Gold Dust's divan. The blush of her nipples stood out against the ivory of her skin. With her eyes closed, she revealed no sign of the arrogance he detested. Narcissus called upon the spirits of the dead to help him overcome the yearning to creep next to her, savor the touch of her fresh skin, the breath of youth. The wrath of Rebekah and the Shah was a dangling ax above him.

He set a stone mortar and pestle on the carpet. From the pockets of his pants, he took three pouches and emptied them into the bowl: the brains of seven serpents, the yolks of seven ostrich eggs, and dried camel dung mixed with human urine. He crushed them with the pestle, sniffing the concoction until the odor convinced him the mixture was ready. Circling Gold Dust's divan, he smeared the blend under her mattress. He closed his eyes and summoned the black spirits.

Gold Dust wrapped her arms about her stomach as if to

shield her child. In his deep stupor, the eunuch did not hear her sigh contentedly.

He muttered incantations, feeling weightless, the beat in his arteries vigorous, the flow of blood refreshing. The room was awash in colors—the emerald necklace on the dressing table, the strands of pearls, the silver perfume bottle, the black roses enveloped by ethereal shades.

He looked down at her. He drew his scimitar out of the scabbard. A golden moonbeam tumbled on her face. A content smile parted her lips. The veins at her neck throbbed. The shadow of his raised hand fell on the velvet drapes. The blade flashed in the moonlight.

With one quick blow, he severed one of her long tresses.

At the stroke of midnight, in the Courtyard of Horses, he rose to his full height and lifted his hands up to the roaming clouds. A black rooster dangled from his hands. His fingers seized the bird by the throat, choking its cry. The cock had never crossed a hen, so its masculine vigor would not be wasted. Once the force sealed in the rooster was released, it could stir any curse to life. He held the live rooster above his head, and with his bare hands tore the rooster in half. He voiced the ultimate curse:

"May the child be born a girl."

The Great Black Eunuch stole out, calling back the words he had memorized from his book of necromancy: Thou shall acquire a strand of hair from the head of thy foe and burn it in the Altar of the Jinns. If that foe has powerful allies who are aware of the dark secrets of magic, thou shall burn the hair in flames that rise in the proximity of that person's lodging, wherein he has lived for many years and where his heart lies. As the smoke rises and turns to clouds, so, too, the powers of your opponent and his allies will forever turn into the smoke of nothingness.

ᦒ

Narcissus rushed past the palace gates and through the narrow alleys, toward the small house with the warm bed and sultry scent of life. For the first time he entered the Jewish Quarter at night. He felt the strand of hair in his pocket. The fire should belong to the foe's protector, his book had warned. Rebekah had a kiln she refused to light even when tears froze. Did she have a wood-burner in her kitchen? Would a lantern, a candle, an oil burner suffice?

A strong vinegar smell floated from the houses of the wine makers who worked late, safe from the frequent raids of the Jew beaters. The only house with oil burners hanging on pegs on both sides of its door was the merchant's at the end of an ancient maze of alleys; the one Rebekah often spoke of. He recognized another house, buried under bougainvilleas as if surrounded by a holy fire. He rushed past it. Veiled by darkness, he feared the lingering presence of the Ancient Zoroastrian whom Rebekah revered.

He had left his horse in the palace courtyard, afraid the clatter of hooves would wake the populace. As he passed the garbage pit, he thanked Allah, sure that the stink would have sent the horse into a canter. Loosening a flap off his turban, he covered his face to protect it from poisonous mosquitoes.

Rebekah's street was muddy from the overflowing gutters. He stared at his red kid boots. The ermine hem of his cloak soaked up soiled water. Chewing on mastic to sweeten his breath, he descended five steps to her door and knocked. The slush in the landing rose to his ankles, drenching his pants; worms crawled up the silk.

Rebekah appeared naked at the threshold. Mint leaves peeped from behind one ear. He had never seen her stripped of her layers of lace. She had confided in him that when alone with her memories, she walked around naked because she couldn't bear the heat of the past.

Bathed by the halo of an oil burner that hung from the ceiling, she sang, "Why, sweetlove, you've come in the dark. To what do I owe this honor?" When he did not answer, she reached out. "Are you coming in, or spending the night by the pit?"

In a daze, he stepped in. He didn't know whether to stare at the blinking flame of the oil burner or at Rebekah.

"Look what you did! How will I wash this off?" she cried at the slush that flooded her carpet. "At least brush off the worms!"

He stared at the mark between her breasts.

"What's wrong?" she cooed. "Haven't you seen a naked woman? Ah!" She touched her chest. "The gift of the Devil. It gives me powers beyond your imagination."

The mark glowed like a throbbing heart.

"What powers?" he mumbled to himself, fearing her reply would toss him back to the ranks of apprenticeship in magic.

"Let me bathe you," she said, leading him into the backyard and unclasping his ermine cloak.

No, he thought, the mark resembles the smiling lips of a newborn child.

By a pool of dark water, she removed his scimitar and uncoiled the sash, as she stepped on the white worms that fell to the ground. She untied the jar of brine from his waist and placed it next to him on the skirting of the pool, then folded his pants neatly, laying them by the jar.

No, he thought, his eyes fastened to her bosom, not like smiling lips, like a dove in flight.

Her breasts rippled with laughter. "And you thought you had seen all the wonders of this world."

She pushed him into the pool and tossed a cone of olive

soap after him. Gathering his cloak, his boots, and his scimitar, she returned into the house.

Narcissus scrubbed his body, his mind preoccupied with the mark. Had his eyes played opium tricks on him? Had the shape changed in front of his eyes? Surely it's an emblem from a universe beyond the human realm. The thought that she had kept other secrets from him rattled his core. He tried to climb out of the pool. The dirt steps gave way under his weight. He kept slipping until he caught the edge of the pool and hauled himself up. His fingers twitched with the desire to touch her bosom. But first he must search the yard for wood, branches, something to light. A fire would look suspicious in this heat. A candle would do. Shivering with anticipation, he waited under the hot sky for her to return his cloak. First he must accomplish his task, then he would ask Rebekah about her mark. Surely no mortal was awarded that honor without having gone through the highest indoctrination. She might reveal to him secrets from a superior universe.

☾

Rebekah washed the cape but not the ermine lining. She brushed the boots with wood shavings and plunged the sash into pure water delivered once a week from the Karoun River. She glanced through the curtains. A pox on his house, what in the plague did he want now? Why had he come at night? Was Gold Dust well? Rebekah searched the lining of his cloak, unaware what to look for, save for a sign that he was here for a reason other than his lust. The veiled look he had thrown at the oil burner, the secret glance he had cast at the kiln, the mysterious way he had searched the yard told her he was after something.

Gold Dust was nearing her last month of pregnancy. She

was not her usual spirited self. She seemed sedate. The hakim had assured her this was due to the calming herbs. Rebekah wiped and polished the handle of the scimitar, dried the blade, and checked it for spots. Was it true that a single blow from the scimitar could sever a bull's head? Passing a finger over the blade, she tested its sharpness, scrutinizing the metal.

Two strands of hair clung to the edge.

Raising the tresses, she examined them, hurried to the oil burner, and held the strands under the light. Her breath caught. They were Gold Dust's hair: thick, shiny, the color of Turkish coffee.

She ran out to the yard and stared down at the eunuch. "What did you do to my daughter?" she cried, her voice shaking the Jewish Quarter.

Her brand pulsated, changing shape and flaming like a blazing dagger. The eunuch's skin turned a sickly brown. He raised himself to his full height. What right had this woman to scream at the chief eunuch, the third most important man of the empire, the man who held the power of life and death? He could force her pretty Jewish head under the waters of the pool and throw her corpse into the river and no one would dare object. No one, he reminded himself, except the Shah and the cry of his own gland, which even now begged for her. "How dare you try the chief eunuch's wrath?"

She reached out and pinched him between the legs. "Now that you've tasted the joys of consummation, you who are the master of the harem have become a slave to this Jewish whore."

He slapped her hand off and twisted it behind her back. The fire in her eyes was inhuman. She was a sorceress. She would put a spell on him that would shrivel his lust gland and maim the rest of him. The mud walls of the yard closed around him. He had a vision of himself, turning into a pillar of baked mud, a permanent spectacle for many Jewish generations.

He released her, picked up the jar and his pants, and rushed past her into the room, searching for the rest of his attire.

She dashed in after him, removing the sprig of mint from behind her ear and sniffing on it. "You stink worse than the Devil I lived with."

The last trace of his dignity vanished. The Devil was known to await eunuchs and hurl them into the abyss of hell if they did not carry their severed organs to the afterlife. Narcissus curled one leg around the other as if to hide his bareness.

She laughed bitterly. "Have you forgotten I've seen all of you? Now before I lose patience, talk!"

He pursed his lips, searching the room for the slightest sign of fire, a flame, a candle.

She pounced on the jar in his hand.

They wrestled, the eunuch for the remains of his manhood, which would assure him a space in heaven, the woman for the life of her daughter.

"Have you killed her?!" she cried. "Have you?"

He freed himself from her clutch and wailed, "I swear by all the imams, I didn't touch her. I made a potion to scare away her protecting spirits. I cut a lock of her hair to burn in the altar of the jinns."

"And you dare come to my bed?" Rebekah pointed to her flaming bosom. "By this brand of the Devil, if you lay a hand on my daughter, I'll deliver the black plague of ancient times on you!"

⚬ঌৎ

The Shah locked himself in the inner chamber to await Narcissus. It was a sad formality that the king should be sequestered in his quarters until the Great Black Eunuch arrived with tidings. The Shah felt a twinge of guilt. He should have been more lenient the last time he visited Gold Dust. She had asked his permission to allow Rebekah to be present at the time of delivery. But although he had begun to appreciate Rebekah's candor and, at times, invited her to discuss simple matters, he could not permit the bad luck of a bundle woman to taint the crown prince's first hours.

"Our son," he had replied, "will become king. He must never find out about his mother's lineage."

The harshness of his words had thrust Gold Dust into labor.

The Shah went out to scan the skies. The magi had assured him that on the day of his son's birth the skies would be clear and the sun bright. Clouds roamed above. The air was stagnant. Peacocks shrieked in the gardens.

ço

Rebekah locked herself in the stable and went through the ritual of decking Venus. "Soon," she whispered, "you'll not be the only male in the family."

The donkey whined and spat in the air.

Rebekah pressed her ear to the straw floor, awaiting the blast of cannons that would announce the Shah's acknowledgment of the birth and finally make known to the public the gender of the child. Her disappointment at not being allowed to attend upon her daughter had not lasted long. She had learned to accept the scraps fate tossed her way. Why complain? Gold Dust was the favorite of the Shah. And she was giving birth to Rebekah's grandson, heir to the throne.

ço

In anticipation of the royal birth, the town criers sang poems and flowery prose; the inhabitants of the city kissed one another on both cheeks and on the tip of the nose in a show of endless happiness. Soleiman the Agile and his acrobats blocked the alleys with a new addition to their show. Adults gaped and children cried in fear of a Giant Man who held thirteen acrobats on his head, shoulders, and arms. The Ancient Zoroastrian abandoned her house of bougainvilleas and joined in the revelry, her eyes twinkling with the secret knowledge that a new marvel that would change the course of history would be born to a daughter of the Jewish Quarter.

19

"Push!" the harem cried. "Push harder!"

The Shah had made it clear that if the favorite died at childbirth, no one would be spared.

Eunuchs parted the circle of women and handed the midwives pots of hot water and muslin. The palace dwarf, his mouth painted in an eternal smile, his cheeks dripping ruby tears, his hat chiming with silver bells, danced around Pearl Hall.

Gold Dust sat in a birth chair, hollowed in the center, under which sparkled a bowl of ashes. The ladies-in-waiting wiped her brow with muslin soaked in the essence of jasmine and sprayed her face with rosewater. They puckered their mouths, blowing in the air to scare off evil spirits. Turquoise beads dangled from the ceiling to ward off the evil eye.

Gold Dust's face turned the color of the garnet powder she used to pumice her body. Even in her worst nightmares, she had not imagined such pain. She was about to break in half. She would not survive. She had no strength left to push.

A hush fell over Pearl Hall. The women raised their heavy-lashed eyes in a prayer to the heavens. Although they had collectively put a curse on the infant, they had taken precautions to protect the mother. And the mother seemed to have surrendered. They cried out with terror in their voices. "For the love of the Shah, push harder!"

At the present, Gold Dust did not feel much love for the Shah. He had not allowed her mother to look after her at her time of need. Yesterday, in the glare of his stare, and before the first pangs of labor, with great clarity, she had realized that her only deliverance from a world where she constantly followed orders was to wear a queen's crown and secure the privilege of defiance.

Yes. She would bear an heir. Make him proud of his lineage. Recount how his grandmother had single-handedly risen above the decaying conventions of her home, how she had struggled to earn a living, forced fate into submission, and with great cunning had introduced her daughter to the harem. She would remind her son that poverty was not a shame, embracing it was.

She would raise a warrior who would prepare his empire for the inevitable invasion. He would study the ways of the Tartars, Mongols, and Turks. Learn that wisdom eliminates fear. And that every warrior conceals a lover in his soul.

She would teach her son that he was fortunate to carry royal blood combined with Jewish blood in his veins—this she would whisper in his ear—the blood of a people who have mastered the art of survival.

No one would dare lock her son in the Cage.

Gold Dust invoked the names of all the prophets she had never learned to pray to and pleaded for one last surge of strength.

"Push!" she heard from afar. "Push harder!"

She inhaled deeply, held on to the sides of her chair, and thrust her strength along the straining muscles of her stomach.

The sigh of tearing flesh.

The baby fell into the bowl of ash that would insure against infection.

Entered the world in silence.

Guarded whispers. Dying tinkle of clown bells. Flutter of fans. Buzz of a fly.

Newborns are supposed to cry, Gold Dust thought, before panic had occasion to settle.

The women elbowed each other. Pressed closer to steal a first glimpse. Was the child stillborn? A great kicking of the infant's blood-smeared legs startled them and brought a smile of relief to Gold Dust's lips.

"It must be a girl," a sultana whispered, before she had seen the child. "She didn't even cry. Boys have weak lungs. They cry to ease their first breath."

"Only a boy shows such vigor," Honey declared.

His head bowed in prayer, Hazel-Boy concealed himself in the corner.

As if she had never been in pain, Gold Dust's body filled with a delicious calm. Surely she had lived her life only for this moment. The ceiling, inlaid with shards of mirror, multiplied the scene below into miniature festivities. Her arms reached for her son.

The Great Black Eunuch raised the newborn's legs and held them wide.

The sultanas tiptoed closer.

A murmur filled the hall.

It was a girl.

The ensuing silence hurt Gold Dust's marrow. She bent, the umbilical cord still hanging from her, and gazed at the baby Narcissus had placed back on the ashes.

On her daughter's head, her brows, the rims of her eyes, and all the way down her spine lay snowy hair, and the rest of her body was carpeted with a colorless down. She checked her surroundings with wide eyes that changed color under the glow of lanterns, at times turning ashen and at other times pink, revealing the flow of blood under the orbs.

Gold Dust's screams cracked her heart and sent the slivers flying past the ornamental orbs, past the torches, and past the lanterns that illuminated the palace in preparation for the weeklong celebrations.

"Albino!" "Albino!" "Albino!"

She prayed to God to help her produce tears to wash away the pain. She rubbed her tearless eyes, dry cheeks; her barren sobs hacked at her throat.

Her bones turned into glass flutes that shuddered, exhaling a sigh of resignation. And her body stopped playing music.

The Bibi Sultana stormed out. Honey's purple lips trembled with fear. Hazel-Boy bowed his head in grief.

Moon Face, who had tired of sewing and unpicking her own shroud one hundred and twenty times in the span of a year in the House of Tears, hid her smile behind perfumed palms. The eunuchs coughed and spat and clapped orders, but locked their delight in the caverns of their hearts.

On a satin cushion embroidered with pearls, Narcissus carried a dagger, the shaft inlaid with gems. He approached the chair of birth, raised the dagger to his lips, pressed the blade to his eyes, and murmured a blessing over it. He cut the umbilical cord. The wet-nurse raised the infant from the ashes.

The newborn's shrieks shook delicate eardrums. Strange, the sultanas giggled; such a small creature with such a shrill cry, and she had entered the world as if she were mute. They tiptoed closer to take a better look at this eccentric creature who, to their great chagrin, was beautiful beyond belief. Her eyes changed from gray to pink to red, each shade alive and vibrant and embellished with silver lashes. Her skin was settling into the lucid shade of tulips.

Gold Dust held the sides of the birth chair and raised herself up. Her unyielding stare checked the wet-nurse. "Give her to me!" she ordered. Blood flowing down her legs, she took two weak but determined steps down and grabbed her daughter, securing her against milk-swollen breasts. "I'll nurse her myself."

And against all the vehement protests of her reasoning, she named her daughter Raven.

20

Narcissus took a deep breath, pressed his hand to his galloping heart, and began his journey to the king's quarters. He had no choice but to follow decorum and announce the birth of another daughter. This one colorless. The guardians of cannons awaited the king's acknowledgment of the birth. The eunuch passed the Hall of Lanterns, the Prayer Room of the sultanas, the Courtyard of the Favorites, past the Secret Passage and knocked three times on the door.

He threw himself at the Shah's feet.

The Shah gazed down at this half-man who roused a rare cruelty in him. He both hated and admired this eunuch. Detested him for his ability to grovel shamelessly, liked him for his ability to spark his anger. Anger, which he would later learn he mistook for courage, and which momentarily eased his grief at not having inherited his late father's valor. But since Gold Dust had begun voicing her sentiments, he started to question his outbursts. "My shah," she had whispered, "don't confuse cruelty and anger with courage. Irrational anger stems from weakness."

Raising the eunuch's face with his satin-clad toe, the Shah

aimed his metal-capped finger at his right eye. "Why so late at a time of happiness?"

The eunuch kissed the king's slipper. His glance swept past the Shah's well-shaped thighs, the broad chest, to the royal eyes. He squeaked with the voice that never ceased to embarrass him, "Your Highness, may I be sacrificed for you. I have bad news."

A flutter disrupted further the disquiet of the king's heart.

"Crown of my meager head," the eunuch muttered, "the favorite gave birth to a little stranger, a veiled one."

The Shah struggled to smother his shock. Not another girl. How could Gold Dust fail him like the rest?

He stared at the mumbling eunuch, prostrate at his feet. "We can't hear a word. Raise your hairless face."

"The princess has no color. She is white . . . like a swan."

ഛ

Hazel-Boy notified Gold Dust that the Shah had decided to visit her.

Gold Dust inserted a smoothly filed seashell inside her to plug the trickle of blood. She faced the emerald-framed mirror and examined her swollen breasts and protruding belly. Her waist had almost disappeared, turning her young body into a woman's. Soaking muslin in ambergris, she washed her underarms, rubbed almond oil on her elbows, and brightened her cheeks with the concentrate of peaches. She bathed Raven in milk of donkeys, groomed her white hair, and painted her lips with cherry extract. With a duster of ostrich feathers, she powdered herself and Raven with crushed gold.

Her lady-in-waiting changed the sheets and swung perfumed censers in the chamber. Gold Dust ordered her away for the rest of the evening.

From the incense table she took a silk scarf and cut it into long ribbons and placed them on her bedside.

Reclining on cushions, she waited, Raven cradled in her arms.

She ran her fingers over her daughter's soft forehead, upturned nose, dimpled chin. She had prayed for a boy, an heir to the throne. This fragile girl with the mysterious eyes and translucent skin would only be an heir to her mother's love— and maybe her father's. Could he learn to love this bleached girl? This girl whose beauty was of another world. Since her birth, in only a week, her luxurious hair had grown to her shoulders, scintillating like a waterfall of pure silver. She traced her daughter's lips, the plump mouth that resembled her father's.

The Shah entered with steps of iron. "You brought shame to our kingdom. A colorless curse, an offspring of Jews, not of royalty."

She glided under the covers, Raven secure against her bosom. "She is ours. No shame, only different, like a rare jewel. Only a man like you can accomplish this." She reached out Raven to him. "She has your strong mouth and sad eyes."

She set Raven on the covers closer to him.

He stood bolted in place, his stare riveted upon her. She had nothing in common with his daughters, whom he had lost count of. She was only a week old. How had her hair grown so long and full? Did her unconventional beauty mesmerize him or the force of her curious gaze that followed him? One moment she smiled at him, another she chastised. What color were her eyes? She must be a sign from Allah. A message he could not decipher. He paced the room, fierce sounds rising from his throat, his face dark with anger he did not understand. Gold Dust unwrapped the gauze from her shoulders. He took in her ripe curves and female tenderness. The shadow of her veins trailed her breasts. She had never seemed so generous. He longed to touch her pigeon-white arms, to inhale her scent of ambergris. His daughter's stares paralyzed him.

Kneeling at the bedside, he confronted her unyielding gaze, red, burning eyes, boring into his secrets. No. Gray, cool eyes, pacifying his demons. He had to confirm her gender for himself. He released her blanket. She was a girl.

He removed the dagger from his sash, undid his cloak, and uncoiled his turban. He would have Gold Dust with all the rage and frustration she had caused.

Gold Dust trembled at the sight of him, the straight-blade hair, the proud cheekbones, the arrogant nostrils, the addictive scent of black roses. She had missed his smell, the wrestling that had become part of their lovemaking, and which had stopped once she had grown with child.

He tossed the satin off her and dug his fingers into her flesh, all the time murmuring that she had to be punished. "Albino!" he moaned. "How will we face our people?"

"Albino is white, pure, a sign of rebirth." She struggled to contain his furious hands, lead them along the curve of her neck, across her milk-swollen breasts, and down her soft belly.

His tongue traced the path of her veins, tasting ripe fruit and sun-warmed spices. His teeth crushed her earlobes, her shoulders, the inside of her arms, puncturing the delicate skin.

She sucked her own blood from his lips. The tip of her tongue probed the indentation of his cheeks, the cleft of his chin. Her nostrils flared to drink the scent of black roses.

He crushed her under his weight, forcing her thighs wide.

She slid from under him. "I'm not pure. We must wait for forty days."

She reached for the silken cords and tied his hands. Whispering promises of fulfillment, she plugged his ears with silk balls. In the silence that extinguished the world and height-ened his senses, she lubricated him, softening every knot, tracing his body with familiar ease, skipping, scratching, teasing until he groaned with anticipation. She did not breathe from her nose to reduce the dizzying effect of his smell. Her tongue slithered over his eyelashes, the beat of his temples, the moisture in his armpits, the hair between his legs.

He could have snapped the silken cords with a slight pressure of his wrists, but he did not. He savored this surrender forced upon him. A moment of trust and abdication he would allow no other. An instant when he stopped being the ruler of an empire. He shut his eyes and pressed his lips to plug the rest of his senses and concentrate on her touch. Her rhythm quickening, she lowered herself and took him in her mouth. He broke the silken shackles.

The cannons blasted at dawn. Three rounds of fire announced the birth of a girl, seven had it been a boy, repeating the fire five times in twenty-four hours, once for each call to prayer. Each palace sacrificed three rams; five had it been a boy.

21

None doubted that the demons of Raven's grandfather, the late shah, and of her grandmother, Rebekah, had found home in the child. She matured faster than any mortal. At six months, her small body erect, she took her first steps. With eyes that shunned color and a touch as strong as a warrior's, she shot fear into the hearts of the sultanas. Her voracious appetite reminded them of man-eating dragons that guarded ancient caves. Her intense gaze was so piercing the women questioned her mortality.

Their collective curse had befallen the princess, but not in the fashion they had predicted. Yes, she was born colorless, but her beauty and grace outshone even that of Gold Dust. Raven's white curls, streaked with silver, fell to her knees and framed skin so translucent her pleasure and anger reflected on her dimpled cheeks in hues of sunsets. Her sentiments and the display of light transformed the color of her eyes from a lucid to a stormy gray or to the soft pink of her cheeks or, in an instant of anger, to a flaming ruby. She exuded such range of emotions even the Chief Eunuch felt trepidation at her presence.

Gold Dust went to visit the king. She set Raven in his lap. "The princess misses you."

Gripping the arms of his chair, the Shah glanced down at the daughter who would not be ignored. Every corner he turned, every room he entered, he heard talk of her. Now he saw why. She did not resemble an infant of seven months. Her hand rose to the armchair, and her fingers grasped his with painful force.

"Shah"—she uttered her first words with ardor and clarity— "Pedar."

"She's destined to a life beyond the seclusion of the harem!" he announced.

ço

Smoke of jealousy curled around the halls and seeped into cracks. Plots and the cry of murder raged on embers in braziers. Gold Dust set out on a long journey to preserve her life and that of Raven.

Rebekah the Bundle Woman came to see her granddaughter. She leaned over the crib of emeralds and stared at a child who resembled no other, demanded as no other, and inspected Rebekah as no other ever dared. "My Raven," she whispered, "you're much like myself, but fortunate to be born into a world of possibilities. Use your power to your advantage and to your mother's. Show no pity to men, but in the process don't lose your soul."

One day, Raven would vindicate her, Rebekah, by ripping the rational fabric of the world, defying fate, and transcending the binding rules of men.

Glancing around to make sure she was not being observed, Rebekah unbuttoned her blouse, baring her brand. "Secure emotional and financial freedom, so no Devil will ever reign over you."

Raven reached out and with great accuracy traced the edges of Rebekah's brand, caressed the inner ring, lingered in the warm center, cupped her palm over the mark to conceal it from the world and transform it into her own treasure. She raised herself and, with tenderness, pressed her lips to the brand, licked it, blew on it, whispered to it in an alien language. A deep baritone reverberated in her chest.

Rebekah sprang back in surprise. The voice echoed in the room, off the ceiling and walls. Then a soft, loving murmur, a feminine whisper replaced the baritone. Rebekah marveled at the trumpeting of elephants, chatter of nightingales, bleating of sheep, and at the gush of pouring rain Raven imitated when she saw Rebekah's joy.

"Bless your heart," Rebekah said. "Keep this our secret. It will come in handy."

Raven rose on her toes, kissed Rebekah's forehead, and plucked the sprig of mint from her ear and settled it behind her own.

"Smell it when cruel men threaten," Rebekah said. "And remember that coupled with feminine cunning, even the benign scent of mint can turn into a weapon."

ço

Rebekah welcomed Narcissus and his ever-rising need to quench his obsession. She bathed him in witch hazel oil and aromatic waters, formulated a concoction with eggshell powder and aphrodisiac blends to strengthen the power of his lust gland, dried cockscombs and crushed them into a powder he poured into hot tea and drank for virility, and mixed a fine grit of fern seeds and employed it with the proper incantations, assuring him his organ would grow back before his death.

But she did not submit to his constant pleading to touch the brand between her breasts to secure magical powers from it. Fully dressed, and with an unerring touch, she played a teasing dance on his body until his agonizing pleas pierced the pillow stuffed in his mouth. Then, at the height of his passion and when it seemed his heart would stop, she paused, moved away, rearranged her attire, and ordered: "Promise to protect my Gold."

Narcissus promised again and again, more out of fear of the child, Raven, than of the woman, Rebekah. He had watched Raven pat Rebekah's mark and kiss it reverently. He had seen her sniff on the sprig of mint and stick it behind her own ear while Rebekah narrated stories of the Devil and his disciples. He had seen Rebekah brush and sprinkle her granddaughter's hair with powdered gold and draw her brows with kohl as she urged her to hone her supernatural powers.

Narcissus was certain two giants of the underworld had come together and no mortal force could ever defeat them.

༽༄

Flanked by a pair of gazelles and by walls of ancient cypresses, Raven and the Shah visited the gardens. Raven's hair glistened like sunlit glass. Her dress and veil, made by the harem seamstress from Rebekah's fabrics, glittered with silver threads. Her velvet collar and waistband were encrusted with rubies and emeralds from the Shah's coffer. She demanded attention from nature, the peacocks, guinea fowls, flamingoes, and ostriches that roamed around. She petted the birds and fed them, hunted their eggs and delivered them to the chief confectioner at the jasmine kiosk. He offered her freshly baked sweetmeats, prepared daily for her.

The Shah watched his daughter feed the birds, examine their feathers for signs of malady, raise their wings as if to uncover the secret of their flight. He was learning to appreciate nature with the same insight he had temporarily acquired when in love. He was restless to retire from his daily duties to join Raven's world, to ride the waves she stirred, trusting they would lead him to rewarding shores. He felt content. Her presence nudged to the background the constant distress he carried of an empire with no heir.

"Let's pray," he said, kneeling in front of the Fountain of Crystal.

She knelt next to him and bowed her head.

He noticed the leaves of mint hidden under her hair. "Remove this ridiculous thing. Leave this kind of behavior to common people like your grandmadar."

Raven pressed her hands to her ears to shut out his words. The herb was sacred, a symbol of her love for her grandmadar. She rose and dusted herself. "Grandmadar is not common people. You discuss important matters with her."

The Shah plucked the mint from behind her ear and tossed it into the fountain.

She fought to stop her tears from flowing in his presence, whirled on her heels, and rushed into her mother's quarters.

Gold Dust was stringing ruby beads on to gold wires, coiling them into buds, and holding each against her hair to create the illusion of a blush. Raven would like that. Last month, Gold Dust had discovered a new trick. On her private terrace, she had scattered ash berries to dry under the sun, then pounded them into a fine crimson powder to color Raven's face. The week before, she had sewed scarlet and lavender veils to toss over Raven's head to reduce the intensity in her eyes.

The bonfire in Raven and her feverish eyes caused her such agony, the eyes of a happy mad child. Her effort to make Raven up, so her startling beauty would seem more conventional, invariably failed. She darkened her brows and lashes, painted her cheeks, streaked her hair. But Raven would run to the fountain and wash her face, reappearing pure as nature and as if sprinkled with silver dew, and Gold Dust would again blink at this exotic stranger.

At the sudden appearance of her daughter, Gold Dust stabbed the needle into the carpet.

She controlled her urge to hold Raven in her arms. Raven would free herself again and race to the gardens to chase the peacocks, ride the ponies, or admire her image in the pool.

Gold Dust wiped off her daughter's tears. She brought her fingers to her mouth and tasted salt and water and anger and a multitude of feelings trapped in a single teardrop. Did every tear encapsulate a distinct emotion? She touched her lips to Raven's wet lids and once again longed for that time before Raven's birth, before her bones had stopped playing music, even before she had lost her ability to cry.

Freeing herself from her mother, Raven whirled around the room hurling objects into partitions, tearing the covers off the divans. "I want my mint! Just like my grandmadar."

"But even she follows her elders' advice," Gold Dust pleaded, helpless against this kind of outrage.

A hookah pipe came flying over her head.

Gold Dust shared her concerns with the Shah. "Raven's anger is some kind of a lunacy. One day it will destroy her."

The Shah smiled. "My dear, what you call lunacy is the natural process of growth and the strength to break away from female inhibitions."

Gold Dust drowned herself in books of history that talked of ancient feuds and of families who were torn apart because of some hidden secrets. She pored over the lives of heroes whose tainted blood had destroyed them. She leafed through her own childhood memories, wondering if Raven's temperament was inherited from the lineage of the Shah or from her own. Bitter memories resided in a clouded past. She was three. She had caught her mother dancing. Silver chains dangled on her. She drifted in and out of flames. Her eyes were sad, her dancing merry.

There was a spectator.

A man. He had mad eyes. Like Raven.

Moon Face's words resonated in her mind: "One thing is certain. Children inherit the madness of their fathers."

The next time Rebekah came to the harem, Gold Dust called her into her bedchamber. "Tell me about the man with the smell of iron."

Rebekah clutched at her chest; a flush tinged her forehead. She snatched the herb from behind her ear and slapped it against her cheek. "He was a demon who came into our lives, then disappeared, leaving his stink behind! Forget him!"

Gold Dust took Rebekah's hands in her own. "Was he my father?"

"Child!" Rebekah cried. "He was my husband and your father and neither of these. Go on with your life. The past is quicksand. Don't linger in it. You've got a future ahead of you. Bear the Shah a son."

Gold Dust squeezed at her temples to crush memories that were impossible to unravel. Was her daughter mischievous, rebellious, or evil? Would she follow the path of the late shah, who had ended his life by drinking bull's blood that coagulated in his throat? No. Never.

She could only think of one way to save herself from repeating the mistakes of the past and giving birth to offspring who inherited madness.

In the privacy of her chambers, she inserted into herself a lining made of the delicate white membrane from under the rind of a pomegranate to protect her from the Shah's seed.

22

The harem convened in the fields. Clad in his most magnificent cape, trimmed with ropes of gold, and carrying his bejeweled staff, the Shah faced his daughter and announced: "We will present you with your first untamed mare."

Sons normally chose horses from the royal stud, but daughters received white donkeys from Muscat—and only if they were favorites. Raven was five. Gold Dust wondered if her daughter had the wisdom to tame the mount.

Narcissus stood in a corner with a stack of mirrors in his arms. He seethed with resentment. The princess had demanded he carry these mirrors, and the king had consented. He did not appreciate standing there in the capacity of porter.

A stable boy led a mare toward Raven. The sultanas gasped in disbelief. Hazel-Boy could not resist stroking her rump. She was the most regal mare he had ever seen. The color of shiny tar, with a flowing, silver mane, eyes the shade of sunflowers, neck swaying and hooves drumming, she was oblivious to the crowd. The delicate princess could never tame such a strong horse.

Raven piled her hair on top of her head and shackled the

curls with a clip of rubies, the color of her eyes. She grabbed the bridle, forcing the mare's nose down to her level.

The king held Raven's hand in his. "If you tame the animal, we will start training you for your future duties."

Gold Dust wondered at the deepening affection between father and daughter.

The Shah and his women retreated to gather behind a skirting of low hedges to watch the princess from afar.

The reins tight in her grip, Raven strode down the path and deeper into the field, aware of her father's gaze behind her. With her deep and assertive baritone, she commanded the horse to behave. "You don't want me as your enemy!"

She straddled the mare and led her in circles around the field, her voice demanding restraint, coaxing submission. Bursting into a full gallop and before Raven had time to draw the reins, the animal shied, rising on her hind legs and tossing Raven off the saddle. Raven swung by the horse's neck, clinging to the reins. With her boot, she gave the horse a powerful kick under the belly. She gathered her strength and vaulted the saddle, yanked at the reins, jerking the animal's neck back toward her. "Enough," she warned, "or I'll choke you."

The mare's nostrils flaring and foam bubbling at her mouth, Raven goaded the mount into a canter, the horse's body beginning to conform to hers, her haunches beginning to sway into rhythm.

The mare sped around the field, her mane the color of Raven's hair, whipping the air and sending the stable boys and grooms scurrying for shelter. A vision of scintillating silver, Raven held firmly, the proud outline of her back carved against the wind, a fluid arc that seemed to mold into the animal and in the span of minutes balance and sway in harmony.

An awesome silence fell on the fields as the seraglio watched Raven abandon the stirrups, vault the horse, and with the dexterity of circus riders release the saddle and hurl it onto the meadows.

The Shah rubbed his hands in glee. The sultanas followed suit. Hazel-Boy sipped nectar of poppy seeds from his silver bottle. Gold Dust wondered if her daughter would love this magnificent purebred, as she herself had once loved the donkey named Venus.

His heart expanding with pride, the Shah watched Raven bounce off the horse, pat its flank, and approach him.

"Can we go into the gardens now?" she asked.

They wandered into the gardens. She skipped from tree to tree; Narcissus followed, nailing a mirror to every trunk she pointed to.

"Lower," she ordered. "No, higher up."

When the last mirror was secured, she stepped back, checked their level, then removed the sprig of mint from behind her ear and smelled it. Tenacity and a few outbursts had persuaded her father that she would not give up the herb.

The Shah's hand lingered on her arm. "Why the mirrors?"

"Now I won't have to inspect my reflection in the pool."

"Why is that important?"

She did not reveal to her father that she had acquired the habit of scrutinizing her chest in pools and fountains. One day she would grow a mark like her grandmadar's. Then she would become strong and willful like her, with the power to force her wishes on fate, and on others.

"Pedar, it's pure vanity," she replied, enjoying the ring of his laughter.

Narcissus asked permission to leave, so he could calm himself with opium.

With a piercing trill, Raven summoned a savage peacock she had tamed. The peacock came wobbling from around the fig tree and began pecking at the seeds in her palm. The king settled on a stone bench. The head gardener brought a bunch of freshly picked mint. Neglecting the peacock, Raven began sorting the most fragrant sprigs to tuck behind her ear.

From the back of her hand, drops of blood colored the dirt. The peacock had stabbed her with its beak. The red flush left by the sun on her cheeks darkened as she chased the bird past the fig tree, in and out of the hedges, around the fountain courts, and cornered it between two columns. She edged forward, her eyes dulled by sunlight.

She grabbed the bird and dragged it to the stone bench, next to her father, squeezed it between her thighs, and plucked the feathers from its tail. Grabbing the shrieking peacock by the feet and dangling it upside down, she raised it in front of the king. "I hope peacocks don't grow feathers again. I'd hate to punish it twice."

He gathered her in his arms. "By God, Raven, I promise to raise you as a man. Strong and ruthless, and able to protect yourself."

23

Raven was vacillating between childhood and womanhood, when she discovered the naked divers. During her habitual roaming through the Secret Passage, in her tireless search for a path to the outside, she stopped by a porthole and stared out. On the highest cliff, facing the River of Dreams, a young man, his brown body shimmering with oils, lifted his hands in graceful arcs, stretching his muscles to the limit, poised to dive.

Surely the diver was trying to impress someone, pretending to dare the voracious sharks. She craned her neck and located another man who prepared to dive.

Swift as a falcon and accompanied by a shrill whistle, he plunged into the river.

She counted the seconds. Soon waves would agitate the water; it would turn red; eventually his bare bones would rise to the surface; the last ripples would die; the river would return to its usual calm, the squawk of vultures the only sound.

Did he end his life because he was a helpless commoner and had no command over others? Did not have the power to transcend fate as she would one day soon?

The water split open and the diver burst through. With

strong strokes, he swam to the lip, scurried up the cliff, and once again faced the fall beneath. Toes raised, chest heaving, drops glistening on his body, he plunged back down.

Excitement pounded in her chest and blood rushed in her veins. She pressed her palm to her wild heart. Out there was a world where men had the freedom to defy the elements and were not answerable to higher authorities. Surely the monotony of the palace was alien there. If she ever learned to tame sharks, she could tame anyone, even her grandmadar's Devil. But the palace walls restricted her.

The urgency to learn the magic of the divers turning into obsession, she went to the royal library and devoured all the information she could find about the River of Dreams. She frequented the Secret Passage, inching her way through the routes that branched from the main hall. She stroked the walls, feeling for hidden apertures and calling out in different voices, hoping the echo would bring back clues from the outside. Her mother went to visit the Shah. Raven followed in the distance. She returned, disappointed that after so many years her mother had no desire to find the way to the outside. How could anyone be content among these walls?

Raven went to Hazel-Boy. He had lived in the palace forever. He was intimate with every dark niche and hidden porthole. She could rely on his help and discretion.

In the gardens, away from curious eyes and surrounded by sunlit mirrors and the rustle of peacocks, Hazel-Boy's lips brushed against Raven's forehead. "You have blossomed, my princess. Even more beautiful than your mother." He was the maturing princess's ally, encouraging her ambitions, pacifying her outbursts, watching her with interest. He could decipher the longing in her eyes with accuracy. She had her mother's eyes, only different, mysterious colors. But neither the grandchild nor the daughter had the grandmother's violet fire, eyes that had once ruffled his innermost soul until they had unearthed all his secrets. He longed to once more embrace Rebekah's ample body and stroke her brand. He would do anything for her granddaughter, but he would not divulge the hidden way out of the palace, endanger her life, and cause Gold Dust sorrow. "My princess, for safety reasons, there's no path to the outside."

Raven flung her arms around his neck. "How can that be? You know this place like the beat of your heart. Tell."

His unbridled laughter joined the rustle of leaves. "Don't ever tell a man he knows everything, my princess. He'll become too arrogant."

"Hazel-Boy, I'm not here for a lecture. Please, tell me."

"It's the truth. I've never had any desire to sneak out; neither should you."

"I'm going on my own, and I won't stop until I find the way," she announced, marching toward the Secret Passage.

A candle lighting her path, she had tiptoed through corridors and retraced her steps the numerous times she had faced a dead end. The heat was suffocating in the mazes. She wiped perspiration off as each trip underground turned the heat into a more formidable enemy. Once she had enjoyed the sun, but the unbearable temperatures in these passages were beginning to rob her of her ability to pursue her goal.

One day she found herself in an unusually narrow corridor. A breeze agitated the candle flame. A faint smell of algae drifted through some crack. She searched frantically, her hands patting the walls, her feet testing the ground. The candle would not last much longer. She would have to blow it out before it burned her fingers. Once again, she would have to return to the harem, the secret of the divers gnawing at her. Letting loose the frustration of many months, she stomped her feet. Hard. Again and again. The whole palace shook under her. Had the force of her anger generated an earthquake? She crouched to protect herself. With a sharp crack, the ground gave way. She tumbled down, rolling and bumping on what felt like stone steps, hard against her back, legs, arms. The candle rolled away. A palpable darkness. She plunged lower, the echo in the tunnel adding vigor to her screams.

She crashed against a landing, her knees pressed to her abdomen, the boundaries of a small cubicle confining her. She had fallen into an alcove. She raised herself with difficulty and pounded her foot on the ground until she had covered the surface on which she stood. Then she lifted her leg and pushed with her boot on the lower exterior of the walls, testing for traps. When her legs could not reach the upper walls, she thrust with both hands and, with all her might, examined every block of stone. She heard the splash of divers; she smelled fish; she detected threads of light through cracks in the stones. She bolted against the wall from where light blinked through.

She sprang back at the squeak of springs, the groan of metal and wood and stone.

She emerged washed in sunlight, a miniature woman of silver and ivory and cream.

She had found freedom.

The river faced her, an expansive forest on the other side. The cliff was on her right. Herons sailed overhead.

Two divers stared at the bewitching child-woman who bore herself like a queen.

She approached, announcing in her ripest voice, "I am the Princess Raven."

The divers prostrated themselves. That commanding tone, silver hair, and those piercing eyes left no doubt that she was the princess.

One of the men bowed low and introduced himself as Cyrus. His skin was like polished leather, his head shaved to add speed to his swimming. Light bounced off his golden eyes and large teeth. A jar rested on a rock by his feet.

A splash of sunburn tumbled across the other diver, peeling the skin on his nose and shoulders into delicate stripes. The tilt of his mouth gave him a sad air.

A royal gesture of her hand told them to continue diving. She settled on a rock and watched them plunge into the river, agitating the logs, and the calm of the herons. The sky was a turquoise blanket. The roaming summer clouds eased the heat. A breeze ruffled her hair. The pebbles under her feet smelled of algae and wet earth. The divers, honored by her presence, flaunted their talent. Was the existence of the sharks a lie to discourage escapes? Or was this calm a facade for the lurking danger underneath? The men scrambled back up the cliff and settled next to her.

"What are you diving for?" she asked.

"For the rare seeds of the black roses your father breeds."

"They're found in the river?" she asked, surprised.

"In claws of blood-oysters."

With steps as light as a mountain goat, Raven clambered up to the top of the steep cliff, raised her arms, and announced, "I'm diving!"

Cyrus held her hand and, with an unerring stride, led her back down to the riverside. "My princess, the sharks will tear you to pieces."

"Why don't they tear you?"

"We have a secret."

"What is it?" She tossed her hair back and cocked her head to one side, subduing her habitual proud stance, and in one of her most inviting voices said, "Tell me, I'm your friend."

"Take off your clothing."

She discarded her robes and stood naked, her silver hair a diaphanous veil. From the jar, Cyrus scooped an ointment, the color of algae, and rubbed it over her face, arms, hands, the soles of her feet, covering every part. She shivered under his palms, and he smiled at the hardening of her nipples. What he had heard was true that by some miracle her body had matured beyond her years. Lifting her on one shoulder, he skipped up to the highest peak and set her down, allowing her time to take in the landscape.

"Calm down, my lady. You'll be safe for fifty seconds in the water. After that the ointment will wash off. While your body is covered with it, the sharks won't attack you."

She stood there paralyzed. Down below, the river was like a sheet of glass. It would cut her to pieces. She was tempting death. What if the divers were lying, what if the sharks reacted to her female scent?

Cyrus tapped her on the shoulder.

Glancing down, she nearly lost her balance. The ointment had turned invisible on her skin.

"You don't trust me?"

Why should she? She didn't even know them. But numerous times she had watched the men dive and reappear from the depths without a scratch on them. What if her child-body repelled the ointment? What if only men were immune to the sharks? What if she lost count and did not surface in time?

What if she conquered the voracious mammals? If she survived, nothing could ever stand in her way. Not even kings.

"Headfirst," Cyrus warned behind her. "Remember. Only fifty seconds."

The hiss of parting air in her ears, she shut her eyes, preferring the dark to the reality of the shark-infested waters, rising to meet her with cruel speed. The velocity of her fall stung her face and caused her insides to collapse. A single thought flashed in her mind: she would have liked to be present to relish her father's tears when he received news of her death.

Her small body slashed the river.

Terrifying stillness. Her eyes sprang open. The river was collecting its power, readying itself for a massive assault. Her limbs shook. Her gaze swept the deep.

The water was sapphire clear, the river walls upholstered with a carpet of Persian sponges and corals. An emerald jungle of giant kelp sparkled below her. Diamond corals, the shape of daggers, swords, and scimitars, rose from between whip gorgonians and pointed their blades up at her. Horned river dragons with yellow, bulging eyes swam with great speed. Silvery fish wove past velvet fish. Handfish gripped the sand with their wild, dancing fins and dashed away, pursued by tails of sand. They were all in constant flight.

Her father's black pearls nestled in bloody mouths of giant oysters. Seeds of his beloved roses. She would learn to harvest them. She averted her gaze from the threatening world underneath and prepared to propel herself up to the surface.

Liquid, pensive eyes circled her like a chain of marbles suspended in water. Her heart slapped against her chest. Hundreds of voracious riverain sharks gauged her. They were smaller than she. Their skin the color of bile and covered with razor scales, they lashed their fan-like tails, spiked with bony arrows.

Daggers scrubbed against her thighs. Her flesh stung. Was she bleeding? They would react to the smell of blood.

With all the might of her legs, she fought and kicked to rise up and escape. But the river had awakened and she could not grapple with the momentum of the waves. She must conserve her energy and oxygen and try not to swallow water. Her lungs about to burst, she willed her body to calm down and float weightless.

The sharks glided away, abandoning a trail of froth and fear behind.

She shattered the surface, emerging for air, and swam to

shore with all the speed she could muster. Cyrus rushed to hoist her out.

He lifted her on his palms, high above his head, an offering to the sun, to melt the rest of the ointment and dry her. Afraid to puncture the miraculous bubble she floated in, she remained silent. Had she mastered the sharks? Would she dare tell her father what had happened?

Ferocious sharks had observed her, had reeled away, not one had attacked. Soon she would learn their language and tame them. If she could last underwater for fifty seconds, might she not prolong her stay?

The diver rested her on the warm sand. Her hair spread out like silver feathers; she circled her arms around his neck and lowered his face, brushing her lips against his cheek. "Thank you."

Cyrus offered the jar to her. "A gift for the fearless princess."

She raised her hand to shield her eyes against the ruthless sun. "What's the secret?"

"Sharks don't like to die in their own natural habitat, especially in fresh waters, where riverain sharks live. When a shark senses the end is near, it will swim to shore and die on the bank. Once we find the carcass we remove the liver and layers of fat under the skin and boil them in algae and create an ointment that lasts for fifty seconds in water. Since large sharks feed on smaller ones, it's essential to their survival to segregate themselves by size. Smaller sharks keep clear of larger sharks that endanger their lives. In sharks, sense of smell dominates the visual. Covered with the ointment, down there for fifty seconds you were one of them, but larger and more dangerous."

24

$\mathcal{M}$essengers were dispatched to the four corners of Persia, inviting satraps and heads of provinces to the capital to celebrate the twelfth birthday of the princess. Palace cooks began preparations two months in advance; gardeners lost sleep in fear of bad weather; royal seamstresses called for extra hands; shoemakers searched the bazaars for fine leathers.

The date arrived—a dry Persian evening. A breeze from the mountains flapped the banners on gilded posts. Viceroys, dignitaries, and generals strolled into the gardens. They brought sweet words, gem-studded jewelry, and child crowns. The Herald of Salutations announced the arriving guests. Torchbearers escorted them down a road paved with turquoise that led to an artificial lake of many fountains reflecting images of Corinthian pillars and lanterns encrusted with rubies.

Beyond, a world of roses unfolded. The Shah had allowed a pick from his private gardens—the flaming roses of Passion; the blushing buds of Gold Dust; the velvet-black, for Pari, the lost favorite; the most fragrant white ruffled roses with yellow fringes, named after Raven. Long-stemmed roses coiled around tree trunks, hung from branches, floated in pools. The footpaths were strewn with black petals. The night was fragrant with jasmines warmed by the heat of braziers.

Behind the royal throne lay a grand circle of couches with ivory feet, on which Gold Dust and the Shah's harem would sit. Next to the throne, a smaller replica awaited Raven.

Guests strolled to stations to amuse themselves while awaiting the royal entourage. In one corner, philosophers discussed marvels of creation; in another, the royal laureate recited poetry. Dancers entertained in tents. Palm readers divined the future.

Stacks of wood saturated in palm oil burned in corners. Freshly gathered ears of corn, soft-shelled almonds and pistachios, melon and watermelon seeds roasted on ember-filled braziers. Giant tortoises and turtles, with candles affixed to their carapaces, crawled about the gardens.

Trumpet bearers heralded the arrival of the Shah.

The guests prostrated themselves.

Tinkling preceded the royal procession. Raven, crystal bells bouncing on her anklets, led the Shah and Gold Dust, followed by the harem and eunuchs. The princess radiated in a flurry of emerald silk, golden lace, and hand-embroidered gauze. Her smile betraying the dimples on her cheeks, she snapped her hand up in a formal salutation. And none mistook her for a child.

She plucked a black rose from behind her ear. After days of sniffing different flowers, she had pretended to give in to her father's request and had agreed, only for that evening, to replace the sprig of mint. Still, now she felt a certain thrill to wear the rose he had bred for his beloved Pari. As if the gardens were not moist with fragrance but with an offensive odor, she waved the flower under her nose.

Gold Dust eyed Raven as she strode toward her small throne and sat, striking one hand upon the chair arm in a sig-

nal for the flute players to announce the commencement of festivities. She did not know her daughter, never understood her
fury, her fire, the need for the world to bow at her feet. And her
obsessive, almost smothering love for her father.

On the Shah's face shone the brightness of pride. Never,
not even before he was imprisoned in the Cage, had he dared
display such zest and spirit as his daughter did. Her existence
was proof that the days in the Cage had not emasculated his
seed, that despite his inability to produce sons, he was not a
weakling. If only his late father were present to appreciate his
granddaughter's spirit. The Shah sat back and struck one hand
on the chair arm as his daughter had done. He had shown his
support for the princess.

After midnight, fire baskets were brought in to heat the air.
Rebekah the Bundle Woman entered, followed by a trail of
scarlet velvet. A flourish of sequins on her veil enveloped her
in a glittering halo. A bunch of mint lodged behind each ear as
if the usual sprig no longer staved off the haunting odor. She
flipped her head back, let her chador slip off her head, and with
an exaggerated shake of one hand, fluffed her curls. "Good
evening, sweetloves," she cooed to the guards. "Do you see that
beauty on the Shah's right? That's my granddaughter. Oh! And
on his left is my daughter."

Even if Rebekah had planned to enter the celebration mod-
estly, Raven would not allow it. Marching down from her
throne, she grabbed a horn from one of the trumpet bearers and
sounded it with all her might. A hush fell over the gardens.
The guests turned their gaze to the entrance.

Rebekah, knowing how to behave in the Presence, fell prostrate at Raven's feet, circled her arms around her granddaughter's ankles, and planted loving kisses on her toes.

The Shah rubbed his chin with some shock. Why did
Raven allow this woman to peck at her toes like some kind of

preying bird? With a wave of his hand he could banish Rebekah from the gardens. But he did not want to anger Raven. After some reflection, he realized that his daughter was only responding to her personal desires and that that was the ultimate prerogative of the king's daughter. With that realization, he let out a pleased roar and pardoned Rebekah for the spectacle she created.

Raven helped Rebekah up. "Grandmadar," she whispered, "he wouldn't let me wear my mint tonight."

Rebekah removed a sprig from her ear and stuck it next to Raven's rose.

"When I grow," Raven whispered, "I'll have a mark just like yours."

Rebekah clamped a palm over her granddaughter's mouth. "Bite your dumb tongue back. What do you think this is? To ward off the Devil, who lurks in every corner. Don't let him cremate your flesh like mine."

"Grandmadar." Raven held her head high and pointed to her father. "You see that throne? One day I'll occupy it, and you'll sit on my right."

25

$\mathcal{T}$he once-passionate nights of love and wrestling turned into an almost mournful battle, as if the king were slipping back to his old, weary days. Gold Dust wondered if Hazel-Boy had come back into the Shah's life. It was not a secret that at trying times, he sought Hazel-Boy for comfort and pleasure. Surely, a eunuch must satisfy the Shah in ways no woman could. Hazel-Boy was not her rival, but her mentor, friend, and protector. To her demand that he tell her if the Shah had lost his desire for her, Hazel-Boy replied that lately the king seemed lethargic and tired.

But with Raven his vigor was boundless. He summoned her to the Hall of Politics, where he sat twice daily and granted audience, receiving complaints, petitions, personal grievances, and announcements of births and deaths.

He invited her to the sitting of the Royal Court of Justice with the vizier, various elderly mufti of the law, and visiting emissaries from other provinces. Criminals were tried; citizens came with complaints to be heard or boons to be asked. The Shah, his vizier, and other officials listened to the charges, pleas, and supplications. The final decree belonged to the Shah, who specified damages to be paid to a plaintiff or extracted from a defendant. Raven waited impatiently for the final judgment.

To her great disappointment, he dismissed the whole affair of a petty thief, and the case closed forever. "You are too lenient," she scolded.

He patted her white hair. "What would you have done?"

A glint of iron sparked across her eyes. She pointed to the terrace outside the hall where a giant brazier warmed up the surroundings. "I'd place a large cauldron of bubbling oil on that and put it to use on convicts who bring false charges, spiteful complaints, or give untruthful testimony."

A playful tone to his voice, the Shah asked, "How would you use the cauldron?"

"I'll order the guards and the executioner to pitch the convict alive into the oil, of course."

The Shah's throat constricted to stop the lurch of bile. In his childhood, his father would force him to attend executions, aware that his young son did not have the heart for such brutalities.

The late shah had held on to his son's hand and had threatened to lock him in the Cage if he did not control his "womanly" inclinations. "Watch with your head up and your eyes open," his father had ordered.

The prince, who craved his father's praise, resisted the flow of tears, but could not contain the urine that trickled down his legs.

The late shah had come down to the level of his terrified son's ear and had whispered that he was not worthy of the throne.

The prince had been locked in the Cage.

Now the Shah realized that to deserve the throne one had to have the courage to stare at death without compassion. In a country that lived with the threat of invasion, the secret to sur-

vival was to destroy the enemy first. If a king did not have the
heart for executions, before long the one who had would eliminate him. What he himself lacked, his daughter had in abundance.

His voice filled with pride. "Your sons would be worthy of
the throne."

"Pedar, why my sons? Why not me?"

The king was taken aback by this novel notion—the defiance of his mores—and had no reply.

Raven raised her gaze to the sun and wondered whether it
was the sun or the heat of thwarting predicaments that caused
havoc in her head. The summer was blistering. Why did the
sun, this abnormality of nature, generate such upheaval in her?
A relentless "summer thirst," she called it, because it came with
her anger and with the sun and would not be quenched until
she triumphed over hurdles raised in her path.

"Come," the Shah coaxed, "let us visit the secret watchtower." He threw a black chador over her head. "We will cross
the outer courtyard, where you will survey the attitude of the
common people."

They concealed their faces, Raven with the hem of her
chador, the Shah with a loosened flap from his turban. They
circled part of the palace where official buildings stood, and
they passed through a gateway, entering a courtyard crowded
with wagons, carts, carpenters, plasterers, guilders, and bargaining tradesmen. The salty smell of fish rising from wagons,
the sweet scent of herbs wafting from handcarts, and the tangy
aroma of spices floating from braziers mingled with the sun-
warmed fragrance of mulberries.

The chatter of people mixed with the rumble of wagons and
cartwheels, punctuated by the jingle of bells that hung from the
necks of mules, camels, and horses. Above the clamor rose the
cry of vendors of fruit, poultry, and dry goods. Flower girls

hopped to the tune of their own songs, waving ice flowers with slender mahogany stems and translucent buds the color of lemon rind.

Above hovered a fawn-colored dust that forever blew from the northern mountains, but did not settle on the inner palace because of the plethora of vegetation that protected the grounds.

Raven walked toward the center of commotion to join the excitement with which the merchants held up their goods and shouted their prices, waved their fists in the air when a price was not right. The languor of the harem was suffocating.

The Shah grabbed her arm, craving to share in her contagious fire; instead, he coaxed her toward the opposite end of the courtyard. "Never mingle with common people. In time, we will introduce you to every official and courtier, instruct you of his duties. Set aside a few hours each week when you will report to us. One day you will become queen regent until your son grows to claim the throne."

She slipped her arm around his waist, a masculine act of gratitude and bonding, so different from her mother's, which had become cloying and needy.

"Pedar, why do you believe in my sons more than in me?"

Crows took flight from the top of plane trees and darkened the skies. The aromas and cheerful noises of the bazaar were fading. A vibrant ring encircled the sun.

The Shah pressed Raven to himself, feeling the germinating of her young breasts. "Alas, the law of our empire does not allow a woman to become king. But you, our dear Raven, coupled with the right man, would surely give birth to sons worthy of the throne."

"You are the king," she said. "Change the law."

"This is the decree of our fathers and forefathers."

"Have you selected my man, then?"

"Not yet," he said, stroking her hair.

"Can I choose him?"

"When the time comes." Could he ever share her?

"Promise."

"We cannot promise you the future."

They entered a passage concealed by tall cypresses and climbed a flight of steps to the top of a tower, flanked by two gold-capped minarets. On the landing, he wrapped her in the veil so her hair and shimmering scarves would not attract attention. "Watch through the grilled window. That's our Registry, where preparations and inspections of council documents and notices of tax levies take place. Taxes. The lifeblood of the empire." He pointed at the vast hall below. "This is where our people, even our most trusted attendants, cheat us. Sometimes we punish them, most of the time we do not. It's a daily occurrence."

Her eyes sparkled. "If I were you, I'd punish every one."

"It is dangerous to have too many enemies. It scares away sleep and makes us suspicious of every morsel we put in our mouth. These larcenies are an inevitable part of our government." As a child, every week, in the Courtyard of Horses, he had gazed up at severed heads putrefying on stakes under the sun. The eyes went first, then the raw flesh on the cheeks as pestilential flies had fought over the rotting trophies.

Raven asked, "May I determine the punishment, Pedar? No one would suspect me. It's better to punish one severely than to punish many leniently."

Although she constantly amazed him, he was never prepared for the complexity of her mind and the fearlessness of her young heart. "What do you have in mind?"

Her brows came together in a frown. "Your Honor does not trust the daughter whose sons will occupy the throne?"

"If anyone cheats us today, you select the sentence."

They did not have to wait long. A hand dipped into a pocket and came out with coins. A man glanced around, accepted the gold, and stuffed it into his own pocket. His plume dipped into an inkwell, and in fine hand, with a few strokes, the royal coffer was cheated of hundreds of dinars.

With wonder akin to joy, Raven whispered, "What happened?"

"He is a wealthy merchant of saffron. Every year, he bribes our men to reduce his taxes to one fraction of what he owes. We relinquish him to you."

The Courtyard of Horses was cleared of animals; the two gates on both sides were secured. A scimitar hung from a hook fastened to one of the gates. A drummer sat cross-legged on top of a lone platform. A dais set with the royal couches, and circled by many levels of benches occupied by distinguished spectators, overlooked the arena below.

The Shah held his daughter's elbow as they entered. He was amazed at the energy coursing through her small body.

Iron Heart, the chief executioner, watched the royal entrance. He had implemented many horrors ordered by the late shah, but his hands had never trembled. Today they did. His usually flushed face was pale, and for the first time in his life, he almost wished he were not in such excellent form. After the late shah, executions and punishments had become rare. Iron Heart had watched this king grow with a penchant for peace and quiet. There had been times throughout his reign when, in order to preserve his throne and his pride, the Shah had been forced to go against his grain and order punishments. But this was different. It had to do with the princess. What would her mother think? She was the kindest sultana in the harem, smiling at him on her outings, asking after his health while blushing as if his profession shamed her. After this, he would ask the Shah to allow him to return to his village. Surely the Shah would honor the demand of an executioner who had the kindness to walk the child-heir to his quarters to change after he had wet his pants at the sight of a hanging. Yes. He would retire. He had seen enough misery and bloodshed.

It was one thing to be commanded by a shah to perform an execution; it was another for a child to mock death.

The gate on the right side of the courtyard opened; the two convicts, the spice merchant and the officer of registry, entered. The executioner was familiar with the signs of fear that men on the brink of death exhibited: the dark stains on the crotch, the glazed eyeballs, the dragging footsteps.

The herald of executions announced the sentence. The first convict was positioned next to the chief executioner. The drummer sounded three beats; the Shah felt the painful resonance of the third in his chest. Had he allowed too much?

Silent rancor hung in the air. None doubted the outcome of the race the princess had devised between the executioner and the two convicts. It was rumored that the exotic princess had demanded the merchant's hands be severed before his head was, so no one would cheat the royal coffer again. But the Shah had refused her wish.

The merchant and the executioner began the race toward the opposite gate where the scimitar hung. The merchant fought to control the violent shaking of his legs. Finding the struggle futile, he collapsed and began to crawl. But the executioner had long reached the end line and had removed the scimitar from its peg. The one who arrived at the gate first would be accorded sanctuary, but only if he had the time and the strength to draw the scimitar and sever the other man's head.

The Shah waited for Raven to give the order of execution as previously planned. All turned to her.

A child in appearance but carrying herself as no adult ever had, she lifted herself from her couch. Her voice boomed at the convict. "Stand up and say: 'Long live the king.'"

The Shah was stunned at the resonant voice of his daughter. But he was more alarmed by her callousness. Even in his most violent moments he could never rob a man of his dignity, as his daughter was doing, oblivious to his humiliation as he struggled to rise, hanging to the last moments of life. "Relieve the man of his embarrassment!" the king commanded.

Intoxicated with glory, she cried out, "Let him live!"

The scimitar dropped from Iron Heart's grip, wrenching a groan from the air. The convict's eyes gaped as if begging for further forgiveness; urine wet his pants—a spreading stain on the earth.

Raven realized that from now on she was no longer answerable to anyone but the king himself. And his rule she did not mind. She would have prostrated herself at his feet if he would not have translated it as an act of weakness. Her hand rested on his thigh. One day, only for her, he would change the ancient law.

The next morning, when the people of Persia went to observe the heads that were promised to be displayed on stakes over the gates of the Courtyard of Horses, they wondered what had thwarted the executions.

Gold Dust was unaware of the events that had transpired in the courtyard, a domain of men, where horses were kept and tamed, where men were once punished and beheaded. But Narcissus, who never hesitated to bear bad news, gushed the story to her with relish and embellishment.

Gold Dust prayed that the late shah's madness had not flared with more intensity in her daughter.

That night, for the first time, Gold Dust drew from the opium pipe and drank a steaming infusion of hallucinating herbs to calm the mute clamor in her bones. In her opiated dreams, her mother, naked and without the sprig of mint, cuddled Gold Dust and murmured, "Forgive me for robbing you of your childhood. Don't do the same to your daughter."

26

"Is it true, my child, that you planned the execution of two men and wanted their hands cut off?" Gold Dust's tongue was dry in her mouth. What if her daughter parted her lush lips and narrowed eyes that sparkled in her porcelain face and replied that she had done just that? Then Gold Dust could no longer fool herself into believing the eunuch lied, that these were tales the sultanas fabricated out of jealousy, that her daughter was only rebellious. Although she had summoned Raven to hear the truth, now Gold Dust froze under the spell of the scalding embers that were her daughter's eyes.

Raven's voice was gentle, even soothing. "Madar, everything you heard is true. Next time I'll be less lenient." Leaving the echo of her words behind, she turned on her high heels and left.

Gold Dust's palm sprang to her chest to hold on to the shreds of her pain. Raven was not at fault. She had not been born like this. The confines of the palace had created her. For too long her only companions were deceptive women, and a father whose every move was calculated to harden and hone his daughter's mettle to prepare her for some higher mission.

Gold Dust had tried but failed to convince the Shah that Raven had ample relentless tenacity and that, if anything, he had to strive to quell her violent nature.

Recalling her dream, Gold Dust decided to follow her mother's advice and invite a distraction from the outside to remind Raven that although in her own small world she was the king's daughter, in the scheme of the universe she was only a child.

ৡ

Gold Dust sent messengers to search for a competent acrobatic troupe and invite them to the harem on the first day of spring, the New Year.

Pearl Hall buzzed with anticipation, with preparation, with a rush that blew life into the seraglio. Large velvet curtains the color of sapphire hung on temporary railings around the hall so the ladies could watch through gauze insets without being seen. Rebekah brought muslin and ribbons of silk so the seamstress could make Raven a special robe. The Shah gave a cluster of pearls the size of pigeon eggs to attach to her cap. The shoe-maker made kid boots that laced up to her ankles and accented her small feet.

When the day came, Raven stared at the garments. "I hate silly frills," she announced, tearing off the ruffles from the stitching of her skirt and sleeves. She longed to return to the sharks, the bloody oysters pregnant with black pearls that transformed into roses when planted into the earth, the rebellious corals that snapped shut at her touch.

Gold Dust watched her daughter tear all embellishment from her attire. Helpless in her solitary fight to force Raven to behave like the child she was, Gold Dust stuffed a doll in her lap.

Raven flung the doll on a cushion on the front row and sat

on it. Feet tapping impatiently, she shut her eyes, forbidding further intrusions.

From up on a balcony, the palace musicians, blinded so as not to set eyes on the sultanas, announced the show. The women slipped closer to the curtains.

Gold Dust pressed her eyes to the gauzed window.

An acrobat stood in the center of the carpeted hall, his arms folded against his chest. A black mask framed by peacock feathers erased all clues to his identity. A clinging fabric the color of polished leather covered his entire body. He was of average height with a proud way of carrying himself. Brass-tinged curls fell on his shoulders, defined by lean muscles that extended down to firm arms. Acknowledging the sultanas, he pressed the tips of his fingers upon the cat-like slits of his mask, which concealed his eyes.

Gold Dust contained the urge to release the drapes. The fire of his hair and a glance of his mouth sent her scrambling to re-create the acrobat of her childhood, the blue eyes and fair complexion, provide him with all the attributes the Shah and her mother's men lacked—gentle touch, sweet words, a tender heart. Finally, to the music of his melodious poem, which she soon learned was composed by himself, she drew the man from whom she would not shy, neither in the dark nor in the brightest light of day.

With his poem resounding from the many arches around the hall and bouncing back to recount stories of fantastic loves that time did not fade but nurtured and blossomed, he arranged a wooden wheel, sturdy ropes, a metal structure, his gaze piercing the partition to locate the opening from where the women watched. Although to most eyes only lighter-colored patches were detectable in the velvet, his keen vision identified the shadows of many women. Thought of the king's sultanas behind the curtains sent a shudder through his steady legs. He would arouse their souls. Capture their hearts. Maybe they would choose him as the entertainer of the palace.

He clapped his hands. His acrobats, twenty young men, leaped into the room, warming up their muscles and preparing for the unseen audiences. The acrobat opened the gate to a cage and a bear roared. The women let out shrieks. Raven leaned forward with interest. Three men vaulted the bear, another two climbed the shoulders of the first group, and one balanced himself on top. The acrobat wrapped a cobra around his waist and under his armpits and coiled it about his neck. The fangs of the snake shooting at his lips, he clambered about the acrobats, on their thighs, on their arms, around one shoulder, then the other, dancing, leaping, bouncing, his feet tapping, flying, never landing. With a single leap and a warrior cry, he sprang on top of the head of the last acrobat and raised his hands triumphantly. The cobra stole a kiss from his half-masked lips.

Giggles and delicate patting of hands assured him his performance was appreciated. He bounced down and thrust his head in the bear's mouth. The animal let out muffled grunts; the sultanas hugged each other in excited fear; Raven gave a joyous yell.

The glint behind the feline slits of the acrobat's mask ruffled through Gold Dust's marrow. His flame obliterated the vast room and all its multicolored carpets and oil burners.

Raven watched her mother press her eyes to the gauzed window. She saw her flushed cheeks, the dreams on her face. Pity, her father was not here to observe his favorite blush like a flustered maiden. Raven brushed her mother's forehead with the tips of her fingers. "Madar, you're hot."

"There's no air here."

"But a cool breeze is coming from the windows. Do you have a fever? Let me walk you to your room."

Gold Dust's tone rose with irritation. "I've arranged this for you. Now sit still and watch."

Raven toyed with the cluster of pearls she'd removed from her cap. "You're suffering, I'll get Pedar."

Gold Dust's fingers clamped around Raven's knee and pressed her back onto the carpet. She thought she heard a chuckle rumble inside her daughter, roll off the ceiling, one corner of the hall, then another. She stared back at Raven, around the hall. There was silence. Raven had turned her attention back to the acrobats. Gold Dust was almost sure that inhuman sound had originated from her daughter.

The acrobat checked the metal structure. All twenty of his men, each playing a different musical instrument, hopped from one tier to another, creating a symphony that sent the sultanas for their opium pipes. Reclining on the carpet, they lolled in a euphoric daze, building their own private world with the bricks of their imagination.

Gold Dust watched the men continue their juggling tricks with ropes, loops, and blazing torches. Objects flew, spun, and hung in the air; goblets full of sherbet swiveled and twirled, never spilling a drop, fashioning a fantastical world that defied all rules of nature. Objects did not fall and shatter; men did not slip and break their bones; animals did not crush human skulls between their jaws; it was a universe where poisons did not exist, where kings did not wrestle to raise their passion, where there were no Bibi Sultanas whose words cut like blades, where your own daughter did not turn into a mesmerizing demon.

Folding the structure, the men prepared for their last act. They constructed a pyramid, each man standing on the shoulders of the men below. The acrobat lifted the bear and like a nimble panther hopped from one shoulder to the other until he had occupied the apex, standing tall and erect, the bear draped like a fur shawl around his shoulders.

The ladies sighed in their opium-induced universe. Gold Dust parted the curtains.

The acrobat saw amber eyes.

He came crashing down.

QQ

Gold Dust's heart became rebellious on that day. The acrobat's agility, light complexion, and feathered black mask remained suspended in her fantasies. She was thirty years old and had only experienced one man, a man who grew more melancholy with every act of love because despite his belief that human bonds were created and strengthened in bed, he had failed to find them there. For years she had probed the depths of his eyes, searching for the man who had loved Pari. Beyond the surface of his anger, she had discovered only doubt and despair disguised as anger and scorn.

Now she had, at last, met the man in the promise of her mother's fairy tales.

The need to glimpse under his mask became an obsession. She had to share the ache in her bones. She sent for her mother.

Cursing herself for having encouraged Gold Dust to invite the acrobats, Rebekah listened to words that hacked at the foundation of her dream.

"I'm suffocating in the Shah's dark eyes, dark skin, dark voice. I've forgotten the difference between wrestling and love. He rules an empire, has all the wealth and power in the world, but Raven manipulates him with her small finger."

Rebekah toyed with one of her daughter's braids. "And this acrobat? Is he different?"

"I have to find out for myself."

The relaxed smile on Rebekah's lips did not betray the turmoil in her heart. She had to think hard so she would not open her mouth and spill words that would drive her daughter into the acrobat's arms.

"Madar, I'm afraid of Raven. I rarely see the Shah. I miss the outside."

Rebekah's violet eyes were calm. She had spent enough time in the intimate company of youth to understand their minds. One word about the dangers her daughter would have to face if she went against the Shah would only propel her into a disaster she would translate as adventure and relief from the confinement of the harem. She must not add the excitement of danger to Gold Dust's infatuation.

She would not yet remind her daughter of the lethal rage of the Shah, whom she thought weak. She would not remind her of the cutting pain of the bowstring. The fire of poison in her belly. The sting of scorpions. The shame of being dragged by her hair around the Courtyard of Horses.

She would encourage the acrobat back. Let him try to sustain his allure through repeated presentations. There was no difference between a tightrope walker like the acrobat and a man who had to, for prolonged periods, uphold his performance in bed. She had yet to meet a man who could charm a woman for too long. The acrobat was no different. Let him uncover his face and strip off the mystery he had skillfully created.

27

When the acrobat lay on his straw mattress and stared at his gray walls, he saw golden eyes glancing through velvet. A consuming fever followed him day and night and his heart turned cold in fear of having fallen in love with the Shah's sultana.

The acrobats asked why he was flushed and why his legs had lost their grip. He mumbled under his breath and continued to struggle with his daily chores. He could not explain that his world had lost color and everything seemed past its prime. He could not explain that he was trapped in the eyes of a sultana he would never see again. How could he explain that he dared not whisper a word in fear of its reaching the Shah's ears?

One early morning, a knock awakened the acrobat.

The sultanas were pleased with his last show and invited him back to the seraglio.

In his eagerness, he did not ask why he was invited back so soon. Could his act have pleased the brave sultana who had dared release the curtains? No. It was the thirteenth day of the month of Farvardin, he told himself, the last day of the New

Year feast. The sultanas and their daughters had decided to end the celebrations with a show.

The fever left him and in its place anticipation permeated his body. He would dazzle the sultana with his chimerical universe, so she would call him back again and again. He would adore the image of the woman behind the partitions; cherish the sound of her applause, the scent of her body. He would continue loving her in his dreams, but he would never express his true feelings to a living soul. He had heard of heads displayed on the gates of the palace, and he was aware that if he revealed his love he would lose his life.

He began a strenuous rehearsal with his men, the bear, and the cobra. This time, the Giant Man would join the show. He picked small morsels and fed the Giant Man, who stared at the chipped bowl that held more food than he was used to. The puffed-up cheeks of the giant trembled, and a smile contorted his face. His unintelligible words slurred as he expressed his delight at the possibility of serving his master. He did not know that his master hoped the breeze of his giant steps might flutter the curtains open and he might glance at the sultana's unveiled face.

Gold Dust crouched over a tub of marble, her muslin skirt a tent capturing the aroma of embers of sandalwood, frankincense, and myrrh. To increase her seductive powers, she rubbed cloves and ginger behind her knees. She went to the Hall of Entertainment, her long train sweeping the ground behind her, a girdle of diamonds hugging her waist, and strands of pearl nestling between her breasts. On her head, at an angle, lay a cap embroidered with satin and damask.

In the hall, before the sultanas' arrival, Rebekah had relocated the burners in odd corners and raised the flames into unflattering glares. The women followed Gold Dust in and lounged on the cushions. Oblivious to the world, Gold Dust rearranged her seat next to the curtains and reclined.

Rebekah whispered, "I've convinced Raven to stay away. I'll remain with you."

Gold Dust nodded her approval. No one could shatter her sweet solitude. She pressed her eyes to the gauzed window.

Cloaked in a skin-tight garment the color of coal, the acrobat bowed to the invisible audiences. The mask concealed his face. He blinked at the oil burners and wondered why the flames were turned so high and positioned at such unflattering angles. The scent of sandalwood and frankincense drifted to him. His gaze penetrated the gauzed window. A flash of honey. Her eyes. He sensed her warmth; heard the sound of her breathing, the flutter of her heart. She sat near the curtains.

Rebekah cursed his cunning. He was clad in a cat costume that emphasized the elegant line of his body and added mystery to his every move. And he still wore that enticing mask.

The acrobat folded his knees in a humble stance, coming down to kiss the fringe of the drapes, and Gold Dust knew this show would be for her.

A wheel strapped to his right foot and a flaming staff rotating in his left hand, he spun around the hall, gathering momentum, transforming into a whirling rainbow, into a powerful storm, agitating the velvets, and Gold Dust's heart, who feared he would turn into a spirit and disappear before he revealed his face. As he slowly swiveled on his toes, his body found form, coming together. Had he tried to free the curtains? She released herself from her mother's grip and moved closer.

He snapped his fingers. The Giant Man started to the center of the hall, his steps rumbling as if his boots were cast in stone. His frizzy hair, supported by metal springs, stood out. His gray eyes harbored the simplicity of innocent children. The acrobat and his wooden wheel bounced on the Giant Man's shoulder, rolled around his other shoulder, then down his outstretched forearms as he marched around the hall, closer and closer to the partitions, the curtains fluttering in the breeze of his stride.

The acrobat's stare tried to penetrate the fleeting gap in the flaps. Did her knees almost touch the partitions? The Giant Man's frustrated steps racing uncontrollably, he reached out his hand; from his unlocked fist he produced a garland of golden flowers, tossed it at the curtains. The velvet refused to yield. The acrobat bounced down onto the carpet. A somersault. He balanced on his head. His legs bent in a graceful angle with his body. One leg folded from the knee, he retrieved something from the cuff of his other leg, spun on the crown of his head, thrust his toes between the hangings, parting the flaps.

Gold Dust held her breath. A single rose lay at her feet.

Rebekah clawed at her chest.

As if he had invisible wings, the acrobat vaulted high on the metal structure—from rod to rod—flying in the air—glass balls juggling above him—around him—a sword in one hand—the orbs bouncing—there was fire in his mouth—sparks flared and erupted—the crystals turned amber—the sword blazed—carved a luminous wreath above his head—softly, as softly as a cat, he landed on his feet—the balls came down in one hand—the sword in another—puff, the fire was out.

One single sweet call: "Marvelous!"

One hand pressed against his heart, the other lifted the mask.

She saw in his lazuli-blue eyes and beneath his fair skin the current of emotions he could not contain. The smooth lines around his mouth had not hardened. Time had embellished his copper-colored hair, the patrician brow, his fingers that had once danced on a tambourine. Did he save her cherry anklet?

His branch of cherries lay dried between the pages of her history book. Was the scar under his chin a memento of a love clash, the cut of a dagger? Tears glistened in his eyes.

Soleiman the Agile. Her acrobat.

୯୨

Rebekah watched her lifelong plans blown to the River of Dreams. She ripped her vest open and beat on her chest. "This is the last time I visit the harem."

Gold Dust stared at her mother with glazed eyes. "You were the one to teach me the value of love. Did you see the tears in his blue eyes? He's not afraid to love."

"What else is he not afraid of? Endangering your life? Do you know the feel of Iron Heart's scimitar?" With the pointed nail of one forefinger, Rebekah traced a line across her daughter's throat.

Gold Dust did not flinch.

Rebekah's brand flared. "How can you toss away your dream?"

"*Your* dream, Madar. For years I held stubbornly to the link that locked me to the Shah, an heir to make me queen and let you settle down." Should she reveal to her mother that every evening, she faithfully changed the membrane from under a pomegranate rind to keep it intact and protect her against pregnancy? "Your dream is lost forever! I'll never give birth to another Raven, the image of my mad memories."

Rebekah understood. Had she herself not done the same in the past? Had she not plugged herself with a cork soaked in the juice of weeping willows to stop the seed of Jacob the Fatherless?

"Gold, it's not too late. You're still young. Don't shut yourself to the Shah. Barren women are thrown into the Cage. Die in oblivion."

"Even if they hang me from the tower, I must meet Soleiman."

∾

Rebekah the Bundle Woman went to the Jewish Quarter, past the Muslim bazaar, where the air was heavy with the perfume of nard and myrrh, where apothecaries stocked jars and phials of cosmetics: green malachite, brown sumac, and red henna. As she approached the garbage pit, the odor of putrid food replaced the fragrant air.

Her daughter had forgotten the agony of living by the stinking pit, behind the baths, where lame beggars deloused their starving children. She had never known the pain of becoming a whore-wife.

Soleiman's wooden-planked door gave way to Rebekah's touch. She entered a gloomy room overwhelmed with books.

Soleiman the Agile's trade took him around the city at night, so he slept during the day—a sleep that had become light and unsettled since that day in the harem. He sensed a shadow over him and opened his eyes, facing an apparition he thought had descended from heaven—passionate eyes, and dewy skin framed by hair the color of sunshine. He reached out to touch her.

"Not me, sweetlove," she sang. "Unfortunately, I've come about my daughter."

He sprang up—leaped into the air—came down and grabbed the sword that leaned against the books—circled it above his head—bent his knees—raised one arm and aimed the blade at Rebekah.

She fluttered her fingers over her bosom. "Don't try to impress *me*, I'm not in a very good mood."

He gazed at the shrunken glove of her hand. The Jewish

Quarter was a small place. Everyone knew Rebekah, who her late husband was, and where her daughter now lived. But was the sultana, whose heat he had felt from behind the curtains, whose eyes he had seen, whose solitary clap he had heard, whose cry of "Marvelous" had, for days, reverberated in his head, this woman's daughter and the girl with the cherry anklet who had vowed to become his wife?

Rebekah pointed a flirtatious finger at the books. "I see you've brains to complement your good looks." She paced the room in silence, the message she was about to deliver locked in her throat. "I was forced to make this trip because of a flaw in the king's character," she said at last. "He has passion in his heart, but can't use it wisely."

Soleiman struggled to hide his fear and exhilaration. The blade carved a circle in the air above his head, crowning him with an invisible wreath, then came down stiffly at his side, exaggerating his lean silhouette. Why was this woman torturing him? When would she voice the sultana's name and break the shroud of mystery, give life to her in his modest room and confirm that miracles could happen in the Jewish Quarter, too?

"The Lord decided to shine His countenance upon you," Rebekah cooed to his dramatic show of silence. "Gold Dust, the Shah's favorite, wants to meet you. Next week when the sun hits the center of the sky, on the day after the first of the week, come to the alley behind the baths."

She waved a hasty farewell and hurried toward the exit. She pitied this young artist who was born in this godforsaken place, but she had her own troubles to tend to. As if she had remembered something, she walked back and faced him, her gaze scrutinizing.

"Sweetlove," she said, her voice brimming with consideration. "You're as pale as a corpse. The favorite dislikes fair men.

Lie under the sun, rub yourself with some coloring ointment, do something to darken your skin and give it a healthy look."

She turned on her heels and swung through the flimsy door, past the stinking pit, the phosphorous flies, and ravenous rats, vowing under her breath that she would not allow this acrobat even to carry Gold Dust's coffin on his shoulder.

Soleiman hardly slept, but his body was alert and nimble. He lost his appetite, so he fed his cobra and bear his own food. The animals grew stronger, and his acrobatic feats opened a different world to his audiences, who remained suspended in his universe as he spun in the air as if he were a fantastical bird who juggled objects, swallowed fire, and twisted his body in the most precarious angles. The ushers had to shake the viewers out of their reveries and remind them that Soleiman's world was only a world of fantasies where things were not what they seemed and dreams vanished at the end of the show.

After his performances, he strolled the night, his thoughts and the song of nightingales haunting him. Repeating his own poems in his heart and tasting unfamiliar longings, he experienced the intensity and harrowing pain of a love that would only bring doom.

During the day he rested under the sun, his face smeared with a mixture of Turkish coffee, henna, and black olives to darken his complexion.

Then the sun hit the center of the sky on the day after the first day of the week. Soleiman went to the baths and sprayed himself with attar of sandalwood. He stole a branch of cherry blossoms from his neighbor's yard and tied a ribbon around the stem. He wore his Sabbath attire and checked his image in a brass tray. The ointment had worked. His blue eyes shone in a face as dark as burnished leather. His polished sword swaying by his side, he hurried to the alley behind the baths.

                              ❧

"Let's take the shortcut to the baths," Gold Dust said, conscious of Rebekah's grip around her arm.

"It's been years since you've seen your home, and the waiting will whet the acrobat's appetite." Rebekah led her daughter through the crowd. Gold Dust had not mingled among the public for so long, she walked in a straight line as if the populace would part in her wake.

She did not mind visiting the Jewish Quarter. Some lingering memories were sweet: the Ancient Zoroastrian, who called her "Tinkling Child" and whose prophesy of jewels and passion and intrigue had come true. The baths where the more affluent women sat on large silver trays that protected them from the bath slush, and whose children, as a show of respect, poured rinsing water over their heads. The large watermelons that crackled when cut open by butcher knives, the sherbets of rosewater and grated apples, the large bath glasses sweating steam.

She sprang back at a hand, clutching her robe.

"One dinar, *Khanom?*"

The beggar was no older than five. Flies covered his head, feasting on the open sores. His bony legs wobbled under the strain of his bloated stomach. Gold Dust searched her empty pockets. She glanced at her mother, angry with herself for not taking charge of her life. She could have filled her pockets with gold and distributed it among the needy. But like the spoiled sultana she had become, she, once again, depended on her mother, who planted a coin in the beggar's hand.

Women washing clothing, pots and pans, and bathing small children occupied the *joubs*, streams of water at both sides of the alleys. A boy urinated in the same water in which fruits were washed. They moved south, farther from the baths, closer to hovels and shanties with tin sheets for roofs and flaps of cloth for doors. The air was biting, the stench of manure unbearable. Stray dogs trailed at their feet. Gold Dust did not remember these scenes.

The smell of putrid ice flowers assaulted her with bitter memories. Her mother's nights, the moans, the tar-colored men. The acidic smell of Heshmat the Matchmaker's armpits that lingered in the house long after she was gone. The scent of rosewater she sprayed on her mother to wash off the stink of manure. The cry of whore. "Madar, I'll ask the Shah to buy you a house. You won't have to live here anymore."

"I'm bound to remain here by forces you'll never understand. Look around, Gold, these are my people and that will never change."

Slapping flies away and sidestepping rodents, they skirted the pit. Gold Dust wondered how people could live with this stench. Her mother must be walking her through the worst parts of the Quarter to scare her away. Where did Soleiman live? A man who composed such lofty poetry could not endure this filth.

Rebekah pointed at a broken door on the opposite side of the mound of garbage. "Soleiman's home."

A shudder scurried through Gold Dust's body. Although she had often heard of the miseries of the Jewish Quarter and the horrors of the pit, her mind had become incapable of imagining such poverty. In Pearl Hall, Soleiman the Agile was a prince with his entourage. Even the Giant Man was clay in his hands. Gold Dust turned to steal another glance at his house, which seemed part of the pit itself, lopsided, cracked, lonely. She had forgotten the world of the acrobat, cholera, smallpox, worms that find their way into intestines. Where scorpions rule over

human flesh. She had forgotten the smell of urine, of decom-
posing bodies, horseback riders who whipped Jewish children.
But she remembered the orphans who crouched behind the
baths, their imploring hands eternally extended. They were
still here, boys and girls Raven's age.

What would happen to Raven? Would the explosive energy
in her daughter, which she liked to believe she had a hand in
containing, spring loose and wreak havoc? Then the world
would whisper that she orphaned her daughter for nothing but
a whim.

What arrogance made her believe she could control her
daughter's temper?

Gold Dust freed her arm from Rebekah's grip and sped
toward the baths.

ॐ

Soleiman waited. He waited until rosebuds bloomed at his
feet. He waited until clouds shrouded the sun. When he had
lost hope and was about to turn back, he saw two women clad
in the drab brown robes the sultanas wore on rare occasions
when they went out—uniforms that made it impossible to
identify one woman from another. But Soleiman recognized
them. He had once seen, and would never forget, Rebekah the
Bundle Woman's swinging hips as she had left his home that
day. Her daughter had the same inviting sway. And from the
slits of her veil, her eyes, warm and scintillating, were the color
of honey.

Soleiman tightened his muscles, as he did when he prepared
to grab ceiling ropes, and he lifted his body to four fingers taller
than his usual height. As they approached him, he sucked in
his stomach, squared his shoulders, and patted his burnished
curls into place. A face the color of burnt almonds over-

whelmed his azure eyes. He reached out his hand with the branch of cherry blossoms.

Gold Dust saw a changed man. Bewildered, she turned to her mother. "He removed his mask that day. You saw him. He was fair!"

"Our minds deceive us in strange ways," Rebekah replied. "We see what we want to. I was there. He is dark."

They glided past Soleiman, one woman clasping the arm of the other, who glanced back in shock.

His gaze pierced their backs. Rosebuds teetered at his feet. Bees plucked at his frayed cuffs.

28

Arabs, Mongols, and Teymour the Lame marched toward Persia. Throughout history, when Persia had begun to flourish, assaults on her frontiers had often occurred. But this time an overwhelming fear filled the hearts of the Shah and his people.

The Tartar, Teymour the Lame, known as Tamerlane in other lands, was rumored to be leading an army of strange species never previously encountered: a massive legion of heavyset creatures, half human and half beast, with scaly chests, stocky arms, short legs, and long muzzles that spewed noxious gasses. Although the enemy had not yet crossed the frontiers of Persia and was many *farsangs* away, a pestilential cloud caused by the fumes the creatures exuded floated past the house of the wealthy merchant Rouh'Allah the Spirit of God, all the way past the garbage pit, infesting Soleiman the Agile's bare room, Rebekah the Bundle Woman's small house, and the Ancient Zoroastrian's home of bougainvilleas. A reeking blanket of vapor and fear levitated over the kingdom.

The mere mention of Teymour, a man whose eternal dream was to conquer the Persian Empire, was enough to send a chill through the country. Talk of his strange beasts added a sense of panic that was lethal to an army that must organize for war.

It was one thing to be threatened by warriors from other lands, but to have his people deceived into believing his empire would fall to peculiar fiends was an insult the Shah could not endure. He sent for his war minister and unleashed his fury. "The enemy must have spread this rumor to paralyze our soldiers."

The war minister rolled bulging eyes and slipped a palm over his shaven head. "We must stop these lies before they cause irreversible damage. Agents will be dispatched to the frontiers to investigate the circumstances."

While the Shah awaited news from his agents, Gold Dust pored over war journals recorded by royal historians. She studied the lives of Arab and Tartar leaders, their many triumphs and massacres.

Monumental sadness clouded her days. Memories of that afternoon behind the baths were still fresh. How could her heart so utterly deceive her? Or had her mother devised one of her ruses? That day, she had returned to the palace and to her private quarters, removing from her inner self the lining from under the rind of a pomegranate that, for years, had stopped the Shah's seed. She had planned to conceive again, give birth to a son, even if he were to be like Raven. Maybe then she would have realized her mother's wish and freed herself of her eternal grip. But she was punished. She remained as barren as the desert of Karbala. And the image of Soleiman's love-stricken eyes thrived in the fertile land of her imagination.

She drowned herself in current problems, hid behind partitions while the Shah met with his men. Recording in her mind the path of the army, she later traced it from memory on a map she had smuggled from the Registry. Her mother's stories churned, sifted, and rose to the surface. She awaited Rebekah's next visit to establish the veracity of her own memories. She would present the king with particulars neither he nor his advisers would discover in books or from their spies.

৩৩

Rebekah cupped her daughter's face in her hands and asked, "What now? Why this sudden interest?"

"To rediscover ways to captivate the Shah. Conceive again—maybe this time I'll succeed."

"Dear child, you *have* succeeded. Raven is your trophy, she's far superior to a son."

Gold Dust was aware of the futility of arguing with her mother about Raven. The two had developed a bond she did not comprehend. "Madar, the Shah is going to war. Tell me about habits of warriors who came to you, so I can impress him."

"That is clever, Gold, but be careful you don't appear more knowledgeable than he, or he'll spurn you."

Rebekah submerged herself into memories she did not want evoked. Throughout the years, soldiers from near and far had visited her because her name had traveled far beyond the Quarter—a Jewish whore who would not reveal their whereabouts at their most vulnerable. But the warrior who had impressed her most had knocked on her door a few weeks ago, at the beginning of winter, when putrid winds had began to blow toward the capital, foretelling the enemy's approach. He came at midnight, his dagger-thin mustache and razor-sharp hair flaked by snow. He wore boots and leathers the color of mud; a sword swung at his side, stirrups on one shoulder. His turmeric complexion, slit eyes, and flat nose told her he originated from Mongolia, a place that bred terror, and his pestilential smell was further proof that he came from the enemy's camp. His gaze bore through her brand and she recognized that curiosity had attracted him to her. She was pleased at the opportunity to conquer another man, this one, by all indications, himself a ruthless conqueror.

He took one look at the sprig of mint behind her ear and a river of tears splashed down his face. He pushed her away and marched into her house, past the makeshift partition, and entered her space as if he were the true owner. He instructed her to discard the herbs or it would send him into terrible convulsions. She saw his twitching face, awash in tears, and she realized that if she treasured her life, she would have to comply. For the first time since Jacob's death, she put the mint aside.

He blew out the candles and the oil burners and undressed in the darkness. She climbed onto the pallet next to him and shuddered at his chill. He murmured in his rolling Mongolian accent that he had just sent his fourteen-year-old son to war.

"What startled me, Gold, was that I heard no trace of remorse in his voice."

Rebekah harnessed her fear and passed her hand over his ice-body and discovered his short leg and the two stump fingers that didn't know how to caress. She realized he was the great Teymour the Lame.

She learned that his thin lips never parted in a smile and that he knew how to fight but not how to love, and that he had sent his spies to assess the military situation in Persia in order to determine optimal tactics of invasion. His emissaries had supplied him not only with essential strategic facts, but with a fascinating tale, which he felt compelled to verify for himself. When inspecting the Jewish Quarter and its surroundings, his men, seeking respite from their demanding schedule, had called on prostitutes who had carried on about a legendary violet-eyed whore who nurtured the fire of youth between her breasts.

He took her fast, ferocious, silent, stabbing at her again and again.

At the height of climax, his body stiffened up as if ready to release an arrow, and he prayed to be stricken down again and again.

Death! he bellowed, challenging Ezraeel, the Angel of Death.

"At that moment, without thinking, I reached out for a bunch of mint."

His eyes leaking, he grabbed the herbs and crushed them under his flat foot and stormed out into the snow.

He had left behind as payment miniature jade warriors copulating in strange postures, their women defeated under their swollen bodies. In fear of spies discovering his presence at her home, she had not had his figurines appraised.

"His most precious gift, Gold, was the reaffirmation of my power. That night one of the fiercest conquerors allowed himself a measure of vulnerability others must never have witnessed. What pleased me even more was that I led him to believe *he* had subdued my fire with his male weapon."

෨

Gold Dust decked herself as she used to when she was first chosen as the Shah's favorite and when she still danced to the music of her bones. The Shah's nights were not occupied with other sultanas or with Hazel-Boy, but with the effort of educating Raven and preparing his empire for battle.

Gold Dust started toward the royal chambers. She had become familiar with every turn, step, and notch of the underground tunnels that led to the king's quarters. She knew which part had more light and where she had to feel her way through the dark. Depending on the intensity of the odor of mildew, she calculated her distance from the river, a hole, or a possible opening that might lead to the outside. According to the layers of spiderwebs, she guessed the number of visitors the Shah had had since her last visit. Even when she smelled the scent of tree barks and sunshine, which told her she was close to a portal that might unfold into freedom, she never dared digress. But the layout of these passages was sketched in her mind and made her dream of the possibility of Soleiman the Agile skipping through them like a panther.

At the threshold to the chambers, she chased thoughts of Soleiman away and waited for the king's permission to enter. He raised his head from a massive map spread before him. Colored flags marked strategic positions and different-sized blocks followed the future progress of the army. She let herself in and slipped next to him. She remained silent not to disturb him. He rose and paced the chamber, his eyes radiating determination. The thought of being forced to fight an invading army of strange creatures instead of honorable soldiers mortified him. He was beginning to harden into a warrior.

"My shah," Gold Dust began, "you, of course, are aware that Teymour is a renowned horse- and bowman."

"Yes, yes, we are. Do you know he invaded Esfahan, beheaded seventy thousand men, and constructed minarets from their skulls? In Neishabour and Harat, he erected lighthouses made of human skulls. This time we will display his own Tartar head!"

"And you are aware, my king, that he sent, with no remorse, his fourteen-year-old son to war."

The Shah stroked his falcons. "Rumors are dangerous. We don't pay attention to them."

Gold Dust heard the tremor in his voice; saw the flutter of the thumb that caressed the bird. "Are his handicaps and how he makes up for them rumors, too?"

"No, they are not."

Gold Dust went into a detailed account of the sword her mother had described that must have made up for the loss of the soldier's two right-hand fingers and conjectured on how he must have mastered the art of fighting by wielding the sword with his left hand. She described the stirrups—one side shorter—that held Teymour's injured right leg, and she reminded the Shah of what he must have known, that the Tartar was a man who never smiled.

"We will annihilate him with no difficulty," the Shah replied.

"Of course, my lord, I do not worry about your tactics. I am trying to grasp the mental state of a man who never laughs. He must be cold and ruthless. For him war must mean survival and death the climax of his life. Does any other solution ever form in his mind?"

"Other than?"

"Victory. Or death."

The Shah's fierce laughter sent the falcons into a flutter. Gold Dust lowered her eyes. Had she offended him? The falcons' heads stooped to touch the Shah's chest, and she realized his heartbeat must have escalated. Now he would banish her.

"My shah, may I share a detail you might find interesting?"

"Amusing! Yes, yes, continue!"

Gold Dust paused to allow the king time to collect himself, turn his ear to her, and maybe even prepare himself for his next response.

"Your Honor, Teymour the Lame detests sprigs of mint. Their sight brings tears to his eyes and causes his collapse."

"And why is that important?"

"I am not a soldier, my lord; you will know how to use this information."

The Shah heard Gold Dust confirm his own deductions, shape a formidable enemy he could not defeat unless he comprehended his every strength and weakness, and unless his empire supported him as one. But this last intimate detail was beyond his books and strategists.

"How did you find this out?"

"From my mother," she replied simply, the warmth in his eyes coloring her cheeks.

He, too, had learned a fact or two from Rebekah. Lately, led by the Master of Ceremonies, she had been allowed a few visits. He was beginning to trust her, sometimes more than his own men. She was bold and intuitive and now she had imparted another valuable piece of information to him.

He reclined on massive cushions. Removing the falcons from his forearm and shoulders, he set the three in her lap. She was not prepared for this tenderness and the upheaval it created in her. She could not suffer the love of two men. She pressed her lips on each of the falcons' heads. She bent toward the map at his feet. "It must be difficult to advance through these passes. Would you explain your plan to me?"

He drew a deep breath. "We will try in simple terms."

Gold Dust smiled gratefully. Who would have thought a bunch of herbs could soften the heart of her king?

They studied the sketch of Persia—an empire that possessed the manpower for the making of an army even greater than the one his father had boasted of. The Shah set to strengthen and unite his soldiers and was hoping to launch an attack against the invaders in six months.

"Our army will climb steep, rocky passes toward a strategic position from where we will attack the enemy exactly when it sets out to cross the valley toward the opposite stretch of mountains. In case the enemy attempts to advance up the mountains for a direct or flank attack on us, we will stop it at any price." He uncoiled one of her braids. "Our name will forever adorn history."

She cast her eyes down as she used to when she was infatu-ated by his power. "What about the beasts that spew poisonous gasses?"

He waved his hand, concealing the fear that the nameless had instilled in him. "It would be less difficult to destroy them than to fight our way up narrow passes that hardly accommo-date a single goat and around a volcano that spews fire."

As if his words had just sparked an idea, she asked, "Then why not use this fire against the enemy?"

It took him awhile to grasp the significance of a woman, still his favorite, having thought of a complex plan he and his strategists had been devising for months. She spoke with humility, as if the thought of using the rage of nature against the enemy were a simple recipe for halvah. She would have made a better partner than many of the cowards who sur-rounded him.

He explained how he had chosen the army's encamp-ment—a flat stretch of land, well hidden from the enemy by the colossal chain of the Alborz Mountains. One of his main concerns was whether the assault should take place in the evening when the enemy did not have the advantage of light in an unfamiliar terrain, or at dawn after the Persian army was rested from a long and arduous march.

"Speed is of the essence," the Shah said. "There is a chance of treachery among our own men." He remembered a past when soldiers in his father's army had joined the enemy in hope of extravagant rewards. But he had to wait for the beginning of spring to melt the ice from the tortuous paths of the mountains and to avoid the destructive avalanches. "We must sustain strict secrecy. Post pickets around the Rostam Valley to stop spies from sneaking in or out of the area."

After many long evenings with his military officers and with Gold Dust in the privacy of his quarters, the Shah had a solid strategy and an invincible army. The battle line of the Persians, now that it was assembled, would prove to be an undeniable force. "For the enemy who lacks the sophisticated tactics of our army," the Shah boasted, "attempt at retreat along those rugged passes would be disastrous."

And he did not reveal, even to Gold Dust, how her casual statement about a bunch of mint had sent his apothecaries into a frenzy of preparations to enhance his already complex and monumental war plan.

29

The ice began to melt on the mountains when agents of the Shah returned with news from the frontier. They had seen the strange creatures from afar as they held their daily practices around the hills.

"Contrary to rumor, they are tall," the agent announced, stroking his sparse beard with his plump, freckled fingers. "They have scaly chests, and although their bodies don't resemble the heavyset Tartars, they joust their swords and string their arrows as Tartars do. But, Your Honor, we can't explain the muzzles that spew gasses at intervals and why the fumes don't trouble their partners."

The Shah's shout drained the blood from the agents' faces. "What are we to make of this? Are these men? Half-men? Monsters? What lies under their masks?"

"We could not move closer," the agent replied. "If detected, we would have endangered our plan of secrecy."

In the space of fifteen days the entire empire lay under severe bondage, while the military recruited young men and supplies. Arms were fashioned, provisions stored, and taxes levied.

Tons of mint was gathered from farms and villages around the capital.

The Shah summoned the palace apothecaries and ordered them to concoct means to nullify the effect of the gasses.

Advised by his apothecaries, the king and his soldiers, for months, gathered around sulfuric bonfires to accustom their lungs to putrid vapors. They consumed powdered bezoar and hyacinth-stone with large amounts of freshly baked bread to be able to absorb toxic elements and to counteract the effect of the fumes.

The masters of artillery and the royal apothecary worked together to construct pebble-like balls made of phosphorous and combustible matter. Compressed into compact pellets and wrapped in nonflammable pouches, they were first soaked in the poisonous sweat from the back of green and black frogs. The pellets were then allowed to saturate for weeks in oak barrels filled with distillate of mint. Once the pouches found the enemy, they would bore deep holes and explode inside their bodies, releasing poisons into their bowels.

His eyes ablaze, the Shah declared he would personally lead his men into battle, and as hard as his generals tried to dissuade him, warning that he might endanger his life and consequently the unity of his army, he would not listen.

"My shah," Gold Dust pleaded. "Mongols make war as naturally as others make love. They cry when they drink wine and laugh when they wield the sword. You are your men's unifying force. You must live."

"Another one of your mother's tales?" The Shah growled, "We shall prove to future generations that Mongol warriors fell on their knees in front of this Shah." He slapped his chest, rising to indicate that the hours of debate were over. When the generals filed out of the hall, he held Gold Dust by the hand and led her to his private quarters.

Intoxicated with his new goal, he felt his past ardor return, and his body, which had for some time lost the strength and vigor to gratify her and had succumbed to need rather than to passion, now vibrated with life. She skipped around the maps that lay about and stepped out of her robes with such speed that she entangled herself and burst into laughter she had believed forgotten.

One by one, with unusual care, the Shah unraveled her garments. His gaze swept over her every strand of hair, her every alluring curve and slant. He caressed, smelled, and tasted her with the voracious appetite that emerges after long stretches of abstinence. He fell to his knees and pressed his lips to her thighs. The aroma of desire rose from her flesh. His forehead touched the ground under her feet.

Again, as in the past, they embraced with their eyes and wrestled with all their strength and made love with their every breath, their only audience three hooded falcons, blind to the couple's passion but listening intently to their desire.

Gold Dust tussled to blot out the image of Soleiman in the alley as she had last seen him, his outstretched hand, offering a branch of cherry blossoms. She relived the incident behind the baths, not the way it had transpired, but the way she had longed for it to happen. She would rush to him—her footfalls light—soaring—borne on a breeze—tossing her chador to the skies—her body soaking up the sunlight—drowning herself in him—free from her past and from her mother's clutch.

The Shah struggled against Gold Dust as she buried herself in Soleiman's arms.

Moaning at the strong flow that drained him, the Shah gripped her with his thighs in a painful embrace.

Soleiman the Agile lodged deeper in her soul.

Resting from their love struggle, she caressed the Shah and wished she had not, that day, surrendered to her mother and had instead trusted her own memories. She had sailed past the acrobat, her hips keeping rhythm to the beat in her chest. But the stunned glance she had thrown him had tattooed in her soul the image that would populate her nights and lock her womb to the Shah. She pressed her body to the Shah's to scare Soleiman away.

The king, in Gold Dust's arms, dreamed of Raven. In the royal kayak, they floated on the river. He pointed out species of trees that grew on the hills surrounding his palace. He labeled the numerous varieties that had invaded the land, some tall and fair with delicate branches, others stocky and tar-colored with heavy stumps. A howling wind had blown their germ from other shores, spreading their tentacles deep into Persian soil, finding permanent residence, assaulting the space of primal foliage, and infecting the natives with a peculiar malaise. The alien plants bore holes into the once-flourishing earth and strong gusts transformed the river into muddy, worm-infested torrents that overflowed, mounting the hills, up to the alabaster palace, and poured into the harem, snaking into Raven's quarters.

The echo of his nightmare resonating in his head, the Shah sprang up, groping for his scimitar. "Raven! Where is Raven?"

"It's only a dream," Gold Dust whispered, touching a finger to his lips. Raven everywhere, even in his nightmares. Gold Dust gathered her skirts and ran from the room.

The king's mouth clamped into a determined line; his eyes darkened. No invader would be allowed the abundance of Persian soil. He had summoned the help of every man and beast in his kingdom. Now he would demand the help of magic and spirits of the dead. Striding to the corner of his room, he yanked at a silk cord.

Narcissus appeared and waited, a shadow at the entrance.

The Shah signaled the eunuch to pick up one of the maps

that lay about the room. "We have to make sure our plan to vanquish the enemy is foolproof."

Narcissus knelt down and examined the symbols sketched on the frontiers of Persia and on the tortuous mountain paths. He recognized the favorite's fine strokes at the borders of the parchment, retracing the trails from which an attack by the army would take place. Had she helped devise this strategy, a direct assault on the army of Teymour the Lame, while he was trapped in the valley?

Rage flamed in the eunuch's putrefied guts. For months, war counselors, generals, the Shah, and his sultana had been planning war strategy without consulting him. The sultana had involved herself in matters she had no right to. Now it would be impossible to curtail her power. Narcissus fought to contain the bitterness about to spill onto the deerskin parchment. He raised his head and, summoning his courage, he announced, "Gold Dust, the favorite, must accompany Your Honor to battle."

Monumental quiet fell over the chamber. A breeze from the mountains agitated the curtains and fluttered the feathers of the falcons. The Shah pointed his finger dagger at the eunuch's eye. "Before we endanger the favorite's life, we will pluck out your eyeballs and feed them to the birds."

Unbelieving, the Shah stared at the dagger cap he aimed at the eunuch and confessed to himself that he was very close upon acting on his threat.

Narcissus rushed his words. "My lord, I would never suggest this unless I could assure the sultana's safety. I fasted for three days, anticipating a vision to illuminate a path to our success. I saw the favorite, on our fastest stallion, leading our army into a vast arena of fire and rubble and into the heart of the enemy. The favorite, the Persian army, and the enemy fought under a cloak of smoke. Then the favorite, a crown on her head, emerged from the inferno. She galloped victoriously, abandoning the enemy in their molten grave."

The Shah concealed his surprise. Unaware of his plan, Narcissus had had a vision of the enemy's demise in molten rubble.

Narcissus fell on his flabby stomach and kissed the tips of the Shah's slippers. "Your name shall live forever as the greatest Persian conqueror."

30

wo of the finest blacksmiths of the country labored for weeks to fashion silver-burnished armor with the likeness of the Shah embossed on the breastplate. The Shah surveyed the armor as he would a work of art, then descended in person to the royal coffers and chose a bejeweled belt that had once belonged to Alexander the Great and had brought the Macedonian leader great luck and unparalleled triumphs. The Shah handed the armor to Gold Dust with a gorget he had ordered to match the belt.

"You shall accompany us," he announced, turning on his heels.

She stood in a daze. Who could have persuaded the king to take her to war? It was a conspiracy. She must stop him. She rushed after him, tapping him on his shoulder. "My lord."

His boots drummed impatiently on the carpet.

"I won't go!" She stepped back from the anger in his eyes. "I can't leave Raven alone."

"She is more capable than most of us. She will take care of herself."

"She's only a young girl."

The king stared at his favorite's grip, but felt the soft touch of Raven's tongue graze his arm as if it were an accident she regretted. He heard her voice pleading in the garden where they walked, in the watchtower where they spied, near the fountain where they prayed: Take me with you, Pedar. I'll fight like a lion.

Gold Dust took a deep breath. "My lord, what would your men think of a woman escorting you? This behavior from a warrior they respect."

He bent his knees, his face a finger-space away from hers. Their eyes clashed. "You are not any woman. You are our favorite. We will do as we please with you. And no one would dare question us. And rest assured a squadron of our best men will protect you at all times."

She parted her lips to protest.

He was gone.

꧁

Gold Dust stepped into her suit of armor. Narcissus checked the fit of the helmet, the visor, and the knee pieces. He had an urge to yank the jeweled gorget from the sultana's neck and hide it with the secret treasure he had compiled throughout the years. He felt no guilt in stealing from those who were blessed. He needed all the luxuries in the world—sweets, spices, musk, and prying eyes—to fill up the bottomless well of his life. He touched impulsively the jar of brine, hanging from his waistband, his most cherished possession, which would ensure his transition to heaven. Men and women who were whole could never understand the bitterness in his curdled blood.

Holding up the sword he polished, he checked it for spots, the smallest specks of dust.

Gold Dust took the sword from him. "Narcissus, why didn't my mother come to say good-bye?"

The eunuch shuffled behind her to fasten the rear brace. "My lady, the departure of the army is top secret. I was ordered not to reveal it." At sunrise, he had left Rebekah's bed, his lust gland temporarily satiated. An alliance of rage, envy, and revenge had blasted his passion, leaving him breathless. When he had informed Rebekah that due to the extreme secrecy of the war strategies no stranger was allowed into the palace until further notice, he did not experience regret. His plan must be executed smoothly. Rebekah must remain ignorant of the cause of her daughter's death, so she would continue performing her miracles on his gland.

Gold Dust locked her buckler. It would be useless to ask Narcissus why the Shah had decided to take her to war. She must not provoke him now that she was leaving. She offered a forced smile. "I worry about Raven."

"My lady, I shall take care of her." Soon after the Shah had decided Gold Dust would accompany him to war, the eunuch had noticed the king avoiding Raven. He could not bear to admit to his daughter that he had succumbed to magic and to the help of women to win his battle. Raven had retreated into her own solitude. Now the eunuch would not have to deal with her curiosity while her parents were gone. He turned to lock the skull of Gold Dust's helmet to the visor.

She removed the helmet. "Every soldier will see that a woman accompanies the Shah to war."

Gold Dust noticed the eunuch's chin tremble and heard his teeth rattle. A spark lighted his lifeless eyes. The slimy octopus was imagining with pleasure another conflict between her and the Shah.

"*Khanom*," the eunuch said. "Do as you choose. You don't need advice from a half-man. Now I must rush to make sure your horse is readied and the saddle properly fastened."

Narcissus had ordered the saddle himself. The seat was

sturdy, sewed together in double stitches and with the thick-est horsehair, the reins of the strongest hide and decorated with gems. The girth was made of calfskin, the most inferior leather.

It would not hold a cat's weight, let alone the sultana's.

31

On the fourteenth of the month of Farvardin, followed by
the last trace of the winter winds, the Persian army embarked
on an arduous march toward the outskirts of the northern
mountains. The Shah had prepared well. It was an organized
force, and its like had never been seen in Persia or anywhere
else. Philosophers, historians, geographers, and scientific men,
such as botanists, were among the royal retinue. A most
revered man, Davoud the Red-Haired, a renowned scholar, was
among the civilians invited to join the troops. He kept a daily
journal, secured information about routes and camping
grounds, and recorded distances traversed. Following the soldiers came a train of sappers and miners skilled in the con-
struction of siege towers and rams on wheels, invented by a Jew
who had been forbidden to join the army.

Behind the final cavalry rumbled engines set up on giant
wheels and clad with hide, each with a row of catapults, massive open-jawed bows. Farther around the bends stretched hundreds of mules, carrying equipment for combat. Camels heavy
with tents and food supplies followed.

A company of royal pages, the finest marksmen in the army,

stood guard over the tents where the Shah and Gold Dust would sleep.

The Shah had sent the archers ahead to hold the enemy at bay if they changed plans and moved around the mountains in hope of trapping the Persians from behind.

Taking precautions to use stony tracks so the dust of their march would not alert the enemy, the army started up the mountains.

The left flank was held by Arsalan the Magnificent, a general who had defeated none other than the White Div, a giant whose scaly hide resisted the strongest impacts and whose only vulnerable spot was his navel. General Afrasiab, whose bellowing war cry had once, with one inhuman outburst, deafened the ears of a whole army of Macedonians, commanded the right flank. His sharp gaze could pierce through the surface of objects and uncover the truth beneath.

The side columns were two kilometers apart and much heavier than the center, which was intentionally thin and only a few ranks deep in order to deceive the opponent into attacking the center phalanx, after which the flanks would crush the enemy in a pinching motion.

The rear phalanx was commanded by General Darius, the war minister, a silver-haired, melancholy man known not for his strength but for his gentle ways and great wisdom and lack of desire to appear heroic. He was the oldest officer in the army and indispensable.

At his side, her braids unleashed into wild curls that tumbled to her waist, rode Gold Dust on the Shah's favorite stallion, Dor, a dumb but handsome animal, with hazel, blister-like eyes, snow-white mane, and a sweeping tail. Around them were the Shah's Imperial Guards, holding their leather-encased shields high overhead to protect the sultana.

The silver-haired general thanked Allah that the sultana's

burnished armor, gorget, belt, and her untamed curls were hidden by the raised shields and did not dazzle in the bright light.

The Shah on his midnight horse, two falcons poised on his shoulders, another on his heavily gloved arm, was in supreme command of the columns that filed toward the rocky plains of the Alborz Mountains to cover the embarkation of another portion of the army, which filed from behind the mountain range in a fork-like march. Next to the Shah rode his bow-and-arrow bearer.

Morning advanced and the sun appeared above the mountaintops, casting its rays into the valley and melting the mist.

The Damavand volcano towered behind, a tongue of smoke fuming from its crater.

After the army started its ascent and was well up the mountains, General Darius pointed at the lowest bend of the opposite stretch of mountains. "Our timing was flawless, my lady. See the last tail of the enemy disappear from that turn and appear from the other. They're pouring into the valley."

Gold Dust curbed her fear and savored this moment. Soon the enemy would be low in the valley and far enough from the Persians not to suspect their approach from behind the opposite chain of mountains. She covered her lower face against the rough winds and the stench that swept up. Even as she was awed by the soldiers who proceeded at the Mongol's war march pace of canter and walk and canter and walk, impressive when watched from afar, and even as she dreaded the creatures whose erupting fumes were coupled with monstrous roars, she was furious with the Shah. If he wanted her by his side, that's where she should be. Not in the rear, a useless ornament concealed by shields. She toyed with the idea of bolting through the protective circle.

General Darius reached out for Dor's reins. "My lady, settle

back. Under the sun you'll be a sure beacon to the enemy. Let
the Shah concentrate on the enormous task ahead."

The last trace of mist evaporated. The fawn-colored rocks
at the bed of the valley took shape and so did the massive
downpour of soldiers.

The Shah galloped around, reining his horse to a halt next
to General Darius. The general made a mental note to com-
mend the Shah, on a more appropriate occasion, on having
trained his birds to keep their balance without restricting his
movements.

"Look at the sons of dogs!" the Shah roared.

Below, an ocean of steel and leather stretched in the ancient
ravine of Rostam. The Arabs, Mongols, Teymour the Lame,
and his creatures had come together in a joint pact. The Persians had counted on fighting three separate groups of assailants
that had appeared to have no natural cohesion and were con-
tinually at odds. Now they faced a formidable and united army.

"What are these monsters?" the Shah asked. "They howl
like wolves and their shiny chests are like fish scales."

The general's voice was calm, with no trace of consterna-
tion. "We won't know until we get closer."

The Shah stared at the molten sea at his feet. The situation
was more dangerous than he had predicted. He did not know
whether to thank or curse his belief in the supernatural, which
had caused the hairless eunuch to influence him into bringing
Gold Dust along. Now, even if she proved to be the sole cause
of a spectacular triumph, he wished her safe in Pearl Hall. He
slapped the rump of his horse. The Imperial Guards stirred
their mounts and freed a passage for the Shah to approach his
favorite.

Dazzling with color and with the fierceness of her convictions, Gold Dust announced, "My shah, it's proper that I ride
by your side."

The Shah's horse stood nose to nose with the sultana's stallion. The king lifted his visor and locked his gaze with that of his favorite. In her defiance, she had bared her face and uncovered her hair, and she was more beautiful than ever. He could not bring himself to reprimand her. In an act of surpassing tenderness, he touched the tip of his sword to her epaulet.

She detected the scent of mint on the blade.

"Stay in the rear at all times!" he commanded.

Sacrificial sheep were brought and their throats slit to run sanctified blood over the path of the soldiers. The Holy Book was held high over the heads of the advancing men. Cries of "God is great!" bounced off the rocky cliffs.

General Afrasiab decided to keep his silence. It was not judicious to inform the king that his stare had traveled the distance and penetrated the helmets and masks of the creatures. To reveal what lay under these guises would only add fear and weaken the king's resolve. General Afrasiab turned away from the tribe of the Wolf-Men, who had yellow blood and were known to go through the ritual of sharpening their teeth at the age of eleven to initiate their boys into manhood and cannibalism to prey on people from other lands.

The center column of the Persians charged. One wing ready at the left, the other at the right, waited their time to move in to reduce the threat of hand-to-hand conflict between the center columns of the Persians and the enemy.

Taken by surprise from the rear, the enemy let out a ferocious war cry that struck the Persians with terror. With Teymour the Lame in command, the enemy advanced to music that set the alternate canter-walk-canter pace for the army behind. Mongols rode using the long stirrups, enabling the hard-riding bowmen to stand for better aim with their arrows.

Turbans flapping behind them, Arabs followed on horseback amid their continuous ululating battle cries.

Guttural snores originated from the belly of the creatures, reverberated in their masks, rising into a grating screech.

The Shah loomed at the head of his center phalanx. Although he had prepared for this moment, his eyes and lungs stung. He heard war cries; saw fierce faces, strong bodies, taut arrows. He sent a prayer to Allah, spirits of other worlds, powers of black magic, and to Raven. She was the single most valuable product of his life. He must live to savor the culmination of his toil.

He slapped his horse into a gallop and lunged headlong into the heart of the enemy, his men in close pursuit.

Amid whooshing winds, a myriad of fluttering wings darkened the valley. Flight after flight of arrows overlapped, assaulting the center column of the Persians.

The center column gave way before the best of the enemy, who, according to their custom, gathered heaviest in the center. Once the enemy had concentrated their force on the nucleus of the Shah's army, his side columns attacked with a sudden enveloping movement. A massive howl rose as the enemy felt itself being crushed from the flanks.

Excitement razing fear, Gold Dust grew bold. She deserved to ride in the open and observe their strategy unfold, to share in the credit. General Darius had not left her side. Soon he must. He was in charge of the Machine and time was of the essence.

The general glanced at the favorite, restless on her saddle, the reins coiling and uncoiling around her fingers, her boots tapping against her horse. Twenty guards surrounded her, but he did not dare leave. Her body quivered like an arrow strung to the limit and poised for release. "My lady, you've worked hard to assure our victory. One wrong move, one distraction, and we're doomed. Please stay under protection until my return."

Gold Dust relaxed her posture and bowed her head in obedience.

General Darius's horse galloped toward the giant war machine looming next to a deep underground abyss. Through holes at the sides of a crater, a constant draft flamed a roaring fire. A pile of stones scorched over the blaze. The general bent down and brought his palm close to the stones, feeling their heat. He raised his lance and with all his might cried, "Ya'Allah!"

A massive wooden ladle, contained with ropes and pulleys, creaked, slipped under the pile, loading a mound of scalding stones.

The general brought his lance down.

The soldiers severed the ropes. The coiled irons sprang loose. A hail erupted. Flaming orbs filled the mountains. A torrent of rocks charged into the valley. Horses of the enemies reared. Scorched bodies fell; barebacked animals bolted. The valley suffocated under noxious fumes.

Although the center column and the best warriors of Teymour the Lame had been weakened in the first round of attack, with the aid of the Arabs and Mongols he assembled his soldiers for another charge.

Teymour the Lame led the middle column. He wheeled around to outflank the enemy's left. The Shah rushed to send his soldiers to prevent the assault. Luring more of the Persians to the left, Teymour the Lame began thinning out their center. Then he called up the reserves and with himself at the head, cried out a curdling war yell and came thundering for the Shah.

The Shah faced the man who never smiled. A man with the face of shadows, prominent cheekbones, and hooded brows. A wide nose and flaring nostrils. Slanted eyes shiny as black marbles. A mouth pressed to a blade, framed by a thin mustache that hung down to his chin. In his dark eyes, which could cut through the heart of the boldest warrior, the Shah saw towers built with skulls of his people.

The Tartar did not face a feeble king. The Shah, poised on a most regal stallion, had the testament of war and death etched on his strong features. Teymour the Lame had committed a grave mistake. He had trusted his spies, who had drawn a languid Shah in love with roses, a man who, like women, turned his eyes away from executions, a man who had spent most of his youth in the debilitating confines of the Cage. Now the Tartar was forced to fight a formidable enemy, whose manner of fighting was a mystery, in face-to-face combat on unfamiliar terrain.

The Shah glared back at the warrior, at his right leg held in a stirrup shorter than the left, and the sword in the left hand. Although still a superb bowman, having lost two fingers from his right hand, the Tartar must not be the splendid swordsman he had once been. The Shah stirred his horse toward the Tartar's disadvantaged side. Drawing his sword, the Shah slashed his horse's rump and bolted to meet the leader. They locked in a ferocious fight, muscles strained, blades clashed, inhuman roars testament to iron wills.

Shrill screams burst against the mountains and reverberated inside the valley. A burst of Persian toxic arrowheads, with pierced holes that whistled and shrieked to scare the enemy, surrounded the Shah and Teymour the Lame. The Shah was prepared; so was his bow bearer. They held tight to their reins. Teymour the Lame's horse bolted. The Tartar lost his stirrups. He struggled to curb the animal. With acrobatic suppleness, he dodged the blade of the Shah and the Persian arrowheads. During another avalanche of stones from the Machine, the Tartar backed off down the valley to ready himself for another assault.

He faced another devastating scene.

The pellets the royal apothecaries had constructed hit the Wolf-Men. Once the distillate of mint and phosphorus mixed with fumes of jealousy and the acids of hatred that brewed inside the Wolf-Men, they erupted into lethal explosions.

With thunderous groans the beasts fell. Their masks cracked at the seams and scattered about. Fragments of flesh, hot gravel, and splatters of amber blood flecked the surroundings.

The Shah recognized the tribe of the Wolf-Men, who had thin blood, wiry red hair, and sun-starved faces. Their green, bulging eyes had no whites to soften the violence in them. Snout-like noses and flared nostrils emitted noxious gasses. Sharpened teeth glared in the sun. They came from wet and cloudy climates, where women did not cover their faces and were permitted to roam freely among men. They came from a kingdom surrounded by water and without fertile land to till and cultivate fruits and grains, so they plundered and invaded other worlds to pillage and sack their goods.

These were resourceful soldiers, the Shah realized. They concealed their faces to hide their identity, aware of the disadvantages of fighting the unknown.

Once again, the Shah faced Teymour the Lame. The king saw that his favorite had recounted the fact. Tears splashed down the warrior's face and further handicapped him. The anger of the past apparent on him, the Shah kneed his horse toward the Tartar, and lunged. Blades clanged and rang in a furious clash. The king aimed his sword at Teymour's right stirrup and severed the leather straps.

Teymour the Lame lost his balance, swayed on his saddle, wiped his eyes. Tears flowed down his cheeks and darkened his leather breastplates. His leg dangled against his mount. Prone on his horse, he goaded his mount into a canter down the valley and away from the Shah, where the Persians had gathered force again.

From his vantage, the Shah glared at the leaders of the Mongols, Arabs, and Teymour the Lame. This was his moment. All three warriors faced him. The Shah's bow bearer reined his mount to an easy trot next to the king.

With no more time than the fleeting seconds of thought to act, the Shah felt his heartbeat begin to mount. He thought of his empire, of the constant invasions that had robbed her dignity, of the tribe of the Wolf-Men and their insatiable greed, and of the many years of lost youth in the Cage. His heartbeat accelerated. The falcons bowed their heads to their master's chest. They flapped their wings against the leather straps. In three fast motions, he lifted the hoods off the falcons' heads. A soft tune he whistled kept them in place. He pulled the brails, freeing their claws. The bow bearer recognized his cue. He aimed his bow. Three scented arrows shot toward their targets.

The falcons trailed the odor. Each pursued an arrow. They flew with the speed of wrath, soaring in wider spirals, in greater swiftness, assaulting the air, the howl of the wind behind them. Within a few palms of their quarries, they snapped back their wings. A flash of feathered lightning; they aimed their sharp claws and darted down.

The birds were fast, their aim accurate. The leaders of the enemy fought with their swords to fell the falcons. They staggered, let go of their blades. Their hands sprang to their eyes. Blood gushed from empty sockets. They fell from their horses. The earth was soaked crimson.

Claws loaded, the falcons soared back, tearing the air with their beaks. The wind gave way. Closed behind the birds. Propelled them onward. Each falcon released two offerings into the Shah's palm. He placed the veined, gelatinous balls in a silver box and into his pocket. Trophies of war to present to Raven. The birds settled on his shoulders and arm.

Chaos erupted in the valley. A headless dragon, the enemy drowned in its own turmoil.

The Imperial Guards who surrounded Gold Dust raised their shields and thundered a cry of victory. Gold Dust flicked at the reins. She dug into the stallion. Charged past the guards toward the base of the mountain and the Shah. Hair flying, the breeze stinging her eyes, she strained to clear a path. She had not realized how far she was from the foot of the mountain. But she would manage. Her heart felt solid in her chest. Her hands were steady. Surveying the scene around her, she goaded Dor forward. So quick had been the advance that the Persians had suffered little. In the valley, the enemy scurried to amass their power and ready themselves for another attack. Useless. They would rise no more.

Her body slipped to one side. The saddle swayed. It seemed to slide from under her. Her heart fluttered. The ground shook. Rocks tumbled. She was losing her grip. She let go of the reins, pulled herself up, and grabbed the horse's mane. She had not been prepared with powdered bezoar and hyacinth-stone to bear the putrid gasses. Her lungs would have burst if not for the soothing effect of essence of mint that infused the air.

Down below, the king was about to give his last signal. She knew every detail intimately. This would be the lethal blow. Where did the saddle go? She clung to Dor's mane, her thighs gripping his panting flanks, his eyes two trembling blisters. Narcissus had checked her saddle. These things were not supposed to happen to the favorite. The animal's mane cut into her palms. Her fingers were bleeding, losing their grip. The stallion was defeating her. Her bones felt hollow. Hopeless isolation replaced her marrow. She was alone among the Persians, towering mountains, the volcano. Not even the music of her bones. Only the thunder of her heart.

The king raised his sword.

A battalion started to ascend the mountains toward the back of the Damavand volcano. The rest of the army circled the Alborz Mountains, away from the canyon. Engineers who had for months dug trenches to redirect lava down the sides of the mountains scrambled out of their hiding places. Cranes lifted boulders that had for years directed the constant flow of lava toward man-made paths away from the valley.

An echo spiraled up the volcanic crater and convulsed against the feverish mouth. A column of ancient smoke ascended. Havoc flowed down from the northern slopes. Horses bolted, muzzles frothing. The trapped enemy rushed to one side of the valley. Others scampered up the opposite direction. In a body the men dashed back to the center. There was no escape. Lava flowed down from all directions.

A molten river snaked down the valley—liquid iron on the move and gone wild, an immense rush of scalding fire; everything in its path smoldered, bursting into flames, sputtering when coming in contact with terrified bodies.

A scorching cloak of gray buried man and beast.

32

Rebekah embarked on a visit to the harem. Since the eunuch had last called upon her, nightmares had overwhelmed her sleep. She could not take her mind off the shrouded look on the eunuch's pig-eating face.

The guards at the palace portals unlocked the gate. She gazed into their eyes and fear churned at the pit of her stomach. She planted a kiss on each of their noses. "What's the problem, sweetloves? Have you lost your mistresses to the black plague?"

"Not us," one of the guards replied. "But you might lose your daughter to Teymour the Lame and his beasts."

Rebekah slumped on the dirt, her tongue unable to form a single word. Gold Dust had never even whispered the possibility of going to war! "I'm not through with you, Narcissus," Rebekah murmured, rising and dusting herself off. Untying her bundle, she searched among her fabrics, finding the velvet pouch that held her valuable baksheesh. She did not know what awaited her in the harem and it was wise to remind the guards of her friendship. She offered each man a roll of opium.

She ran through the halls, burst into the harem, and stopped in the center of the main vestibule, as if it were her private domain. Her heart twisting like laundry wrung by the riverside, she shouted at the top of her lungs: "Narcissus!"

The name reverberated against marble columns but did not startle the sultanas out of their languor and narcotic trances that drained them of petty concerns.

Honey murmured from a smoky corner, more to herself than to anyone else, "The news reached you, at last."

Followed by murmurs afloat on hashish breezes, Rebekah marched through the halls, into the quarters of the eunuchs, and burst into Narcissus's room. He lay on his mattress, a sickly pallor on him, clutching a gerbil. Disbelief swept over her as she stared at his drugged eyes and sweat-drenched face. Disgust contorted her face. She spat on his naked body. "You miserable low pervert! And I expect *you* to protect my Gold. You don't even know what's good for yourself!"

He hurled the animal at her feet and cowered under the bedspread to shield himself from her assault of curses.

With her sandals, she kicked the squeaking gerbil, then bent and touched the eunuch's cheek so softly, he slackened his grip off the edge of the blanket. Her voice was slippery and scathing. "You're blushing! I didn't think blood flowed in your rotten veins. Next time use desert rats. They're larger, hungrier; they'll tear you apart."

He whimpered; ejected beastly sounds; pulled the covers over his head.

"Get up, Narcissus! Did you think rats could find your lust gland? Did you think you were done with me? Why did you send my daughter to war?"

He bolted upright. "That's a lie! Who told you that?"

"Sweetlove," she whispered, easing down to the edge of his mattress and rebelling against the fatal vapors of his body. "Don't make me yank the truth out of you. I'm tired."

"It was the Shah's decision."

"You lie," Rebekah said, glancing around the room. "I know the Shah. He's the slave of words. Did yours sway him?"

"Gold Dust convinced him to take her."

"Why would she?"

"To share in the trophies of war. To ride next to her man. You are more competent in deciphering love. . . ."

"Was it love? Is this the truth?" She glimpsed the top of the divan, where a low table held the eunuch's jug of water, bowl of raw sugar, opium suppositories, and a silk sash. Her glance rested on the sash. "Accept my apologies," she purred. "My blood is too quick to boil. When will the army return?"

"Allah knows it might take weeks before they reach the mountains. The trip back depends on the outcome of war, the weather, and the condition of the soldiers."

Her hand slithered under the covers. "Why didn't *you* warn me?"

"I didn't know." He sighed as Rebekah found him.

"Poor Narcissus, the gerbils tore you to pieces." She shifted to the head of the mattress. "Some opium to ease the pain." Her hand slid over the sash, lay briefly on a hard object under it; a tap of her fingernail told her it was glass. Her fingers crawled away and into the bowl of opium, selected three dome-shaped pieces. Inserted one after the other.

He sprang up, terrified. "Not two, I'd never wake."

She pushed him back on the mattress. "It was one, sweet-love."

Her fingers grazed his buttocks, which trembled like mounds of lard, kneaded his shoulders as she hummed a soft tune, checking his breathing, the movements of his puffy lids. "Where is Raven?"

He fought to raise his languid eyelids. "In the gardens or the watchtower. . . ."

His chest settled into rhythmic purrs. The occasional convulsion of his fingers betrayed the rush of opium in his blood. Rebekah brought her ear to his mouth. "Narcissus?" she whispered. "Sweetlove?"

His nose ejected whizzing sounds. The beat of his heart was steady. A screeching snore startled her and sent the gerbil scurrying for shelter. Deep opium sleep had overcome him. Rebekah approached the stool. Her hand rested on the object under the sash. Lifting the stretch of yellow satin, she smiled to herself. His pickled organ was safe in brine. She grabbed the jar and stuffed it in her bundle. Storming into the gardens, she searched for Raven.

Raven slumped on a stone bench; peacocks roamed around her. Rays of sun tumbled on her hair. There was no sign of her once spirited grandchild. Her eyes were dull, her hands limp at her sides, her lips lifeless and cracked. Rebekah gathered her in her arms.

"My father invited my mother to war and now I'm so thirsty. I gave him courage. But he took her."

"Child, the thirst is in your mind. Neither the sun nor your father caused it, but your own unhappiness. Don't rely on others to quench your thirst. You want to fight? Come with me. I'll show you a world where every breath is an endless fight."

୨୨

The One-Eyed Rabbi kissed the single scroll of the Torah, housed in a tall wooden casing that stood on a wide shelf in the ark above the pulpit. With only a single Torah, his spacious ark was pitifully bare. If he had had the means to obtain six more holy books for his synagogue, he would have been a contented man. He bowed reverently to the Torah, shut the doors of the ark, shuffled around and leaned on his cane, squinting to bring into focus the blurry images impinging upon the sanctity of his temple. Before he could place her, he recognized the offensive shimmering of her chador, the impudent tap of her sandals, and the shameless halo of her golden curls. He pounded his cane on the pulpit, his frail body swaying like a willow branch. "Impure woman! How dare you come here?"

Rebekah approached the pulpit, Raven marching by her side and observing this curious world through the slits in her mask. The strangeness of the dusty alleys intoxicated her, the shabby synagogue, the One-Eyed Rabbi who shook with anger and age as if he would die in front of her eyes.

"I've come to beg for shelter," Rebekah shouted for the rabbi to hear her.

The One-Eyed Rabbi brought a fingertip to the corner of his sightless glass eye and wiped a lingering tear. "Wash your mouth! Don't utter such blasphemy. This place shelters angels and their holy books, not whores!" His hand sprang up to his mouth as if to shove back the word he had just vomited.

Rebekah had an urge to bare one shoulder, to narrow her eyes and lower her lashes, maybe whisper in his ear promises of fulfillment. "Soon the palace guards will be after us. They'll hang us. A temple is a house of mercy. Where else could we go?"

"What have you done now?"

"I have loved," she declared.

"Bite your indecent tongue back!" He limped down from the pulpit. "Not only have you slept with our own but with the uncircumcised. That's what you've done!" He slapped the crown of his head, where a skullcap clung to a few gray hairs. "Woe unto me and unto my ancestors for uttering such words in the dwelling of the Lord." He pointed a gnarled finger at her. "Remove your unholy self!"

Rebekah grabbed Raven's arm and swept past the kneeling rabbi to the end of the hall, thrust aside a single flap of cloth that separated the hall of prayer from the rabbi's private quarters, and settled on a straw mattress in the center, Raven by her side.

Rebekah's hand fluttered on her brand, the padlock of her memories. In this synagogue, her mother had once held a parchment, a decree to end her childhood, proof that Jacob the Fatherless had taken her as his wife. Neither she nor her mother could have predicted the cruel abruptness with which Jacob would end her innocence.

Now, her mettle hardened by the rancor of time and bent on twisting religion to her fancy, she had returned with her granddaughter, the Princess of Persia.

The rabbi lifted his hands in a prayer and thanked the Lord for sending the whore away. Wobbling to his feet, he limped to his room, which held a mattress, a washbasin, a few prayer books, and an oil burner for light, heat, and cooking. He bent close to Rebekah's face. His hands shot up to his eyes to erase the image of the barefaced woman, her mouth the color of evil. Sickly heart beating against his bony chest, he mumbled a chain of absolving prayers to a Lord who had forsaken him.

Rebekah nudged Raven, who removed her mask, suddenly transformed into the image of virtue. "Will you offer this child to the butchers?"

He flapped his hands in the air and called out to the ceiling: "She's like cotton! The curse of the parents shall descend upon their offspring."

A grape-wine flush darkened Raven's cheeks. She planted her palm on the back of the rabbi's neck and forced him into obeisance. "Express the proper respect to your future queen. We are staying and that's it." She spread her chador on the mattress and lay down next to her grandmother.

33

$\mathcal{N}$arcissus's eyes sprang open. His body, heavy as lead, buzzed as if ants swam in his blood. His stare turned to the mantelpiece to check the hourglass. Had the sun risen and set once, twice, or three times? He extended a hand to the table at the head of his mattress and with much difficulty lifted the jug of water and emptied it on his face. Gasping, he tried to recall the past days: The Shah had gone to war with Gold Dust. He had visited the stables and had chosen Dor, the fastest and dumbest purebred. Rebekah had come to visit. He sighed. The opium. She had used more than one suppository. His mouth was as dry as an ink blotter. Rebekah was here. She had inserted the opium. No, he had. When did she leave? Had he helped plan the war strategy? Gold Dust would never return. Not with the inferior girth and the stallion's speed and temperament. His lust gland throbbed. His rectum burned.

He must go to the baths to wash off the stink of opium, blood, and rodent. Blurry-eyed, he stepped into his pants and buttoned his vest. Reached out for his sash. Snatched his hand back. He stared, stunned. The stretch of satin lay flat, lifeless. His jar!

They cut him from the roots. Clean-cut. They offered him his manhood pickled in brine. Be thankful, they had said. He would enter the other world a whole man, virgin angel-houris of paradise and a myriad of concubines would lick the soles of his feet.

He flapped the sash in the air. Threw himself on the stool. The jar! His hands plunged into the water jug. Bowls of sugar and opium crashed to the ground. Shards of glass cut his feet. He dove under the covers, searched beneath the stool. Falling on the chest of clothing, he flung red, yellow, and green pieces about the room. "I'm doomed!" he shrieked, bashing his head against the wall.

✺

Narcissus dug his heels into the ribs of his panting mount as he cursed the world and all its inhabitants. He could not believe Rebekah's audacity. She had led Raven through the main gates of the palace in clear view of the guards. She had become so powerful the guards did not question her. His horse squeezed through the narrow alleys of the Jewish Quarter. The populace scurried away, recoiling from the steaming breath of the animal and from the obscenities that spilled out of the eunuch's eggplant-colored lips.

Coming to a dusty halt in front of Rebekah's house, he sprang from the saddle and with all his might charged against the door that had once sheltered his most intriguing fantasies. His shrill screams sent a pack of hungry dogs yelping for shelter; a cloud of flies buzzed around his ears. Rebekah's door stared back unyielding.

He vaulted back onto the saddle and galloped toward the pit, the heart of the Quarter, where news of local happenings first circulated. The massive horse circled the pile of garbage as the eunuch cried at the top of his lungs: "Hear ye! Hear ye! A worthy reward awaits anyone who reveals Rebekah the Bundle Woman's hiding place."

Like metal eyes, the stalls slammed down their lids. The owners found it prudent to shut their stands as a safety measure against a foreboding in the air.

His nostrils flaring, the eunuch shouted Rebekah's offense: "The whore kidnapped Princess Raven. If she isn't found before the Shah's return, the Quarter will be set on fire."

More booths shut down and the owners stole away through back doors. Peddlers held tight to their sacks of goods and hurried from the bazaar. Wives latched padlocks to their homes. Wet-nurses stuffed their nipples into mouths of infants to stop their crying. Rodents and stray dogs that fed on the garbage scampered away.

"Honorable *Agha*, are you looking for Rebekah the Bundle Woman?"

The eunuch stared down at a heap of flesh stuffed in a wheelbarrow. An emaciated man who seemed on the verge of abdicating his last breath lugged the wheelbarrow. An acidic smell rose from the woman as she struggled to control a phlegmy cough that shook her bloated folds.

Narcissus checked her suspiciously. "Where's Rebekah the whore?"

The emaciated man unfastened the leather straps from his waist and collapsed on the ground. "Heshmat," he pleaded. "Let's mind our own misery."

"Shut up or I'll cut off your tongue," the matchmaker shrieked, turning to the eunuch, a sudden smile contorting her face. "Respectful *Agha*, my husband is a simple man; he doesn't understand. I, on the other hand, am Heshmat the Matchmaker. I'm the glue between men and women, familiar with the mysterious labyrinths of love." She lowered her voice. "Many years ago, I thought of marrying Rebekah's daughter to a respectable butcher, but I decided she was destined for a better life. I was right."

Hugging her ankle in his bony clutch, her husband groaned, "Please, Heshmat, don't sell your own people to goyim."

Narcissus fished into the pockets of his pants and presented a fistful of sovereigns. "Tell the truth. You'll get more."

The matchmaker snatched the coins and stuffed them under the folds of her stomach. "Take the alley on your right. At the end, you'll find the synagogue of the One-Eyed Rabbi. Moses protect your every step."

☙

Rebekah heard raging curses, violent hooves, neighing horse. She slipped the jar of brine in her pocket and hurried into the main sanctuary. Her fingers locked around Raven's wrist, feeling the pounding of her pulse. "Calm down, child."

An impish smile leaped on Raven's lips. "*You* be calm, Grandmadar."

The clatter of hooves came to a halt at the door. Rebekah heard the shake of the horse's bridle and knew that the eunuch had dismounted. She started up the stairs of the pulpit toward the ark and opened the double doors. Raven climbed the ark and flanked one side of the Holy Book; Rebekah huddled on the other side and brought the screens together.

The eunuch's holler advanced as he ran into the synagogue and approached the pulpit. "Rebekah! Give back what is mine and you're free."

The commotion brought a pleasing wetness under Raven's tongue, calmed the thirst that had overwhelmed her since her father's departure. She pressed one ear to the partition. The tap, tapping of a cane on the stony floors punctuated the eunuch's shouts.

The voice of the One-Eyed Rabbi struggled through his weak lungs. "You are in the house of God. Do not mention the name of whores."

"You have given sanctuary to one, old man," Narcissus cried out. "Now you cringe at the mention of her name?"

The cane pounded the floor. "Who gave you this blasphemous information?"

Rebekah smiled. Maybe, after all, she had found God in a glass-eyed rabbi.

"That does not matter," the eunuch squealed.

"But it does, my friend. I have many enemies around here—as all men of God do. We try to bring order to the community; order is restrictive; men rebel against it. An enemy must have lied to you."

"Out of the way, old man!"

Rebekah and her granddaughter heard footsteps, one soft and hesitant, aided by the cane, the other fast and angry, propelled by loss, striding around the sanctuary—into the single room—back into the hall. Voices neared—climbed up the steps—onto the pulpit—came to a stop in front of the ark.

"What's in here?"

"The holy Torah."

"Let me see this book of yours," the eunuch ordered.

The rabbi half-opened the two flaps of the ark to reveal the Torah standing high at the center of the ledge.

The eunuch gauged the size of the Torah. If the scrolls were removed from the wooden casing, Raven could hide in there. "What's inside?"

"No one is allowed to unlock it."

"Move. I'll open it myself."

The rabbi's voice became strong, blotting out the quiver of

age. "You'll have to kill me before you touch and defile the Torah, and you'll never get out alive."

"Are you insinuating that *you* will kill me?" The eunuch's laughter grated against Rebekah's eardrums.

"No," the rabbi replied. "The Jews will."

"Unlock the casing yourself!" the eunuch snickered. "Protect it from the infidel touch."

The rabbi shrieked, "I cannot! Only the Cohanim, our holy leaders, can touch the scroll. If anyone who has sinned sets eyes on the Torah, he will be struck down."

Rebekah felt the rush of blood in her temples. She imagined the two men facing each other, one, whose faith in his Holy Book had transformed him into a warrior, the other, a believer of black magic, his soul a fertile ground for terror.

The rabbi's voice resonated: "If you've never sinned, come forward and unlock the casing."

Rebekah heard the shuffle of the eunuch's slippers, the labored breathing of the One-Eyed Rabbi. She flattened herself against the walls of the ark, holding tight to one flap of the door, Raven to the other. Would the eunuch dare remove the book from its sanctuary? It was heavy; he would have to struggle under the weight, and in the process fling the doors of the cabinet wide open and discover them there.

Narcissus scratched at the knob, cupped the polished wood in his palm, turned it a notch, paused, as if expecting some admonishment from a Supreme Being.

The doorknob squeaked dryly.

The rabbi's voice became weak. "You won't dare."

Narcissus cleared his throat. "I am the chief eunuch—I'll do as I please."

A deep baritone rumbled inside the ark, rising with stupendous force and echoing off the corners of the hall. "Beware of the Lord!"

The rabbi fell down, burying his head between his arms to plug his ears from Jehovah's wrath.

The eunuch let go of the knob, inching backward, away from the ark.

"Narcissus!" the voice blared. "Of all the sins thou hast committed, this one I shall not forgive. Depart from my temple and never darken it again!"

Rebekah heard the rabbi's sobs, the eunuch's harried footsteps retreating down the steps, subsiding. She could imagine the spark of triumph in Raven's eyes. Bless her mischievous heart.

Rebekah waited for the rabbi to leave. He had not detected herself and Raven in the ark. No need to add yet another offense to his sacred convictions. She would return later and offer him a bouquet of mint.

The rabbi tapped on the doors. "Rebekah, my son lives close by. His place is safe. If the Lord finds it proper to raise His voice in your presence, who am I to send you away."

34

From his vantage, on the peak of the mountain, the Shah searched for Gold Dust. He would share his intoxicating triumph with his favorite. The universe was at his feet, the clouds his crown, the enemy vanquished under the scorching vomit of the volcano. If only his father were here. Even with madness distorting his faculties, he would have applauded his son's victory.

If only Raven were here. Her praise would have been sweeter than the music of houris. The two of them were of the same blood, but she was merciless, strong, and courageous. His character had been formed by the solitude of the Cage, hers by the heritage of her ancestors. When he returned to the city, he would discuss the future with her. He had promised to raise her as a man, strong and ruthless, and able to protect herself. Yes, he confessed to himself, he had. He did not want to repeat his late father's mistake. Smother his daughter's soul in the dungeon of solitude. He would allow her free rein to act upon her ambitions. She was capable of handling bolder experiences. His late father's blood flowed in her veins.

He would allow her to choose her man. He would endure

his pain at having to share her with another and accept her gratitude as his reward.

A dead crow crashed in front of the horse, a stain of black feathers on rusty rocks. Vultures swooped down and fought over the bird. They were everywhere—the cities, deserts, mountaintops—a bad omen, these funereal birds. Why this premonition after such victory? He tore his eyes from the carcass and cast them upon the horizon. Gold Dust's chestnut stallion stood barebacked against the skyline. General Darius's horse grazed nearby. The imperial guards had lowered their shields. The Shah's brows came together.

He spurred the stallion into a gallop around the rocky pass, where hooves of beasts had worn the steep tracks. Amid a cloud of dust, he drew the reins next to the two idle mounts, leaped from the saddle, and dashed toward the general and the royal guards.

Gold Dust lay at their feet like a heap of burnished metal on a boulder. Her body sprawled on the rock at strange angles—arms twisted, legs tangled. None had dared remove her armor, which seemed the only support that held her together. Her eyes were shut.

The Shah fell down on his knees. How could she have died? How could Allah defeat him after such a triumph? Damn Narcissus! Damn himself for following a eunuch's advice. The Shah cupped Gold Dust's head in his hands.

A torrent of tears splashed down her cheeks. The king's heart raced with fresh hope. This must be a good sign. He had never seen her cry before. He passed his fingers over her face and neck, felt her skull for fractures. He did not dare remove her armor. Why was her body so twisted? Even the worst fall could not have broken so many bones. The armor should have protected her. She must live, he repeated to himself, as if the words had healing powers.

"I lost my saddle." Pain contorted her face. "My bones feel heavy."

Head bowed, General Darius stood behind Gold Dust. Her saddle dangled from his hand. He had checked the favorite's saddle and had noticed the inferior girth. The general decided to spare the king more grief and keep this knowledge a secret until the army returned.

Refusing help from his men, with great care, the king removed Gold Dust's gorget and breastplate. She gazed at him, melancholy tears washing down her face.

"You have to see the graveyard of the enemy," he said.

At the sight of her body, his face went white. He recoiled in horror at what was left of her once inviting curves. Her spine was a pliable bow that could not support her body. Her arms and legs lay useless at her sides.

She shut her eyes, tears spilling out. "I can't stop crying."

The army hakim examined her. His brow creased in thought. It was as if the favorite's bones had turned to rubble. Had an obscure disease putrefied her bones, robbed their sturdiness, changed their consistency? He knelt and smelled her joints. The scent of roses emanated from her. He located her heart and heard a strong beat. He plucked a weed from the rocky cracks and made her blow on it. The strength of her exhalation was proof that her lungs were not punctured. He remained in silent meditation. Then he faced the Shah. "Your Honor, in my long years of practice, I've never encountered anything like this. Something beyond the fall has gone wrong, something inside the favorite's body. We have to speed back and seek additional advice."

A stretcher was constructed to hold Gold Dust. An awning overhead kept away the fierce sun. The water bearer with his donkey walked by her side and sieved water through charcoal to purify it and quench her thirst.

Amid inaccessible clefts of rock, where hardly a passage might be secured to allow two soldiers to march side by side, the procession of mournful victors began their descent toward the capital. The same route they had taken some time ago now seemed impassable, lined with narrow brooks that carried black cholera, intestinal worms, and lasting fevers caused by the many corpses.

When the melancholy look in Gold Dust's eyes turned to resignation, the Shah lifted her from the stretcher and carried her on his lap upon the horse. When night fell and the sky grew diaphanous, the king furled the awning, so she could count the stars and follow the transformation of the moon.

She gazed overhead. "I feel such despair. The tears I prayed for won't stop now."

He ran a lock of her hair between his fingers and tugged at it softly. "We will invite the best hakims. They will find a cure."

She sighed. "What's the cure for bones that once sheltered emotions?"

The Shah snapped his visor shut and made a disjointed sound of grief, his metallic sobs reverberating inside the helmet. "There must be a cure for a sultana at whose feet the Shah prostrates himself."

But Gold Dust knew that this time the powerful king and all the wealth in his coffers could not heal her. The fall could not have been the only cause for her broken bones. For years, she had listened to the grievance in her marrow as she longed for the love of a humble acrobat, as her mother plunged deeper into her own obsession, as a daughter with no color and with strange passions was born to her, and as she watched her man drown himself in his own daughter, her Raven. Now her bones had, at last, surrendered, like grief-stricken hearts. She averted her eyes from the Shah's. Too late, his tears had lost their healing power.

The army neared the base of the mountains. The narrow passes gave way to goat tracks. On his black stallion, the Shah loomed restless against the gray dusk, or the blush of dawn, as he spurred his soldiers on. Behind him, mountain ranges caught the faint light of the moon or the gold of a rising sun absent of resurrecting power.

During the day, they stopped to replenish their goatskins with water from *ghanats*, or to shoot mountain goats for food. The few hours they rested, watch fires scared wild animals away.

At night the Shah was a dark silhouette pacing the campsite, the breeze shuffling his hair. Occasionally, the tinkling of camel bells punctuated the stillness of the night. The gruff calls of muleteers and the despondent caravan song of men of the desert left behind faint echoes and the grief of an impatient Shah, awaiting daybreak to resume the march, while the ponderous silence and the never-ending tears of the favorite pressed on everyone's heart.

The triumphant army of Persia entered the capital. But there was no sign of gaiety on them. In his eagerness to reach his palace, the king had pushed his men to the limit. Their faces were caked with dust and streaked with fatigue. The horses fought for breath, their mouths foaming, their hooves worn down to the frogs. The populace came out with jugs and filled the helmets of the soldiers with fresh water. Ice flowers floated in the air and rosewater was sprinkled against clattering hooves. Eunuchs of the palace adorned the horses with shimmering cheek rosettes and bridles fringed with silver bullion. Men and women prostrated themselves at the sight of their king.

A whisper originated from one mouth to another and turned into a moan that threatened to poison the fragrant air.

"Is that General Darius at the head of the army?"

"Why is he carrying a saddle on his back?"

"Who is that lifeless body on the Shah's lap?"

"Is she the favorite?"

"Gold Dust!"

The funereal words floated on the wind past Rouh'Allah the Spirit of God's gardens, past the Ancient Zoroastrian's home, past the temple of the One-Eyed Rabbi, and entered the house of the rabbi's son.

Rebekah thanked him, left Venus in his yard, and took the road to the palace with Raven.

It was a long, arduous path filled with people and their words. "The Shah and his men just passed the gates of the city."

"The enemy is vanquished, but the Shah forbade any show of merriment."

Rebekah grabbed one of the soldiers by the arm and asked, "Why?"

"No one is to celebrate the fall of Arabs, Mongols, and Teymour the Lame until the favorite recovers."

The words gnawed at Rebekah's heart. Meaningless gossip. Jealous rumors. Gold Dust was well, she assured herself. She had borne with dignity the brand that heralded her daughter's birth. She had spread her legs to men who smelled of iron, lard, and greed so she could support Gold Dust. She had pressed her mouth to the stinking crack of a eunuch to secure her daughter's future. Her journey must have a different meaning, a different ending. Her daughter would not die in a senseless war.

"Where's Narcissus?" she asked the soldier.

"There's rumor he could not greet the king because he had come down with high fever and great abdominal pain."

The slimy snake was aware that no ailing man, whatever his sin, would be punished and executed before he was ready to stand trial. He wouldn't get away so easily. She would make sure of that. Let him hide. She had his treasure. He would come calling for it.

Because they were cloaked by their veils, none recognized Rebekah and Raven as they pushed their way among the foot infantry. Rebekah struggled to hold on to Raven, who, unaware that the column was many *farsangs* long, was eager to run to the head of the procession and to her father.

She longed to wipe off the smile splashed on Raven's face, press her palm to her mouth and plug the hum in her throat, shackle her legs to stop her dancing gait. Did her granddaughter not realize the enormity of her fear?

Raven buzzed in her ear, "Grandmadar, we won the war. Don't be so sad. No one has won a battle without losing a few lives."

Rebekah's hand shot up and came down against Raven's cheeks. "She is my daughter!"

"And my mother," Raven replied, the imprint of Rebekah's hand a spreading scorpion on her cheeks. "To sacrifice both for the empire is no great loss," she announced, bolting toward the palace.

A white cloud formed behind Rebekah's eyes, turning her mind blank. Nothing mattered, save the effort to move her legs.

A man muttered at her side. What did he say? Did he address her? Nothing mattered. She rushed her steps. A tap on her shoulder. She elbowed the man away. She must move forward.

"I have an urgent message for you."

Rebekah's fist closed over a note the man forced into her palm. Nothing mattered. He held her arm. She jerked around to face him and had a feeling that in a past she would rather forget, she had seen this man. What did he want from her? Even now, they would not leave her alone. She plunged through the chaos toward the palace, oblivious of the elbows thrust at her ribs, the boots crushing her toes, and the odor of bodies that had not touched water for weeks. She struggled to bring concentration into her glazed mind. Entering through the gates would not be a problem. But if Gold Dust was badly wounded or very sick, Rebekah might not be allowed into the infirmary.

At the palace gates, two guards disclosed that, hours ago, the favorite had been carried through the Gates of Bliss into the harem.

Fresh life flowed through Rebekah's veins. Gold Dust had not contracted the plague, or she would have been segregated. She was not seriously wounded, or she would have been moved to the infirmary.

Outside Gold Dust's bedchamber, Rebekah opened her palm and smoothed out the note, wet and crumpled from her perspiration.

"Years have passed, but the violet spark of your eyes and the blush of your naked toes remain my daily companions. With every single breath, I have regretted sending you away that day. Please accept my remorse. May I help?

Rouh'Allah the Spirit of God."

The day she was robbed of the last shreds of her dignity came back to her. The heaviness of the pouch of gold he offered still hurt her lap. They all bought her with coins. Even the honorable merchant. Would his wealth heal her daughter? Why the remorse now? Had he married his son, was the daughter of a whore no longer a threat? Her eardrums echoing the gallop of her heart, she entered Gold Dust's room and stood over her. Her daughter lay on the crumpled divan, tears rolling down her cheeks. This lifeless body did not belong to her daughter, her Gold, the girl she paraded around the Jewish Quarter, the girl who had a sweet wandering eye, the girl who never cried. No. This was a bag of shapeless bones. A face of tears.

35

A hacking cough and a stream of tears replaced Gold Dust's sweeping laughter. The hakim announced that the cough was due to the accumulation of powdered marrow in her lungs, but he did not know what had caused the flow of tears. Five times a day, she was ordered to drink an infusion of quince seeds to relieve the cough. In the evening, she endured cupping, where hot suction glasses extricated evil demons, which left purple marks on her skin.

At dawn, she woke to the pain of leeches, bleeding her of the tainted blood that was believed to cause her malady. She gazed at the leeches, gorged with her blood and many times their original size. "Soon they'll drain me of my last drop."

Rebekah realized the leeches were also draining her daughter's will. She went to the Shah and pleaded with him to dispose of that hakim and invite another.

The second hakim, a short, round man with a tinted, curly beard, visited the harem every sundown. He fed Gold Dust a spoonful of the oil of *taryak*, made from petals and pods of poppy flowers, to stop her tears. He never left the *taryak* with the favorite. An extra dose could rid a patient of the misery of an unbearable life.

Since no male was allowed to touch the sultana, every day, through a tube, the hakim smelled her properly cloaked body so as to detect any putrid odor. But apart from the lingering fragrance of black roses the Shah left behind, there was no unusual smell on her. The hakim straightened his back and puffed up his cheeks. "It is clear the favorite is suffering from leprosy of the bones and a mysterious malady of the tear ducts. I'll order an active sweating-out of the toxins."

On a figurine, he demonstrated to the female slaves how to rub Gold Dust with floured apricot kernels to clear her pores and to facilitate the expunging of the plague, then sprinkle and rub flaxseed flour over her body and roll a number of goatskins around her to facilitate sweating.

Gold Dust's body became so haggard she seemed to have lost even her soft bones.

Rebekah planted her hands on her waist and cried out, "It's time to try a different remedy!"

"We must fumigate the harem against the evil eye," the doctor advised.

Rebekah dismissed him on the spot.

The third hakim, a literate Jew, had long, thin legs, dangling arms, and wiry fingers that scribbled marginal notes in a book of apothecary. When he was informed that he could not touch Gold Dust's wrist, he tied a string around it and held the end from where he counted her pulse. "Sluggish," he concluded. "Phlegmatic. Evidence of a neglected digestive system."

He mixed a purgative blend of powder of magnesium, castor oil, and sulfate of sudd to purge the favorite's bowels. The week after, he ordered permanganate baths and a hard scrub with clay soap and ashes to destroy the malicious elements that had found their way onto her skin and multiplied there. On the third week, he gave the sultana a bowl of a strong purgative, the stink of which sent Honey running from the chamber.

Rebekah grabbed the hakim by the collar and shouted, "You are killing her! She has coughed, teared, and sweated out every last drop of her life!"

The hakim pounded the floor with his cane, his stringy beard shaking. "I can't do any better when I'm not allowed to examine her properly. Look at your daughter! She's cloaked from head to toe as if she were shrouded for burial. If a hakim is not a *mahram* and a confidant of the harem, who is? Do I have to cut off my member before I examine her?"

Rebekah clung to his sleeve. "Don't give up. There's no other doctor left in the empire."

"Go tell the Shah," the hakim shouted, "that I'm a Jew, and like all other persecuted Jews, I've long lost my manhood!"

In the Hall of Ceremonies, stifled by heavy drapes the color of blood, Rebekah waited at the threshold. On a dais, in the center of the room, Raven sat on a high-backed throne, layers of peach muslin tumbling down her shoulders. A snake of gold with ruby eyes twisted around her bare arm. The king, wearing a cape of royal blue trimmed with silver braids, stood next to her.

Since the day her daughter had returned from war and now that Narcissus was incapacitated, the Shah depended on Rebekah's daily visits to take care of his favorite and to bring the truth and outside gossip to him.

The Shah motioned Rebekah to approach. She glided to him with a sway that sent soft ripples into her chador. Although the veil fell loosely over her head and covered part of her hair, her face was exposed, and she still enjoyed the look of embarrassment men exhibited at her presence.

She cast her eyes down but did not prostrate herself. "My shah, please allow Gold Dust to be examined properly by the hakim without her hampering attire."

The Shah stabbed the air with his finger. "No stranger will set eyes on the naked body of our favorite."

With a flurry of fabrics, Raven descended from her throne. Sparks of anger colored her cheeks. Her father behaved like a lovesick adolescent. Why was he protective of her mother? Why did it matter if another man saw her naked? "Your favorite's body doesn't resemble a woman's," her voice of velvet reminded. "It has disintegrated. It will arouse only pity in a man."

Rebekah watched this child-woman, who had never been a child, and who defied age, slither a hand down her neck; a red fingernail outlined the mature cleave of her breasts. The golden snake flickered in the light; the jeweled eyes winked in conspiracy.

The Shah stepped down from the dais. He would not be swayed. He would not allow a male stranger to touch the sultana and forever spoil her.

Raven was at his side; her hand lingered on his shoulder, her words pained whispers in his ear.

Rebekah watched the tip of Raven's breast stab the king's arm. Her tongue sweeping her lips, she went to a jug of water and drank long and hard. Breathless, the color high on her cheeks, she faced her father and, as if he held some secret potion that could cure her never-ending thirst, she asked, "Aren't you concerned that I'm always dry?"

Rebekah did not care to wait for the king's reply. Raven and her convenient thirst must not steal the moment. "Your Honor, six weeks have passed. No hakim, potion, incantation, prayer, or spirit cured my daughter. She's crying herself to death. She can't be healed with blind guesses."

There was sadness in the Shah's voice. "We have done and will continue doing all in our power for the sultana. But we will not permit another man to touch our *namous*, our most intimate belonging."

Rebekah fell down and kissed the Shah's feet, waiting for his grief to ebb and for Raven to storm out of the hall. Only when the Shah asked what else she wanted did Rebekah glance up. "Our last hope is the Ancient Zoroastrian. She might save my Gold."

"Not Gold. Gold Dust. Gold Dust." He stressed every syllable and rolled it under his tongue, as if that would bring her back. He gazed at the woman in front of him, in a humble stance he knew went against her grain, and he accepted this alternative.

Rebekah left the royal halls, aware of shuffling steps behind her. So the eunuch had dared steal out of his hiding place. She veered around to face him. "I've got your pickled cucumber, Narcissus," she hissed, poison spilling from her mouth. "I won't give it back until Gold Dust stands on her feet, a sound woman."

He emerged from the shadows, a fearful man who had abandoned all hope, a bloated man with eyes almost invisible above morbid cheeks, caked sugar on puffy lips. He extended a begging palm, shaky with the overuse of opium. She almost pitied the ruins of the once powerful eunuch whose life now depended on the Shah's mercy and on what was preserved in brine.

His hands sprang out and patted her in a desperate search. General Darius had forewarned him that the moment the Shah turned his attention from the immediate problems of the empire, the general would show him the inferior girth. Narcissus had to have his organ back before that happened.

"Do you take me for a fool?" Rebekah hissed, slapping his hands off. "Would I hide your precious meat on myself?"

"Years ago," he mumbled, "slave traders deprived me of this life; now you've robbed me of the other."

"Sweetlove," she sang. "You should have thought of that

when you sent my daughter to war. Your rotten penis is safe with me. You'll go entire to that world when my daughter's health is restored." She turned on her heels and breezed out of the palace and directly to the house of bougainvilleas.

The Ancient Zoroastrian's purple eyelids snapped open at the intrusion. Her opal gaze fixed on Rebekah, then returned to the brazier in front of her.

Rebekah cleared her throat. "My Gold is dying, Holy One."

The old woman cackled. "It was not an accident. Gold Dust fell from her horse because the saddle was not secured properly."

The Ancient Zoroastrian recalled the day Gold Dust had visited with her mother; Gold Dust's skin had the glow of a girl who had experienced her first menstrual period. Her own supernatural powers had heard the silent hum in the girl's bones. Such sweet music, the source of so many emotions, melodies untainted by time and harsh experiences. The Ancient Zoroastrian's tongue struggled between dry, pleated lips. "Does your daughter still make music?"

The jingle of Rebekah's bracelets sounded funereal. "Not since Raven's birth."

The Ancient Zoroastrian smacked her lips. "Take me to your child."

✣

The Ancient Zoroastrian huddled on a stretcher carried on the shoulders of two young men. This was the only means of transportation she accepted because it allowed her a leisurely pace of life. Up to the time her legs had grown too feeble to support her, she had only walked from place to place and from village to hamlet, answering questions the young asked. Legend has it she not only predicted one's fate but had the power to change it and that those who helped carry her stretcher were repaid by the holy fire.

Rebekah, who could not differentiate between the song of birds and the cry of her heart, suffered while the old woman instructed the men to stop at every corner so she could study the peeling barks and the spreading branches of the plane trees, the sunlight shining off the phosphorescent flies, the many colors of the fluttering butterflies, and the child faces she encountered for the first time.

She averted her gaze from the offensive columns of malachite, the intricate faience, and the lush carpets in the palace. She had lived too long to be fooled by transitory wealth.

In Gold Dust's quarters, Honey helped the old woman down and set a hill of cushions around her. The Zoroastrian smacked her tongue and mumbled, "I need solitude . . . the mother, the daughter . . . no other."

Petulantly Honey walked out.

The old woman wiped off the favorite's eyes. "Why tears?"

"I'm dying," Gold Dust sighed.

"Don't mention death in my presence. Talk about the moment your bones ceased singing."

Gold Dust shut her eyes. Did the ancient one know that it was the moment of birth that had shattered the harmony of her bones? She had bent to greet her daughter. All white, like virgin doves, her red-bright eyes rimmed with swan feathers. Her screams of "Albino" had shot through the halls, bounced back, pierced her bones, and killed the music.

"It stopped with Raven's birth."

"Poor child," the Zoroastrian moaned. "That's a long time for bones to remain idle. They became so weak, they couldn't support you any longer."

"Holy One," Rebekah said, "you're talking in riddles."

"When part of the body is not regularly used," the Ancient

Zoroastrian said, "it becomes brittle and eventually crumbles. After Raven's birth, your bones gradually grew weaker. When you fell from the horse, they collapsed, spilling your emotions every which way and causing chaos. But your soft bones also saved you. If they were strong and singing, when you fell your rigid bones would have punctured your heart, your liver, or your spleen and killed you."

Rebekah wrung her hands as if she had the old woman's tongue between her palms. "What's the remedy, Holy One?"

"There is a remedy for all ailments; it's the desire we lack."

"Gold," Rebekah pleaded. "Assure the Holy One you have the will."

"Madar, I've lost the support that holds my emotions together. I don't know how to summon any feeling but grief."

The Ancient Zoroastrian raised a triumphant finger. "Yes! Without the protection of your bones, you can't contain your sadness, or look beyond the present into a better future. That's why your tears flow unchecked.

"Child, do you have love in your life?"

"Of course," Rebekah interrupted, "the Shah's, Raven's, mine."

The woman waved her hand in Rebekah's face. "Let your daughter talk! I've remedies from the beginning of time that cure any malady, but I can't cure lies and false hopes."

"What is love?" Gold Dust sighed. "I love like a sultana, like a daughter, like a mother."

"Have you loved like a woman?"

"I don't know. I've known one man."

The Ancient Zoroastrian rested ravaged fingers on Gold Dust's head. "Your first step to recovery is to find a patient lover to teach you to minister to each emotion separately, not only acknowledge pain and sadness, but joy and eventually hope. Hope is the mortar of our bones."

She turned to Rebekah. "Gold Dust's bones didn't deteriorate without the silent collaboration of you, the Shah, Raven. Free your daughter. Take her to the one who's not consumed by his empire and his daughter. Prove to her a man can care."

"You've all gone mad!" Rebekah screamed, no longer able to contain herself. "Gold Dust is the Shah's favorite! No man is allowed to see her face. How in the world do you propose she meet with a stranger? The Shah will kill her!"

The Ancient Zoroastrian's opal gaze settled on Rebekah. "I know you well, Rebekah. You will find a way, or your daughter's misplaced emotions will kill her before the Shah will."

⟨⟨ 36 ⟩⟩

Rebekah guided Venus toward the pit and Soleiman the Agile's shack. A bitter smile stuck on her lips as she freed a curl from the fringes of her chador and stared at the golden strand. The color was vibrant and without a trace of gray. The skin on her face and body was smooth, the brand between her breasts had not lost its vigor, and the shine of her violet eyes had not diminished. It pleased her to look in the mirror and confirm that the natural ravages of time sped past her. But today her insides felt old and a blanket of gray enveloped the flowers, the leaves, even the sun. A palpable gray she tasted.

"A few hours of harmless entertainment would lift Gold's mood," she had pleaded with the Shah.

"What kind of entertainment?" he had asked.

"Performing acrobats," she replied, while thinking bitterly of the Ancient Zoroastrian's assurance of the acrobat's love for her daughter. But would Gold Dust still want that sun-baked man she had last spurned behind the baths?

"Nonsense!" the Shah thundered. "Who proposed this strange remedy?"

"The Ancient Zoroastrian, who witnessed the fall and rise of many Shahs."

"Absurd."

"To divert her mind from her body."

"Foolishness!"

"My lord, only a few hours of solitude. Pearl Hall must be emptied of the sultanas and their eunuchs."

He directed his amazement at her. "Why?"

"To feel she is the sole inhabitant of a temporary dream world."

The king fell into deep thought. "Is it not enough that she rules as our favorite?"

Rebekah's voice cracked. "Because of you, my lord, Gold has everything a woman could desire. Please don't consider me thankless when I say this life was imposed on her rather than chosen by her. I am to blame." She had been on the brink of kissing his hand and begging for compassion, but she had looked him straight in the eyes and had assured him that the favorite would remain behind curtains and no stranger would see her.

He had paced the hall, the aigrette on his turban flashing. At last he had approached her, towering over her. "We will allow this nonsense on the condition Raven be present at the time."

"Yes, my shah," Rebekah had promised, marveling at Raven's ability to have established herself as the king's agent.

Now, with every gallop closer to the garbage pit, Rebekah's dream died a little. But she could not blame Gold Dust, who had been tutored in the importance of love by a mother who did not believe in the alliance of marriage and who was ignorant of the convoluted ways of love. How often had she cuddled her daughter on her lap and, feeling utterly helpless and defeated, whispered fantastical lies: "Love is not what you see or have seen in this home, not the way Jacob was, not the way these men who come and go are. Oh, no! I'm talking about men whose touch is soft, whose words are sweet, whose heart is tender." Yes. She had known, in the back of her mind, long before it had happened, that Gold Dust would one day feel in her marrow the need to experience the man in her mother's fairy tales.

The Shah had fed her daughter with passion, while starving her for love; so her bones became weak and brittle. The Zoroastrian was right. If not a fall from a horse, one day a single snap of a finger would have crumbled them.

For some women love resided and was nurtured in their heart; for Gold Dust it lived in her marrow and had not been fed properly. Rebekah understood. That need had been her companion all her life.

Years ago, when she had launched Gold Dust into the world, she had never imagined a day when she would ride to the pit to beg a petty acrobat to save her daughter. What would she tell him? "My daughter is dying from lack of love. It's my fault. I taught her to be ambitious, but forgot to pluck all emotions out of her bones. Now her bones broke and her feelings spilled out."

Rebekah did not knock on Soleiman's door. Today she did not have patience for such formalities. She walked straight into his dark hole.

Soleiman the Agile opened his eyes, resenting the intrusion into his light sleep. But he did not spring up and clutch the sword, bouncing into a fit of acrobatic outbursts, as he had done on Rebekah's first visit.

Rebekah caught her breath. He had changed. He was heavier. His body had lost its attractive suppleness. "Soleiman, what have you done to yourself now that I need you?"

He raised himself, recognizing Rebekah the Bundle Woman.

Curse her. How dare she question his health? "What did you expect? I spent an eternity waiting. Unused muscles decay."

"Bless your heart, sweetlove. You and my daughter suffer from the same disease, only hers is in the bones." She saw a cloud pass over his face. At the thought that he still wanted Gold Dust, fresh hope filled her and she purred, "I've the remedy for your muscles, but you must promise me one thing."

He folded his bedding and piled it away in a corner. He would not allow this woman to deceive him again. Was it not enough that he had rubbed his face raw with dyes only to be stared at as if he were a clown?

Rebekah's gaze glided over his body. Despite the softness around his waist, she was certain youth and a strong incentive would restore his firmness. "Promise me, sweetlove."

Pale sparks darted from his eyes. "I trusted you once. That was enough."

She understood. She, too, had once trusted a respected merchant, offering with sincerity her daughter's hand, forgetting she had been repeatedly rejected by all the forces that once mattered: by her mother, by her husband, by God himself. "Soleiman, please accept my apologies and don't blame my daughter. I'm to blame."

He remembered rumors his acrobats had brought him after the army had returned from war. The favorite was not well. She could not stop crying. She had contracted the plague. He never knew what to believe. "Is your daughter sick?" he mumbled.

"No, oh, no, God forbid. She's just not well in her spirit. She's young. Youth needs the company of youth. Come to Pearl Hall and perform for her. But first work your muscles. Wash your hair. Go to the barber. It's such a shame, sweetlove, you're buried under a blanket of stinking indifference."

"I waited until bees plucked at my cuffs, until rosebuds teetered at my feet. . . ."

She blew kisses into the air and shook her bangles. "I'll mend all the hurt."

He controlled the urge to repeat the words she had once thrown at him when she had first invited him to the harem: "Don't try to impress me, it's my daughter who wants you." But he remained silent to hear the exhilarating beat of his temples, the rush of blood in his ears, the thumping of his heart. He was alive again. He would rather confront the dangers ahead than remain a living corpse.

She saw hope and fear in his eyes. "Soleiman, I'm close to the Shah. I'll protect you both. But remember, you've no future with her. Don't attempt to become intimate. One touch could lead to another, then you'll find yourselves in such trouble no one could save you."

Soleiman did not say that he was a patient man, that he never rushed his emotions, and that while seeking out his lost love, he had remained a virgin and would continue to remain one if he had to.

Rebekah's fingers traced Soleiman's cheeks, the cut under his chin, the delicate curve of his neck. "Don't paint your face, Soleiman. The sultana prefers pale men."

೧೪

Thirty-five days after Rebekah had visited Soleiman, the Shah called for *khalvat*, the seclusion of the gardens. The gates were locked. The guards kept watch outside, the eunuchs inside the gardens.

The sultanas poured out of the harem and fluttered behind the Shah like vibrant butterflies. Apart from Honey, no sultana cared to miss this day. The Shah had not had a woman since his pledge to Gold Dust. Now each sultana prayed she would be the one the king would spend the night with.

Metal railings and velvet partitions went up in the Hall of Entertainment.

Raven had been ordered to remain behind, at her mother's side, but against her father's instructions, she now ran to catch up with him. She brushed her lips against his shoulder. "May I join you, please?"

His arms circled her waist and, feeling her young body, he drew back. Why did her touch, her scent generate such contradictory responses in him? She was his blood and flesh. Why did that matter? Throughout Persian history fathers had wedded daughters and had produced heirs to the empire. He faced her. "You had orders not to abandon your mother while the acrobats perform."

For some time now, Raven had noticed a certain turmoil in her father. Although he invited her to his quarters, he dismissed her without addressing any specific subject. He was restless, snapped at her for no particular reason. He shied from her touch and visited the harem more often, his glazed eyes following the sultanas. The determination now etched on his face told her she must not argue.

໑໑

Moon Face followed the Shah into the gardens. Fresh hope blossomed in her heart. This time she would make sure he noticed her. Then she would entangle him so completely he would never discard her again.

She had prepared meticulously for this outing. After rubbing rice paste on her face and cherry extract on her lips, she had examined herself in the mirror. The contrast of her red mouth to her pale face was feminine and mysterious. The way the Shah liked his women. Stepping back, she had touched her powdered face, bent forward and studied her reflection. No. The Shah's taste had changed. Had she not noticed Gold Dust's blushing cheeks, golden eyes, chestnut hair? Plunging her face in a bowl of water, Moon Face had scrubbed until her skin was raw. She painted her cheeks bright, used less kohl on one eye to duplicate Gold Dust's wandering eye, and tinted her black hair with saffron to give it a lighter tinge. Out of her faded satin pouch, she spread out her tools of passion. Dear Gulf Lily, he had fashioned these gadgets for her, the artificial penis molded after the size of the Shah's erect member, the incense burner that permeated the room with the calming effects of hashish, the lubricants extracted from the roots of aphrodisiac plants.

The entourage sailed toward the marble pool, on which miniature rowing boats floated. Moon Face searched for the carriage that would transport Gold Dust into the gardens. Why was she absent? Would she join them after they left the pool? Moon Face's jaw locked in anger at the thought that this excursion might have been planned for a reason other than the Shah's desire to select a woman. Standing on the skirting of the pool, she watched the Shah slip behind an arabesque. Afraid the water would rinse off her makeup and electing to stand apart from the other women, in order to attract the king's attention, Moon Face froze into her most alluring pose, the pouch swaying from her bare arm.

The Shah reached out a hand from behind the arabesque. A spray of pearls, their glossy shells luminous in the sunlight, splashed into the water. The sultanas plunged after the pearls—rose above the surface, wet-haired, breathless—naked bodies gleamed, dove back under, searching. The Shah willed his body to respond. In the Cage, the most important lesson the eunuchs had buzzed in his ears was that if his glands were not used regularly they would shrivel, he would lose his hair, and his voice would become squeaky. In fear of an heir rising from the Cage, girls, stripped of their childbearing organs, kept the young prince amused, busy, and obsessed. It was hard to erase the everlasting scars of youth, the beliefs carved in his innermost being. He had not joined a woman for a long time and had not rid himself of the stagnant seeds.

But his mind and body clashed with the two women in his life. Who owned his body? Who his mind? Had Raven sowed the germ of desire in him? Had Gold Dust watered it until it sprouted? When had it flowered and the roots burrowed deep? They were with him, around him, in him. He could not free himself from Raven's constant whispering, her touch, her insistent hands. And from Gold Dust's melancholy, tearful eyes. He must find diversion, drown himself in work, distance himself from them. He concentrated on Moon Face's muscular breasts, thick, pointed nipples, lean hips, and the pronounced triangle between her thighs—a sign of passion, the ability to bear boys. She stood out, tall and lanky among the many large-breasted, amply curved sultanas. Like an ugly weed, disturbing the landscape of a rose garden. But he had vague recollections of a past when she had burst upon his bleak life with a host of tricks stashed in her satin pouch.

Moon Face felt the Shah's stare tingle her body. A pearl between her small teeth sparkled. Her tongue danced, skipping the pearl from her teeth into her mouth, back to the tip of her tongue.

To the Shah, from behind the arabesque, the skin of all the sultanas seemed painted a frosty white, their hair silver and wild scintillated in the sun, and their pink, mischievous eyes blinked against the light.

∽

In Pearl Hall, Rebekah piled cushions and helped Gold Dust recline on them. She could press her eyes to the gauze inset or the slit between the curtains and watch the show, her body concealed behind the screens.

"Stay," Gold Dust pleaded.

Rebekah tucked a curl behind her daughter's ear. "I'll wait by the doors. In case of danger, I'll carry you out. Don't part the curtains." She tiptoed toward the door, wondering why Raven had not appeared.

The groan of partitions and a chain of vehement protests announced Raven's tardy entrance. Rebekah stepped back into Pearl Hall.

Raven searched for a comfortable place to settle down. "Where are the servants? Why haven't they arranged my cushions?"

Feigned surprise tainted Rebekah's face. "I arranged the cushions. I didn't think you'd miss this day of outing."

"Pedar left me no choice."

"Choices are made by us. The secret is to select the least dangerous ones."

Raven's eyes flashed. This language she understood, respected, was the reason she admired her grandmother. She adjusted the gold chains that cascaded from her neck and shook the bangles that hiked up her arm.

Rebekah approved of her granddaughter's exaggerated demonstrations. The princess was frustrated, and the world must heed. "Don't disobey or ignore your father's order, alter it to accommodate yourself. Enjoy the outing from a safe distance, and he'll never know. I'll stay here and cover for you."

Raven stifled a chuckle. She would follow the events by the pool. She would keep an eye on her father. And before the end of the acrobat's performance, she would lead the king to Pearl Hall.

The urgent race of Gold Dust's heartbeat replaced the echo of Raven's retreating footfalls. What if Soleiman was no longer

the man she had tattooed in her mind with fine needles that
had left such an imprint even time did not fade? What if the
face she had glanced at when he had removed his mask was no
longer full of pride? His eyes no longer an ocean of tears. His
passion no longer transparent beneath his fair skin. What if
that leather-brown face she had sped by in the alleys was his
true color? No different from her mother's night-men. No different from the Shah. Taking a deep breath, she approached
the gauze inset.

In the center of the hall, framed by the borders of her private window, he faced her. Her own intimate portrait. No
props, no bear, no cobra, and no Giant Man. His magnificent
body, gleaming with oils, shamed the image of her memories.
His burnished hair reflected the copper light from the many
torches around the hall. His eyes were pure blue. His complexion the shade of compassion.

She must plead for his forgiveness. She should not have
believed her mother that day in the alley behind the baths.
Unable to clap, she changed the tone of her voice and whispered, "You may start."

Soleiman the Agile was disappointed. This voice did not
belong to his sultana with the amber eyes. She had lived in his
heart forever, but she still considered him a stranger from
whom she had to hide her true voice. Then he realized that
they must not be alone. Eunuchs must be watching from
behind screens. It was prudent not to exhibit any sign of inti-
macy. He, too, must respect her and conceal his emotions.

In his mind he subtracted certain notes and added others to
re-create the voice of the shy girl with the cherry anklet. And
to that composed melody he began to perform.

Lids half-mast, head bowed, his hands curled above his
head in the pose of love idols, the rise and fall of his chest the
only sign of life on him—eternal silence—his hands aban-

doned their dazed stance, trunk rooted in place, limbs, waist, and neck twisted in a miraculous show of power and resilience and in absolute command of his body—an expert craftsman with a fine chisel, his fingers carved each posture against the outline of his silhouette and paused in each stance to acknowledge the admiration of his master. Then his legs folded; finding the carpet, his palms came together; his forehead rested on the dome of his fingertips.

She began to understand the posture of supplication, of prayer, of pleading. "Please, continue," she begged.

He heard the ring of her true voice, the sadness, the many questions. His heart pounding with fear and pride, he rose, spinning on his toes, his hands extending in a meditative stance, curving, praying, imploring, conquering the hall as if it had no boundaries, as if he would fly through the walls like a spirit, leap through time and never come back, yet he always returned to the center, an innate grace infusing his every move, folded down, his forehead kissing the ground on which she walked.

Then as if an internal band of minstrels created music for him, he began reciting the tale of a poor boy who had the divine face of angels and the stunning body of wrestlers. But his eyes were not rimmed by lashes and were too large for his face, eyes a livid purple that penetrated the souls of the populace and forced them to reveal their most intimate love stories, in hope he would find his lost love in their tales. He read their minds from near and far, whether they spoke or not, and learned that his beloved had abandoned their small town. He could not handle the enormity of his loss, could not sleep at night, nor eat or rest during the day as he prayed for a normal vision that would not betray the enviable love lives of others.

One morning, the One-Eyed Rabbi, who visited once a week to comfort the boy, found him lying faceup in his garden on a patch of dried grass. His wide-open eyes stared intensely at the sun. He was dead.

An outcry rose from the hakims in town. They wanted to perform an autopsy to discover what gave the boy those enormous eyes and that intense color and gaze. Since the boy had no relatives to protest the dissecting of his body, soon a gathering of acclaimed doctors assembled at the morgue.

They cut the boy's chest and stomach open. They shrank back in horror. Some mysterious disease had ravaged the boy's organs, leaving behind a feverish and inflamed heart.

No book of medicine explained what had plagued the boy. But the One-Eyed Rabbi knew. The enormity of his lost love had consumed him.

A sigh lodged in Gold Dust's throat. She felt a great affinity to the boy. Then she realized Soleiman was that boy. Suddenly, he was too far away. "Come closer," she whispered.

He danced toward her, closer to the curtains, to the gauzed inset, to the shrine behind where she sat. Genuflected. Extended both hands. His playful fingers skipped about the inset, stroked the imprint beyond the curtains, the outline of her cheeks, the bridge of her nose, traced, and worshiped, asserting himself with greater assurance.

She did not dare release her sigh. Did he smell her presence, feel her warmth, hear her heart? Did he realize he stroked her face through the gauze inset, that she felt his breath? Why had he shared his story? Did his gaze rip the curtains and penetrate her thoughts? Her brave acrobat, in a few moments, had revealed more than the king with whom she had had a daughter, more than her mother, who had shut out the past—no childhood tales, no recalling of family events, left her with only dull memories to trace her past.

"Marvelous!" she cried, his presence obliterating all fear.

He withdrew.

Forgetting the infirmity of her bones, she tried to create music. Her bones refused, but it did not matter. Hope had stirred her marrow.

She thrust her head through the slit in the curtains.

He fell at her feet, shocked at being allowed to observe her naked face, not even a transparent veil hiding her. He pressed his palms to his eyes. She was even more stunning than the portrait in his mind. Soon the guards would burst in, take him to the courtyard. This would be his last vision. He must etch this instant into his final moments.

The silence was not interrupted. No footsteps to yank him off his feet. No scimitar hacking the life out of him. The glimmer of torches fell on his spine, arched like a moonlit wave, rising to her, his face level with hers, their eyes fusing.

"Soleiman, how do you master your body?"

He stared at her velvet-framed face, his lips a breath away. "You, my *Khanom*, are my tutor."

"The truth . . ."

"For years, you've lived in my thoughts and instructed me to perfection."

"Why can't I do it for myself?"

"The task belongs to your love."

His pale face turned crimson; drops of sweat glistened on the bridge of his nose. He was almost child-like, with the pale body of city craftsmen. How could she, at another time, have been attracted to wrestling, falcons, and the massive body of men of the mountains? "Caress my face," she murmured.

Soleiman stepped back. He would not endanger her life. And he would not reveal his clumsiness. He had lived too long with the silence of books and with his audiences who were shadows in the dark. When he performed acrobatic feats, he was the king of his private universe. But faced with the favorite of the Shah, the lessons in his history books came to

his mind and magnified the dangers. "What about the Shah?
My lady."

"Are you afraid?"

"For you. I've nothing to lose."

"Open the curtains!" she ordered.

Soleiman stood motionless. Never. He would not. The
eunuchs. The guards. The sultanas were hiding behind partitions.

"I want you to see me."

"My lady, you are the favorite of the king."

"I am no longer a woman!"

Soleiman saw the suffering in the golden gleam of her eyes.

"Must I beg like a servant?"

He sucked his breath in and gripped his muscles tight. His
eyes, filled with dazzling clarity, locked with hers.

He released the velvet flaps.

37

Above the spreading branch of a plane tree, a pair of ruby eyes surveyed the Shah as he gazed at the wet bodies of his women in the pool. Raven watched the sultanas while her touch glided over her own curves. The sultanas paled in comparison to the ripeness of her breasts, the inviting shape of her thighs, the voluptuous curve of her buttocks. But to her father she was still a child.

Shielding his eyes, the Shah stared at the sky, calculating the position of the sun. Gold Dust had been entertained long enough. He stole from behind the arabesque and started toward the harem, past the hedges, bordering the garden paths, and the plane trees that filtered out the rays of the sun. He came face-to-face with Raven, her nipples imprinted against the sheer fabric of her vest. He growled, "We told you to remain with your mother!"

"The show is almost over. Why didn't you invite me to the pool?"

"These outings are for the sultanas."

"Am I not a woman?"

He gazed at her. She had grown tall, almost to his height.

Her silver hair bounced on hips that had honed her mother's sway into perfection. Her breasts challenged the world with rage and defiance. The shadow of her nipples, her parted lips, eternal thirst, and husky voice were proof she had grown to become an exceptional woman. He was furious with her for testing him, with himself for his inability to acknowledge her maturity, and with Gold Dust for becoming incapacitated when he needed her most.

Raven flung her arm around him and led him toward the harem.

The Shah's steps grew urgent as he approached the ominous silence that shrouded the hall. He threw open the double doors. The velvet curtains were drawn. The acrobat was about to leave. The Shah stared at the lean body, pale eyes, and copper curls. "We had been informed you would bring a cobra and some Giant Man. Did you think you alone could entertain the favorite?"

Soleiman prostrated himself. He struggled to control the tremor of his voice. "My shah, I came alone because I was told the sultana suffers from lethargy. To cure the spirit one must proceed with caution."

The Shah burst out in his mocking laughter. "Are you an acrobat or a healer of souls? Have you learned this from your Giant Man, or the bear?"

"The soul, my shah, is more fragile than the body. The slightest turbulence can throw it off balance. There are hundreds of reasons why the spirit can lose its wholeness, but only a few known cures."

"What is the sultana's spirit suffering from?" Raven asked, her eyes searching the hall.

"Lack of natural light, my princess, sunshine, the essence of life."

She plucked the sprig of mint from behind her ear and

brushed it against her nose. "How, may I ask, did *you* help her?"

"My princess, I'd never boast of the ability to heal like nature. Since the favorite is not allowed to leave the harem, the next best remedy is entertainment, an opiate of the soul."

Raven's lungs felt heavy. The air was stale. Nothing stirred. She could not breathe. She parted the curtains. The impression of her mother's body lingered on the cushions.

The Shah had the urge to spit out the truth about Gold Dust's fall and make an ass of this insolent acrobat who spoke of strange matters. The king was comfortable with the tangible, the flesh, and needs of the body. The soul belonged to the realm of Allah, and he preferred not to tread unknown terrain.

The Shah waved a silver-capped finger. "We won't need you any longer."

Soleiman the Agile started toward the door. At the threshold, he turned on his heels as if he were a graceful sculpture gyrating on a carpeted platform. "The real remedy, Your Highness, is sunshine. Light to the soul is like air to the lungs."

"Our immense love for the favorite is sufficient."

Raven gathered her skirts and breezed out of the hall.

ဢ

Moon Face crushed the pearl between her teeth and spat out the shreds. The Shah had sneaked away from behind the bushes as if he were a squeaking eunuch, guilty of fondling women. He had hardly glanced at any of the sultanas, nor acknowledged her efforts to please him. Holding her breath, she dived down to the glazed bottom of the pool and picked more pearls. Her lungs bursting, she shot back up. Even with silent bones, Gold Dust held magical powers over the king. Like vicious mills, Moon Face's teeth ground the pearls in her mouth until the fine powder was about to choke her. The pain in her throat was easier to bear than the rage in her veins.

She coughed up the pearl dust and climbed up the steps of the pool. Gulf Lily rushed to wipe off her running makeup.

"My bladder's bursting," she whispered.

Gulf Lily, the color of the Persian Gulf on moonless nights, glanced around, bewildered. His hand flew into the air in a wild, pleading dance: My lady, you can't leave now. The gates might be open; there might be men around.

Moon Face shifted from one foot to another. "I can't hold it. I'm going to die from shame."

He threw a veil over her body and clasped her hand in his.

"No, you stay here and cover for me. I'll be back soon." She crawled behind the jasmine bushes and ran past the courtyard and beneath the silk underpass. She recognized the burnished curls and the lithe body of the man leaving the harem. Securing the chador around her face, she sped toward him. Two fingers in her mouth to change her voice, she barked through puckered lips, "By Allah, it's the acrobat from the Jewish Quarter!"

Soleiman turned his pale gaze to her one dark eye, visible from the parting of her veil. He bowed slightly, a palm against his chest. He did not like the murky shadows inside this woman's head.

"Have you come to perform for *her?*" Moon Face coughed in her manly voice, her eye combing him from head to toe. "So that's why we were banished to the pool! Did she enjoy your acrobatic feats?"

Soleiman was a poet, a master storyteller; he knew how to create believable lies. "Princess Raven? Yes, she enjoyed the show."

Moon Face squinted one suspicious eye at the acrobat. "Since when is the harem evacuated for Raven?"

"The poor girl suffers from . . ." Soleiman looked around and whispered, "Pardon me. For a moment, I forgot my promise to honor her secret."

Moon Face pointed to her heart. "Her secret will be safe here." She probed his eyes, trying to claw at the truth. "When Gold Dust and the Shah left for war, I took care of Raven. Now they keep secrets from me." She aimed a wad of spittle into her palm and stared at it sadly. "This is what I deserve for considering her as my own!"

Soleiman watched her wipe her palm against her chador. "I did not mean to upset your ladyship. The truth is that the princess suffers from a lethal consumption of the liver, which is the cause of her colorless appearance. She is wasting away."

Moon Face imitated his secretive tone. "Are you a doctor?"

"A different one. I distract the mind so the body can wither away painlessly."

He had whispered with such genuine grief that Moon Face felt a catch in her throat. God was merciful. He had decided to punish the favorite through the loss of her daughter. Moon Face shuffled back to the gardens.

38

*H*iding behind the balcony of blind musicians, Gulf Lily observed the meeting between the Shah, Rebekah, and the Ancient Zoroastrian. Gulf Lily was amazed at the power of the supernatural, which had transformed the king into an obedient servant who remained standing in deference to the old woman.

"King!" The woman's gnarled fingers grazed her hairless head. "Allow Gold Dust time out of this prison you call harem. At least once a week, until she grows stronger. Or you'll be left with a bag of useless bones. She must experience the healing powers of the sun outside the palace where light is not smothered by plane trees and weeping willows."

The Shah kept his distance. "We shall allow these excursions on the condition Your Holiness never leave her side."

"No need for my presence, King," the ancient one cackled. "Don't make life more complicated than it already is."

Irritation crept into the Shah's voice. "You're closer to Allah than any mortal. With you, the favorite will be safe from men who harbor vile desires."

Gulf Lily saw the Ancient Zoroastrian's mouth flap open and shut like that of a dying fish. Was she laughing at the king?

At last, she caught her breath. "As you wish. I'd benefit from the sun myself, before I'm buried in darkness."

"The outings must cease in one month!" the Shah ordered. "Ample time for nature to prove itself."

With hushed footsteps Gulf Lily hurried to Moon Face.

༄

Moon Face secured the latticed windows. She had seen two young men carry Gold Dust and the Ancient Zoroastrian's fleshless frame on a stretcher. "I'll sneak out from the Courtyard of Eunuchs," Moon Face pleaded with Gulf Lily. "I won't be recognized behind the mask. I'll be back in no time."

With arms folded against a muscular chest, and a fierce fire burning in his stomach, Gulf Lily remained rooted, his tar eyes fixed on his mistress.

She softened her voice. "Gulf Lily, you love me, don't you?"

He raised both palms to his eyes to hide his dark yes.

"You want me like a man wants a woman."

His ebony skin turned crimson. He planted his feet apart to steady himself and control the violent quake that began to shake him. He had been a father to her. He had taught her to hone the Shah's curiosity, and to handle the envy of the sultanas. He had fed her boiled chestnuts to plump and soften her lean flesh, so it could be dented with loving fingertips. He had served her a diet of goat milk to lighten her skin. He had shared her most personal concerns. He was the one to assure her it was normal to bleed every month. He fell down to his knees, sobs shaking his immense body.

"Dear, dear Gulf Lily." Moon Face pressed his shaven head to her raw, pumiced cheek. "It's all right."

No, he thought, it was not. He had raised her like his own child while wanting her as a lover. He should have plucked his eyeballs out before they had begun lusting after her. Now that he had revealed his true emotions, he would have to find a way to preserve the integrity of his soul.

Moon Face felt the beat of his temples, the shudder in his limbs. She locked her mouth to his, forcing his eggplant-colored lips open, her tongue searching for his. "You are the only one I have in this world. Help me!"

Gulf Lily went to the chest of clothing and selected a cloak and a mask of black leather. He helped Moon Face conceal herself in them. He wrapped himself in his mantle and hid his face with a flap of his turban.

∞

"Delight in the glory of nature," the Ancient Zoroastrian said to Gold Dust as they moved toward the Jewish Quarter. "Savor the beauty of dawn and dusk. Choose between the forces of good and evil. Ahura Mazda gave you free will; use it wisely. Above all, love intensely. Love is the mortar of your bones."

Gold Dust kissed the old woman's hand. "Holy One, you've given me back my life."

The talon-like fingers clawed the air. "Don't spit blasphemy! Have *I* given you life? *I?* When will you learn, child? *You*, your will, your heart, your mind give you life, joy, strong bones."

A smile colored Gold Dust's lips and the old woman realized that nothing mattered to the young girl but the end of this journey. Not the danger of a looming Shah. Not the threat of her daughter who hovered between genius and madness. Not even the breaking of her mother's heart.

"Devour these transient moments with all your senses," the Zoroastrian said. "In a month, you'll grieve for passions you didn't fulfill. Now go! Soleiman is waiting."

As the young men, loyal followers of the old woman, carried

the stretcher, not once did the Ancient Zoroastrian worry that the inhabitants of the Jewish Quarter would reveal where Gold Dust spent half a day of every week. No one would dare try the wrath of the Ancient Zoroastrian and Ahura Mazda, her God.

Two shadows, draped in black, stole behind Soleiman's shanty. Moon Face could hardly curtail her joyful chortle. She had caught Gold Dust in the act of adultery.

Gulf Lily's heart was heavy. He had come along to protect his beloved, but the route she chose was dangerous. She would not stop at anything to destroy the favorite. In the process she would lose her own life. The Shah did not reward those who bore bad news.

39

$\mathcal{S}$oleiman the Agile had searched the alleys and had picked wildflowers from the cracks in the walls and from under fences of private yards. He arranged daisies and tuberoses in a glass of rosewater against which he rested a parchment engraved with his own handwriting. He inspected the room for signs of dust and spiderwebs. He had gathered stray feathers to stuff a casing he had sewn from threads unraveled from pillow covers. He had piled his books against the walls to make room for Gold Dust's mattress.

His chest too small for his expectant heart, he waited at the threshold of his house. The stretcher bearers appeared at the opposite end of the pit. He stopped himself from rushing to Gold Dust and carrying her inside. His fingers locked in a nervous grip. The favorite was a breath away, her amber eyes questioning. He had felt at ease in the presence of the girl with the cherry anklet, but he did not know how to behave in the presence of the favorite. Was he allowed to lift her off the stretcher?

The voice of the Ancient Zoroastrian startled him. "Son, don't stand there and stare. You don't have much time."

He lifted Gold Dust and held her in his arms, surprised at

her frailty. Inside, he settled her on the cotton-cloaked feathers, piling cushions behind her and arranging her legs and arms.

She longed to wrap the veil around her body to conceal herself from his penetrating gaze.

Kneeling, he gathered the veil and tied it around her shoulders.

Had he read her thoughts?

He went to the windows and threw them open. Sunlight tumbled in. Fresh air filled her lungs. Here there were no partitions, no boundaries, no dark corners.

Soleiman raised the parchment. "I composed a poem for you."

Here there were no cutting words. No fear of a king who dangled from the talons of his daughter. Here, in the light of day, she was not afraid to touch this pale-faced man, who in her silence had felt her embarrassment and had covered her up.

"Will you recite this poem?" he asked. "I'd like to study your voice."

In a voice laced with passion and longing, she read what, she soon discovered, was the continuation of Soleiman's story.

Even in death, the boy with the lashless eyes did not find peace. As hard as the angels who guarded the gates of heaven tried, they could not find a place for a man who had lost his inner organs and had entered heaven with a lovesick heart. The angels congregated to decide if his soul was worth saving. They raised their wings in a unanimous show of approval. A man who had spent his life searching for love deserved a place in heaven. Each angel would donate to the boy her own organ and a few drops of ambrosia that flowed from the fountain of love.

When the boy heard them, a storm formed in his purple eyes, and his lashless lids fluttered in grief. His gaze had penetrated their ethereal bodies and had learned that each angel owned one organ; one had a heart, another a liver, another a kidney. They functioned as a unit. He struggled to free himself from their grip; he would not enter heaven at the cost of their lives.

Soleiman cast his eyes down to hide the tumult she created by rendering life to his story.

"Did he enter heaven?" she asked. "Why didn't you end the tale?"

"He was allowed into heaven for a very short time." He reached out to her, then withdrew his hand. "Your voice rises from the depth of your throat with an assurance rare among sultanas. It's seductive, filled with promises, and powerful. Not smooth. That's monotonous. But rich with lows and captivating highs, validating itself through obstacles. Husky notes concealing defiance and unresolved emotions. The outcome of a harsh childhood. Child, do you understand?"

Amused that he addressed her as the Ancient Zoroastrian had, she burst into her contagious laughter, pleased she had not lost it with her persistent tears. "Can't you see I'm not a child?"

"I see everything," he murmured. "Have you noticed your tears have stopped?"

She touched her cheeks. In his company, she had forgotten her grief.

"An old pain in your bones has not been acknowledged."

"You're too serious, Soleiman. Forget old pains. Put your hands on my joints to solder them and bring back my music."

"Soon," he whispered, noticing her trembling fingers. "Your bones will heal. Now they're buried under confusion. Lift the burden and your bones will sing again. I'll be your guide."

She wondered at a love so selfless he insisted on her healing, despite the awareness that it would be the end of her visits.

꩜

Soleiman struggled to complete his story, but the knowledge that today would be the last time he would see Gold Dust dulled his creativity. He had tried to accelerate the healing process, but when he mentioned her childhood, she folded into herself. From rare glimpses of her past, he had learned that a cross-eyed man with a bloated belly who smelled of burned metals figured prominently in her memories.

He searched his books for help from Socrates, Aristotle, and the canons of the great physician Ebne Sina. He racked his brain for an approach to help her brave her past. Suddenly he rose and leaped in the air, hands applauding, toes tapping. He had, at last, located the problem and the solution had followed.

The yodeling of the Ancient Zoroastrian floated through the window. The sultana was at his door. He drew the drapes. He would receive her in the glow of a lamp he had made by blowing a camel's bladder into a sphere and painting it with lacquer to hold the shape.

With the help of a cane, Gold Dust stepped down from the stretcher without help. Soleiman followed, arms extended, ready to support her. She walked slowly but steadily toward the cushions, her face golden in the light. Even in that fragile state, he preferred her to any woman. Yet not once had he touched her, not even a brush on her lips. It had nothing to do with her frail body. Her fearless temperament and expansive laughter made up for all else. To him love was like composing music. He imagined himself and Gold Dust as two players creating a tune with their emotions, notes that ripened, surged, and soared into waves that would wash over them in an inevitable climax. He was a patient man who did not have the luxury of time.

He helped her recline. His mouth lingered, a breath away from hers. Her lips parted. She pressed her expectant eyes shut. She felt a stirring. He withdrew.

"Touch me," she pleaded.

He saw that, despite her request, she was scared, too. And she was disappointed. Should he disclose that he did not dare touch her because he feared for her life, because he had promised her mother? Should he tell her he had read her mind? Yes, he was still a virgin and he was courting disaster, and she was aware of that, too. He must not tempt her into an emotional tangle worse than she already was in.

He placed on her lap his writing board, a bleached collarbone of a camel. "I found your cure. Last night, remembering our discussions, a name that populated your childhood memories came up again and again."

"Forget the past." Her childhood must not intrude into her last hours with Soleiman. She had locked her memories in a safe place. Memories that had hibernated to spark sporadically. They would lead to others and others that would crack her protective shell. Then she would return to the harem more vulnerable than before.

"Memories don't go away," Soleiman sighed. "Who was Jacob the Fatherless?"

Her hand struggled toward him. "Don't stir the filth of my past."

Soleiman sprang up and danced around the room. He had a feline quality, a sensuality like a panther. Removing the sword that leaned against the wall, he drew graceful figures in the air above her head. With his blade, he lifted a curl from her shoulder and planted a kiss on the tip. He made her laugh even as she hurt. His words were like a balm. "First acknowledge, then sever yourself from your past so you'll be able to greet future possibilities."

"I don't have a future without you."

He was tempted to encourage her to remain here. They could flee the empire, far from the Shah, where even eagles would not find them. He would till the land to produce fruits and grains, and she would grow strong and bear him children with chestnut hair, ringing laughter, and sweet, wandering eyes.

What right did he have to indulge in senseless fantasies? What could a penniless acrobat offer to a past favorite? In his home, with columns of malachite, she would evoke the palace where eunuchs had bowed to her every wish and servants had scrambled to bathe and dress her, where a powerful Shah had flung jewels at her feet, and her daughter awaits her return.

"Your future is in Pearl Hall," Soleiman said. "It's a wondrous place. Like a pearl hidden in an oyster. Pry the shell open, prod the pearl from layers of slime, hold it up to the sun, and discover the laminate with all its shimmering colors."

Her laughter permeated the small room. "You're a hopeless dreamer, Soleiman."

"Tell me about Jacob the Fatherless."

An acrid smell stung her throat. Something burned in her stomach. Flames lashed in her bones. "My mother rarely talked about him. 'He was a blacksmith,' she said, 'that's all you need to know. He melted iron. That was his passion.' If I demanded more, her hand sprang to her chest and grief contorted her face. Once, I asked why she did not light the furnace at home, even in winter. The mark between her breasts flared. She said the fire reminded her of married life and whore-wives.

"I remember heavy hands. Maybe they belonged to Jacob the Fatherless. They tied me up with wires. Through a funnel, they forced steaming liquid down my throat, but it didn't burn me. My bones began to sing, but my eyes became dry until the day I fell from the horse."

Silence formed icicles around Soleiman's lamp. The mystery began to unravel. Jacob had used liquid iron, the oldest weapon known to blacksmiths. However, Rebekah had protected her daughter well. Books of apothecary mention a certain potion of cypress, myrrh, and magic mushroom, which coats and shields the insides from scalding matter.

They were out of time. The Ancient Zoroastrian was at the door.

Soleiman buried his wet face in Gold Dust's lap, praying his love had brought back the health of her bones. Gold Dust pressed her mouth to his eyes to drink from his tears.

Soleiman removed an object from his pocket and placed it in Gold Dust's hand. She stared at a bracelet of dried, shriveled fruits. Her cherry anklet.

40

No! No!" Rebekah cried, as if the word would change her daughter's fate. What happened to the Ancient Zoroastrian's prophecy? Mattresses stuffed with stinking feathers of fowl were replacing the jewel-encrusted thrones.

Had someone turned the Shah against Gold Dust? Warned him of her obsession with the acrobat? Why else did the Shah refuse to see Gold Dust or herself? She must visit Narcissus. He had access to the most intimate gossip of the palace, even as he remained in hiding, knowing full well that his absence would only delay his inevitable fate.

The eunuch listened to Rebekah. His eyes flashed hope, anger, vengeance. Once he secured the jar with his severed organ, he would be ready for trial and accept his punishment. "I know why the Shah is furious."

Rebekah slipped closer. "Why, sweetlove?"

Narcissus stepped back. "There's only one thing in this world you can bribe me with."

"I know. Your manhood. But if I give it back, and you lie, I'm left with nothing."

The eunuch opened his cloak, unbuttoned his waistband,

and released a cord from around his midriff. Raising the rope, he dangled it in front of Rebekah. "This is priceless. Keep your side of the bargain. When you're assured of the truth, return it to me."

Nestled in a vibrant emerald the size of an egg was the likeness of the Shah's face etched with fine strokes. The stone was precious, so was the splendid carving, the aesthetic toil of many years. Rebekah secured the rope around her neck, lodging the jewel between her breasts. "Don't go anywhere, Narcissus. Before dusk, I'll be back with your treasure."

On her way to the temple of the One-Eyed Rabbi, she removed the sprig of mint and sniffed as if she were the Devil and in pursuit of herself. She resented the fact that, once again, she was forced to invade the rabbi's peace.

The One-Eyed Rabbi crouched under a window, his feet immersed in a bath of permanganate. With a heated skewer, he seared his corns. The smell of burnt fungus filled the air. At the tapping of feminine footsteps, he focused his good eye at the approaching luminous blur. He groaned. The whore was back.

"I won't stay long," Rebekah hastened to assure. "I've come to pray and ask forgiveness."

"Go to the women's section, maybe Hashem finds pity upon your soul." The rabbi struggled up the stairs to the ark. His body swayed and his cane tapped as he asked the Lord to pardon his transgressions.

When it seemed the rabbi's prayers would never end, Rebekah called his name. But he seemed to have lost his contact with this world. Short of knocking him unconscious, she could not get to the jar while he stood there, his head resting against the doors of the ark. She had not come so far to surrender to a blind rabbi's religious eccentricities. She climbed the pulpit, gazed at his glass eye, reached out, and fondled his crotch. Her red mouth parted to suck on his dry lips. He must suffer from severe hernia, she thought as she stroked and squeezed two exceptionally large lumps.

He did not gasp, did not sigh. He fell. His tongue clamped between his teeth.

She had squeezed too hard and killed him. Now she would be charged with the murder of a rabbi. She felt tired, longed to go home, undress, lock her doors, and never again allow a man into her bed. It was time to retire, give up on a world that had defeated her every move. Give up on Gold Dust? Give up on Raven?

She pressed her ear to the rabbi's chest and heard a faint beat. She pried open his jaw and held on to his tongue so it would not fall back into his throat and choke him. She propped him against the ark, dashed into his bedroom, brought back a bowl of water, and splashed it on his face. He convulsed. Sucked his breath in. He would live.

She flung the doors of the ark open and reached out to the far corners. Her frantic hands slid into the dark alcoves. She moved the Torah, slid her palm under it, around it, on top. She swept the shelf with her fingers, climbed up and took a closer look. The jar was gone.

The rabbi did not allow anyone close to the ark. He was the only person who removed the Torah, unlocked its wooden casing, and dusted the ark. She shook him, rattling his false teeth. He opened one eye and slipped back into oblivion. She dashed into his bedroom, flung his mattress against the wall. There was not much furniture, not many places to hide the jar. To whom could she turn? Gold Dust was consumed by the acrobat. And Raven, perched on a steeple of power, was unpredictable, and could not be trusted.

Rebekah sat down on the bare floor and waited for the rabbi to regain consciousness. Kilns flamed in her chest as her eyes swept the room, fell on a broken mantelpiece under which rested a stool with the rabbi's washbasin. The jar stood on the mantelpiece.

The lid was absent and the container filled with water. A branch of orange blossoms stuck out from the center of a bunch of herbs. The brine had settled at the bottom. She flung the branch and herbs out and emptied the water carefully. Plunging a finger in the jar, she stirred what she thought was brine, but found out to be sand. Where was the organ? She rushed back into the hall.

The rabbi sat cross-legged on the floor, his chest wheezing.

She raised her hands in a gesture of complete submission. "I'll leave and never look back if you tell me what happened to the contents of this jar."

The rabbi fluttered his hands on the crown of his head. "Now you want to steal the Lord's miracle from me?"

Rebekah brought the jar closer to his good eye. "Where are the contents?"

"What contents? The Lord placed this in the ark. I hosed it down in the backyard." He grabbed the jar. "It's a gift from Him—a receptacle for the *boreh ismeh besamim*—the prayer of herbs and scent."

Rebekah wrestled the jar away from him and ran into the backyard. She plowed the dirt with her fingernails, shook every thorny bush, every blade of dried grass. With bare feet, she padded through the slosh at the bottom of a grimy pool, then came down on all fours and searched with her hands.

The eunuch would never go entire to the afterworld.

∽

Rebekah took the Alley of Beggars toward the butcher's shop and left with a sweetbread still warm inside the wrapping. For the first time since Jacob's death, she ignited the kiln in her bedroom. She set a stool next to the kiln and sat counting the minutes. Fiendish tongues licked the soot-blackened walls. Her nipples shrank against the heat. Smoke and cinder burned her throat. The translucent skin on her fingers glowed. Bloody and veined, the sweetbread glistened in her palm.

Would the day come when she could look at a fire without evoking the Devil, without wondering why Gold Dust's bones had started singing? Weeping. Crying out for help. She could still hear the first melody of her daughter's body: the moan of harps, the trill of nightingales. She had examined her daughter's mouth and had found no trace of liquid iron, or had seen it and not recognized the poison. Had the Ancient Zoroastrian's concoction saved her?

Had she been absent when her daughter had needed her most?

The sweetbread dried up and shrank. Like her hand. Now it was the right size and consistency. She dropped it in the jar of sand, went to the corner of her room, and searched through the many parcels. She pulled out old veils, faded pants, crumpled skirts. Each piece revived memories: the day she buried Jacob; the day she became a bundle woman; the day she initiated her sweet Moses into manhood. But none carried the importance of the dress she wore on the two most significant occasions of her life: the day she seduced Narcissus, so he would allow her daughter into the harem, and the day she reappeared in the Jewish Quarter with Gold Dust on a journey to visit Rouh'Allah to offer her daughter to his son. His rejection had caused a shame greater than she had ever experienced, greater than the shame of spreading her legs to Jacob and barking like a dog. But that incident had sparked such a monumental dream; its success had become as essential as breathing.

That day was the beginning of her life. Today might be the end of it, and she wanted to dress appropriately.

The crumpled silver veil and the glass-studded skirt were stained with years. She had worn this glittering skirt and vest on the same day the merchant had found her daughter unworthy of his son. She pressed the garments to her nose. The scent of ancient cypress had drifted from Rouh'Allah's cloak; his melodious voice still populated her nights. She clasped the old glass beads around her neck. Had the cheap necklace offended him, too?

The skirt and vest fit her as they had in her youth, hugging her waist and flaring out at the hips. She sprinkled them with water and sat by the kiln for the heat to dry and smooth them out. She wondered if the eunuch had a heart for memories to soften, if he would recognize the garments she had worn when she first introduced him to his lust gland and the joy of an orgasm.

The flames crackled. Fire sparks of iron flashed against the kiln. The blaze turned orange, the color of the amber prayer beads Rouh'Allah the Spirit of God had toyed with the day her life took a different turn. Sparks flared, sputtered, hissed, died. Yellow. The color of the pouch of coins Rouh'Allah had thrown in her lap. It had hurt. The fire emitted the odor of greed and fat. She gazed into the hearth. A pool of yellow appeared at the bottom. Her stomach lurched. Bile stung her throat. Liquid gold.

Her late husband's wealth.

Poor Jacob. He had first melted his gold in the fire and had then stepped in to join it. Years ago, when she had searched the house, she should have thought of the kiln. I'm a rich woman, she thought, and felt no joy. She slumped back on the stool and waited for the flames to die and the yellow river tainted with Jacob's fat to harden.

She tossed a bucket of dirt into the kiln and buried Jacob again.

41

The Great Black Eunuch stared at Rebekah's stained vest and moth-ridden skirt. The past, faded and rusty, was imprinted on her, a nymph pulled out of an ancient coffer. Her steps were light and full of promises; tarnished glass studs shimmered around her. His heart ached with anticipation. The pain was unbearable. His knees wobbled. He did not dare take a step toward her. Once she gave his treasure back, he would regain his strength. The first time she had introduced him to his lust gland, he had felt such vigor, a euphoria greater than opium's, sweeter than the hypnotic sway of her hips as she approached him now, an apparition who would restore his manhood. She levitated, an angel of mercy in antiquated clothing. A mirage. Not again. Not the bleating calf. They cut him from the roots. Clean-cut.

At last, she was at his side. Pleasant warmth filled his groin. His lust gland swelled as he remembered her lubricated fingers teasing and probing him. He reached out his begging palm.

She untied her bundle. Unwrapped the jar. Held it up.

He stared at it, snatched it, circled it in the air, pressed it to his heart, removed the cap and surveyed the contents. His marble eyes, hidden under puffy lids, darted from side to side as he burrowed a finger into the jar and poked the organ. Stroked it. Weighed it. His stare flicked back to her.

"Thank you!" he croaked, pain tearing at his chest.

"What does the Shah know?" she asked, clutching the emerald in her hand.

"Beware . . . Moon Face . . . the Shah. . . ." His hand vaulted to grab the stone.

Rebekah dodged him. "Has the order gone out?"

"The date is set. . . . Gold Dust will die . . . " he gasped, doubling over.

"When?" she cried. "When's the date?"

The eunuch's fingers clawed at his chest. The jar crashed onto the marble. Rebekah sprang back. Glass, sand, and shriveled sweetbread scattered about.

Narcissus saw his hope strewn to the dust. He buckled. Collapsed.

"Talk!" she ordered.

His eyes gaped at her.

"Talk," she pleaded.

Saliva dribbled from his mouth.

She slipped her sandals off and pressed her heel to his artery. Narcissus the Great Black Eunuch was dead.

Rouh'Allah the Spirit of God cuddled the emerald in his palm. Such a pure green. Such a flawless stone. Such workmanship. But he was taken more by the woman than by the stone that dangled from a rope around her neck. Not a line on her face had changed, not one strand of hair had lost its luster, not a spark had diminished from her violet eyes. And she was wearing the same dress she had worn when she came to offer her daughter. That day was carved in his heart. She had left behind an aura that warmed his home for years. He had propped that parcel of coins on the shelf in his bedroom. A token of his shame. At times, he had weighed it in his palm and had thought of her. In a world that could not tell valor from vanity, the pouch remained a symbol of her courage. He had cherished it as if it held a part of the woman. Now she had returned, wearing around her neck the glass bead necklace she had worn that day, and nestled between her breasts an emerald worth more than his wealth.

"Keep the stone. I'll give you all the gold you need."

She colored. The man had not changed. When would he realize she would not accept charity? She had come to plead once again on behalf of her daughter. This time to bribe a whole contingency of spies and guards to learn when and how her daughter's life would end. Although the Shah did not have the heart for executions, Rebekah knew he could not allow an adulteress free among his sultanas.

"No charity," Rebekah whispered, amazed his voice had not lost its hold upon her.

"My wealth is yours," the merchant said, rejoicing that the years had not reduced her pride.

Rebekah felt the man, his scent of rain-soaked woods. The silver at his temples had spread to the rest of his hair. The lines at the corners of his mouth had deepened. His smoky eyes harbored a sadness that came from living alone.

"I won't lose you again," he whispered.

He was only being kind, Rebekah was certain. It was his nature. These were words of charity, not passion. "How is your son?"

"He's well. He went to other lands, became a doctor, is married, has five children. All boys. I would have liked a granddaughter."

Her eyes lighted. "I have one. She will become queen."

"And Gold Dust?" He reached for her hand.

Her fingers grazed the lines on his palm as if her future was carved there. "She's too sensitive. Not ruthless, ambitious . . ."

He squeezed her fingers. "Not like her mother?"

"My ambitions are for her."

He wrapped a protective arm around her waist.

She welcomed his embrace. She was tired. Tired of pride and vengeance and aspirations. Tired of the Devil and his mint and the smell of iron that never went away. She ached to lean against Rouh'Allah and cling to the melody of his voice.

Words of love he had locked up for years poured out of him.

She realized this was not kindness and charity, but a love that had had time to ripen and sift out doubt. But her life had been directed for too long on her daughter. She did not know how to shift her emotions.

"Stay," he pleaded.

What did he mean? Was she still a whore to him? Didn't she deserve to be properly proposed to? She would not "stay" with any man, not even Rouh'Allah, who was the only man who sounded right to her, the only man to whom her nipples responded even in anger.

She dashed into the alleys.

42

We will sever your adulterous head!" the Shah roared to Gold Dust's blushing roses. Uprooting them, he snapped their necks, ripped the petals, crushing their tenderly fed buds into the earth.

"How dare you!" he bellowed, stomping his flowers deeper into their graves.

From behind the hedges, Raven watched her father transform into a demon. Guilt-ridden emotions assaulted her. And an unexpected sadness. The most severe punishment she had anticipated for her mother was to be locked in the House of Tears. Then she would have made sure her mother had all the comforts she needed, save her lover. But the thunder of her father's voice, and Hazel-Boy's whispers, told her the king would execute his favorite. Faced with the possibility of losing her mother, Raven realized the extent of her love for her.

She was baffled by her father's violent reaction. Was it the outcome of deep affection for her mother, or of injured pride? Thorns drew blood from Raven's bare feet and intensified her thirst as she hurried away.

When there were no more roses to raze and no more curses

to hurl, the king wondered if Gold Dust's execution would cause Raven grief. A king had to do what the empire expected of him. And after all, Raven had been the one to confirm his suspicion.

At first he had shut his ears to Moon Face's words. How could Gold Dust have fallen in love with another man? Had he, the king, not fulfilled her every desire, indulged her with every extravagance a woman could fancy? Then Gulf Lily had repeated the accusations. Still, the eunuch was loyal to Moon Face, the Shah had reminded himself. There was no truth to their allegation. But when Raven had hugged him, pressed her lips to his ear, and whispered, "Watch Madar. She's slipped back into her own world," he had ordered his spies to follow the sultana and the Ancient Zoroastrian. The news that came back had set him on fire.

He abandoned his graveyard of roses and went to the palace to find refuge in Hazel-Boy's arms.

The Shah tenderly squeezed Hazel-Boy's organ. "We shall twist her pretty neck until no life is left in her!"

Hazel-Boy walked the Shah's spine with light fingers. "My lord, Gold Dust is faithful to you. Don't listen to jealous words."

This eunuch had a soothing quality to him, suppleness no man possessed and firmness no woman had. It was good to feel his hard penis, the expert touch familiar with his body. He was man and woman in one, without each gender's complicated intricacies. "You are not with us tonight," the Shah said, sensing his softening.

"I worry for you, my shah," Hazel-Boy replied, willing himself to harden in the Shah's hand. "It's a conspiracy to eliminate the favorite, then the princess. The two women closest to you."

Hazel-Boy's fingers, dipped in salve, grazed the king's scrotum, slipped down the tight cord and around the shaft. The

Shah moaned, struggling to delay his release. He didn't want to talk about treachery and death. He longed for an hour of rest. The emollient was cool on his shaft, the pressure right. No woman could master him with such precise rhythm. His passion was about to erupt. He must contain himself. At times of anger and sadness he preferred to spill himself in Hazel-Boy. Not in the impersonal vastness of a hand.

His seed flooded the eunuch's palm.

Hazel-Boy's lips brushed the Shah's forehead. "Rest, my king, you will feel better."

"Stay!" the Shah ordered.

Hazel-Boy rubbed the king with a towel soaked in oil of sandalwood. His mind raced, but his touch was attentive. He did not mind Gold Dust's love for the acrobat. Long ago, in that opium dream preceding his castration, he had promised himself to help those who found pleasure in each other. His heart lurched at the thought of Gold Dust's head gaping on a stake above the Courtyard of Horses. Could he beseech the Bibi Sultana's help? She despised him, but he could use that to Gold Dust's advantage, argue that without her the king would surrender completely to him.

"Talk to us!" the Shah ordered.

"You are tired, my lord."

The Shah seized the eunuch's arm. "Our orders have gone out. At dawn, the bowstring will slash her throat. Our last respect a quiet burial in our rose garden."

"And what will the princess think? The favorite is her mother." Hazel-Boy's arm did not flinch in the Shah's clutch.

"We will raise Raven on our own. As is befitting the mother of kings."

Sadness swept over the eunuch. Was this all the compassion the king could muster for his favorite? A swift death by the bowstring, a dignified death, an eternal home next to his beloved roses? It was hopeless. There was no retrieving the order, no time to go to the Bibi Sultana. He must warn Rebekah before dawn. He shifted about with light steps, arranging the covers around the Shah. Hazel-Boy felt the shock of the king's stare on the length of his naked body. He relaxed his muscles. Stroking the Shah's forehead, he felt the beat of his arteries. "My king, you have a fever. Allow me to pour your nightcap."

Hazel-Boy stepped into his silk garments, locked the chain around his neck, and mixed a brew from the roots of the eucalyptus tree and wild berries. Turning his back to the king, he added from his silver bottle six drops of the nectar of poppy seeds. The Shah would sleep deeply through the next day.

Hazel-Boy slipped out into the Secret Passage and sped through the labyrinth of damp corridors. How could the Shah end Gold Dust's life because she had fallen in love? Had he not shared his king with hundreds of sultanas and rejoiced at his pleasure? But he was only a half-man. Did true men react differently? What about women? How did Gold Dust and the other sultanas feel about sharing the Shah? And Honey? She was like him, half-woman, half-man, desiring other women, weeping when a lover was indifferent, but having the generosity to forgive. Honey! She was the only one he could trust in the harem. He would seek her help before he hurried to the Jewish Quarter.

The guards at the inner entrance made way for the lover of the Shah and the confidant of the sultanas. He took the halls to the harem and entered the sleeping quarters of the sultanas. Honey's bedroom was at the end of the corridor, another ruse of the eunuchs to keep her far from other women.

He approached her pallet and laid his hand on her shoulder.

She sprang up, the black tear at the corner of her eye wet with her dreams. He pressed his hand on her mouth. "The Shah found out about Gold Dust."

Her teeth punctured his palm; her lids fluttered like miniature wings.

"At dawn, the bowman will go to her. Warn her! Tell her to
leave her quarters and wait for me in the Secret Passage. Spend
the rest of the night in her room. Don't fall asleep. Stall.
Deceive the executioner. Steer him toward the gardens."

"What if she refuses?"

"Convince her if she flees she'll have a chance to save
Soleiman."

Hazel-Boy ran out, hearing the rustle of Honey's attire
behind him. On the horizon, the moon was high and the vast
branches of the plane trees cast ominous shadows. The hoot of
owls punctuated the silence. He climbed the path behind the
watchtower, from where the guards had often seen him leave to
take care of personal errands for the king. He must get to
Rebekah before sunrise. He gazed up at the watchtower. Moonlight flooded one of the four arches.

Framed by the arch, a silhouette dangled in the breeze.

He squinted, trying to make sense of the sight. He did not
need new troubles. He must hurry on. But he could not tear
himself away from the black vision carved against the stars. He
dashed up the stairs to the top of the tower.

He came to a halt at the landing on the peak. A dark hulk
dangled from a rope tied to a hook from the ceiling. The neck
twisted at a grotesque angle against a shoulder. Hazel-Boy
moved closer and turned the body toward the full moon.

A shaft of light hit Gulf Lily's face.

The loyal eunuch had preferred to take his life before his
mistress was punished. It was not a secret that Moon Face, having borne bad news about the favorite, would lose her life.

℘

Rebekah heard the banging on her door. She pressed her naked body to the rough wood, her palm cupping her heart. No one came to her this late anymore. Something had gone wrong. The wood cut into her back. She would not open. She would lock herself up, crouch by the kiln until the Ancient Zoroastrian came for her.

"Rebekah, open up!"

She squeezed her ear to the door. The urgent voice did not belong to men who wallowed in the bearing of evil news.

She unlocked the door.

Hazel-Boy stepped in, held her shoulders to steady her. "At dawn, the executioner will go to Gold Dust."

Rebekah slipped down to the floor. Her cheeks were wet. When had she last cried? Not even when she was branded. There must have been other tears. When her doll had caught fire? When the kiln would not stop roaring? When Gold Dust's bones moaned with hunger?

Hazel-Boy took into his arms the naked woman, his tutor of love. Her polished skin gleamed. The hair on her pubis and armpits glistened. Her brand radiated the pride of her youth. Nature had treated her well. She did not need any embellishments, other than the sprig of mint that had become part of her. At another time, in a bare room with a cold kiln, she had converted him into a man. Even castration could not rob him of the gift she granted him. "Honey will warn Gold Dust. She'll wait in the Secret Passage. We have to find a way to get her out."

"Her legs won't carry her too far."

"She's much stronger than you think."

Rebekah's mind raced as she willed her body into action. She needed brave hands and lucid minds to plan her daughter's escape. Her fingers sprang to her chest, weighing the emerald. Rouh'Allah the Spirit of God would give her daughter refuge.

For a short while, until she found another place, another land. "We must wake the merchant," she announced, racing to toss a chador over her body.

The howl of stray dogs broke the silence of the alleys. Hazel-Boy led Venus by a rope as Rebekah pointed the way. Stripped of his usual trimming and headstand of ostrich feathers, the donkey appeared old and shabby. Rebekah flanked the limping animal with her bare thighs. This was her third trip to the merchant. But tonight she had left behind her pride and the vow to refuse his help.

Despite the late hour, the merchant's servant did not question Rebekah's presence, but went into the house to awaken the *Agha*.

The merchant's usually brushed hair tumbled down his forehead, hiding the gray and giving him a younger look. Her skilled glance determined he was naked under his robe. "This is Hazel-Boy, a friend of Gold," she whispered. "Rouh'Allah, my daughter is in danger. She's fallen in love with Soleiman."

He held her by the hand and led her in, thinking this woman's daughter was even braver than Rebekah, certainly much braver than he. "We'll find a solution."

His presence, his serene voice, his firm grip, and his unwavering gaze calmed her. She turned to Hazel-Boy. "Will the Bibi Sultana help?"

"The order of execution has gone out," he replied. "No one can change it now." Hazel-Boy thought of the possibilities. There were too many jealous women, too many eunuchs loyal only to their own mistresses, too many guards who feared for their lives. Only Honey could be trusted. And she had been warned. Hazel-Boy drew the plan of the harem on a parchment and pointed to all the gardens and gates that led to the outside. The only unguarded part of the palace was the back, which was skirted by the river, where the voracious sharks patrolled.

"Even if we manage to get her out, where will she go? What will become of Raven?" Rebekah slumped, disheartened at the enormity of the task.

"Get Gold Dust out of the palace," Rouh'Allah said. "Leave the rest to me. My son is familiar with roads that lead to other lands. We'll send Gold Dust to a place where not even the Shah and his men will find her." His eyes swept the length of her body.

"What about Raven?"

"Raven will stay behind," Rebekah said. The Shah would pursue Gold Dust with the force of his pride, but he would hunt Raven with the vigor of his passion, and that was dangerous and infinite.

"I know the way out of the Secret Passage," Hazel-Boy said. "If we could cross the river, we would lose ourselves in the woods before the guards are alerted."

"The river is full of sharks!" Rebekah cried out.

"Yes," the merchant replied, summoning his servant. "But every problem has a solution." A plan was forming in his mind. It would not be difficult to win the cooperation of the men of the Quarter. They would be pleased to repay him for his never-ending kindness. He had been their benefactor. If the palace refused to help, the Jews would not.

He would awaken the carpenters, ask them to collect their tools and set out toward the river. They would work feverishly to construct a raft from logs that drifted on the river. From the side of the river bordered by woods, they would row to the other bank, where the palace stood. Before dawn, they would pick Gold Dust up and row back with her and advance deep into the forest.

Hazel-Boy was up and ready to leave. Rebekah became conscious of her chador. She had to wear something that would not hamper her.

"You must disguise yourself," the merchant said. "Would you mind wearing my robes?"

She flung her clothes on the carpet and stepped into a pair of pants he handed her, rolling the cuffs up. She felt their stares on her and realized she stood with her indignant nipples exposed, the pants sliding below her mound. She pulled up the pants and drew the waist string tight, flinging his shirt over her breasts.

Rouh'Allah walked out to dress. So the tales about her mark were true. It had blushed under his gaze. Was this miracle what gave this woman her rare qualities? The ability to undress in front of men as if it were the nature of things, to call him by his first name as if they were longtime lovers, to fight for her daughter as if her life was fused to hers? Rouh'Allah strode into the night, aware that only through saving the daughter might he claim the mother.

Soleiman sprang from his bed and clutched his sword. The end was here! The palace guards were at his door. They had exe-cuted Gold Dust. He could not hear the thumping of his heart, nor feel the tears in his eyes. He was ready for death. He flung the door open and faced ghosts glaring condemnation. It was a dream. These wells of disapproval were the product of his imag-ination. His conscience had caught up with him.

"Get ready, Soleiman."

He pressed his lids shut to squeeze out sleep and bring into focus the presence of Rebekah and the shadow of the merchant behind her. He did not recognize the other man, cloaked in lavish silks.

Rebekah held Soleiman by the shoulders and shook him. "Wake up! We don't have time. Venus is outside. Feed him.

Prepare a bundle of food and go wait by the gates of the city. You're going to *yengeh donyah*."

Soleiman opened his mouth to say that even if the Shah's men were after him, he did not care to flee to the edge of the earth. He would stay here, be buried next to Gold Dust. But his visitors had vanished into the night.

43

Behind the partitions, countless stars bled through the dark canvas of the skies. The din of Raven's thoughts disturbed the calm. Her heavy breasts, erect nipples, and the response of her flesh to her exploring fingers were alien and sweet. The craving. The thirst. The demons in her mind blotted her of the last drop of moisture. She consumed large amounts of sherbets, teas, and wine. She took long baths and swam often in the river. It was useless. Her body was a desert.

She had slept with lethargic women and eunuchs who roamed the harem, half-men whose organs had been left intact although their testicles had been removed. She preferred these eunuchs to sound men because they knew how to prolong her pleasure. They had groveled between her legs and feasted on her with their tongues. They had promised to quench her thirst without piercing her maidenhood. But the drought in her veins persisted.

Yesterday, after her swim with the sharks, Cyrus, the naked diver, had carried her to the top of the cliff and licked the shark ointment off her body, his tongue circling her underarms and nipples, teasing her navel and mound, and darting in and out of her until her screams had exploded.

But the thirst persisted. So she fabricated another excuse, another urgent reason to visit her father. A drop of sweat in the cleft of his chin, or an accidental kiss from his lower lip, where saliva gathered, would momentarily replenish her with moisture. Why did he resist her?

Her eyes swept the skies and stopped at the horizon. She threw her arms up, turning her back to the window. She didn't understand the sadness she felt for a mother who refused to accept the truth, who refused to acknowledge that her daughter was no longer a child. If not for her mother, the king would have noticed the drought in her. Last week her fingernails had a healthy sheen to them. Now they were brittle and yellow. Her scalp felt taut. Her skin was losing its suppleness and threatened to strangle her. She would not stand idle while this demon robbed her of her youth and beauty.

Spreading her thighs, she rubbed the lips with the balm of musk and sprayed a mist of the essence of cloves, nutmeg, and ginger on her body. Wrapping a diaphanous veil of lilac around her breasts, she fastened the gold chain with the jar of shark ointment around her waist. In the straps of her sandal, she adjusted a dagger. The snake of gold with ruby eyes clasped her arm.

She glided through the dim corridors of the Secret Passage. The night was hot and humid, which made it difficult to breathe. Hardly acknowledging the presence of the eunuchs who stepped aside, she slipped into the royal chambers.

She stood at the foot of the bed and gazed at the sleeping king. Was her mother in his dreams? She threw off her veil and unlocked her ornaments, her movements cautious but hurried. Through the drapes, the moon glared at her naked body. Her boldness disappeared. She fluttered around her father's pallet to escape the moon's castigating stare. Silver hair tumbled down her hips and slashed the dark. She leaned down to sweep her tongue over the moist bush under her father's arm. The moon scrutinized her. She rose and danced around its beam, skipping to the left and right, under the windowsill, behind the ottoman, in back of the drapes. The chilling light was at her side, under her toes, trailing her, daring her.

She searched the room for a hiding place, behind the partitions, the cushions, the sculptures, but the fear of being alone behind some inanimate object stopped her. She slipped under the covers, sinking into the scent of black roses.

Eyes heavy with narcotic sleep, the Shah wrapped his arms around her waist and crushed her to himself. Her lips parted, embracing his tongue, sucking the wetness. Her mouth clung to his, replenishing her cells, rejoicing at the increasing hardness against her belly. She inhaled the tart odor of hashish on his breath and was saddened that he needed opiates to calm him. With all her inhuman strength, her thighs held him in their grip, and in fear of missing the moment when he awakened, she did not blink.

Through gauze and veils and curtains, the Shah had illusions of being immersed in ivory flesh. He felt the softness of thighs, the smoothness of arms, the tap of fingers. Was this a dream? Had opiates taken over? His eyes were heavy, but he felt with exceptional sensitivity. He inhaled a scent he could not place. The perfume embraced him as if he had spent all his life swimming in it. His palms cupped perfectly round mounds. Had Gold Dust come to ask forgiveness? This was not her fragrance of jasmine. His fingers trailed the indentation of a slim back, up to the curve of a lean neck. Moon Face? She had never felt warm to the touch, never had soft lips, and she wore the essence of crushed aphrodisiacs. His hands crawled into a harvest of silk; lush strands streamed through his fingers as he raised them to his nose. The scent of wild spices filled his nostrils. Only one woman wore this daring perfume.

His eyes sprang open. Silver strands cascaded through his fingers. Only one woman had hair this color.

He saw ruby eyes.

Only one woman had eyes of fire.

"You are mine." An urgent whisper. A pledge. An order.

Only one woman owned this strong yet feminine voice.

He moaned, the narcotics rushing his blood.

He had to rise. Break away from her. Rush out. Call the guards. Order them to remove her. He searched for the bell to summon his men. His hands were paralyzed, his legs dead pillars.

Her thirsty tongue aroused a desire for the forbidden. Her eyes were warming torches that held him in their grip. She was connected to him with her thighs and arms and lips and through lineage. The kernel of his soul. His body dissolved into hers like warm wax. She was consuming him, and it seemed an innate act that should have transpired long ago.

She sat up, turned around, and straddled him, facing his feet. Her core exposed, she bent to drink from the source. A drop of salty liquid at the tip burst in her mouth. She went back for more and more, always careful to slacken her lips and trail her tongue around the edges so as not to drain him of all his fluids.

When he gasped, no longer able to endure her thirst, she faced him, taking him between her breasts. She felt his experienced hands tease her body and was angry with the many women he had had. She rose on her knees, then lowered herself on him, again and again, crushing him under her until he moaned that animal sound he had locked for years. The cry she had been awaiting. The plea of a king rendered helpless by the enormity of his desire. A cry of submission no other woman had evoked.

Moonlight flooded his face and the white of his teeth. He was smiling.

She no longer shunned the moon.

"I will bear you sons."

Her father. Her lover. She would bear him sons and obliterate the shame he had endured for so long.

She lifted herself and planted her legs at his sides, looming above him. Milky thighs spread wide over him, she had a regal quality that assured him the strength to support both love and loss. The loss of Gold Dust. The love of Raven.

She lowered herself.

A roar welled up from him. A cry of pain. His pain. Her pain. He shot into her the seeds that would become his sons. The heirs of the empire.

"Pedar," she moaned. "Don't force fidelity with death. Let your favorite go."

44

Honey glanced at her reflection in the mirror in Gold Dust's room. Layers of black concealed all but her bewildered eyes. Her mind raced, and the rhythm of her heart was broken, but determination propelled her on. For too long, she had desired women who disliked her or was refused by those who feared the Shah. She was thirty-six, an old and tired woman, who had experienced more than women twice her age. Gold Dust's charm and candor had enriched her life. She was thankful for that.

The chatter of crickets entered through the window. Bright-colored drapes static in the heat; gifts of silver and crystal glittering in the moonlight. She slid her fingers over Gold Dust's hair.

Gold Dust sprang up. All of last week while the Shah had avoided her, while the eunuch was in hiding, while Moon Face sported an eternal smile, and Raven's glances were secretive, Gold Dust had wondered if the Shah had found out about her and Soleiman. Now she gazed at Honey's eyes and knew she bore bad news.

"Get ready," she whispered. "Hurry!"

Prisoners don't hurry anywhere, Gold Dust thought. They drown in the smoke of opium until nothing is left. "Where to?" she asked.

"The Shah found out. We've got to get you out of here."

Where? To the Jewish Quarter, where she would be trailed by the executioner? To a foreign world she did not know? Certainly not to Soleiman's shack, where she would be discovered before dawn.

Honey threw the covers off Gold Dust and dragged her to her feet. "Hazel-Boy will meet you in the Secret Passage. Move!"

Smell of the passage filled Gold Dust's nostrils. The odor of mildew and humidity, the scent of rain and tree barks. Dear Hazel-Boy. He was raised in the palace. He must know secrets none but the Shah knew. She trusted him, but she didn't have the strength to dare the unknown. Her bones were weak and aching. "I can't leave Raven," she murmured, watching Honey rummage through her coffer of clothing, choosing pieces and setting them aside.

"Are you blind?" Honey said, dressing Gold Dust in layers. "Do you think Raven needs you? You've no choice. The Shah will execute you. Soleiman will be next."

"I won't leave him behind."

"He has been warned. He's in hiding," Honey lied.

"Where?"

"I'm not aware of the details, except that you're going there, too."

Honey tucked a dagger inside Gold Dust's belt. "I have to say good-bye to Raven."

"Over my dead heart." Honey's lips trembled. "She must not find out until you're many *farsangs* away."

Above the pain she felt, Gold Dust had to confess to herself that Honey was right. She must leave without embracing Raven.

Honey cupped Gold Dust's face in her palms and took her lips in her mouth. Her tongue glided over Gold Dust's lips, teeth, the roof of her mouth. She tasted salt. Her own tears. Gold Dust's grief.

On Honey's breath Gold Dust smelled wine and the smoke of hookah pipes. She pressed Honey to her heart, felt a love she had no name for. She would miss her friend and all the forbidden things she symbolized. "If they find out you've helped me, they'll kill you!"

Honey's gaze fell on Gold Dust like a shock of burning water. "They're after you, not me. Now go!"

She shut the door behind Gold Dust and secured the curtains, darkness falling on the room. She was at peace, almost happy. When Gold Dust had first burst into the harem, a girl indifferent to riches and class distinction, a virginal girl with alabaster skin and flaming cheeks, hair cut short and face bared, she had known she would become an important part of her life. She had been right. One of the few sultanas untainted by opium and wealth, Gold Dust had left an imprint in her otherwise gloomy life.

∾◌

Gold Dust walked through the Secret Passage. Cobwebs did not net her face. The Shah had just had a visitor. A man? A woman? She would miss the king. He had shared intimate secrets with her; he had guarded her against the plotting of the harem; he had loved her in his own way, with all of his passion and the fierceness of his beliefs. In his palace, she had grown into a woman, given birth to Raven, and discovered the world through the eyes of two eunuchs as different as good and evil.

She prayed Hazel-Boy would be waiting. Her bones made the walk difficult. She glanced through a porthole. The moon shone at a northern angle. In a few hours the sun would rise. She turned her eyes back to the Secret Passage. A blush of lilac drifted in and out of the shadows. A wave of silver. A flash of gold. She slowed down. A snake of gold coiled around a white arm. Ruby-jeweled eyes. Raven.

She walked toward the gold snake with bloody eyes and crushed her daughter against her breasts.

Raven circled her arms around Gold Dust and kissed her on the neck. Her mother must be on her way to the Shah to beg for his forgiveness. Her father's breath was still on her. Never again would she allow another woman close to his quarters.

"Madar, the order has gone out. You must escape."

"I know," Gold Dust murmured.

"Pedar won't change his mind!" She did not understand her mother, her hands sliding over her hair, securing the snake around her arm, twirling her belt, toying with the buckle. She seemed detached from the world and her fate. "Madar, don't you understand? You're in danger!"

Gold Dust's fingers traced her daughter's face to sear in her mind the outline of her features, the border of her eyes, her brows, her lashes.

Like a wild animal sensitive to the smell of weakness, Raven's nostrils flared.

Gold Dust withdrew. She must not tarnish these last moments. She must leave behind a courageous image. "Hazel-Boy will meet me to help me escape."

Raven's eyes flickered. She could deal with the sultanas who vied for her father's attention. But she did not know how to handle a ravishing eunuch who had been the Shah's companion of many years. She stroked the snake that hugged her arm. "I'll help both of you. But Hazel-Boy must never return to the palace. If it's found out he assisted you, both our lives will be in danger."

"My princess, your life will always be honored." They had not heard Hazel-Boy approach from behind.

Raven and the eunuch latched stares in an understanding that springs from being bound to the same man. Gold Dust took in Raven's stares, poisonous vipers aimed at a rival, and her suspicions were confirmed. For years, she had lived with a gnawing premonition that had made her life bitter, but not hopeless. Now she didn't want certainty to replace doubt. Then despair would render her helpless. Her bones had just grown stronger. They could not take another blow.

Hazel-Boy's mind raced. He would not reveal the merchant's plan to Raven. But he must find out her intentions. Assure her sincerity. Was she an ally? "My princess, I'll disappear, but after your mother is safe. How shall we accomplish that?"

Triumph flushed across Raven's cheeks. "You know there's only one unguarded route out of here. The river. Your enemy, my friend."

Hazel-Boy did not understand, but he was relieved that they both had the same destination.

For years, Gold Dust, too, had had the impression that one of these passages must lead to the river that skirted the back of the palace. But she would rather die by the bowstring than be torn to pieces by sharks. Still, she did not dare question the two who led the way, bent on getting her safely out. She allowed herself to be guided toward a branching passage that sloped down and was narrower and darker than the main one. The *click-click* of rattlers rose above the heat that entered through the portholes. Flanked by two forces that understood each other in a way she did not, she followed the sparkle of Raven's dagger. The assured steps of the two told her they both knew where they were headed. How well they silently communicated, familiar with the passage—the eunuch, surely, through long years of living with the Shah, and Raven through curiosity, obsession, and fearlessness, which had helped her discover mysteries she was unaware of. This was the same passage she had frequented and had never dared follow the scent of changing seasons that might have led her to the outside.

Raven held her back. "Count to eleven, then step aside."

Gold Dust did as she was told, marveling at their accurate calculations. She watched Raven and Hazel-Boy stomp on a spot under their feet.

"One!" Raven called, not a drop of moisture disturbing the lucidity of her face.

"Two!" Hazel-Boy heaved, his chest rising and falling with the effort.

A rumble jolted Gold Dust. The ground shifted, creating a quake that shook her whole being. She stared at a cave gaping at her feet. Slabs of wood had been painted to duplicate cobblestones. She descended a narrow flight of stairs. The air was heavy and stifling. Raven's voice was at her side: "Watch your step. There's a turn here. Another one here." Gold Dust collided with a wall, lost her balance. She was being lifted. She surrendered to Hazel-Boy's arms. He set her down in what she thought was a narrow landing. Her lungs filled with welcome freshness.

Raven measured a wall with her outstretched fingers and pushed on an invisible crack. The groan of shifting boulders startled Gold Dust. The ground under her feet shuddered. Stone and wood and iron ground against each other. Immense iron jaws unlocked to reveal a world she had forgotten.

The river coiled against land carpeted with sawgrass. Beyond the river many *farsangs* of dense woods stretched into an impenetrable darkness. Gold Dust heard the hoot of an owl. Then another. And another. A bad omen, the Shah had believed. She resisted turning around and racing back to the

harem and sneaking into her quarters. Here she was faced with
the dense night, fierce sharks, and sawgrass that would cut like
a hundred blades. Another hoot punctured the night.

Hazel-Boy touched her arm. "These are signals. They're
sending a raft from the other side."

She did not care to ask who. It did not matter. The sharks
would devour them, raft and all. What mattered was to keep
her dignity so her daughter would remember her as marching
away like a warrior.

"What kind of a raft?" Raven demanded. From the beginning of their journey, she was certain the eunuch would not
dare the dangerous waters without a carefully devised plan.
Now he must reveal it so she could help assure its success.

Hazel-Boy believed he understood Raven's concern. The
tenacious princess was bent on helping her mother escape so
no one would thwart her aspirations. He understood Gold
Dust's silence. The favorite was still as proud as the day he had
tutored her in the erotic arts. Now she refused to utter a word
in fear of revealing her dread. "The merchant and Rebekah are
sending a raft. We'll row back to the other bank and advance
into the forest before we're missed."

"Have you lost your mind?" Raven hissed. "The sharks
would destroy the raft in seconds."

Hazel-Boy held on to Gold Dust's arm. "At the mouth of
the river the blood of other fish is keeping the sharks busy."

The white of Raven's teeth flashed in the moonlight. This
plan might succeed. Then she would return to the Shah's quarters, entertain him until her mother distanced herself from the
city.

And the king and the empire would belong to her.

The horizon was turning purple, and stars were beginning to
fade away, but the raft had not arrived. Raven's fingers snapped
impatiently. "We can't wait any longer. Come, I'll send you

safely to the other side! But I can't lose both my mother and grandmother. You must send Rebekah back to me. I promise no harm will come to her or to the merchant. Now take off your clothing."

In answer to Hazel-Boy's questioning glance, Raven unlocked the jar from the chain around her waist. "With this ointment covering your bodies, the sharks won't approach you. You'll have five minutes to swim to the other side before the ointment washes off. It's ample time. I've tried it." She had helped the naked divers create an ointment with the binding qualities of gum that would not melt as fast as the previous one.

The courageous mask Gold Dust had painted on her face crumbled. She did not dare swim in these waters with only an ointment for a shield. She felt helpless against Raven's admonishing stare.

Hazel-Boy flung away his vest and stepped out of his pants. Something had gone wrong with the merchant's plan. They had to trust the princess or turn back. He preferred to die in the deep, a clean, honorable death, rather than have his throat cut and drown in his own blood.

Raven undressed Gold Dust, all the time whispering, "I've swum the river many times. Control your fear. Or you won't be able to swim fast enough."

Gold Dust watched this vision of silver and lilac and gold, her daughter, apply a greenish oil on her body, spreading it meticulously on her face, behind her ears, in the creases of her armpits, under her breasts. This woman who remained a stranger. Now that she was leaving, her fate unknown, she felt her daughter's love in the caring pressure of her fingers as she rubbed the balm on her body. Gold Dust shut her eyes to treasure Raven's touch, the warmth of her breath, the closeness. For too long she had longed for this union.

Raven's lips touched her mother's shoulder. "Madar, good-bye."

Gold Dust's gaze followed the swell of her daughter's veil, the silver wave of her hair, the pat of her footfalls, as silent as a cat's. She was gone. Her daughter. The queen.

45

$\mathcal{G}$old Dust plunged into the river. She swam as vigorously as her bones allowed. Ahead, Hazel-Boy's body sliced through the water, a beacon for her to follow. Her arms and legs moved of their own accord, no longer at her command. Fear had been replaced by resigned expectation of sharp teeth tearing into her flesh.

She had failed her mother. A daughter, destined to occupy jewel-encrusted thrones, devoured by sharks, so humiliating, so final. If only her mother would have realized that for a short time when she had reclined on Soleiman's torn mattress, she had truly felt like a queen. Was this not what her mother had aspired to? Love? What was left to propel her forward now? She had tried to please her mother. But the constant paradox of her instructions left her helpless. Rebekah herself could not have followed her own ideals: be ambitious but don't become hard to the world; seek power but don't let it cloud your humanity; join a man but refuse to be trapped in the prostitution of marriage; surrender to love but remain the master of your body.

Now there would be no body left, only memories, dreams, longings that had turned into her killers. Her lungs were about to burst. Did longings die with the body, or remain forever in the universe? Tombstones of memories. Her private legacy.

What would become of Soleiman? She was angry with him. She was dying and had never felt his touch. Such lofty beliefs: Absence is the aphrodisiac of the soul. Never rush your emotions. Didn't he realize danger lay around every corner, and each breath might be the last? Just when she was done with coffee-colored faces and had found her lost love, he had deprived her of his touch. Did he find the meeting of flesh with flesh too binding and final?

The pounding of her heart was unbearable. She could hardly follow Hazel-Boy's shadow. She struggled to keep her head above water. Feed her lungs with air. Her strokes were beginning to weaken. Rough scales scraped her skin. Pain flamed up through her body. The sharks had found her. She struggled to keep afloat. A surge under her agitated the water and raised the odor of algae. The fish were gathering force. She filled her lungs with air and shut her eyes.

The waters settled around her. She opened her eyes and felt her legs. They were intact. Had the ointment worked? Surely the sharks would be back. What could there be in some green oil to deter sharks? Three consecutive hoots came from the woods beyond, another, then another.

Struggling to muster the last vestiges of her strength, she fought the river. Hazel-Boy's specter vanished and she felt even more alone in this massive, frozen universe. A spinning force gripped her and began dragging her down under. Had the allotted five minutes elapsed? The river tasted bitter. Her lungs were about to explode.

Her body scraped against sand, stone, solid ground. She was hauled out of the water. They had survived. The ointment had worked.

She stood lost and shivering in Hazel-Boy's arms. On the

horizon clouds carved a smile into the moon as it began its descent. Hoots punctuated the calm of dawn. They walked toward the sound.

Hazel-Boy wondered if the king would find compassion in his heart for the two lovers he had cherished. Love had become a weapon of destruction between partners, between fathers and sons, mothers and daughters. He did not care where he went from here and what his future held. If not for Rebekah and Gold Dust, he would have surrendered to the River of Dreams.

Sawgrass cut into Gold Dust's toes. Sadness replaced fear. She should not have left the harem. She should have accepted her fate with dignity. Then she would have been mentioned with respect in history. Now she was nothing but a coward with silent bones.

She hooked her arm in Hazel-Boy's, her faithful ally banished from his home because of her. He had been her companion in Pearl Hall, and now in this lonely universe. Her cheek brushed against his bare shoulder. She became aware of her nakedness.

She repeated his teaching of years ago: " 'Don't smile too broadly, lest it be taken for brashness.' Look at us now, completely naked."

"And never stare, lest it be taken for arrogance, and not even Allah would forgive that." He gazed down at her, remembering a time when a direct stare or a broad smile mattered.

Their laughter rang out into the night.

"Gold Dust." A whisper among the trees.

"Madar?" Gold Dust hurried toward the voice.

Rebekah gasped with delight at the sight of her daughter. "It took us longer than expected to assemble the raft. We were beginning to lose hope."

She saw Hazel-Boy. Stared at his naked chest, his spare heart, another heart to love with. Her gift to him. They had

castrated him. Her Moses. That's why he had disappeared from
the Jewish Quarter and from her life. She had never questioned
his loyalty. She pressed her palm on his henna-heart, the
tattoo-heart she gave him to support his grief. In return, he had
taught her to differentiate between good and evil, sadness and
joy, the scent of flowers and the stink of iron.

He traced her brand with his fingers. "Will it still burn my
eyes?"

"Not if you care," she whispered.

"I'll always care, wherever I go, whatever the future, but
yours is with Raven. She wants you back and promised to protect you and Rouh'Allah."

Rouh'Allah wrapped his cape around Gold Dust's shoulders. "We should distance ourselves from here before daybreak."

Gold Dust spun toward the man whose face brought back
memories of a brick house with lace-framed windows, cherry
trees, saffron rice, roasted pistachios, and baked chickpeas. The
recollection of her mother's face when she had left his home.
Their lives had changed after that day.

Rebekah guided her daughter into the pine-choked woods.
"We must reach the city gates before sunrise."

It did not matter that in the layered darkness of the woods,
branches scratched and insects stung; Rebekah hurried, Gold
Dust at her side, the merchant, Hazel-Boy—now covered in
one of the men's cloaks—and the carpenters keeping pace.
Rebekah thrust aside the branches that blocked her way and
stabbed at her flesh.

The vegetation turned awash in a startling brightness. Light
bleached the tree barks of color and painted the leaves a luminous sapphire. Rebekah's brand, a beacon illuminating her
path, impressed itself deeper into her flesh.

She followed the lucid glow of her chest that bounced

ahead, on dirt tracks, over undergrowth, around wildflowers, on treetops. The sprig of mint felt heavy behind her ear, the throbbing between her chest unbearable. She longed to rid herself of both. She did not know how to discard the brand, the mint; she was afraid to. For too long she had associated it with safety, its scent capable of warding off evil.

Lightning streaked the skies, and the howl of wild animals filled the heavens.

"Open your eyes, sweetlove, devils are roaming among us." Rebekah's past words echoed among the branches. A message she had thought belonged to another time. She was wrong. Although she had witnessed many miracles, and would encounter more, none would erase the need for her sprig of mint.

The boundaries of the city scintillated in the first light of dawn; early sun bathed the gates amber. A breeze whistled among the ancient plane trees. The gardeners had unlocked the watering dams. Water lapped at the stout roots. The city was still asleep.

Soleiman leaned against the trunk of a cherry tree. The mask he had first worn in the harem covered half his face. Despite a few missing feathers, the mystery behind the disguise had not diminished.

Gold Dust slowed her steps. She saw the shine of his blue eyes through the slits of his mask and nothing else mattered. She would embrace him. No words. No memories. No poems. No past. Only the urgency of the present. She had contained herself for too long, had heard too many philosophies, too many stories, too many words.

He folded her in his arms, the pressure around her waist urgent but not harsh, firm but not demanding, his eyes comforting torches, and still she recognized that his touch could not wipe out her past, the palace, the king, or Raven.

Rebekah watched her daughter, perched on Venus—Soleiman flanking her on one side, Hazel-Boy on the other—ride into the horizon to the edge of the earth. "Farewell, Moses," she whispered. "I owe you much more than my daughter's life."

A sweet music sailed toward Rebekah, a melody that danced on the wings of the breeze and sent the nightingales into a cheerful chatter. Gold Dust's bones had healed.

Rebekah raised her finger to wipe a tear from the corner of her eye. Wrinkles had formed there. Would she now grow old like everyone else? She raised the burned glove of her hand. The skin had acquired a comforting suppleness. A cool wind fanned her breasts. She parted her vest and glanced down. Would her brand ever fade?

The merchant circled an arm around her shoulders. "Come home with me."

She stroked the silver hair at his temples. She had always longed to do that. She rubbed her nose against him to take in his scent of ancient Cyprus.

He opened the flaps of his cloak and wrapped her in his warmth.

She crushed her breasts against his chest, against a man who was a true man and who loved her because of what she was. A man for whom her nipples swelled. A man who would help her cast away the curse of her brand, extinguish the flames of her kiln, and smother her memories.

He sighed, "Marry me."

She allowed herself to relish the moment. She would invite the populace of the Jewish Quarter to hear Rouh'Allah the Spirit of God propose to her. Never again dare call her a whore. Never again splatter her with horse manure. Even the One-Eyed Rabbi would welcome her to his synagogue. She would ride a regal, coal-black stallion into the center of the Quarter—

savor the praise tossed at her, the bowed heads, the envious stares. Dealers in the bazaar would compete to sell her fabrics for her personal use. "Does this please your eyes, *Khanom* Rouh'Allah the Spirit of God? How is your honored husband, my lady?"

She burrowed her nose into the hair on Rouh'Allah's chest. Yes. He did smell right to her.

HAREM

DISCUSSION POINTS

1. Set in the Jewish Quarter of Ancient Persia, *Harem* follows the lives of three generations of courageous and cunning women—Rebekah; her daughter, Gold Dust; and her granddaughter, Raven—who are determined to realize their dreams despite the limitations of their forbidding society. How do those limitations change over the course of the novel? How do their dreams differ? How successful is each woman in achieving her dreams?

2. At the opening of the novel, *Rebekah of the violet eyes heard a voice that would haunt her the rest of her life.* As she hugs her doll, tossing on her pallet suspended between wakefulness and sleep, ten-year-old Rebekah is captivated by the stranger with a voice like music, who she is convinced will be chosen as her future husband. In a sense it can be said that Rebekah falls in love at first sound. What does the man's voice represent for her? Why do you think Rebekah's dying mother believed she was choosing a better future for her daughter by choosing Jacob the Fatherless? Do you think the stranger continues to inhabit Rebekah's fantasies more because of the brutality of her marriage, or because Rebekah and Rouh'Allah the Spirit of God are fated to be together?

3. Alarmed by the growing madness she can see in her husband's eyes, Rebekah yearns to escape. Yet when Jacob slyly tells her she can leave but reveals that her mother is dead, she elects to stay. Why? *"You've nowhere to go. I'm your only hope,"* he taunts her. Is that true? *You are a weakling, afraid of freedom, Rebekah,* she taunts herself. Is that true? What choices does she realistically have? Why, when she becomes pregnant, does Rebekah fear having a son? Why do you think she sees giving birth to a girl as a sign that God has forgiven her? What was your reaction to Rebekah's deliberate goading of her increasingly delusional husband into flinging himself into his flaming kiln in an attempt to make himself immortal? Was there any other way to free herself and Gold Dust from Jacob's violence?

4. With no family and no money and a child to care for, Rebekah eventually sells her favors to carefully selected, mostly wealthy, men. When her daughter, Gold Dust, hears the names her mother

is called and asks what a whore is, Rebekah replies: "A whore is a woman who has the honor to sacrifice her body and soul for the comfort of her child." Do you agree or disagree with Rebekah that there can be honor in becoming a "whore"? Why? Does she believe she had other choices? Do you think she did?

5. Even though Gold Dust has announced her own intention to marry the acrobat Soleiman the Agile, Rebekah still insists on choosing a husband for her. Discuss the irony of Rebekah following the path that made her feel so betrayed by her own mother. Rebekah is sure she can choose more wisely than her mother did. Instead of selecting the wealthiest suitor, she will search out the most educated bachelor in the Jewish Quarter. *Wisdom, she had decided, granted a man confidence and ease in his relationships with women. Illiterate men like Jacob made up for their ignorance by stifling a woman's soul.* Do you think this is true? Why or why not?

6. When Rebekah visits the merchant Rouh'Allah the Spirit of God in an attempt to arrange a match between her daughter and his son, she discovers that the father is the man with the voice that haunts her. Discuss the irony of Rouh'Allah turning down Rebekah's daughter for his son the way her mother had turned him down as a husband for Rebekah.

7. Unable to secure a suitable husband for Gold Dust, Rebekah turns to the world of the harem as the perfect solution for her daughter's life. How do you think Rebekah is influenced by her own view of marriage, which she has described to Gold Dust as "an alliance to enslave and shame women"? How is her choice for her daughter influenced by the knowledge that if Gold Dust is admitted to the harem, she, Rebekah, will no longer have to earn her living as a whore? Did the world of the harem in fact offer Persian women of that time advantages they could not gain elsewhere? Did the exotic, conspiratorial, mysterious world of the harem portrayed by the author seem enticing to you? Why or why not?

8. How does Gold Dust's life in the harem change once she becomes the chosen one? How does she learn to cope with stares that stab like daggers and words that poison like hemlock? When her mother visits, she shares with her daughter the secrets of men, the hidden weaknesses of kings, and the power of the heart over the body. *"Seek power but don't let it cloud your humanity,"* her mother cautions. *"Men are fickle; they come and go. You and only you must remain the ruler of your heart; that's the secret to survival,"* Rebekah reminds her. And she adds: *"In the end, life is judged by highlights not by days."* What does she mean? Do you agree or disagree? Why?

9. Gold Dust gets rigorous training in palace etiquette, dance, poetry, music, and Islamic culture, but it is palace gossip and lessons in the art of lovemaking from the eunuch Hazel Boy that help to set her

sights on a new ambition: to become queen. How does Gold Dust plan to advance her power in the court? When she gives birth to the child who she is convinced will be heir to the throne and it turns out to be *not* the Shah's first son, but an albino daughter, how does Gold Dust manage to get the king to accept this odd-looking but very beautiful girl child? And how does their extraordinary daughter, against all reason named Raven, capture her father's heart?

10. While Raven's teaching the Shah to see women as equals may strike many modern readers as admirable (told by her father when she is twelve that the law doesn't allow a woman to rule, Raven's hard-to-refute logic says simply: "You are the king. Change the law."), her lack of compassion alarms both of her parents. *"Is it true that you planned the execution of two men and wanted their hands cut off?"* Gold Dust confronts her. When Raven gleefully responds, *"Next time I'll be less lenient,"* Gold Dust prays that the late shah's madness has not flared with even more intensity in her daughter. What do you think of Raven? How do you think the author intends the reader to view her?

11. Suffocating in the Shah's dark moods and melancholy lovemaking, afraid of her own daughter, Gold Dust yearns for Soleiman the Agile, the acrobat whose love-stricken eyes have thrived in the fertile land of her imagination. *"How can you toss away your dream?"* Rebekah chastises her. But Gold Dust will not be deterred. *"Even if they hang me from the tower, I must meet Soleiman."* Even though she agrees to help Gold Dust, Rebekah secretly plans to thwart the meeting. Rebekah clearly loves her daughter and wants her to be happy. Yet still she is willing to sabotage her desires. Do you know women like Rebekah—who would manipulate their grown children's lives if they had the opportunity to prevent what they view as a major mistake? Do you think they have the right? Only when she fears for her daughter's survival does Rebekah show a willingness to help Gold Dust as she wants to be helped. How do you think the author expects us to react to the clash between mother and daughter?

12. Under threat of invasion by the legendary Tartar warrior Teymour the Lame, the Shah readies to lead his men into battle. Intoxicated with his new goal, his body vibrating with new ardor, the king makes love to Gold Dust. As she yields to their love-tussle, Soleiman the Agile lodges deeper and deeper into her soul. And as the shah lies in Gold Dust's arms, it is Raven, who occupies his dreams. But it is not until he is back from war that the undercurrents of incest in the bond between father and daughter come to fruition in the cries of a king rendered helpless by the enormity of his desire. Given the strength of the taboo against incest, did reading about their passion make you uncomfortable? What are we to make of their strange, forbidden relationship?

13. When the Shah learns of Gold Dust's infidelity, he orders her executed. Hazel Boy tries fussily to convince the Shah that the accusations are lies. He struggles to understand such violent jealousy. *How could the Shah end Gold Dust's life simply because she has fallen in love? Had he not shared his king with hundreds of sultanas and rejoiced at his pleasure? Is jealousy different for a half-man?* the eunuch wonders. *Did true men react differently? What about women? How did Gold Dust and the other sultanas feel about sharing the Shah? And Honey? She was like him, half-woman, half-man, desiring other women, weeping when a lover was indifferent, but having the generosity to forgive.* What do you think determines how possessive a person is in a relationship? Is sexual jealousy a necessary component of passion? Do people who are generous in other areas of life take a more generous and forgiving approach to infidelity than those who are less generous?

14. John Rechy, author of the bestselling classic *City of Night,* praises *Harem* as an "epic novel that teems with sharply drawn characters and haunting scenes." Novelist Ann Rowe Seaman calls it "an intensely visual book, written in scenes like an exotic movie." And novelist Maureen Connell finds "the despair, danger, and erotic life of the Seraglio stunningly portrayed." Do you agree or disagree with these assessments? Why?

15. How much did you know about the harem before reading this book? As she researched this novel, author Dora Levy Mossanen found herself powerfully drawn into the intimate and secret dealings of the sultanas. "I studied the psyche of women whose lives revolved around the one night the Shah might invite them into his bed and about their sexual relationships with eunuchs who were supposed to be their guardians. I found myself lost in these women's tormented worlds of smoke and opium and poisons. I studied different forms of castration and how the process physically and psychologically scarred the eunuchs." Does the author succeed in communicating her own fascination with this world? Does her novel make you want to learn more about life in the harem?

Q & A WITH DORA LEVY MOSSANEN

1. *You paint such a vivid, detailed landscape of life as it was lived in the harem, the Jewish Quarter, and ancient Persia. How much research did you conduct, and how did the process of researching for the novel shape the story and the characters? Are Rebekah, Gold Dust, and Raven based on real people?*

   Research for *Harem,* although voluminous, was so fascinating, I look back at the learning process with great fondness. My education about the Jewish Quarter, harems, sultanas, and eunuchs began early after I moved to Iran from Israel. My grandfather, a historian, would relish recounting astonishing stories that he assured me were true. As I grew older, the tales I heard and books I read became more complex and so did the characters that took shape in my imagination. I've known Rebekah, Gold Dust, and Raven first in real life and then embellished them in my imagination.

2. *Your research yielded some very surprising facts about life in a harem. What were some of the most surprising to you? How did they change your view of women's lives in that era?*

    Facts I found most surprising, which also altered my view of women in harems, were the power sultanas often wielded over their men and the politics of their countries, despite their restrictive environments. I was also astonished at the sexual desires and skills of eunuchs in spite of the general belief that castration deprives men of the need for and ability to perform.

3. *Many women will recognize themselves in the loving but sometimes conflicted relationship between Rebekah and Gold Dust, especially by the clash between Rebekah's ambitions and Gold Dust's dreams. How did your experience as a mother and as a daughter inform your writing?*

    Both as a daughter and mother of daughters, I have experienced the intricate web of love, ambition, and dreams that often translate into rebellion and a clash of wills that, if not handled delicately, could lead to disaster. Rebekah's aspiration for Gold Dust did not mesh well with Gold Dust's vision for herself, but, in the end, Rebekah's wisdom and courage might have saved the day. I, too, like all my characters, have been faced with challenging decisions that might have altered the course of our lives.

4. *You've just completed a second novel called* Lyla. *Can you tell us about your new heroine? Do you plan to continue the story of Rebekah, Gold Dust, and Raven in this book or another?*

    Lyla is a modern Iranian woman who in many ways is similar to Rebekah. Lyla will not tolerate her husband's infidelity and betrayal, but Rebekah's dream is for her daughter to join a world where hundreds of women compete for one man's attention. Both Lyla and Rebekah are obsessed, cunning, and powerful and, despite all odds, refuse to be discouraged. I hope to, one day soon, continue Rebekah and Raven's story after Rebekah returns to her beloved granddaughter, the Queen of Persia.

5. *Today, Iran is a very different place from the land you describe in* Harem, *yet it is still a very restrictive society for women. Are there any similarities between your experience as a modern Iranian woman and that of your characters? What parts of the culture have endured? What has changed for women?*

    After the Islamic Revolution of 1979, Iranian women were forced to retreat into a more restrictive past like the one I recount in *Harem*. Like my heroines and myself, Iranian women have often managed to rise above the limitations of their societies. But, in order to succeed, we had to be more resourceful than women in liberal countries. Iranian women are still a strong force who hold important jobs, are represented in the parliament, and are highly educated, but now they're forced, whether they concur or not, to conceal themselves under chadors.

6. *Having lived in Israel, Iran, and the United States, you have a unique perspective on women's lives in very different societies. What are some of the misconceptions we have about women living in Iran today? And about Iranian women living in the United States?*

   The misconception we have about women living in Iran is that their spirits have been broken down by this male-dominated society. Although this is true in some cases, overall it's difficult to break down an Iranian woman's will. She will find a way to educate herself, work, and expose her hair or ankle. The younger generation of Iranian women in the United States has become a major player in all aspects of society, and it would be a misconception to dismiss them.

7. *Many of the women in* Harem *are quite powerful despite the severe limits imposed upon them by Persian culture. In fact, they are often as ruthless as the men who dominate them. Do you think there are any lessons contemporary women can draw from them?*

   Yes! It is exactly this, the power these women had, that fascinated me in the first place. And what we must learn from them is that our sensual, intuitive, and cerebral traits, coupled with perfect timing, can be a very effective tool in all aspects of our lives.

8. *You were born in Israel and grew up in Iran, so it seems no coincidence that the novel's main protagonists are Jewish women in ancient Persia. In addition to theme and location, how have your Jewish and Iranian cultures inspired and sustained your writing?*

   Having been raised in a culture rich in poetry and sensual imagery, it has certainly influenced my voice and style. The stories communicated to me throughout the years are so ingrained in me on conscious and subconscious levels that it's hard to separate what I write about from the reality of my life.

9. *What inspired you to write about the world of a harem? Why did you decide to depict it in a novel instead of a straightforward history? Did any particular book or author influence your choice?*

   I was inspired most by histories I read about sultanas who ruled empires from behind and beyond their golden cages. Not too long ago, Reza Shah, the late Mohammed Reza Shah's father, had a harem on a smaller scale, and I was intrigued by the intricate circumstances of these women's lives. To write a straightforward history, I would have had to curtail my creativity, an impossible task. Alev Lytle Croutier's book, *Harem: The World Behind the Veil,* supplied captivating facts that influenced my choice.